P9-EGM-710

Praise for *The Last Place You Look*

"Lepionka's debut confidently portrays complex characters with multiple, sometimes contradictory, motivations and offers an unusually naturalistic perspective on sexual identity." —*Kirkus Reviews*

"Lepionka reboots the thriller genre with her troubled hero, Roxane Weary, a private eye with little concern for her own safety (or the gender of her shifting sexual partners). *The Last Place You Look* riffs off Raymond Chandler and Mickey Spillane but finds a way to make detective fiction relevant again, in 2017. I have never read a more confident debut." —James Renner, author of *True Crime Addict* and *The Man from Primrose Lane*

"In *The Last Place You Look*, a talented new voice in crime fiction gives us the seedier side of a midwestern community—and a character worth following anywhere she trespasses. A wonderful debut." —Lori Rader-Day, Mary Higgins Clark Award– and Anthony Award–winning author of *The Black Hour* and *Little Pretty Things*

"Utterly superb—can't remember when I last read such an expertly written and perfectly constructed book that gave me so much pure reading pleasure." —Sophie Hannah, author of *Closed Casket* and *The Monogram Murders*

"*The Last Place You Look* is a sharp, timely, and assured debut. Lepionka's got a real knack for character. Her protagonist, private eye Roxane Weary, manages to honor her literary predecessors while still crackling with originality and life."
—Chris Holm, Anthony Award–winning author of *The Killing Kind* and *Red Right Hand*

SOUTH PARK LIBRARY
2575 BROWNSVILLE ROAD
SOUTH PARK, PA 15129
412-833-5585

"Just when you think the PI novel is dead, Kristen Lepionka brings it roaring back to life. Roxane Weary is a richly drawn protagonist who proves that 'hard-boiled' and 'feminine' aren't mutually exclusive. This book is so good it makes me jealous."

—Rob Hart, author of *New Yorked* and *City of Rose,* and associate publisher at MysteriousPress.com

"*The Last Place You Look* is a beautifully written mystery, one I devoured in a single sitting, late into the night. I'll now follow detective Roxane Weary anywhere: into her hopes and fears, into her past, and—especially—into danger. An extraordinary debut novel."

—Christopher Coake, author of *You Came Back*

"The PI at the heart of *The Last Place You Look* may be troubled and still green, but Kristen Lepionka's debut mystery is as confident and deft as they come. A moving, arresting novel."

—Michael Kardos, author of *Before He Finds Her*

"In her daring debut, Kristen Lepionka blends traditional mystery with heart-stopping thriller elements to create something plenty original. The down-on-her-luck PI Roxane Weary battles her emotional demons to track down a human one, stumbling into plenty of trouble along the way. But she overcomes doubt in all its ugly forms, succeeding where others have failed. Lepionka exceeds expectations, as well, in this ambitious novel. With its memorable characters and surprising twists, *The Last Place You Look* will stay with readers long after they turn the last page."

—Erica Wright, author of *The Granite Moth* and *The Red Chameleon*

"Seriously, this is a must-read. I loved it."

—Martina Cole, author of *Close* and *Betrayal*

"Kristen Lepionka spins a twisting, turning, enticing tale that keeps the reader guessing and turning pages to find out what happens next. *The Last Place You Look* is a promising first novel by a remarkable talent and you won't be disappointed if you look here first."

—*The Oklahoman*

The Last Place
You Look

Kristen Lepionka

Minotaur Books
New York

SOUTH PARK TOWNSHIP LIBRARY
2575 BROWNSVILLE ROAD
SOUTH PARK, PA 15129
412-833-5585

0 5   2018

To my parents,

who listened to my never-ending stories

This is a work of fiction. All of the characters, organizations, and
events portrayed in this novel are either products of the author's
imagination or are used fictitiously.

THE LAST PLACE YOU LOOK. Copyright © 2017 by Kristen Lepionka.
All rights reserved. Printed in the United States of America. For
information, address St. Martin's Press, 175 Fifth Avenue, New York,
N.Y. 10010.

www.minotaurbooks.com

Excerpt from *What You Want to See* copyright © 2018 by Kristen
Lepionka

The Library of Congress has cataloged the hardcover edition as
follows:

Names: Lepionka, Kristen, author.
Title: The last place you look / Kristen Lepionka.
Description: First edition. | New York : Minotaur Books, 2017.
Identifiers: LCCN 2017005604 | ISBN 9781250120519 (hardcover) |
    ISBN 9781250120526 (ebook)
Subjects: LCSH: Women private investigators—Fiction. | Missing
    persons—Investigation—Fiction. | BISAC: FICTION / Mystery &
    Detective / Women Sleuths. | GSAFD: Suspense fiction. | Mystery
    fiction.
Classification: LCC PS3612.E62 L37 2017 | DDC 813/.6—dc23
LC record available at https://lccn.loc.gov/2017005604

ISBN 978-1-250-18130-5 (trade paperback)

Our books may be purchased in bulk for promotional, educational,
or business use. Please contact your local bookseller or the Macmillan
Corporate and Premium Sales Department at 1-800-221-7945,
extension 5442, or by email at MacmillanSpecialMarkets@macmillan
.com.

First Minotaur Books Paperback Edition: May 2018

10 9 8 7 6 5 4 3 2 1

No one's ever lost forever.

—*Amanda Palmer*

ONE

"Matt said you find things. For a living," the woman said on the phone.

I was lying on the carpet underneath my desk. I'd only answered the call to make the shrill ringing stop. The inside of my mouth tasted like whipped cream and whiskey, and the sound of my breathing was like a roaring thunderstorm in my head, but at least I was alone and in my own apartment. "That's right," I said.

"What kind of things?" Her tone was suspicious, like her main objective was to debunk whatever my oldest brother told her.

"Objects. People. Answers. Whatever needs to be found."

"You good at it?"

I hadn't worked much in the last nine months and didn't want to start now. But my bank balance had other ideas. "I am. Matt doesn't like me much, so it's a vote of confidence he gave you my number in the first place."

That was the best sales pitch I could manage. Illusions didn't serve anybody in the detective business—not the client, and not me.

The woman chuckled. "He said you'd say that. Can you help?"

I thought it over. People give the worst advice about lost things. *Retrace your steps. Pray to Saint Anthony. Think about where you last saw it.* But that doesn't apply to the things that matter. Those are right in front of you, except they can't be found by looking for them. Only by looking at everything else. "What do you need to find?" I said, finally.

"The girl who can get my brother off death row."

Ninety minutes later, we were sitting in the front room of my apartment, which served as an office of sorts. Three cups of green tea with mint had fortified me enough to turn on a single lamp. I still chose to sit in the armchair farthest away from it. Midday Monday light streamed in from the west-facing window near the ceiling but I kept the miniblinds firmly closed on the others. If my new client noticed the cave-like atmosphere of the place, she didn't let on.

"Until that night," Danielle Stockton was saying, "I hadn't seen her in fifteen years. Nobody had."

She was about thirty or so, pretty and put-together in a royal-blue cardigan and jeans. Her hair was pulled back into a tight ballerina bun and she had a leopard-print scarf looped artfully around her slim neck. She wore no makeup except for a dark red lipstick. She worked at American Electric Power, she had told me, and was here on her lunch break. "Sarah Cook," Danielle added. "That's her name. White girl. She and my brother were going out—that's what they claimed this was over, her nice white family not liking him."

They were the prosecutors in her older brother's case, which Danielle had just finished briefing me on. Bradford Stockton was almost twenty when he had been convicted of murdering his girlfriend's mother and father fifteen years ago. Of stabbing them to death in their living room with a Kershaw folding knife that the police found in the trunk of his Toyota hatchback, wrapped in one of Sarah's shirts. The seventeen-year-old Sarah, meanwhile, disappeared that night. The prosecution alleged that Brad had killed her, too, and had concealed her body somewhere.

The defense hadn't put up much of a fight, ignoring the built-in alternate theory of the crime, that the absent Sarah had committed the murders and then run. Brad had just finished his shift at a Subway at the time Elaine and Garrett Cook were killed, and he claimed he was waiting for Sarah in his car in the parking lot. She'd been in the restaurant earlier that evening—confirmed by Brad's coworkers—and the pair had plans to see a movie when he got off work. But Sarah never came back, and by the time Brad went to the Cook house to see if she was at home, the police were already there and his life was already over. He was convicted on two counts of aggravated murder and had been on death row ever since.

"She still looks the same," Danielle said.

She'd brought me a binder of newspaper clippings and photos, a grim scrapbook of her older brother's troubles. A yearbook picture of Sarah smiled up at me from the coffee table. She looked like a Girl Scout, honey-blond hair cut into blunt bangs, a faint spray of freckles across her nose.

"I mean, she didn't look seventeen anymore," Danielle continued between sips of tea. "And she's put on weight. But it was absolutely her. Not a doubt in my mind. Kenny saw her too—Kenny Brayfield, he's one of Brad's friends from school."

I raised my eyebrows. I'd heard crazier stories, but not recently. "And when was this?"

"Ten days ago. November second. Maybe seven thirty. Kenny and I were meeting for dinner at Taverna Athena and we both just got there when I happened to look across the street and saw her at the gas station, walking out of the little store. I ran over there but the traffic was blocking my view. By the time I made it across the street, she was gone. She must have driven away."

"Any idea what she might have been driving?"

Danielle's mouth twitched. "It's a pretty busy intersection. There were a lot of cars around."

I drew a bullet point in my notebook but didn't write anything else. Other than the blue dot, the page so far was blank. "Can you remember any of them?"

"Well," Danielle said, "I saw a red four-door leaving when I got over there. And like a green pickup, one of those big new ones. And someone on a motorcycle, too. But it was already dark, and I was looking for her, not at the cars. So I can't say for sure about that."

"What was she wearing?"

"A coat, a long wool one. I think."

It was a lot of uncertainty, in an encounter not strong on the details to begin with. I wrote down *red sedan, big green pickup, long wool coat.* "But you're sure it was her."

"I'm positive," Danielle said.

I said nothing, just paged silently through the binder. It seemed unlikely that Sarah would have been so easily recognizable—fifteen years was a big time jump, and Danielle had only seen her for a split second. In the dark, at that. Besides, where had she been all along?

I studied Danielle in the chair across from me. Although we'd just met, she struck me as levelheaded and smart. Maybe it wasn't impossible.

"So suppose I can find her," I said.

Danielle nodded.

"What do you think will happen? How can she help? What makes you think she'd want to?"

My new client was quiet for a minute. Then she said, "Do you believe in God, Roxane?"

I smiled. "No comment."

Danielle smiled too. "Well," she said. "Brad is innocent, okay? I believe him one hundred percent when he says he didn't do it. He'd never hurt anybody. He's a good person—not perfect, but who is? My brother didn't do this."

I could tell she believed that. But her question about God made me think that faith came easy to her. "What does that have to do with God?"

"I don't know what really went down or where she's been," Danielle said. "Believe me, the police tried to find her, the investigator for Brad's lawyer tried to find her—she was gone. But then, all this time later, two days after they scheduled Brad's execution I see her? It had to be for a reason."

I raised my eyebrows. She'd buried the lede a little bit on that one. "What's the date?" I said.

"January twentieth." She wrapped both hands around her mug.

Just over two months away. It was hard to imagine facing that down. I shifted in my chair. "Could she have done it?" I said. "Killed her parents?"

Danielle pressed her lips together. "I've thought so much about that. Brad acted like there was no way—he wouldn't even let the lawyer bring it up at the trial."

"That's love for you."

She shrugged.

"What about you, though, what do you think?"

Danielle said, "I wasn't close friends with her, but she was in my grade so I knew her. She seemed like a nice, exuberant person. Her family was religious, pretty straitlaced, and she was one of those girls who, you know, developed early. Boy-crazy. In high school, she was really into writing. Slam poetry—that's how she and Brad got to know each other, he's a writer too. And I didn't see how she was with her family, only how she was with ours. But I got the feeling they weren't thrilled about her seeing Brad."

I thought about what Danielle had said at the beginning of our conversation. *Nice white family.* "Weren't thrilled because Brad was older, or because he was black?" Then I added, "Or because he was a poet?"

Danielle gave me a slight smile. "All of the above? I don't know. I overheard them in our basement talking, a week or so before it happened. Brad and Sarah. There was some kind of regional poetry slam in Michigan that they both wanted to go to. Sarah was saying that her parents wouldn't let her go with him, but maybe if she went with someone else, they could meet up—that's the extent of it, as far as I know, it's not like her parents ever forbade her to see him. But then at the trial, Mrs. Cook's sister testified that the Cooks had a very contentious relationship with Brad, that they were afraid of him. She's in there, in the back."

I flipped to the last page in the binder. "Stockton: Guilty in Belmont Murders." A grainy photo of an attractive woman in a tweed jacket crying in a courtroom, a tissue clutched halfway to her face. The caption read "Justice for my big sister: Elizabeth Troyan celebrates the verdict." If Sarah was seventeen when all of this had happened, then that meant Danielle had been too. I tried to picture a younger version of her calmly cutting out these newspaper articles and slipping them into plastic sheet protectors and carrying them around for her entire adult life.

"She never even met Brad," Danielle said, shaking her head. "They painted a picture of my brother that just wasn't true."

"And you think Sarah could help with that. Set the record straight, in the eleventh hour."

"I do."

I flipped the scrapbook closed. "You have to be prepared for the possibility that she won't want to."

"I know."

"That she might have her reasons, whatever they may be, for not sticking around."

"I know."

"That you might not like what you find out." I didn't bother to say that what she might find out was that she was wrong. That Sarah was dead, that her brother was guilty anyway. Or that we might find nothing at all.

"That's what Brad's new lawyer said. That I should just move on with my life because nothing good comes of diving back into this stuff." Danielle shrugged. "He inherited the case from his uncle. He doesn't care."

I felt my eyebrows go up. Everybody, innocent or not, at least deserves a lawyer who won't tell family to *move on*. "Sounds like what you really need is a new lawyer, not a detective," I said. "I can give you some names if you want."

Danielle shook her head. "What I want is to find Sarah. Matt said you'd try to talk me out of it." She grinned. "That it's how you get people to trust you."

I did do that. I almost laughed. "What else did he tell you?"

"That you're very determined. And smart." She stopped then, like she wasn't sure if she should tell me the whole truth. But I nodded at her and she continued. "And that you're kind of a mess, since your dad died. But nothing gets past you."

I finished my tea and set my mug down on the coffee table. It was true, what I'd told her about my brother not liking me much. But he sure as hell knew me. "So you want to do this?"

"I do," Danielle said. She reached into her handbag and pulled out her checkbook. My bank account was going to be thrilled.

TWO

It was after one o'clock when Danielle left. I sat for a while in the armchair and flipped through her scrapbook again, pausing on a description of the murder weapon. Three-and-a-quarter-inch blade, available in any hunting-supply store. I didn't need to see crime-scene photos to know that these murders were brutal, that Garrett and Elaine Cook had not died quickly. I tried to imagine their seventeen-year-old daughter doing it, but my head still hurt too much from last night to imagine much of anything. Besides, the bloody knife had been found in Brad's trunk, wrapped in Sarah's shirt.

That was pretty persuasive.

I figured he was guilty.

But Danielle hadn't hired me for my opinion on the merits of the case. In fact, Danielle had written me a check for twenty-five hundred reasons to assume that Brad was innocent.

I swallowed two more aspirins and called Kenny Brayfield at the number Danielle had given me. He was too busy to see me, but he told me I could stop by the office of the event-promotion agency he ran later that afternoon. Then, I spoke with Brad's new lawyer, who didn't give me much besides the contact info for the private investigator who had assisted with the trial. I tried him next.

"Yeah," an old, gruff voice answered on the third ring.

"Peter Novotny?" I said.

"Maybe. Who's this?"

"My name is Roxane Weary. You worked a case a long time ago, Brad Stockton?"

"Oh, that," he said. "Look, I'm retired, I'm not going to chase a ghost all over Ohio anymore. Wait a second. Did you say Weary? Any relation to *Frank* Weary?"

It had been nine months since my father died. But it still felt, as it always did, like a punch to the stomach. "I'm his daughter."

"Well, shit!" Peter Novotny said. The growl was gone. "Great guy, what a goddamn shame. Sure I'll talk to you, honey. Are you a whiskey drinker like your old man?"

"I am."

"Good, because I've been waiting all afternoon for a beautiful woman to walk into this bar and sit down beside me," Novotny said.

"Good luck with that," I said, "but I'd like to talk to you. Where can I meet you?"

"Well, even if you're a hag, I'll still buy Frank Weary's kid a drink."

I closed my eyes for a second, then decided to play along. "Just one?" I said, and the old man laughed.

"I like you already."

I drove to the east side and found Peter Novotny at the bar at Wing's. It was a Chinese restaurant that, improbably, had just about the best whiskey selection in all of Columbus. It was dim and warm, the bar flanked by deep booths upholstered in red vinyl. It was also empty, except for Novotny. He had to be close to eighty, the kind of old man with a full head of pure white hair and a good jaw, and I could tell he had been a heartbreaker at one time. I walked right up to him and sat down and said "Is this taken?" in my best Marilyn Monroe.

He spun around to look at me and broke into a huge grin. "Dreams do come true," he said. He stuck out his hand and I shook it as he took me in. I was nobody's dream, but I was no hag, either. "Real nice to meet you, Roxane." He slid a glass toward me; he was also the kind of old man who ordered for everybody. "I didn't roofie it, don't worry."

"That's not funny," I said, and he laughed.

"I'll bet you ten bucks you can't guess what it is."

I swirled the amber liquid around in the glass and took a sip. "Smooth. Scotch whisky, light, not too peaty but a little salty." I took another sip. "I have to go with something from the West Highlands. Oban fourteen-year?"

"Shit, sweetheart, you *are* Frank's kid." Novotny opened his wallet and slapped a ten on the shiny bar top.

"You were just trying to get me to say 'Petey,' you dirty old man," I said, then nodded at the bar. "Also, the bottle's right there." I threw back the rest of the drink as he almost fell off his chair laughing.

I ordered another and we got to talking. Peter Novotny had been a cop years ago, that was how he knew my father. He retired after his thirty, took the pension, went private. Now he was really retired, except for the occasional records check for the law firm that had represented Brad Stockton. "That case was shit, though. This girl, Sarah? Nowhere to be found. And whether she could have helped the Stockton kid or not, it was the obvious defense, right? Her absence makes for the very definition of reasonable doubt. But no, he didn't want to say one bad thing about his beloved. But you know, in my experience? It's the innocent ones who're the least helpful."

"Really," I said.

"I'm not a lawyer," he said, "nor a psychic. But yeah. I wouldn't have sent this case to the prosecutor without digging a little deeper. Sure, you got that knife, and it's wrapped in Sarah's jacket or shirt, something like that. But her blood's not on it. Her parents' is, but not hers. Not on the knife, and not on the shirt. How do you manage that? Plus, there's no blood anywhere else in Stockton's car or his house. A murder like that, things would have gotten messy."

"So he got rid of his clothes."

"Right," Novotny said, "but then why not get rid of the knife, too? It just felt weird as hell, is what I'm saying."

"You ever meet him?"

"Oh yeah," Novotny said. "Lots of times. Nice kid, he had these long eyelashes, like, shit, no wonder the Cook girl was crazy for him. He was polite, too, real soft-spoken. But I think he must have been stupid, because he didn't understand what he was facing. How often do you see a black kid thinking he could beat the system? He was shocked when the sentence came down, I remember. Tried to hang himself. But he was too tall."

I thought about that. When everything went wrong, that had to be an incredible disappointment: not even being able to pull off giving up. "So you believed him," I said.

Novotny polished off his drink. "I don't know. I'm just saying what I've noticed. A guilty kid, he can tell you the hair color of the cashier who sold him the cigarettes he bought while he was busy not committing the murder, right? An innocent kid, one who actually *was* buying the cigarettes instead of committing the murder—he barely even remembers he bought any until you ask him about the receipt in his pocket. The Stockton kid could hardly say anything to help himself. No alibi, no idea who'd put a bloody knife in his car, no help at all." He paused and looked at me. "I was him, I would have started making stuff up to fill the story in. But he didn't. Like I said, stupid. All he wanted to know was if we found Sarah yet, like she was going to make sense of it for him."

Novotny didn't seem like the type to suggest someone's innocence lightly. Cops never were. "What do you think happened to her?"

"I haven't the faintest," Novotny said. "None of her stuff was gone.

No secret rendezvous in her e-mail. This was before all the kids had cell phones, so nothing there. No activity on her savings account. She's probably dead, that's all I can think. Otherwise how else did she vanish like this?"

"The million-dollar question," I said.

He shook his head, his expression going serious. "This is one of those cases. The ones that stick with you. Nothing makes any sense. There must have been a hell of a secret, that's all I can think. The Cooks were nice people, boring corporate jobs, no known enemies. And we got Brad saying he and Sarah were the love story of the century, but then we got Elaine's family saying she was terrified of Brad. Sarah's not here to settle it for us, so you look at her, maybe she did it. But she'd have to hate both her parents *and* Brad a whole helluva lot in that case, and there's no evidence of that at all."

"So she's gone, and they're dead, the end?" I said.

"Bah," Novotny said. "I don't know what to tell you, kid, if you were hoping for insight. That's all I got. I don't think the case was open-and-shut, not by a long shot. But Danielle Stockton would tell you she saw Jesus Christ himself if she thought it would help her brother out," he added, shaking his head. "You're wasting your time."

"The execution is in two months," I said. "I think it's important to her to know she tried everything. There's something to that, you know? So listen. What if I wanted to visit Brad Stockton in prison?"

"Then you'd fill out a form and wait to get put on the approved-visitor list like everybody else. Believe it's form DRC twenty-ninety-six."

"Are you saying I'm like everybody else?" I said.

He chuckled. "Okay, no. As a licensed private investigator, you— wait, you do have a license, right?"

"Petey, what do you take me for? Of course I do."

"Okay, so you'd be entitled to visit in an official capacity if you have a written statement from the attorney of record."

"Is that something you think you could help me with?" I said. "I'm impatient."

Novotny grinned. "Yeah, okay. I can call the law firm." He looked at me for a long time. "What did your daddy think, you being a detective?"

"He thought I was wasting my time too," I said. "He thought I should have been a dental hygienist."

Novotny laughed. "Good as they come, Frank was," he said, although the anecdote I had just shared was not one of my father's finer moments. Most of my anecdotes weren't. "They got the guy, right? The guy who shot him?"

"Dead at the scene," I said.

Novotny nodded. "Good, good. That has to be a relief."

I nodded, though it wasn't, not really. I didn't like to think about it: the twenty-year-old kid my father had pursued across a housing-project playground, the kid who turned and fired three times before Frank could even unholster his gun. My father's partner shot back, taking the kid down with a bullet to the chest. But it was too late. That bullet wasn't a time machine. Nothing about any of it was a relief. "Thanks for the drink," I said, giving him one of my cards. "Drinks."

"Any time, doll. I hope you have more luck with Brad than I ever did."

"Ten bucks I do," I said.

We shook on it.

My father always had a drink in his hand. It was part of him, like his broad shoulders or his temper or his antifreeze-blue eyes. It was the catalyst to every good time and every bad time he ever had. It was a magnifying glass he put himself under, revealing the truth of him. It was the only thing we had in common, the only thing we ever agreed on.

The last time I saw him was three weeks before he died. We had dinner once a month, my brothers, my parents, and me. I don't remember what we ate or what we talked about. Probably nothing of consequence, because despite the monthly get-togethers, we weren't really close. I only remember the last thing my father said to me, grabbing my arm as I walked past his chair on my way out.

"You turned out okay," he said as he gripped my arm. It didn't sound affectionate. It sounded like an accusation. Frank had been a cop for thirty-eight years. Everything he said sounded like an accusation. "More like me. I was afraid you were going to turn out like your mother."

Andrew and Matt, wisely, had already left. My mother was sitting on the couch. She didn't look up from her magazine. "Let go," I said.

"She's nice, that's what people would say about her, she's *nice*. But you," he said. He looked at me, his eyes bloodshot and whiskey-wild. He was still touching my arm. His other hand held a cut-crystal tumbler, empty except for an ice cube that barely had a chance to start melting. "You know, maybe you could stand to be a little nicer, actually. You're a girl. You have to be nice. But not too fucking nice. That's what you have to do. Be nice but not too fucking nice."

I jerked my arm away from him. "Good night, Mom," I said.

"Drive careful," my mother said, ignoring the tension as usual.

I left without saying anything else and drove home too fast and called Andrew to tell him about it.

"You're always so surprised, when he does something shitty," he said. "But, Roxane, he's *Dad*. He's always going to do something shitty. That's all."

"Yeah," I said. But I'd had a weird feeling that there was more to it somehow.

THREE

Be nice but not too fucking nice. I replayed that final conversation as I drove to see Kenny Brayfield. This was as close to fatherly wisdom as I was ever going to get. There were too many bad feelings between us, about my work, about his affairs, about the types of men and women I brought home. There wasn't any peace. Neither of us ever apologized, and we wouldn't have been interested in forgiving each other anyhow, not all the way, not then. But I thought that I didn't have to decide about my father yet, that given enough time, the past would start to drop off the permanent record like a bad debt or a speeding ticket. I just wanted to wait. I thought there was time. But there wasn't, and the part that bothered me most was how my father said I was like him, and how he was right.

I mentally tabled the matter as I parked my car. Next Level Promotions was in a square brick office building in the Brewery District on the south end of downtown. It was one of those cheaply modern spaces with glass walls, exposed ductwork, and fake Herman Miller furniture. Five young, beautiful employees were sprawled on a plush white area rug, folding T-shirts that bore the logo of a new vodka brand. A Radiohead song was blaring from a pair of iPhone speakers. I approved of the music choice, at least. One of the women looked up at me, twisting her red-lipsticked mouth. I guessed I didn't resemble a potential client enough to merit a warm reception. "Can I . . . help you?" she said.

"Here to see Kenny Brayfield," I told her, raising my voice over the bass line. I pulled out a card from the pocket of my leather jacket and handed it to her. "He knows I'm coming."

"Let me see about that." She took my card and stood up, stepping back into her patent-leather heels. I noticed then that the other four employees on the white rug had taken off their shoes as well.

"Am I allowed to walk on this or should I go around?" I said to the others as she clacked down the polished concrete hallway.

No one said anything. A beat later, the one-person welcome committee returned and pointed in the direction she had come from. "You can go back." She sounded disappointed that she didn't get to throw me out.

I didn't bother to thank her as I stepped over the edge of the rug. I went around the corner, passing three empty offices and a small kitchen with a table stacked high with cases of vodka. At the end of the hallway, I found Kenny in a large office behind a conspicuously clean desk. He was skinny, dressed in a hoodie and dirty Chuck Taylors. His medium-brown hair was buzzed on the sides and slightly longer on top, and a diamond stud glittered from one earlobe. He looked like the type to get pegged by mall security as a shoplifting risk. But he owned this whole enterprise, so who was I to judge? When he saw me, he stood up and gave me a big smile.

"So you're the detective." He shook my hand with an overly firm grip. "Wow. I mean, wow. How crazy is that?"

"It's pretty crazy," I said as I sat down. There was a big window behind his desk, through which I could see the brownish-green Scioto River and the skyline of downtown Columbus beyond.

"Can I offer you a drink?" He sat and reached for a vodka bottle with the same label as the shirts. It was that kind with gold flakes floating in it like fish food. "They're a client, in case you wondered."

I shook my head. "Ingesting precious metals isn't really my thing," I said, and he laughed. "So, Sarah Cook."

"Sarah Cook." He leaned back in his chair and balanced there.

"Did you get a good look?" I said.

He took longer than he needed to answer. "Yeah, I got a good look."

"And?"

"And." He paused again. I had been about to take my notebook from my pocket, but I stopped to stare at him until he finally spoke. "I don't want to mess with whatever Danielle's up to here."

That struck me as a strange thing to say. "Was it Sarah or not?"

"I told Danielle at the time, it just looked like some chick."

My client had not mentioned that part. "So you *don't* think it was her."

Kenny bounced in his chair. "Look, Danielle's really shaken up. About the date, the execution date. I mean, me too. That's crazy. So I get it, she wants to do what she can do. And yeah, this woman we saw, she looked sort of familiar. But Belmont's a pretty small world. Lots of people look sort of familiar. I would have recognized Sarah. But they've always said she's dead. So how could it be her?"

"How well did you know her?"

"Well enough. She was a real sweetheart, good influence on Brad."

I shifted in my chair. It was uncomfortable, clearly designed to discourage long conversations with the boss. "What do you mean?"

"Oh, we used to get into trouble together, me and Brad. Dumb stuff, kid stuff. You know how it is, bored in the suburbs. But when Brad started hanging out with her he mellowed some too. But that's ancient history. Believe me, if I thought there was even a chance that woman was Sarah? I would have hired you myself. Brad doesn't belong in jail."

I nodded. So far I had three votes for Brad Stockton's probable innocence. "So if Brad didn't do it," I said, "who did? You knew Sarah—do you think she could have?"

Kenny sat up and leaned on his elbows. "She volunteered at the food bank and shit. She was, you know, a good girl. And she actually liked her parents, unlike basically everybody else I knew back then." He splashed some of the vodka into a tumbler and tossed it back quickly, wincing like he'd learned to drink from a movie. "So the answer is either no fucking way, or it's no one knew her at all."

I went home feeling a little frustrated. Danielle had conveniently avoided telling me that the other witness to her Sarah sighting disagreed with her, which gave it something of a different flavor. But it was her money, and I figured she could lie to me if she wanted to. I sat at my desk and ran a few database searches in case Sarah Cook's fifteen-year absence had left an electronic trail, which, of course, it hadn't. I did have a fax waiting for me though, a statement on letterhead from the law firm of Donovan & Calvert, authorizing me to act in an official capacity at the Chillicothe Correctional Institution. Peter Novotny worked fast. I liked that.

I closed the computer and stared at the wall of my office for a long time. The previous tenant had painted spirited colors in every room: a dark, shiny teal in the office, burnt orange in the living room, aubergine in the bedroom, bright yellow in the bathroom, chocolate-brown walls and red cabinets in the kitchen, cornflower blue in the long hallway that ran the length of the apartment. When I moved in, I asked the landlord to paint over the craziness, to make everything white. But he hadn't, and then I grew to like it, and then eventually I didn't see it anymore. Sometimes it still took me by surprise.

I got up and cracked a window. Even though it was cold outside, the ancient, overactive radiators in the building hissed and gurgled all day and night unregulated, causing the temperature in my apartment to spike to tropical highs. Almost every room in the place had a window open an inch or two, even in the dead of winter. But the heat wasn't why I felt like I couldn't get enough air. It was getting to be the time of night when the apartment felt like a tomb. Through the screen I heard the rustling of someone in the alley, dragging a sack of aluminum cans. "They all had their blank faces on," he was muttering, "like Jesus Christ foretold."

I put my coat back on and grabbed my keys.

The lobby of the downtown Westin was all marble floors and baroque-looking upholstery, and the doorman gave me a familiar nod as I passed him and cut to the right for the bar. It was medium-busy for a Monday after eight, a few clusters of businessmen with their ties loosened at the tables and an awkward couple that was either on a blind date or was about to break up, but there was only one party sitting at the bar itself and I sat down at the opposite end. Andrew caught my eye in the mirror behind the liquor bottles and broke into a grin.

My brother had tended bar in just about every hotel in Columbus by now. It was a good regular gig when you dealt a little bit on the side, because the hotel bar was the first place out-of-towners would check when they were in the mood to party. In-towners too, sometimes. He finished the drinks he was mixing and passed them to a server, who then carried them to the couple on the verge of breaking up.

"Have you seen our new *fall seasonal cocktail menu*?" Andrew said as he turned to me, heavy on the sarcasm. He was thirty-seven, three years older than me. We had the same blue-grey eyes, the same dark brown hair. Mine hit just below my shoulders and my brother's shaggily grazed his collar. His tattoos were visible from under the cuffs of his shirt. He pushed a narrow sheet of ivory card stock in my direction. "If I have to make another mulled-apple-cider-tini I'm going to kill myself."

I squinted at the menu in the semidark. "I'll have the Winter in Paris."

Andrew thunked two shot glasses down on the bar and filled them both with whiskey. "No," he said.

"It doesn't sound that bad. St-Germain and champagne? Maybe I'm feeling classy."

"You're not." He slid one of the shot glasses to me and held his up. "Friends don't let friends order cocktails invented by social-media interns."

I clinked my glass against his and we drank. "Is Matt dating someone?" I said.

Andrew shrugged. "Like he'd tell me. Why?"

"He sent someone my way," I said, "and I figured it was some girl he was trying to impress."

"And?"

"And, I'm just not sure I'm up to the challenge of impressing anybody."

"You're the smartest person I know."

"Christ, you need to meet more people, then."

"Is this how you get when you're feeling classy? I think," he continued more softly as he refilled our glasses, "that after losing Dad, you just don't want to pick back up and keep going."

I didn't respond right away. Then I said, "That's not true."

"It is."

"Why?"

"You're scared. That it would mean you're as over it as you're going to get."

I swallowed my second shot and thought about that. Neither of us had a good relationship with Frank, but that didn't make it any easier. In fact, it might've made it worse. "Aren't you?" I said.

"Roxane, I'm fucking terrified."

FOUR

At eleven the next morning I meant to be heading an hour south of
Columbus to the prison in Chillicothe. I wanted to get Brad's side of
the story, hoping that fifteen years in prison made him reconsider
his own unhelpfulness. But as I drove I saw the exit for Belmont, and
I decided to take a brief detour. Belmont was one of the city's farthest-
flung suburbs, way out on the southeast side. According to the sign
that greeted me as I veered off the highway, it was also the wildflower
capital of Ohio. I'd lived in the state for my entire life and this was the
first I had heard of such a claim. But it didn't look like Belmont had
much else to pride itself on. It was seventies suburban sprawl personi-
fied, the ranch architecture, the cul-de-sacs. The Outerbelt divided it
in half; everything on the east side of the freeway was the good side of
town and everything to the west was the bad part. The east side had
the bigger houses and the high school, a few narrow blocks that
passed for a downtown, a mall called the Shops at Wildflower Glade,
and a string of medium-nice hotels and chain restaurants. The west
side had a skate park and a railroad crossing and a UPS sorting facility. There weren't any wildflowers to be seen, but then again, it was
November.

The gas station where the Sarah sighting occurred was on Clover
Road, the main drag through the city. I stopped there and went inside

and asked the kid behind the counter if the security cameras worked.

"What cameras?" the kid said.

I pointed. There were four cameras that I could see: one in each corner of the rear of the store, one above the door, one behind the counter.

"Oh," he said. He looked embarrassed now, as if the thought of his every waking move being captured on film had never occurred to him.

"Yeah," I said. "So do they work?"

"Hang on." He disappeared through a door marked *Private* and then reappeared a moment later. "Yes," he said, "they work."

"Do you think I could take a look at the recorded footage?" I said.

He went behind the door again. When it opened, the kid had a young woman with him. "Can I help you?"

"Hi," I said. "I was hoping to get a look at your security cameras."

They both stared at me. They were probably eighteen or nineteen. I took out my license and told them who I was. "Just for one day, a couple weeks ago. I'm looking for a woman who was here, and I was thinking maybe your cameras would show her or if she was with anyone."

"Are you," the boy said, "a cop?"

"She's not a cop," the girl said quickly.

I gave them the most responsible smile I could manage. "I work with the cops all the time."

"She has a badge." The boy's eyes flicked toward my license on the counter.

"That's *not* a badge."

"Should we call Dave?"

"*No,*" the girl said.

"Is Dave your manager?" I said. "Maybe I could talk to him."

They both looked at me, stricken. No one wanted Dave involved.

"Do you have a picture of her or something?" the boy said. "We could probably look at a picture."

I tapped my fingernails lightly on the counter. I did not have a picture, unless you counted Sarah's old yearbook photo, which was obviously going to make canvassing difficult. "Well," I said, "I was hoping her picture is on your security tape."

The girl shook her head. "We're not supposed to let *anyone* in the back."

I didn't press it. Instead I bought a cup of tea for the road and sat in the car, thinking. Tracking down someone who hadn't been seen for fifteen years had many challenges, but especially the fact that I didn't have a photo to flash around. So I called Catherine Walsh at her studio at home. Her husband answered. My instinct was to hang up, but I was calling on business for a change. "May I speak with Catherine, please?" I tried to sound polite and artistic.

Her husband thumped the phone down and a few beats passed before Catherine came on the line.

"Is this Catherine Walsh, the world-renowned professor and artist?" I said in my polite artistic voice. "I have some pressing business to discuss with her."

Catherine sighed. "Roxane, we have caller ID."

She didn't sound happy to hear from me.

"Aren't you curious about the pressing business?" I said.

"I'm kind of in the middle of something." Such as, *her life.* "Or is there actually business?"

"I need a sketch artist," I said.

"Really."

"No expense spared."

"And what would I be sketching?"

I filled her in briefly on Sarah Cook.

"I don't know," Catherine said, but her tone was warming up the tiniest bit. "Sounds intriguing but I'm not sure it's a good idea right now."

"I can just give my client your info and have her call you," I said. "And you can set it up with her directly. You wouldn't even have to see me. It might be easier that way, although less fun."

"Indeed," Catherine said. "Okay."

"I'll have Danielle get in touch."

"Okay."

Neither of us said anything but neither hung up.

Then Catherine finally spoke. "Is there anything else?"

I hadn't seen her since my father's funeral. She'd surprised me by coming, since she had decided the previous fall to go back to her husband again. Meanwhile, I went back to a few men and women myself, and now there was just a sense of unfinished business between us. "Nope," I said. "Thanks."

After we hung up, I called Danielle and left her a voice mail with instructions. Then I drove down 23 with Elliott Smith playing on the stereo of my car, an old blue Mercedes 300D from five years before I was born. I'd gotten it a few years ago in trade when a used-import dealer needed help figuring out who was stealing parts from his shop and I needed a new car. Someone had taken good care of it—the vehicle had forty thousand miles on it when it came to me. Now it had over a hundred. The old-fashioned odometer showed only five digits, so it looked like it only had three. It drove like a car was supposed to, smooth and fast and sturdy. I loved my car. I spent more time in it than in my apartment.

The Chillicothe Correctional Institution sat near the Scioto River on a few acres that could have been mistaken for a small liberal arts college if not for the barbed wire and the watchtowers and the metal detectors and security checkpoints. My letter from Donovan & Calvert cut through a bit of the usual administrative bullshit, but the prison system was still a bureaucracy and I still had to wait for well over an hour in a beige room that felt like the loneliest bus terminal in the world.

Finally I was ushered into a narrow corridor lined with Plexiglas booths, where I waited some more on a rickety metal folding chair. It smelled like disinfectant and basement and grease all at once. A guard on the other side of the glass led Bradford Stockton over to me. Brad sat down and frowned.

The friendly, long-eyelashed kid from the pictures in Danielle's scrapbook was gone. He was thirty-four now, tall and lean and serious-looking in orange prison garb that seemed to glow against his smooth, dark skin. His angular face was still handsome, but now it was also a little bit mean.

I picked up the grimy handset next to the glass and waited for Brad to do the same. When he did, his movements were slow and fluid like we both had all the time in the world.

"Who're you?" he said.

"Roxane Weary. Your sister hired me—"

"What happened to the other guy?"

"Novotny?" I said.

Brad nodded.

"He retired."

"So Dani's paying for the lawyer *and* for you now?"

It was a strange thing to be concerned about, given his circumstances. "Yes, I guess so."

"How much?" He slouched low in his seat. "How much is she paying you?"

"You can ask her that," I said.

He glared at me some more. "Where the hell did she find you, anyway? Because you look a little, I don't know, like you might not be doing all that much better than me."

"Thank you for that," I said. I tucked the handset between my ear and my shoulder and I folded my arms across my chest. It was cold in the prison, like the heat was set to about forty-five degrees.

"Are you here to ask me if I did it? Try to see if *you* can tell if I'm lying or not?"

I ignored the attitude. "Did your sister tell you she saw Sarah?"

Brad gave a slight nod. "So she said."

"You don't believe her?"

"She wants everything to be okay," he said. "She tries real hard. And she can believe whatever she wants, if it makes her feel better. But it doesn't have to make me feel better."

"You don't think I can help you."

"No offense, lady, but no, I do not."

I couldn't blame him for that. Fifteen years of white strangers trying to help him hadn't done fuck-all for Brad Stockton. But I wasn't sure that I believed he meant the *no offense*. I wanted to hear his side of the story but I wasn't about to beg him for it if he was going to sit there and insult me. "Listen, it's up to you," I said. "The date's been set. You're almost done, Brad, and your sister wants to feel like she did every fucking thing she could. Because even though *you'll* be dead, she's still going to have to live the rest of her life. So you talk to me or you don't, but I'm doing this for her, not for you. And I'm getting paid regardless."

He looked a bit startled and said nothing for a while, as if he was trying to decide about me. Then he straightened up a little, brows knitting together.

"Okay," I said. "Where do you think Sarah is?"

"I don't know."

"I know you don't know, Brad. But help me out here. Speculate."

"Help you?" He sighed heavily before he answered. "I think she must be gone."

"Gone?" I repeated.

"Passed on. It took me a long time to accept that she wasn't going to come back, because that meant she had to be gone. But there's no way Sarah would leave me here, to face what I face." He sighed, a short forceful burst of air through the phone. "I don't want to talk about Sarah. How is that going to help?"

"You let me worry about that. This is the easiest thing you'll do all day. It's just answering questions."

He shook his head but eventually he shrugged.

"Did you ever meet her parents?"

"A few times."

"And?"

Another shrug. "They were, I don't know, nice. Polite to me. That's why it was such a shock, everything Mrs. Cook's sister said at the trial. That they were afraid of me? We played Scrabble together once." He sighed. "But, I guess you never know what people say behind your back. My mom used to say, *What people say about you behind your back is none of your business.*"

Unless it gets you convicted of murder. "Do you think Mrs. Cook really said those things?"

"I don't know what I think anymore," Brad said.

"I talked to Kenny Brayfield yesterday," I said. "He told me you guys used to get into some trouble together. The kind of trouble that makes people afraid of you?"

He shrugged. "Vandalism, whatever. Kenny used to sell weed around school. Figures he would bring up that shit—dude still wants to be a gangster. But his parents are loaded. He never got in trouble for anything."

We were starting to get off topic. "Tell me about what went on that day, when you saw her last."

He let out a long breath. "I don't want to think about it. Every time, it's like it rips me open again." He started shaking his head again. "Do you really think you're going to be able to do something nobody could do for fifteen years? Prove anything that nobody could prove? You act like it should be so easy for me to sit here and talk to you, but it isn't. Maybe I'm done talking now. I don't like my sister spending more money anyway."

"You don't like her spending money on trying to get you not executed?" I said. "That doesn't sound like an innocent man talking."

He flinched. "Fuck you." He leaned forward, jabbing an index finger in my direction. "You don't know anything about me or my sister."

"I'm on your side."

"You think sides are going to help me now?" Brad said.

He had a point there.

"Listen. When I got in here at first," he said, "I was so depressed. Everyone said I did these terrible things I didn't do, and it wasn't like some situation that would pass, it was forever. I tried to make a, you know, a noose, from my sheets. Like, no sense in waiting around." He looked up at the ceiling. "But I couldn't do it—I mean, I tried, but I couldn't get it right, what the fuck do I know about making a noose from sheets. Then they put me in the hospital here and I was all fucked up on lithium, and all I could do was stare up at the ceiling. When I went back to my cell after that, I was like, okay, this is happening. It's like that song, you sing it when you're a kid. About a bear hunt."

I knew the song he meant. "Can't go over it," I said. "Can't go under it."

"Can't go around it," Brad said, smiling very faintly. "Gotta go through it."

We watched each other for another long while.

"So I read every single word of every legal document about my case I could get my hands on. I read law books. I got enrolled in this print-based college degree thing, you know, a correspondence course. Wrote about a thousand poems, wrote letters to the lawyers, the cops, everyone I could think of. Trying to keep busy, right? Busy busy busy, fight fight fight." He pinched the bridge of his nose. "But busy doesn't mean shit. There is no *through it*. Through it means I'm dead. And no amount of fighting is going to change that." He shrugged. "The only *real* way through it is to accept it. Otherwise, it'll just tear me up all over again every single day."

I wanted to believe that I was working for an innocent man. I also wanted to believe that if I was wrongfully accused of a crime, I'd be fighting every minute. But there was a sad kind of wisdom to his words. "Okay," I said. "Forget all the other questions, forget every other person who has tried to help you or hurt you or whatever. Nobody knows as much about this case as you do, right?"

"Yeah, I guess."

"So let's start totally fresh. Just educate me about your case. Pretend I don't know anything."

He finally seemed to accept I wasn't going anywhere. "It was a Thursday," he said. "I worked till nine at Subway. Sarah came by after school, it was just a short bike ride. Maybe three thirty, she got there. I took my lunch and we sat in the car and talked. We made plans to see a movie later—the theater's in the same plaza as Subway. She was going home for dinner but she'd come back. And that was it. She got back on her bike and I went into the restaurant."

"What about after your shift?"

"I waited, in the car," he said. "I waited for a long time. I thought maybe she was just running late. I called her house from a pay phone in the parking lot but there was no answer. By then it was probably ten thirty. I drove over to her house, and there were ambulances and all these cop cars, it was just insanity. No one would tell me what happened. They asked me to come to the station and they said I was free to go whenever I wanted, but it didn't feel like that."

"How long were you there?"

"They talked to me for hours, I mean, *hours*. They still wouldn't tell me what had happened, exactly. I thought *Sarah* was hurt or something, I thought that's what it was, they were only asking me questions about her. In the morning they gave me a lift back to my car, and I went home, and it wasn't until I saw the news with my mom that I heard what really happened. We were shocked. Like, we just stared at the TV—and then the cops came to the door. They wanted me to come answer more questions, and their tone was all different, asking me all about knives, do you own any, did you ever go hunting, all this crap. They'd gotten a warrant to search my room and my car, while I was talking to them. And I thought they were making it up, that they found a knife in there. I never had a knife. I honestly didn't believe it."

"So how'd the knife get there?" I said. "What actually happened that night?"

"If I knew, you think I'd be sitting on that information?"

"I think you've had an awful long time to formulate some kind of opinion, Brad."

He looked up at the ceiling again, shaking his head. "I saw this episode of *Dateline* one time, okay? Where this family was killed and there was absolutely no explanation, no reason whatsoever. No one could figure it out. But then, it turned out these guys had been hired to kill some other family, and they had a similar kind of address, like Court instead of Street or something. But they went to the wrong house and killed the wrong family."

"And you think it's like that."

"Yeah."

"It was just a mistake."

"I mean, what else was it? They were nice people. There's no reason for them to be dead, and no reason for Sarah to be gone, and no reason for me to be in here. It's just a mistake."

"But the knife, Brad. The universe got the address wrong," I said, "but somehow got the right car?"

"I don't *know*. I don't know how it got there. Like, I was in the prison hospital all doped up and staring at the ceiling and I got to thinking that *aliens* put the knife there. And that sounds stupid, but that's as good a guess as any."

"Where was your car when you were talking to the police? At Sarah's house and then at your house?"

He nodded.

"When was the last time you were in it?"

"Like after I talked to the cops the first time," he said. "I got a ride back to the car from the station, and then I drove it home."

"And you didn't notice anything weird, like someone had been in there?"

"No."

"Doors locked?"

"The locks were busted. So I had to leave it unlocked."

"Anyone else know the locks were busted?"

"Whoever I gave a ride to or whatever. Sarah knew, obviously. Kenny. My sister. Lots of people."

"And there's no way Sarah was involved," I said.

"No, there's no way. There isn't much I can say for sure, but I can say that. She was a good person. Fundamentally *good*. The lawyer was like, Come on, I know you think you were in love with her, but the fact is, she's not in here, and you are, so be realistic. But I'd rather die than try to save my skin by saying she did something she didn't do."

"Literally."

"Literally," he said.

"I don't think most people could stick to that."

"I'm not most people."

"That might not be something to be proud of."

"But maybe it is," Brad said.

"Maybe it is," I said. "And you're not protecting her."

His eyes crinkled up. "I wish that's what this was."

"Even after all this time."

"Protecting her would mean she was okay. But I don't know what happened. I don't." He rubbed his hand over his face.

I wanted to think I could help him, but it wasn't easy. Not when he didn't think I could. He didn't think he could help himself either, and he'd had nothing but time to come up with a way to do it. I didn't know what to make of Brad Stockton yet. But I also didn't think that was the end.

FIVE

I went to Dirty Frank's on Fourth downtown and placed a carryout order for dinner—a hot dog topped with sriracha cream cheese and Fritos and a side of Tater Tots. While I was waiting, I sat at the bar and ordered a Crown Royal on the rocks. The restaurant was small and pleasantly warm, and the chill from the prison started to fade away. I was staring into my drink and thinking hard about whether I bought Brad Stockton's *I'd rather die than sell out my beloved* routine when I felt a hand between my shoulder blades. I jumped, spinning around on my barstool to see my father's former partner right behind me.

"Hi, sorry," Tom Heitker said quickly. "Was that creepy?"

"Extremely creepy," I said, letting myself smile. "What the hell is wrong with you?"

He grinned at me, stepping in closer to let a waiter squeeze past with an armful of the red baskets that served as plates.

"And what are you doing way down here, dressed in jeans?" I said.

"There was a community policing meeting in Twelve Precinct. I wanted to go incognito so I could eavesdrop."

Even in jeans and a fleece half-zip, he'd get pegged as a cop anywhere. It was his posture, or maybe something about the eyes, a guarded squint. He was in his late thirties, and he'd worked with Frank for his entire career as a detective, till now. He had lost weight

SOUTH PARK TOWNSHIP LIBRARY

since my father died, twenty pounds from a frame carrying an extra forty, and he looked good. But then, he had looked good before.

"And?" I said.

"Pointless," Tom said. "Nobody saw nothing, ad infinitum. Can I sit?"

I gestured at the empty barstool beside me. "I'm not staying though. I ordered food to go. I spent the afternoon at the prison in Chillicothe and all I want to do is get home."

Tom held up his own carryout bag. "Great minds," he said. "What are you working on?"

"Tracking down a witness in an old case. Maybe a witness, maybe not. Double murder in Belmont a while back."

"When?"

"Fifteen years ago," I said. "Ish."

"Married couple, right? Stabbed to death? Daughter went missing?"

"Yeah," I said, surprised. "How do you know that?"

"Cops remember everything. I was working a drug task force on the southeast side back then. I was always down there. Belmont and Columbus have weird borders. That case was closed in record time, I recall. What's going on now?"

"The kid who was convicted is going to be executed in two months," I said. "His sister hired me. She claims she saw the daughter in Belmont a couple weeks ago."

"Convenient."

"Yeah," I said, letting out a sigh without meaning to. "Have you ever worked a case where someone was framed?"

"Nope. That's television stuff. Ditto for faked suicides."

"That's what I thought." I finished my whiskey. "I can't figure this guy out though. The missing daughter—a logical alternate theory of the crime. But he wouldn't let his lawyer talk about it at the trial and even today, fifteen years later, he still won't entertain the thought. I don't know if that's idealistic or delusional."

"Fifteen years is a long time to put up a front," Tom said. "Then again, didn't they have him dead to rights with the murder weapon?"

"Correct."

"Possession is nine-tenths of the law and all that. Goes both ways."

"Sure does."

"So it sounds like you've got your work cut out for you."

The bartender brought over my carryout bag, and I slid off the barstool. "Well," I said.

Tom and I watched each other for a few beats. He was always a little shy around me, and I found it slightly endearing. "So do you want to come over, or what?"

The day of my father's funeral was the longest of my life. There was a full agenda: private prayer service at the funeral home. Procession to Saint Joseph downtown for the Mass. Procession to Greenlawn for the burial. Light refreshments at my mother's house to follow. It was after ten when I finally left, dry-eyed and bewildered. I was wearing a strange outfit that belonged to my mother's neighbor—my own wardrobe selection of a new black pantsuit and flats having been declared unacceptable that morning—and the borrowed pumps rubbed against my heels as I walked down the sidewalk toward my car. As I got closer, I noticed that Tom was sitting on the retaining wall in front of a neighbor's house, staring at his own shoes.

I sat down beside him. "I thought you left like two hours ago."

"I did," he said without looking up. Like the other cops who had attended the service, he was wearing his uniform but he was all unbuttoned, disheveled. His short, dark hair was sticking up like he'd been tearing at it. He had worked with my father for close to a decade and he had spent a fair amount of time around my family in all those years, but I barely knew him personally, wasn't sure if we had ever had a one-on-one conversation longer than a few lines.

I stood up again. "Sorry, you look like you want to be by yourself."

"No, no," he said. He turned toward me, his warm brown eyes full of stunned pain. "I really, really don't."

We went to the liquor store at the end of my mother's street and bought the cheapest whiskey they sold. I had plenty of liquor at home but I didn't want to go home and I didn't want that liquor. We sat in Tom's car and passed the bottle back and forth between us without talking for a long time. The night sky felt heavy, like an X-ray blanket.

"Your mom," he said eventually. "She has people in town, right?"

I took a long pull from the bottle. The whiskey burned all the way down but not as much as I wanted it to. "Two sisters. They're staying with her right now."

"That's good."

"She's had to be strong, to stay married to him. She's tough. And she has a lot of friends. And my brothers."

"And you."

I drew a squiggly line on the fogged-up window and then erased it with my palm. "That'll do a lot of good," I said, trying and failing to use a light tone.

"You know you were his favorite," Tom said.

I stared at him. "He never said that. He didn't even like me."

"That's not true."

"I don't even blame him for that," I said. "How could I? I never listened to a goddamn thing he said."

"Sure you did," Tom said. "Didn't he get you your first job?"

I looked down at my hands. It had never occurred to me that my father had talked about me to Tom. "Is that what he told you?"

He nodded.

"Old family friend used to have a private security company. I worked there through college part-time, in the office, and I kind of stayed after I graduated. I thought I was going to be a psychologist. Frank told me I would make a terrible psychologist. But then I started helping on cases when I was supposed to be studying for the GRE. Which is just as well, honestly, he was right."

"You would have made a terrible psychologist?"

"I'm too nosy. Too impatient." I shrugged. "You know he was always right. Somehow. Even for the wrong reasons, he was always right."

Tom gave me a sad smile. "He was," he said. "But nosy and impatient, those are good qualities for a detective. So I guess that worked out."

"I don't think I really had a choice. It's the only thing I can do."

Tom sighed heavily. "Frank was proud of you," he said again. "For doing your own thing, being your own person."

"Stop it," I said, serious now. I had promised myself I wasn't going to cry and I wouldn't. I pressed my hand against my mouth until the tightness in my jaw eased up. "Change the subject."

Tom was quiet for a bit, gazing over the steering wheel at High Street. Finally, he shook his head. "I got nothing," he said. Then he turned to me. "It happened so fast."

"Don't." I couldn't hear about how fast it had happened, the end of everything. I picked up his hand. "No crying. I can't take it. I'll go home."

"You can't drive like this," Tom said, blinking fast, nodding.

"Then I'll walk."

"In those shoes?"

My face felt too weird to smile. But I would have. I brought Tom's hand to my lips. "I need to feel something else," I said. It was the only other coping method I could think of. The whiskey wasn't coming close to touching the way I felt. "Do you want to come home with me?"

"Roxane." Tom shifted in his seat. "You're upset."

"Yes," I said. "So are you." I placed his hand on my bare knee.

"I know you're feeling crazy but we can't—"

"Sure we can."

Now, just inside my apartment, Tom pushed me into the wall and kissed me hard in the dark. His hands found my shoulders and peeled off my leather jacket and dropped it to the floor with a jangle of zippers and loose change, and I hooked my thumbs into his belt loops and pulled him close to me so there wasn't even the suggestion of space between us. He smelled good, like fresh air and pine, and his mouth was soft and hungry. "I want you right here," he whispered, his voice equal parts intensity and restraint. Our respective carryout dinners were forgotten.

"I have a bed," I whispered between kisses. Everything about the day was beginning to recede from my mind like a tide.

"I want you there too," he said.

He pulled my hands away from his hips and pressed them against the wall at my sides, slowly sliding my arms up over my head so he could hold both of my wrists in one hand. My breath caught in my throat. This was what I liked most, the way he wasn't careful with me. He could be rough and tender at all the right times and he was different in private—assured and almost playful, unlike the reserved way he carried himself the rest of the time. He slipped his other hand under the hem of my shirt, his fingers at once hot and cold on my bare skin as he undid the button on my jeans and slid the zipper down so slowly I couldn't stand it. Then he parted my legs with his knee. I arched toward him, my whole body humming.

Afterward we lay on my bed, looking up at the glow-in-the-dark stars on my ceiling, left over from the previous tenant like the paint colors. Tom was gently brushing the inside of my wrist with his thumb. It was like we were camping, gazing at the real night sky. We hadn't bothered with most of our clothes. "I needed you," he said, "after the last few weeks I've had."

I wanted to be annoyed at him for saying that, but I wasn't. "Do you want to tell me about it?" I said instead.

He tipped his head toward me. Out of the corner of my eye it looked like he was about to launch into something. But then his features relaxed. "Nah," he said. "Just the usual bureaucratic bullshit. A million miles away right now."

"Good." I liked him like this, relaxed and open. The night of the funeral had been a protest fuck, an act of defiance. But we'd seen each other quite a few times in the nine months since. There was nothing to it, just stress relief, pain relief, all of the above. But I still needed those things. I turned toward him and put my head on his shoulder. He slid his arm underneath me and made a soft noise in his throat and I played with the buttons on his plaid shirt. "I like this. It's nice and worn."

"It should be, it's twenty years old," he said. "I'm into dark territory in the closet. Alice in Chains T-shirts are next. Everything else fits like a windsail."

"And it just makes you *furious*," I said.

"Stark raving mad," he said. "It just kills me, the things people say to me sometimes lately, like, I'm thrilled they want me to know I look better now that I'm depressed."

I rested my chin on my arm and looked him in the eye. He was doing better than he had been during the spring and summer, but I knew what he meant. "But just so you know, I always thought you were a stud," I said.

Tom laughed in a way that seemed to take him by surprise. Then he cupped his hand around the back of my head and pulled me in for a kiss, and it said everything.

Maybe it said too much.

SIX

I walked to the patisserie on Oak Street for breakfast and drank a cup of tea and ordered the white African sweet potato tart, which was not a breakfast food, so I got it to go in a little paper box in order to pretend it was for later. The neighborhood was caught in midgentrification right now, and though I approved of the introduction of exotic pastries, I hoped Olde Towne wasn't going to get much nicer. I walked back home in the bright, cold morning air and tried to imagine who I might be appear to be: a rich lady buying a dessert tart for a Tuesday-night dinner party and checking items off a to-do list, instead of a slightly hungover detective inordinately proud of herself for being out and about before eleven o'clock and planning to eat half—no, most—of the dessert tart while driving. But when I got back over to Bryden Road, I saw a slim figure in a vintage-looking green wool coat in the doorway of my building between the two brick-enclosed porches, writing something on a large manila envelope. It was Catherine. I was glad I hadn't started eating the tart as I walked.

"Have sketch, will travel?" I said as I approached her from behind.

"Hi," she said as she turned around. Her long blond hair was twisted away from her face in wavy sections. Her eyes were hidden behind a pair of oversize sunglasses with white frames. She looked, as always, like she had stepped from the pages of an Anthropologie catalogue.

"That was fast," I said.

"Well," Catherine said. "Danielle called me not ten minutes after I talked to you, so I thought I should get it to you quickly."

"Do you want to come in?"

"I can't," she said.

We looked at each other. Or, she looked at me while I looked at my reflection in the lenses of her sunglasses. "Let me see your eyes," I said.

She didn't smile but she pushed the sunglasses into her hair. Her eyes were lovely, pale green and sparkling. "Hi," she said again.

"Hello."

I hoped she wouldn't ask how I was holding up or if I was seeing anyone or say that I looked great or that I looked awful, and she didn't. Instead she handed me the envelope and flipped her sunglasses back down, nodding at the grease-spotted box I was carrying. "What've you got in there?"

"It's not breakfast, I swear," I said, and she finally smiled. "Come in so I can pay you, and we can share."

Catherine lifted the sunglasses again. "I really have to go," she said. "And you don't have to pay me, it only took an hour."

"I'll get dinner then," I said, "the next time we have dinner."

"We're not going to have dinner, Roxane. You know I can't see you right now."

I did know, though this knowledge was somewhat confounded by the fact that she was standing here. She could have sent the sketch with Danielle, but she hadn't.

I placed the tart on the brick ledge formed by the wall of my porch and pried up the edges of the metal brad that secured the envelope. Then I pulled a thick sheet of paper out of the envelope and took in

Catherine's work. As usual, it looked effortless and yet eerily realistic, a charcoal sketch depicting a woman with sad eyes and a spray of freckles across her nose. Her face was fuller than in the yearbook photo, her mouth more pulled in at the corners. But it resembled Sarah Cook, at least a little.

"It's very good," I said. "Which I'm sure you know. Thanks."

"I hope it helps."

"Me too."

"Let me know," she said. "What happens."

We looked at each other for another long moment. There was a lot I wanted to say to her, but I couldn't make myself say any of it.

Then she pulled out her keys and adjusted the strap of her handbag. "Okay. Well. Later."

"I hope," I said.

Catherine kissed her fingertips and reached out and pressed them against my sternum for the briefest instant. Then she turned and hurried down the sidewalk without another word. I listened to the sound of her heels clicking against the sidewalk and waited to see if she would stop and come back, but she didn't. Then I grabbed the tart off the brick wall and got in the car.

Before I headed back to the gas station for another crack at the security tapes, I decided to check in with Sarah's family in case one look at Catherine's sketch could tell me if I was on the right track faster than days of canvassing could. Elizabeth Troyan lived on the east side of Belmont in a big colonial with white-painted bricks and black shutters and one of those little sculpted hedges surrounded by decorative pavers and a water feature. But the pond was full of dead leaves and mud and several pulpy community newspapers. I would have guessed that no one had lived here in weeks, but the curtain fluttered as I walked up the steps to the porch.

The woman who opened the door was blond, late twenties, her thin frame dwarfed in an oversize cowl-neck sweater. Her eyes were ringed in heavy black liner, lashes spidery with mascara. She frowned thoroughly at me. "Can I help you?"

"Is Elizabeth home?"

"It's not a good time," she said.

From somewhere in the house, a female voice slurred, "Cass, who the fuck is it now?"

The young woman in front of me winced a little. "It's no one, Mom, go back to sleep," she called.

Cass turned back to me. "Sorry," she said. She didn't sound sorry. "If this is about the car, you'll have to come back later. Like, next week. And definitely call first. My father just ran out on her and it's, you know, a bad situation all around."

I wondered what had happened to the car, but I didn't ask. "It's not about the car," I said. "I was hoping to talk to her about your cousin, Sarah."

Her eyes narrowed. "No, I don't think so."

She started to close the door. I took a guess that the recent exodus of her father and, also, the car thing might be a cash-flow situation, so I quickly adapted an old gimmick of mine. "I work on a show about missing-persons cases in the Midwest. I was hoping it's in our budget to get an interview on camera with Sarah's family." No doubt Sarah's family had been offered money for their story at some point, but it looked like maybe they needed it now.

"A show?" Cass said. She looked interested. "A television show?"

"Yes," I said, opening my wallet to look for a business card. I hoped I still had some of the ones that identified me as Roxane Smith, production coordinator for a PBS affiliate in Chicago. It was amazing, the things people would tell you when they thought fame or money could be involved. I found one of the cards and handed it to her while I spun through possible titles for this television show in my head.

Cass looked at the card. "You're making a show about Sarah?"

Usually the scheme didn't require much detail. I started to feel a little bit bad for the lie. "We're still in pre-pro but we're interested. I'm authorized to offer five hundred dollars per day of shooting, if we decide we want to move forward," I said.

She glanced over her shoulder but the slurred voice was silent. Then she looked back at me. I could see her weighing the pros and cons, but finally the hint of money won out. "Here, why don't you come in for a few minutes?"

She led me through the kitchen, which was missing the stove—a power cord abandoned in the gap it left like a dead snake. Everything in the house looked like it had been recently zapped with a shrink-ray: a small tube television on top of a footstool in the place where a large entertainment stand should have been; the telltale impression where a sectional sofa had once gone beneath a small love seat. Through the doorway, I could see that the woman sprawled on it was blond and curvy, good-looking in a mature, highly engineered kind of way that could have put her anywhere from sixty to seventy-five. But I knew from my research that Elizabeth was fifty-six. The fifteen years since she had her picture in the paper had clearly been rough ones. She appeared to be asleep now.

"Um, let's go into the dining room," Cass said, quickly steering me away from the spectacle of her mother. The dining room was missing a light fixture in the ceiling, but still had the table. Elizabeth's daughter sat down and got out a pack of Parliaments. Her left hand sported an engagement ring with the world's tiniest diamond. "So how does this work?"

"I'm just going to ask you a few questions," I said, "to see what you might be able to offer."

"Okay."

"Did you know Sarah's boyfriend, Brad?" I said.

Cass lit a cigarette. "Nope, I never met him. None of us did."

"Were you close to your cousin?"

She nodded. "Pretty close. I mean, she was five years older than me. And we didn't see them a ton, because my mom was such a bitch." She looked at me as if waiting for me to be shocked, but I wasn't. "My mom was just always in this one-sided competition with Elaine, like, about who had the nicer stuff. Then she and my dad would fight about it. It got to the point where we barely went over there. But I always liked hanging out with Sarah."

"So they weren't close either," I said. "Your mom and your aunt."

Cass shrugged. "They'd talk on the phone sometimes. But I just remember, when it happened and suddenly my mom was acting like they had been so super close all their lives. I know she was upset, we were all upset. But she was just making shit up."

I crossed my arms. "You thought she was lying."

"Not *lying*, really. You know how it is, when you're a kid and your parents do something," she said, "and it's just like, whatever, but then later, when you grow up, you're like, wait, that was actually really fucked up?"

"I sure do."

"It's like that, I guess. All that stuff she said at the trial about that kid, Brad?" She shrugged again. "I always thought that was so weird. But she wanted to help, which I get. And they had the guy, he had that, you know"—she lowered her voice—"knife. In his car."

"Do you know if anyone has heard from Sarah recently?" I said, the coup de grâce.

"*Heard* from her?" Cass said slowly. Her expression turned wary, like she suspected I might be insane.

"Yes," I said. "So have you?"

"No."

"Your mom?"

"No. Sarah—they told us she was dead. I mean, she has to be. She wasn't the kind of person to just disappear and not tell anyone. Why are you asking if I've heard from her? I don't understand."

"Sorry, there are just certain things I'm supposed to ask." I breezed past it. I certainly didn't want to tell her that Brad's sister was trying to get him out of jail, not when I was already here under false pretenses. "Did you ever hear Sarah talk about running away?"

Her eyes flicked down to my business card on the surface of the dining table. "No."

"She get along with her parents?"

"Yeah, I guess," she said. "Uncle Garrett was pretty strict. Not mean strict, but, like, she was supposed to get all A's all the time in school. And there was a list of words Sarah wasn't supposed to say, like *heck* and *that sucks* and *shoot.* And if she said one of the words on a list, her allowance got docked a quarter."

"*Shoot*?" I said.

"I guess because it's like *shit*?"

"That's nuts," I said, and we both laughed a little.

"And I remember this one time, she was showing us this boy collage she made—you know, like pictures from those dumb teen magazines, how girls used to put them up on the wall. But Sarah had hers on a poster board that she kept hidden behind the headboard of her bed—she said she had to hide it because she wasn't allowed to put boy pictures up. But I always kind of felt like Sarah was lucky. Her parents loved each other, and she loved them, and their house was happy."

Cass looked uneasy again, like she didn't want that sentiment repeated in the television show. I smiled in what I hoped was a reassuring way. "What was she like as a person?"

Cass got a faraway look in her eyes. "She was really lively. A little bossy. She was always writing these stories and songs and scripts and trying to get us to perform them with her. But she was also really cool." She stabbed out her cigarette against the side of a pumpkin-scented jar candle. Then she looked at the filter for a minute like she wasn't sure where it had come from. "You're asking these questions like you think she's still out there and it's really weird."

I reached into my coat and pulled out Catherine's sketch. "I'm going to show you a picture. A drawing. Tell me what you think."

Cass looked down at the sketch. "What is this?" she said.

"Does it look like your cousin?"

She picked it up and studied it carefully, but there was no emotion or recognition in her face. "It just looks like a drawing," she said.

SEVEN

I went back to the gas station, where I found the same pair of employees that I'd talked to yesterday peering into the open front of the soda machine. "Hi again," I said. I held up my sketch. "This is the woman I'm hoping to find on your security tapes."

The girl put her hands on her hips. "We talked about you at our staff meeting," she said. She paused, so I nodded like I was flattered. "Dave said we only keep the video for seven days. Then it records over itself. Was it less than seven days ago?"

It was not. So much for that. "Forget the tapes," I said. "Can you just look at this and tell me if you've seen her?"

The girl glanced at it briefly. The guy gave it a more thoughtful once-over, but he shrugged. "We see a lot of people," he said. "I don't know."

There was no way I was going to find the maybe-Sarah like this, whoever she was.

I thanked them both and went across the street and stood outside the Greek restaurant where Danielle and Kenny had met that night. It was midafternoon and the sun was high, though hidden behind gauzy November clouds. I squinted at the faces of people pumping gas on the other side of the street, and I could barely make them out in broad daylight. Danielle's encounter had taken place well after sundown. I made a mental note to check what the weather had been like. "It's not looking good," I said to myself.

In the lot beside the restaurant, there stood a small plaza offering a tanning salon, a title loan outfit, a pizza carryout, and a liquor store. I went into each shop with the drawing of the woman.

I got nowhere at the tanning salon and the pizza place. At the loan shop, the attendant offered, "Looks sort of like, what's her name. From *Iron Man*."

I looked at the drawing and thought. "Gwyneth Paltrow?" I said. "Yeah!"

"Maybe a little," I said. It didn't look like Gwyneth Paltrow. "But have you seen her?"

"In my *dreams*."

At the liquor store, I did somewhat better: a half pint of Crown and one nibble at the sketch. A partial nibble. The old guy who worked there squinted hard at it. "Yeah, she kinda looks familiar." But then he added, "The lady with the dog?"

"The dog," I said, raising an eyebrow. That made her sound like a regular in the area. I hadn't considered the fact that Sarah might never have left Belmont. It wasn't impossible, but it seemed like someone would have recognized her way before now if this was the case.

"One of those, what do you call 'em, doodles? Something-doodle? Kinda curly and brown?"

"But what about this woman?"

"Right," he said. "I think I've seen her walking the dog before. Maybe. Labradoodle, is it?"

"Do you know her name? Or where she lives?"

"Sorry," the old guy said.

"How about when you saw her last?"

He shook his head. "What did she do?"

"I just need to talk to her," I said. I gave him a card and asked him to call me if he saw her.

I spent another hour knocking on doors on the residential streets next to and behind the gas station. I didn't see any curly brown dogs.

No one else recognized the sketch or did anything to encourage me except for the teenage punk girl who told me she liked my jacket. Then I got back into the car and squinted at the sketch. The more I stared at it the more it did look like Gwyneth Paltrow, if Gwyneth Paltrow lived in Ohio and had never been happy.

I took the sketch back into the gas station. The duo from earlier had been replaced by a middle-aged guy whose name tag pegged him as the famous Dave. He looked at me with suspicion. "I was wondering if maybe you've seen this woman in here," I said, placing my sketch on the counter. "She might live in the area, might sometimes walk a, a"—I was not going to say *Labradoodle*—"brown, curly dog?"

Dave's face brightened. "Sadie."

"Sadie?" I said. "That's her name?"

"The dog," Dave said, and I sighed. He shrugged. "I have a goldendoodle, myself."

I asked if he knew the woman's name or where she lived, but he didn't. "This does look a lot like her," he said. "The lady I'm thinking of, she comes by a few times a week. But I wouldn't put money on it. Too bad you don't have a sketch of Sadie!"

"Indeed," I said. I thought about what Kenny had said, that Belmont was a small place, lots of people look familiar. Either the woman wasn't Sarah, or Sarah hadn't gotten very far fifteen years ago. Either way, it seemed like keeping an eye on the area was the only possible way to find her.

It was after five, and I was due at my mother's house for dinner at seven. But as I pushed outside, I saw that I wasn't going anywhere just yet: a Belmont police cruiser was parked diagonally behind my car. The cruiser door opened and a uniformed cop got out, young, with gym-rat muscles and a smug expression.

"How are you doing, ma'am?" he said. The pin on his uniform shirt said *C. Pasquale*.

"I'm all right," I said slowly.

"Because we got a couple calls. About you, hanging around here all afternoon. What's going on?"

"Just a routine inquiry," I said, wondering which of the unhelpful Belmont residents had called the police on me. I got my license out. He frowned at it, tilting it in the light like it was a lenticular from a Cracker Jack box.

"What kind of inquiry?"

A routine one, I wanted to say, but didn't. "I'm looking for an individual who has been seen in the area." I reached for my license but he held on to it. So I showed him the sketch. Maybe he had a something-doodle too.

"Who is she?" Pasquale said.

"An old friend of my client," I said.

"Who's your client?" he said next.

"That's confidential." It wasn't, but he was annoying me. Some small-town police forces were full of good people who believed in their community. Some were full of glorified crossing guards who had nothing to do but run speed traps near the edges of town and revel in their tiny bit of power. I was getting a pretty good idea of which Belmont's was.

"Well, next time," he said, finally letting go of my license, "give us a heads-up that you're out here. Professional courtesy."

"Sure, of course," I said, trying to sound contrite.

"Have a good night, ma'am."

I got into my car and he got into his, but neither of us went anywhere. After three minutes, he got back out and rapped on my window.

"Do you need directions or something?" he said after I had rolled it down.

"I'm good," I said, and rolled the window back up.

But he tapped on it again and I rolled it back down.

"That's not an open container," he said, nodding toward the whiskey on my passenger seat, "is it?"

"Oh, for God's sake," I muttered, and I put the window up and shifted my car into reverse.

Dinner was steak and fried onions, potatoes, and one of those coconut cakes that you store in the freezer. Although there were four of us at the table, my mother, Genevieve, did most of the talking. She never ran out of things to say. She talked about how she and her neighbor Rita were taking a tai chi class at the Conservatory on Tuesday nights. She talked about the week's excitement in the neighborhood: a traffic accident, a glum kid selling wrapping paper from a catalogue. Outwardly, she was back to herself, more or less: all smiles and the fluffy ash-blond curls she wore to compensate for her diminutive height. But I was still anxious for her, the way she seemed wound more tightly than before behind that layer of bulletproof niceness, the way things could upset her out of nowhere. I wondered what her nights were like, in the house alone. I hoped they were nothing like mine.

"I think I need to call a plumber, for that sink," she was saying when I came back from getting another round of beers for Andrew and me. The booze situation in this house was getting dire. Andrew and I had drunk everything in the once-formidable liquor cabinet. It felt tacky to restock it now, as if my mother needed one more reminder that Frank was gone. So we had since moved on to the beer stored in the garage, but even that was dwindling. "It's leaking again, and it always acts up when the weather gets cold."

Matt set his fork down on his dessert plate, eyes flicking briefly to the beer cans. He was bearded and gruff, stocky as Andrew was wiry, and he'd quit drinking about five years ago. Back then he was a disaster zone. Now he was just a self-righteous prophet of sobriety most of the time. For a second I thought he was going to concern-troll me about the beer, but instead he said, "You know, Mom, we can get you a new sink, that one's as old as the house. You should have a nice new one."

Andrew glanced at me as if to say *suck-up.*

"Oh, no, honey," my mother said, even though she'd been asking my father to replace the sink for years, "that's okay." Something in her expression had changed.

"It's just silly," Matt went on, unwisely, "to pay a plumber to come out again, for a sink that barely works anyway—"

"Matthew, I told you it's okay. I don't want a new sink. I want *that* sink to work right." My mother stood up abruptly and began clearing the plates. Even without my father, or maybe especially without him, every gathering inside this house devolved to an argument. But if there was anything my family was good at, it was not talking about what was really going on.

Andrew got up too. "Mom, let me help with those."

She stopped clattering the dishes around and smiled at him. "Thank you, honey," she said, her features relaxing. Matt glared at both of them. It had always been like this with my mother, Matt trying too hard in unspoken competition to be the favorite, Andrew not trying at all but somehow coming off better. Me staying the hell out of it.

But Matt couldn't leave it alone. He played with the tab on his can of Coke and said, "Would you go in on the sink with me?"

"Hell no," I said. "I'm steering clear of that hornets' nest. You should too."

"Come on."

"No."

"You owe me," Matt said. "For Danielle."

"I knew that was part of your long game to screw with me," I said, and he rolled his eyes. "Thanks, though. She seems nice—how do you know her?"

Under his beard, he blushed a little. "She lives in my building. We talk sometimes in the laundry room."

"Ooh," I said, "like a little laundry-day love affair."

"No, like adult conversation."

"About what, your spin cycle?"

He ignored me, probably thinking he was taking the high road.

He was such an easy target though. He always had been. "Your agitator?"

"You're drunk, stop it," Matt said, trying and failing to contain a slight smile.

"I am not," I said, "I've had two beers. You know I just like to make fun of you. What do you think of her?"

Matt looked at me. I didn't usually inquire as to what he thought about things. "She's pretty cool," he said. "Smart—I think she's an accountant or something, some finance thing. Do you think you can help her?"

"I'm going to try," I said as my mother came back into the dining room. She was carrying a crystal vase full of lilies and miniature gerbera daisies.

"Did you see these, Roxane?" she said. "Tom brought them by over the weekend. For my birthday."

I knew that Tom checked in on her from time to time, which was sweet of him. My brothers didn't like it though, probably because it made them both look bad. Neither of them had brought birthday flowers. And my brothers would have liked Tom even less if they knew I was sleeping with him. "Pretty," I said.

My mother set the flowers down in the center of the table and went back into the kitchen.

"Now we have to do the sink," Matt muttered, turning his glare on the flowers. "You know she'll love it once it's done."

Andrew leaned around the corner, brushing water off his shirt, another victim of the sink in question. He shot the double finger at the flowers. "I'm in," he said. "Rox?"

"Oh, whatever," I said.

The street was quiet and cloaked in fog when I left around ten thirty. As I slid the key into my car door lock, I could tell something was up: I felt no resistance when I turned it. I squinted at it in the dark for a second, confused. The door was unlocked, and I knew I'd locked it when I went into the house. I spun around and looked at the street, but it was still empty and silent. Then I opened the door and peered in.

"Great," I muttered.

At least nothing appeared to be damaged or missing, but the loose change, hair ties, and pens in the console were moved to one side and the whiskey bottle I'd purchased earlier was resting on the gear shift instead of on the passenger seat where I'd left it. A hoodie that had been on the floor of the backseat was now partially draped over the armrest. I checked the latch on the glove box but it was still locked up tight—good news, because my gun was in there.

This was the sort of thing you might expect in my own neighborhood, although usually accompanied by the glitter of safety glass on the curb and, if you were lucky, a complimentary brick left on the seat for your trouble. But my mother's block was usually exempt from petty crime, and nothing had been taken anyway.

Someone who didn't belong here had been in my space, and I didn't like it.

I straightened up and surveyed the street again. Then I walked down the block and checked out the cars that were parked behind me. Nicer and certainly newer than mine, they nonetheless appeared un-rifled-through. I paused next to an Audi that had what looked like an iPad blatantly sitting on the passenger seat. Seriously? Even around here, that was just asking for trouble. I leaned in closer for a better look and bumped the side mirror with my elbow. A blast of sound made me jump a foot into the air as the car's alarm began to bleat into the night. I staggered backward a few steps, one hand over my chest. I had to laugh. Jumpy much? I hurried up the block before anyone came out of their houses to ask me what the hell I was doing, because I certainly didn't have an answer.

EIGHT

In the light of day, I could see that whoever had gotten into my car last night must have used a slim jim or a coat hanger. The weather stripping at the bottom of the window was ripped and the blue paint on my door was faintly scratched. Better than a brick through the glass, but it still pissed me off.

On top of that, I didn't quite know what my next move should be on Brad Stockton. So far there were three votes for Brad Stockton's innocence, two maybes on the unnamed dog owner, one strange encounter with the Belmont cops, but zero corroboration for Danielle's claim that the woman she saw was Sarah. And anyway, locating that woman based on the no information I had about her felt impossible. After all, beyond a credit-card trail and the unlikely event another motorist remembered me, there'd be no trace of me at the last gas station I visited either. But that was still all I had, and I wasn't quite ready to cry uncle.

After I got a cup of tea and a muffin at the gas station, I showed my sketch to the morning clerk with no success, and then holed up in the car in the parking lot. I was hoping to spot the Sarah look-alike, but I'd settle for a brown curly dog, a red sedan, or a green pickup. Something to corroborate even a piece of Danielle's story. But all I found was rain, a thin, icy drizzle that made everyone tuck their chins to their collars and dash in and out of their vehicles. Ordinarily I didn't mind spending a lot of time in the car, even in shitty weather, but I couldn't stop thinking about the fact that someone had been pawing around in here last night, and it made my skin crawl.

By two o'clock, I'd been watching for a few hours—minus a break for lunch of melitzanosalata and pita at Taverna Athena—and I was restless and very cold. Optimistically I had brought my Nikon D750, but so far there was nothing remotely worthy of photographing. I turned it on and clicked through the images saved on the memory card. The last time I had used it was last January, when I had taken pictures of a real-estate broker suspected—correctly—of stepping out on his wife. The good old days, when my cases were straightforward.

Between Novotny, Kenny, Brad, and Cass, I had four votes for the likelihood of Sarah being dead. So far, that constituted an overwhelming majority. But unfortunately none of those four were paying me.

Danielle's endgame was to find evidence that could help her brother, though, not just to locate the woman she saw, and I was starting to wonder if there might be another way I could go about it. The murder of Sarah's parents didn't seem like one of chance. It wasn't a robbery, a random home invasion, or a serial crime—or was it? With one eye still on the scene in front of me, I put away the camera and opened my laptop. Tom said the police had closed the Cook case fast, which made sense, since there would have been a lot of pressure. And regardless of how they made the leap to getting a warrant for Brad Stockton's car, they hit pay dirt with that search. They wouldn't have had to look any further after that, wouldn't have bothered to look at past cases or anywhere else. And if a similar modus operandi had been used since then, I doubted that anyone would have volunteered to revisit the investigation.

I tapped my fingers lightly on my keyboard without typing anything for a minute, thinking. Then I turned my attention to my network of databases and started a clunky search for stabbing deaths in Franklin County. There were roughly one hundred homicides in the county each year. Of them, ten percent had used knives or cutting instruments as murder weapons. I went back as far as 1990, which meant two hundred and fifty stabbings to consider.

It might be easier just to wait for the dog lady.

But I alternated between watching the street and reading through reports for a while. Bar dispute, domestic, domestic, drug-related home invasion, teenage girl charged with stabbing her friend in the arm with a homemade shiv, man stabbed to death in his North Linden home, no suspects. But forty minutes into it, I saw the word *Belmont* in an entry from the year before the Cook murders, and I got excited. The crimes appeared to be very different, but the victim, Mallory Evans, was eighteen years old, close in age to Sarah. To Brad Stockton, too. Wondering if they all knew each other, I opened a new browser tab and searched the *Dispatch* database for Mallory's name.

> *The body of a Belmont woman who was reported missing last May has been found in southeast Columbus. A man hiking in the woods near I-270 and State Route 33 on December 5 discovered the body of Mallory Evans, 18, buried in a shallow grave.*
>
> *Evans had multiple stab wounds, a police spokesperson said.*
>
> *Evans was last seen at her Belmont home at 73 Providence Street on Friday, May 25, at 10 p.m. There had been no confirmed sightings of Evans since her disappearance.*

> *Police are asking anyone with information to call*
> *the homicide squad at 614-645-4730. Detective Frank*
> *Weary is the primary investigator.*

Frank Weary.

I reread it, heat flooding through my face. It still said my father's name.

I quickly clicked through the other search results, but none of them contained much more detail or mentioned my father. The case appeared to be unsolved. Although my objective had been to try to establish a pattern, actually finding a similar crime jarred me a little, especially one that my father had worked. What were the odds? I was still staring at the screen when I heard a vehicle pulling in behind me, and I turned around to see a Belmont police cruiser parking perpendicular to my bumper.

"Now what," I muttered. I put my computer on the passenger seat and got out of the car, too keyed up to sit still. It had stopped raining but the air was damp and cold. The cop took his time getting out of the cruiser. This guy was older than the officer from the other night, fiftyish and tall with short silver hair and a neat goatee. He was good-looking in a reliable sort of way, like he could build you a hell of a cabin. I could see sergeant's bars on his sleeve through his tinted window. "Good afternoon," he said.

"Hi," I said. "Complaint about loitering, right?"

He walked over to me, nodding. His name tag said *J. Derrow.* "Can you tell me what you're up to?"

"I'm waiting for someone. Well, looking for someone. I'm a detective, private."

"Oh yeah?" he said pleasantly. "Can I see some ID?"

I leaned into my car and got out my license. He glanced at it briefly and handed it back.

"What brings you to Belmont?"

Since he'd already asked the same question, I gave him roughly the same answer. "Just looking into something."

Derrow smiled. "Come on, humor me. I always thought about going private myself, after my thirty." He looked skyward. "Four more years."

He would have been a cop when the Cooks were murdered, I realized. "Do you remember a case about fifteen years ago, a double murder here in Belmont? A married couple were stabbed to death, and their daughter vanished?"

Derrow's expression darkened. "Garrett Cook was a friend of mine," he said.

I opened my mouth to respond, but he kept talking.

"Is *that* what you're looking into? We got the guy already, thank God, and he's on death row, where he belongs." He ran a hand over his face. "We get this every now and then, people nosing around here, looking for details on the case. Like their house, before it got torn down. Always people in there looking for ghosts."

"I'm sorry, about your friend," I said quickly, and he nodded. "And I'm not trying to bring back bad memories. Just following up on a lead that Sarah might have been spotted here."

"Here?" Derrow said. He twirled a finger around atmospherically to indicate the general vicinity. "Let me guess. Stockton's sister told you that."

"Yeah," I admitted.

He nodded slowly and sadly. "Nice girl, but maybe not too realistic. She comes in to the station sometimes, to ask about something she heard of, something she saw on CourtTV, what about DNA testing, what about this, what about that. I'll tell you what we always tell her: The case is closed for a reason. Because it's solved. You know he had the knife in his car, right?"

"Yes."

"And he had a record, too."

"Kid stuff, though, right?"

"If you call breaking into a teacher's car and slicing up the seats *kid stuff*, sure," Derrow said.

I felt my eyebrows go up. "Oh?"

"Not sure of the details, but it was over some kind of beef at school," he said, shaking his head. "He got suspended. She left the school, didn't even stick around long enough to press charges. I sure wish she would've, though. Belmont's a nice town, and we never had any trouble before Brad Stockton."

I didn't like the sound of this. But based on what I'd just read about Mallory Evans's murder the year before the Cooks were killed, it wasn't entirely accurate that Belmont never had any trouble before Brad. "I just learned about another case though," I said. "A young woman named Mallory Evans?"

It was his turn to raise his eyebrows. "You know your local history," he said. "Mallory Evans, poor soul. We weren't part of that investigation, on account of where she was found, that was inside the Columbus city limits. But there was always a rumor floating around that it was someone she went to school with."

"Really."

"Nothing concrete, but yeah. Never even could find a name to investigate. The Homicide boys from Columbus didn't want to haul in every student for questioning, which I guess makes sense. Parents would lose their minds," Derrow said, shrugging. "But if I were you, I'd cut my losses. Stockton's not somebody worth fighting for." He added, "People around here get a little jumpy, so I'm not going to jam you up for loitering. But maybe it's time for you to be on your way."

"Yeah," I said.

I was starting to feel that way myself. I was now in the murky middle of the case, where the early intrigue of the mystery had burned off, leaving me with the bitter taste of inadequate facts and loose ends in my mouth. But after Derrow left and I pulled out of the bank parking lot, I drove back across the street to Taverna Athena. It would be easier to blend in there, and I figured it would buy me another hour or so before I gave up for the day. Although I was cold, I knew I only had so long before I was lulled into stakeout complacency, where even if my subject walked right by me, I might not even notice.

Which is almost exactly what happened.

NINE

Shortly after four o'clock, a brown, curly-haired dog strolled into view. I watched it idly for a few seconds, nothing registering in my brain yet. But then I noticed the woman on the other end of the dog's leash: the woman from the sketch.

"Thank you," I murmured to the universe. I grabbed my keys out of the ignition and bolted across the street, narrowly avoiding getting hit by no fewer than three cars. "Sadie," I called, for lack of a better idea.

The woman stopped in front of a ranch house two doors down from the gas station and turned around, smiling expectantly. She was about five-seven, slim, wearing a hip-length grey wool peacoat. Her hair, dark blond and cut into long layers around her ruddy face, was wind-whipped and shiny. As I jogged over to her, the smile turned confused. "Hi?" she said.

"Hi," I said, trying to catch my breath. "This is Sadie, right?"

She glanced down at her dog, tugging on the leash slightly. "Yes? Do I know you?"

"No," I said. "Listen, this is going to sound nuts. I'm a private investigator and I've been trying to locate a woman matching your description." I showed her my license and gave her one of my cards.

"Really," she said. Now she seemed amused. "My husband is going to love this, he reads nothing but mystery novels. What did this woman who matches my description do? Allegedly." She had a wicked little grin. I liked her.

Her name was Jillian Pizzuti. She lived three streets over, and routinely came by the gas station, both to fill up her car and when she walked her dog. "There aren't sidewalks on the residential streets," she explained, "and people around here drive like maniacs. I've almost gotten hit more times than I can count. So I stick to Clover as much as I can."

I asked her if she remembered the night of November 2. "It was a Thursday," I added. "Clear skies, if that helps."

"That was two weeks ago," Jillian said.

"I know."

"It's possible," she said. Sadie whined, straining against the leash as another woman with a dog walked past us. "I really have no idea." She pulled out her phone and opened her calendar for that night, but it revealed nothing. "I'm sorry."

"Do you drive a red sedan?" I asked her, thinking of what Danielle had told me about the cars. "Or a green pickup truck?"

"White hatchback," she said.

I knew it had been a long shot, so I wasn't exactly disappointed, but it felt like a door closing in my face. I thanked her for her time and patted Sadie on her curly head.

"I hope you find her, whoever she is," Jillian said.

I went back to my car—using the crosswalk this time—and slumped inside. It wasn't the same as definitive proof. But it did seem likely that Danielle had seen Jillian Pizzuti that night, not Sarah, which meant that my one solid lead in this case was a done deal already.

The plumber's van sitting in my mother's driveway should have told me to steer clear, but it didn't. When I went into the house I could hear my mother and her neighbor Rita talking at the kitchen table. "Oh, Gen, I know," Rita was saying, "but his heart was in the right place."

"I told him, I didn't *want* a new sink," my mother said, her voice thick.

I froze, hand still on the doorknob. I considered sneaking back out. But I was here on a mission. "Hey, Mom," I called. "Hey, Rita."

"Hi, love," my mother said coolly as I crossed through the kitchen. "Rita brought pizzelles, you remember how you used to go nuts for those."

"The almond ones are a little soft," Rita said, "but the anise came out perfect."

I shoved a cookie into my mouth and looked at the sink, which was partially disassembled on the counter and floor. "Are they just putting in new pipes?" I said.

"New everything," my mother said. "New pipes, new faucet, plus something to do with a P-trap and compression washers. Did you know your brother was doing this?"

I looked at her. I knew better than to answer that. "I think once it's done, you'll like it," I said.

Rita took that as her cue. "I'm leaving the anise pizzelles for you, Roxane," she said, pulling on her coat. "Genevieve, I'll call you later, sweetie."

After she left, my mother stood up and cleared away the coffee cups. But the sink was only a sink in theory at the moment, so she put them on the stove and crossed her arms. "Someone came by for you this morning," she said.

"Someone?"

"I didn't catch his name. A boy you knew growing up, maybe."

I broke another pizzelle in half and nibbled the lacy edge of it. "What makes you think that? Did he look familiar?"

"Well," my mother said, "no. But he asked if you were home. I told him you hadn't lived here since high school and he got a little bit sheepish. He said, right, that makes sense. Then he left."

I thought about that for a second, chewing. "What did he look like?"

"Oh, I don't know, he had one of those piercings in his eyebrow." She reached for a cookie. "And his tongue, too. He kept clicking it around in his mouth. Isn't that bad for their teeth?"

"Probably," I said, impatient. "What else? What was he wearing?"

"A jacket, a camo jacket with leaves on it, like hunters wear. And a knit hat."

The individual she was describing didn't sound like anyone I knew. But my thoughts snagged on the camo jacket. Like hunters wear. The knife Garrett and Elaine Cook had been killed with was a hunting knife. A random connection, maybe. No doubt hunting jackets were just as common around here as Ohio State bumper stickers. But I still didn't like the thought of this person looking for me, especially not after the car-rifling incident last night. "So he just knocked on the door and asked if I was home?"

"He didn't really knock, I guess," my mother said. "I was just walking by the front door and I heard someone opening the storm door. I was expecting a package, so I thought it was the mailman. Why—do you know who it was?"

I ate the rest of my second cookie and shook my head. I didn't want to worry her. She'd dealt with enough this year, and she had never been happy with my career choice anyway. "Probably someone from school, like you said. If he comes back, let me know?"

My mother nodded. Her chilly expression had warmed up a bit, until she said, "So what brings you over here again?"

I sighed. I knew she wasn't going to like my reason for coming. "Dad's files, his notebooks and stuff," I said anyway. "What happened to all that?"

"What?"

"You know he kept everything. What did you do with his old case files?"

My mother's expression went tight. "Well, I suppose it's all still in his office."

"What do you mean, you suppose?" I said.

She crossed the kitchen and began searching through her purse. "I don't know what all is in there. It's locked."

I stared at her. "You mean you haven't been in the office since—" I stopped. "Since February?"

"No, Roxane, I have not," my mother said. "I'm going out to smoke."

She had been a smoker all my life, but my father had hated the smell and always made her go outside. There was no one to stop her from smoking in the house now, but she still didn't do it. She went out through the back door without a coat and I saw her through the window, shivering in the cold, a cigarette poised halfway to her mouth.

Upstairs, I jiggled the knob on my father's locked office door and regarded the cheap wood grain of its surface. The house was small and my brothers and I had always shared bedrooms in various permutations, but this room had always been Frank's office. I guess he needed a place for his record collection and his notebooks and his booze, even though all he did in there was drink and make late-night phone calls. Once, when I was nine, I picked up the phone to call a friend and I heard my father on the line, talking to one of his women. Her voice was breathy and she was crying. My father's voice was just his voice, rough and flat.

He'd always kept the door to the office locked, and none of us had ever dared even to attempt to breach it. So this could have been significant. Should have been. I felt like a thief for robbing anyone else of the opportunity to witness this, the opening of the tomb. We could have left it sealed up for months, years, decades, opening it only on the twenty-fifth anniversary of his death, when all of us had dealt with it already. We could have toasted to him, shared an anecdote or two—*remember the time he . . .* But instead I jimmied the door open with the nail file from the Swiss army knife on my key chain and that was that.

The air inside the small room was dusty and cold and smelled just like my father, like whiskey and Aqua Velva. One wall was mostly taken up by a particleboard desk, the front right corner going gummy from years of a tumbler of melting ice sitting in the same place. A big, nineties-era computer monitor occupied the desk, plus a scratch pad with a single, indecipherable word written on it in my father's hopeless handwriting. The other wall was lined with bookcases, haphazardly piled with random artifacts of his life: baseball glove, a framed picture of my grandparents, rows of cracked-spine Western paperbacks, records—mostly jazz, some in sleeves but some just stacked on top of each other—manuals to long-gone cars and appliances, someone's graduation tassel, and, finally, a dozen whiskey bottles, arranged on the top like trophies from his proudest accomplishments. I took in the labels. He'd been holding out on us all this time, stocking the liquor cabinet downstairs with cheap stuff.

I grabbed a bottle at random and took a long pull and sat down in the black leather executive chair at the desk, opening drawers. A rubber-band ball, a roll of stamps, a matte black Smith & Wesson 327 revolver. I picked it up, expecting it to somehow feel different from the way my own 327 felt, but it didn't. I set the gun down as my phone started vibrating in my pocket.

Danielle.

My stomach flip-flopped. I couldn't answer, not yet. She left a voice mail asking me to call back with an update, which I also couldn't manage. To my credit, I had only been on the case for four days. But to *her* credit, four days was a hell of a long time when her brother only had two more months to live. And four days had been plenty of time for me to debunk her version of events, but not nearly long enough to come up with a new theory. I put my phone away and continued the search.

I found what I was looking for in the filing-cabinet drawers on the other side of the desk: the notebooks I remembered him always carrying, little black Moleskines with pages soft from wear and dense with ink. There were dozens of them stacked in the bottom drawer. I pulled out a stack and thumbed through a couple. His writing was somewhat more legible here, probably—hopefully—because he was sober while working. But his entries didn't appear to be dated, the notebooks basically just endless volumes of one giant list. I paused briefly on a page with an uneven crime-scene diagram scribbled onto it, stick figures like a child's drawing, except they were dead bodies.

My phone rang again. This time the caller ID said *Unknown*. I answered, hoping that it was somebody calling to solve my case for me and not a ploy on Danielle's part to trick me into picking up. But all I heard was the sound of breathing in my ear.

"Hello?" I repeated. "Who is this?"

The breathing continued. A creeping dread began to inch up my spine. I leaned on my elbow, trying to be logical about this, extract information from the sound. But there wasn't anything—no background noise, no clues. Just the rhythmic breath, which got more menacing the longer I listened to it. When I couldn't take it anymore, I hung up. But a few seconds later, the unknown number began calling me again.

"Hello?" I said.

There was no response, just the sound of the breathing.

"Who the hell is this?"

Breathe in. Breathe out.

I hung up again and slammed the phone down in disgust. Funny how a phone call could feel like an intrusion, a threat, even though the caller wasn't anywhere near me.

Right?

I went to the window and lifted the miniblinds, looking out at the street. But nothing appeared out of the ordinary, no camo jackets or suspicious-looking breathers anywhere to be seen.

I glared at my phone and waited for it to ring again, but it didn't.

I paged through a few more of the notebooks and then I went back to the kitchen to get a bag to put them in. In the thirty or so minutes I'd been upstairs, the plumber had put the sink back together, a shiny new faucet in place of the lopsided, rusty one that had plagued dish-doers in this house for years. I flipped it on; the water pressure was instant and even. My mother was sitting in the living room watching Dr. Phil fix everybody up. She didn't look at me.

"Are you taking care of this?" the plumber said to me, holding up a pink invoice.

I took it from him and when I looked at the bottom line I about died. Seven hundred dollars. "Hang on a second," I said.

I walked down the hall out of earshot and called Matt. "I'm at the house," I said when he answered. "Who the fuck hired this plumber? It's seven hundred bucks."

There was a briefly stunned pause. "Well," he said.

"Matt. I'm over here and someone has to pay the guy now."

"So pay him," my brother said, like the whole thing hadn't been his idea. "We can sort out the details later."

"We were supposed to split it. I don't have that kind of money," I said, lowering my voice even more.

"You can't cover seven hundred bucks for a few days?" Matt said. "Didn't Danielle just write you a big old check?"

I didn't need any reminders about that. Nor did I need my brother's judgment. I drew in a sharp breath. Then I hung up on him.

I went into the bathroom and opened the medicine cabinet. Cold medicine, aspirin, a prescription ointment of some kind. I slammed it closed and stared at my own reflection. Either the mirror was filthy, or I was physically turning as blurry as I felt.

I tried Andrew next, but he didn't answer. So I went back to the kitchen and handed the plumber my Visa and tried to give him a withering look. He didn't notice, or didn't care. Then I headed upstairs, telling myself that I was not going to page through all of my father's notebooks before resuming work on my case, or that it wouldn't just be a stalling tactic if I did.

TEN

"Evans, Mallory Lynn," Tom read to me from a thin stack of print-outs that evening. We were sitting on the sofa in the front room of my apartment, a barely touched pizza from Yellow Brick on the table in front of us. I was rolling the rubber-band ball from my father's office between my palms. "Age eighteen. Cause of death, severe blood loss due to multiple lacerations from a single-edged blade. Evidence of sexual assault, fingernails torn like she had put up a fight, but no DNA. She was wrapped in a blue tarp, which was secured around her body with bungee cords. She was buried approximately ten inches below ground and covered with rocks and leaves."

He fanned the pages, summarizing. "According to her husband, she left home after an argument and she never came back."

"Husband?" I said. "Even though she was only eighteen?"

"He was older," Tom said, "twenty-three. Joshua Evans. They had a six-month-old daughter. Mallory dropped out of high school when she got pregnant."

"Oh man." I leaned back against the cushions and pulled my knees to my chest. The story of Mallory Evans was a bleak one all around.

"Yeah." He had come to my apartment straight from his shift and still wore a white dress shirt and tie, his service weapon and gold shield still clipped to his belt. "This was obviously before my time, but

Frank talked about it sometimes. This case. It was the tarp, that's what stuck out to him. That's the work of someone cold as hell."

"For being a bland little suburb, a lot goes on down there," I said.

"Yeah, they've got their share," Tom said. "Pretty heavy drug use going on in the public high school back then, maybe now too. Plus the Brad Stockton case."

"You couldn't have mentioned Mallory Evans to me the other night?"

"Well," he said, lightly tapping the papers against my shoulder. "The only connection between them is *you*."

"I don't know," I said. "A single-edged blade? That's what killed Garrett and Elaine Cook. Feels like that means something."

"You sound like Frank."

I said nothing. Thinking about Frank not as my father but as Detective Weary gave me a sharp little zap, like touching the tip of your tongue to the coil on a nine-volt battery. I didn't like it, but it was also hard to stop. The pulse of anxiety I'd had in the pit of my stomach since talking to my mother that afternoon was only getting worse.

"What about where she was found, any clues there?"

"Nope," Tom said after a second. "Looks like it was a party spot for people in the area—bottles, condoms, vials, the whole spread. So forensics back there was pretty hopeless. And the area itself, it's ten or so acres of woods right on the Columbus city limits, but no specific connection to Mallory."

"So what then? No witnesses, no trace evidence, no obvious link to anyone she knew, so it's just hopelessly unsolvable?" I said.

"Well, no, I'm sure he threw a lot of time at it," Tom said. "But when nothing shakes loose right away, it does get a lot harder, it gets buried under other cases that are easier to close—triage, I mean, that's the only way you can get anywhere. But Frank would revisit old cases from time to time, ask around, call the victim's family to see if anything new happened."

"Which in this case, nothing did."

"Correct."

I sighed. "Frustrating," I said, "not knowing."

"Yeah."

"Why do you do it?"

"Why do you?"

We looked at each other.

"What I do," I said, "is nothing like this. Dead girls left in the woods? Christ." I stood up and grabbed the pizza box. "Want any more of this?"

Tom shook his head. "So how did you land here? I thought you were looking for the missing daughter."

"I was, but that's a dead end," I called on my way to the kitchen. "So I started thinking that the Cook murders might have been part of a pattern." I opened the fridge and tried to make space for the pizza box. In the hallway, the floorboards creaked as Tom walked toward me. "And I found this, which might look unrelated on the surface, but the Belmont cop I talked to said there had always been rumors about a student from the high school being involved. Then, less than a year later, there's another murder and a student is involved in that too? It just feels like it means something."

"Like what?"

Tom leaned against the doorway and watched me.

"I don't know," I said. The pizza box was too big to fit and I abandoned it on the stove. "The crimes are very different, but it just makes me wonder. If they're connected, it opens up a whole bunch of possibilities." I rubbed the bottom of my foot against the ankle of my jeans. The linoleum floor was cold, thanks to the partly open window. The overactive radiator was currently silent. I reached over to close the window and caught a flash of something through the curtain.

Then I froze.

"What's wrong?" Tom said.

"Shh," I said.

I snatched the curtain aside and jumped away from what I saw: behind the ghost of my own reflection, there was a man on the other side of the glass, looking in at me.

Knit hat, pierced eyebrow. Our eyes locked for a second, a ringing sound building in my head.

Then he ducked and started running, his footsteps in the alley audible through the open window.

I darted down the hall and grabbed my gun from the desk in my office. On the other side of the wall, I could hear my neighbor's dog yapping furiously. I ran outside, shoeless, but once I hit the street I saw nothing but a pair of taillights disappear around the corner on Ohio Avenue.

"Dammit," I said to the empty street. I wondered how long the guy had been lurking outside, if he could hear our conversation through the open window. The thought made me shudder. I made a mental note to call my landlord about the heat for the ten thousandth time.

"Roxane, what's going on?" Tom said behind me.

I turned around and looked at him. His hand rested on the grip of his holstered gun and his expression had gone all-business. "I don't know," I said. "I saw someone in the alley, right outside the window."

"So you just thought you'd come charging out here in your socks with a gun?"

"What, you think I don't know how to use it?"

He looked at me flatly. "I know you know how to use it," he said. "But maybe don't tell me to *shh* the next time you think you might get a chance to, okay?"

I sighed. He had a point. "I've been getting some strange phone calls. And someone went to my mother's house, looking for me."

"Who?"

"I don't know. Some guy in a hunting jacket with a pierced tongue."

"A hunting jacket?"

I looked at him.

He went on, "There was somebody hanging around on the corner when I got here. Hunting jacket, shady-looking. I figured he was there to score."

A fair assumption. "Knit hat?" I said.

"Yeah." He folded his arms. "There's always a somebody hanging around on your corner looking shady. I didn't think much of it. Do you want me to take a look out here?"

"No, I'm sure it's nothing," I said, although I didn't know who I was telling since clearly neither of us believed me. "It's cold out here. Let's go back in."

Inside the building, my neighbor Alejandro was on the landing with his dog—a tiny, spastic Chihuahua wearing a little cable-knit sweater—squirming in his arms. "What's going on, darling?" He looked at Tom over my shoulder and added, "Detective Darling."

I climbed the steps and held out my hand for the dog to sniff. "Did you happen to see who she was barking at?" I said.

Alejandro sighed fabulously. He was in his early twenties and flat broke. But he pulled off broke better than anyone I'd ever met. "I don't mean to alarm you," he said, "or disappoint you. But it's probably Richard."

"Richard," I repeated.

"You remember Richard. Wealthy, pathetic Richard. He got a bit, you know." Alejandro shrugged. "We parted ways during the summer and he's having some trouble accepting it. I mean, I can hardly blame him, but still—annoying."

"Oh, right," I said. I remembered Richard. I'd encountered him once a few months ago, drunk and crying on the steps just inside the building, muttering about the remains of his shattered heart. I'd ordered an Uber ride for him and texted Alejandro to be on the lookout for ex-lovers lurking around. But shattered heart or no, a man like Richard would never be caught dead wearing a hunting jacket, so even though it would make me feel better, my neighbor's love troubles were hardly a reasonable explanation for the person hanging around the building. "Well, let me know if you see him. Him, or anyone else." I waggled my gun. "You know I'm carrying."

We went back into our apartments. I switched the safety back on my gun and set it down on my desk. "Well, that was interesting," I said.

Tom watched me from the doorway. "That's one way to put it," he said. "You're worried."

I shrugged. "I'm paying attention, although I don't even have enough information to know what to worry about. But looking in someone's window—you don't do that if you're just stopping by to chat, do you."

He shook his head. "No, you don't. So who is this guy? Assuming it's not Richard."

"No, it's not," I said. "And, I have no idea. I just have a weird feeling about this case. That probably sounds stupid."

"Hey, no," he said. "Actually, that sounds like Frank too. He was very intuitive that way. He'd say, *When you feel it, you feel it.* We could have the whole murder on videotape but if Frank didn't feel it, we weren't making an arrest. If you have a feeling about something, don't ignore it."

I might have preferred he just said it sounded stupid.

I didn't mind listening to Tom talk about my father; many evenings over the last nine months had passed that way. But I started to mind when he talked about my father and *me.* I made sure all three dead bolts on the front door were locked and then I went over to him and hooked my fingers around the buckle of his belt, ready to be done with the entire conversation. "You're looking pretty tough and unapproachable today," I said, "what with all this hardware."

He caught my hand and squeezed gently. "You're trying to change the subject."

"So what?" I tried to undo the belt, but he squeezed my hand tighter.

"You don't have to," he said.

"What, change the subject? Or put out?"

Tom's eyebrows knit together. "What's wrong with you today?"

"*Today*?" I said.

The sex was a high-speed pursuit, breathless, lights and sirens. Afterward we retreated to opposite sides of the bed, silent and panting. The stars on the ceiling seemed to pulse. My hair was damp on the back of my neck.

"I'm sorry," Tom said finally. "About before. It got weird."

I wiped perspiration off my upper lip and listened to the quiet outside, relieved. "I think we sorted it out."

"It's just that—" he said, and stopped. A few more beats of silence passed. "Sometimes I'm not sure how to talk to you," he continued. He turned to me. I didn't look over. "You're so direct, but then there are just places you won't go, you just don't even want to hear it."

I said nothing. He was right, of course, and also, this seemed like one of those places. "Honestly, I do better when no one is talking."

He sighed. "If we weren't doing this, what would happen if I said something you didn't want to hear? Would you just throw me out?"

"That's ridiculous," I said. It wasn't. "But we are. So it doesn't matter." I thought for a second. "Or does it?"

"So there's this woman," he said.

I sat up on my elbow, refusing to acknowledge to myself how much I didn't like the sound of that. "You're a slut," I said. "A different lady every night! Tell me about her."

I saw a flash of his teeth as he smiled in the dark. "I've been out with her a handful of times. A guy from the squad set me up with her. She works for the school district."

"What's her name?" I said.

He looked at me like he thought I would probably Google her, which I would. "Pamela. Pam."

Tom and Pam. Nope. "What's she like."

He thought about that. "Upbeat," he said.

There was nothing funny about it, but we both laughed a little.

"She's very nice," Tom added. "Normal."

"Well, that has to be a blessed relief."

"I don't want to be unfair to you, Roxane."

"No," I said, "no, there's no fair here, no one is keeping score. We're just two people, helping each other out."

"Helping," he repeated.

"Are you saying I'm not helpful?"

"You're very helpful."

"Thank you." I leaned toward him and kissed him. I suddenly needed a drink, and to not talk about this Pam any more. There was a whiskey bottle on the nightstand, but no glass. And the bottle might have been empty.

I couldn't help myself.

"So, Pam," I said. "Is she what they call *the one*?"

"Oh, shut up," Tom said. "I just met her like a month ago."

I really needed that drink now. I said, "Do you like her?"

"Yes, I do," he said after a beat.

"When are you seeing her again?"

"Saturday. She said she has tickets to some chamber music thing."

"Oh, she's a lady of culture, then," I said.

"She's, I don't know, she's a grown-up. She has her life together. It's nice to date someone like that for a change." He looked down at me. "I'm sorry," he said quickly, "I'm not talking about you, obviously you have your life together."

Did I? "I'm getting us a drink," I announced, crawling over him. "Plus, this isn't dating," I called as I walked down the hall.

"Right," Tom said from the bedroom. "It's—what did you say? Helping?"

I swallowed a shot in the kitchen and finally closed that window, gazing out at the alley. Nothing was out there this time. "Exactly," I said, loud enough for him to hear me. "And when it stops being helpful, either because of this Pam or you just get tired of wondering if your car will get boosted when you come over here, we'll stop and it's not a big deal. The last thing I want is to interfere with your life." I did another shot and put the glass in the sink, then grabbed two clean ones from the dish rack.

"You know I like you, too," Tom said when I got back to the bedroom.

"And I like you," I said. This was a conversation we'd had before. "But that's different."

"How?"

I climbed back into bed and sat cross-legged against the wall. "It just is," I said. I poured some whiskey into our glasses and took a sip of mine and tried to imagine it was my first of the day.

"Yeah," Tom said finally. He looked at me in the dark and I looked back for a long time.

"So it's fine, everything's fine," I said. I downed the rest of the whiskey and set the glass on the headboard. "It's just sex. It's not like you have to turn it into something just because we've fucked twenty-five times."

"But who's counting?" he said. He patted the mattress beside him. "Would you come here?"

I lay next to him and let him pull me into his chest. I was going to miss this. "It's just that you've been the only good thing," he said.

"Stop right there," I said, but I didn't move away.

After Tom left, I lay in bed and tried not to assume that every creak and sigh in the hundred-year-old foundation of the building meant that my visitor was back. The radiator was hissing again and I was hot, but I'd already closed all the windows and had no intention of opening any of them, no matter how hot it got. Finally, unable to sleep, I got up and dragged my father's notebooks down the hall to my bedroom.

Tom had given me the key to deciphering them: they were numbered, a small numeral inside a circle drawn on the first page of each one. There were, it seemed, 243 of them in total. I went through them quickly, skimming through dozens and dozens of names.

Finally, in the middle of notebook number 71, I found the one I wanted. *Evans, Mallory.* I let out a long breath.

> *Missing 7 months frm hm, infant daughter Shelby.*
> *Last seen leaving hm after argument re: housework w*
> *husband Josh. *Incl MPR from Belmont PD 5/29 in IR.*
> *Hm w infant night of, cnfrm by 2 neighbors. J. Evans*
> *employed Meigert Auto, North Cbus.*

His entries were written in a jerky shorthand. I had to think about some of the abbreviations: missing persons report, investigative report, home. He drew a line when his notes switched from one case to another, and I had to read through several other investigations to find the place where Mallory's case picked up. He had a list of camping-supply stores in the area, because the tarp her body was wrapped in had been brand-new. Another list of registered sex offenders in the southeastern quadrant of the county, spanning six pages, most of the names checked off and a few crossed out. He had two maps of the woods where her body was found, one scribbled over and redrawn to be oriented north. It had a note in the margin that said *FUCK YOU, HARPER*. I remembered Wallace Harper vaguely; they'd worked together only briefly when I was right out of high school, before Harper dropped dead of an aneurysm in the elevator at the police department headquarters downtown. I had to put the notebook down for a second, spooked.

Ten pages later, the Evans thread resumed. I picked through the messy shorthand to get the gist of it: among the many useless, anonymous tips to the homicide squad, there'd been one report that one of Mallory's former classmates was involved. If she hadn't dropped out, she would have been a senior. I was just thinking that Brad Stockton would've been a senior too when I turned the page and saw his name, written out in my father's handwriting.

I took a deep breath.

That was unexpected.

His name appeared in a list of three others under a heading that said *Follow-up?* Brad's entry read: *Suspended—retaliation? No charges.* All of the names were crossed out. There was no further explanation for it, like there wasn't for most of what Frank wrote down. I thought about what Sergeant Derrow had told me, about Brad slicing up a teacher's car.

I didn't like the sound of anything today.

I paged through the rest of the notebook and the one that Frank started after it was full, but there were no other mentions of Brad and few mentions of Mallory. The case got replaced by newer, easier-to-solve homicides and was eventually forgotten, at least in terms of active investigations.

I got out of bed again, this time for a bottle of whiskey and a glass. I forced myself to look again out through the kitchen window, but the coast was still clear. That didn't really make me feel any better, though. Not about anything. I was beginning to regret falling down this rabbit hole in the first place. Frank had probably crossed out Brad's name for a good reason. But less than a year later, two more people were dead and the murder weapon was found in his car. What did *that* mean?

"Shit," I said.

Danielle was going to be pissed.

ELEVEN

I was dreaming about my father: a wren had flown into the picture window on the front of the house, and we were burying it in a Crown Royal bag. I woke up gasping, some kind of noise yanking me out of sleep. I listened hard for the source of it, then realized it was just the phone vibrating somewhere in the bed. Late-morning light streamed into the room. I dropped back to the pillow and covered my eyes with my hand. I hadn't slept well, and I wasn't keen to start the day with a call from the unknown breather. But I felt around under the covers for the device, finally locating it near my feet.

Danielle Stockton again.

I sighed toward the ceiling. I could still see Brad's name written in my father's handwriting. I still didn't want to talk to my client, not when I'd all but proven she hadn't seen Sarah after all and I'd also just found at least some kind of connection between her brother and another murder. But I had taken her money—I couldn't hide from her forever. So I made a cup of tea and ate a handful of Goldfish crackers at my desk while I called her back and gave her the update she asked for.

"I'm not saying this means your brother belongs in prison," I said, wincing at my own words. "But I am saying it seems likely that the person you saw wasn't Sarah Cook. Two separate people looked at the sketch and identified her as this other woman, Jillian Pizzuti."

Danielle didn't answer for a few beats. "But what do they know? They haven't spent the last fifteen years hoping to see Sarah, that's the thing."

That didn't exactly help her cause. "I spoke to her myself," I said. I got up and cracked the window in my office and then, remembering what had happened last night, closed it again just as quickly. "The resemblance is very, very real."

Danielle sighed. "So you don't believe me either. Great."

"It's not about believing you. It's about what we can prove."

"So that's it."

"No, not necessarily," I said. I filled her in on the murder of Mallory Evans, leaving out the parts about her brother's name in my father's notebook for now, until I had even the slightest clue what it meant.

"And you think all this might have something to do with my brother?" she said, somewhat incredulously.

"Well, not exactly." I chewed and looked up at the ceiling. "I don't know. Did you know her?"

"Me? No," Danielle said. "I mean, she had a reputation as trouble. In middle school she got busted for drugs in her locker and had to go to this boot-camp program that the city runs for messed-up kids. And I remember she was kind of wild. Like, lots of boyfriends. But I didn't know-her-know-her. I was two years behind her, I was a freshman when she dropped out. I heard she was pregnant."

"Did Brad know her?"

"Probably just from being in class together."

"I'm just thinking, Belmont's an awfully small town to have two—well, three—murders less than a year apart."

"I guess I never really thought about it like that."

"Really," I said.

"Mallory . . . I don't know. That was different. I heard all kinds of things about her. Like I heard that she would have sex in exchange for drugs. And I'm not saying anyone deserves what happened to her, but you have to wonder. How careful she was. People didn't really talk about it when she died. When Sarah's parents were killed though, the whole town was just completely shaken. Listen, I have to say, this isn't really what I expected when I hired you," she finished. "I thought you'd, I don't know, be talking to the police, talking to people about Brad."

"I did," I said. "I am." I sounded defensive. On top of that, I sounded exhausted and clueless. I didn't know what else to tell her. I opened my laptop and Googled *Columbus city schools Pamela*. It was ridiculously easy, like all things that don't matter. Pamela Gregorio. Tom's new girlfriend. She was tagged in a photo on the Web site for an annual fund-raiser, caught in a camera-ready embrace with three other women and their glasses of wine. She was a pretty redhead with a coy smile, wearing those hip tortoiseshell glasses and a V-neck sweater. She seemed all right. I was disappointed. "This is just how I usually work."

"And how is that?"

"Exploring whatever comes up," I said as I searched on Pamela's full name: thirty-eight next month, owned a condo in Grandview.

"My brother doesn't have time for you to explore whatever comes up," she said next, and I winced again. She had a point. She was quiet for a bit before adding, "But he did tell me that he liked you."

I slammed the computer closed. "Did he," I said.

"He doesn't like much these days."

"Danielle, I promise you, I'm trying."

She sighed. "I guess I just imagined this would be more like *The Rockford Files* or something."

I would have thought that fifteen years of visiting her brother in jail would have disabused her of any idealism about criminal cases, but maybe it was a coping mechanism of some kind. "What, a fist-fight and a resolution in forty-five minutes flat?"

"Something like that," she said, but I could hear a smile in her voice now. "Just please remember. I hired you to help Brad, not anybody else."

"I'll keep you posted," I told her.

When she didn't tell me not to bother, I assumed that meant I was still employed.

Joshua Evans exuded unhappiness. He was a big guy, fortyish and tired-looking, wearing a faintly grease-stained polo shirt from the car dealership where he worked as a service advisor. He looked like he hadn't shaved recently and hadn't smiled in way longer. It was clear he hadn't had an easy time since his young wife was murdered; even after sixteen years, the pain of it was still fresh on his face, evident in his body language and the state of affairs in his small bungalow house: a haphazard mess, the carpet around his chair barely visible for all the old mail, fast-food wrappers, dog toys, shoes. I was hoping he could give me something to go on as far as Mallory's murder, hopefully something other than Brad Stockton, but I wanted to ease into that particular topic. So I went with a spiel about my father's death prompting me to look into some of his old cases.

"He seemed like a good guy, your dad," he was telling me. "He called me every December. Just to check in, to tell me he hadn't forgotten about her. I talked to a lot of cops when Mallory died. And I realized, cops are just people, doing a job, and some of them aren't great at it. Frank though, he always made me feel like I had his full attention. When I heard about him on the news, I couldn't believe it. I'm real sorry."

I forced a smile. "I'm glad he was kind to you," I said. "It's good to hear."

"But you want to talk about Mallory."

"If you don't mind."

He nodded slowly. "I'm going to need a beer for that. You want one? Or maybe it's too early."

It was four in the afternoon, and not too early by a long shot. "No, a beer sounds great," I said.

He heaved himself out of his beat-up recliner and shuffled off to the kitchen. "Mallory and I met at this bonfire party," he said. I heard the refrigerator door open and close and when Joshua returned, he handed me a bottle of Miller Lite. "She told me she was the same age as me. I was twenty-two then. She looked it, and she sure acted like it. I didn't know she was only seventeen till she and her mother were on my doorstep with an ultrasound photo."

"So her age wasn't the only surprise."

"Nope," Joshua said. "And I was not pleased. But I wanted to do right by her. Take care of her. That's why we got married. She didn't want that, but her parents did, and I did. She wanted to, you know, get an abortion. She didn't want to be a mom, she said she'd be awful at it. I thought she'd change, the first time she held Shelby, like maybe all that mothering stuff is supposed to kick in automatically." He took a long swallow of his beer. "Long story short, it didn't. We were married for about a year, all told, and it was not an easy year. But I was doing my best, for Shelby." Here he smiled, and some of the gloom vanished from his face. "Light of my life."

I remembered how Danielle had described Mallory in middle school: wild. "How about Mallory?" I said. "Was she doing her best?"

Joshua shook his head. "She couldn't handle it. She didn't like staying home with the baby, she didn't like cooking, cleaning. She didn't even like me all that much, I don't think."

"She felt stuck," I said, and he nodded.

"She started using drugs again right after Shel was born, started staying out all night." He finished his beer and set the empty bottle on an end table next to a Wendy's cup. "I knew she was sleeping around, but I didn't know who. I was barely keeping it together though, between work and being here by myself with Shelby every night. So we never really had the conversations we should have had. The last time I saw her, we had this stupid fight about the dishes, of all things. She never did the dishes, and I mean, never. And I snapped at her about it, I told her, I'm supporting you, can't you even wash your own fucking dishes?" Joshua shook his head. "It was not me at my best."

I felt for him, having to live with the fact that Mallory left the house that night because of a fight that he started. "What happened then?" I said.

"Well, she told me to fuck off and said she was leaving and never coming back. But that was nothing new, really. The difference that time was that she really didn't come back. I started calling her friends, but nobody'd seen her. So that's when I reported her missing." He clenched and unclenched his jaw for a few beats. "Shit, I still get so worked up, thinking about it. Sorry."

"No, no, it's okay," I said. "I understand."

"I kept thinking that she'd come back, she had to come back. She was just blowing off steam somewhere. But it turned into months," he continued, "and I convinced myself that she just ran out on us and that was all. I had so much rage inside me, I think that's how I kept it together. And when the police—when your dad came to tell me, that they found her? I fell apart hard. She had a good heart, under all her attitude. She had a good heart, and she was so beautiful." He stood up, roughly pressing the heel of his hand against his eye. "Here, I got some pictures."

He crossed the small, messy room and took a photo album down from a shelf stacked high with VHS tapes and random knickknacks. He smiled faintly. "This one. This is right after Shelby was born."

I took the album from him. Mallory, looking exhausted but happy in a hospital gown, clutching a pink-faced, sleeping infant to her chest.

She had a big, crooked smile and long blond hair cut into blunt bangs across her forehead.

Just like Sarah Cook.

Then I turned the page and drew in a breath as I saw a snapshot of a younger, thinner Joshua Evans posing with a crossbow in the woods, a camo ball cap perched on his head. I jerked my hand away like the page was hot. "Are you a big hunter?" I said.

"What? Oh, no," Joshua said. He glanced down at the album. "I used to go out with my brother, but I'd really just watch. Not my thing."

I nodded with relief, realizing that even if he'd said yes, it didn't make any sense to think Joshua was my camo-coated visitor. He had no visible piercings, for one, and for another, he didn't know I existed until thirty minutes ago.

"Can I look through the rest of this?" I said.

"Oh, sure, yeah," Joshua said. "I'm going to change clothes before Shelby gets home, she should be here soon."

He left me to page through the rest of the album. Mallory looked progressively unhappier as time went on; she got dangerously skinny and her eyes grew dark hollows beneath them. I wondered if my father had looked through this same album, and I wondered if it had imparted secrets to him that it wasn't sharing with me. I set it down on the end table when I heard a key in the lock behind me.

The front door opened and two laughing teenage girls stepped inside. "I can't believe you didn't even get cookies and punch," the blond one was saying, hefting half a dozen plastic grocery bags onto the floor, "isn't that the whole point of those things?"

Her friend said, "It wasn't even a ceremony. We just had to fill out a stupid survey." Her hair was dyed a reddish-violet color that seemed to glow. "Like *On a scale of one to ten, how frequently did he ogle all the girls in class?*"

Their animated conversation expired when they saw me.

"Um," the blond girl said. Her hair was pulled up into a messy ponytail, and she wore a Batman T-shirt under a faded green military jacket. Her friend was tall and willowy and she was dressed thrift-store glamorous: a mahogany-colored leather trench with a patchy ermine collar and a lacy black dress over jeans. The two of them exchanged glances.

Joshua came back into the room. "Hey, Shel." He gave the blond girl a squeeze around the shoulders. "Uh, this is Roxane?" he said, sounding a little nervous. "She's a private investigator. Her dad, uh, her dad was one of the detectives who worked on your mom's case way back when."

Shelby looked from her father to her friend to me. It was clear from her expression that she found this explanation very weird, which I guessed it was. But she gamely smiled and held up a hand in greeting. "Hi," she said. Then she glanced over her shoulder at her friend, almost cracking up. "This is Veronica."

"That's a cool name. One 'n' or two?" Veronica said.

I laughed. "One," I said.

She nodded approvingly. "I like it with one."

Shelby locked the door and grabbed the groceries. "Come on," she said, "we need to get this going if we want to eat before two in the morning."

"Shel's quite the little cook," Joshua said, "aren't you?"

Shelby restrained an eye roll and started carrying the bags through the living room and into the kitchen. Veronica shrugged and followed her.

"She just started working at the Olive Garden, over by the mall," Joshua said. "Four nights a week. She's a hostess for now, but I'm telling you, she's going to be the head cook in no time, right, girl?"

"Maybe," Shelby said. She smiled from behind the pass-through, the kind of smile that said she had no intention of ever being a cook at an Olive Garden. "Vee, can you start pressing the tofu?"

"Veronica doesn't eat meat," Joshua told me. "And Shel's worried about my cholesterol. So she makes a lot of veggies, a lot of that tofu stuff. It's pretty good, actually. You ever had it?"

"Tofu? Yes," I said, and the girls in the kitchen giggled.

"Dad, literally everyone has had tofu," Shelby said.

Joshua waved her off. "Quit eavesdropping, brat," he said. Then he turned back to me. "I got real lucky with Shelby," he said, his voice lower. "She's a good kid, she's never been anything but. And it's always been just me on my own, after Mal left. I've done my best but it's not like I had a good example for a dad or anything. Shelby's great, though. Good grades, real responsible."

I thought it was interesting that he still said *left,* rather than *died.*

"I was so afraid that, you know—that some of Mallory's wildness was hereditary or something. God, that sounds stupid."

"No, I get it," I said. I remembered that last conversation I'd had with my own father, the way he'd said he was glad I turned out more like him. *Be nice but not too fucking nice.* I found myself blinking hard all of a sudden. "So were there ever any leads?" I said, to change the subject. "Any suspects."

Joshua shook his head. "Not that Frank ever told me about," he said. He tried to take a sip from his beer bottle, but it was empty.

Since he seemed more or less comfortable with me by now, I decided to steer the conversation toward my actual case. "Do you know if she was friends with a guy named Brad? Brad Stockton?"

He tipped his head to the side. "That name sounds familiar but I'm not sure—wait, that's the kid who killed his girlfriend and her parents, isn't it?" He leaned forward. "Why? Do you think they were friends?"

"I don't know," I said, "but they would have been in school together."

"Damn," Joshua said softly. "She never talked about him, but I didn't really know her friends that well." Joshua rubbed his eyes again. He didn't seem to want to know more about the connection between Mallory and Brad, so I didn't press it. I wasn't completely comfortable voicing my theory even to myself. "Shelby, hon, that smells great." Then he looked at me. "You oughta stay for dinner."

"Oh, I wouldn't want to intrude," I said. My phone began buzzing in my pocket: the *Unknown* caller. I rejected the call and put the phone away.

"No intrusion at all," he said. "I mean, a good-looking woman like you, I'm sure you got plans on a Friday night. But if you don't." Then he pressed his hand over his mouth, his eyes sad and strained and desperate for something, company or attention or just some kind of reassurance. "Christ, that was embarrassing. Sorry."

My phone started ringing again, but I ignored it this time. Realizing I was not all that keen on spending another evening alone in my apartment, I leaned forward and touched his arm. "Hey, no," I said. "You're sweet. I'd love to stay."

Relief flooded through his features. "There's plenty, right, Shelby?"

"Sure," his daughter replied.

So we ate around their small dinette table in the kitchen. Unlike the living room, the kitchen was spotless and I wondered if that was Shelby's doing. She had made fried tofu and spicy green beans. I told her it was the best meal I'd had in a while, which was true. "I can barely microwave a frozen dinner," I said. "So this is great."

"You don't cook?"

"Not if I can help it."

"It's so rewarding, though." Shelby wrinkled up her nose. "*Rewarding,* that's a majorly uncool word."

"Shelby makes this chocolate cake," Joshua said. "You'd swear it had a dozen eggs in it, it's so rich. But it's vegetarian."

"Vegan," his daughter corrected. "Vegan baking is so cool. Orange juice and vinegar cause a chemical reaction to make it rise."

"Science cake," Veronica said. The girls looked at each other quickly, faces reddening with restrained laughter. Shelby was plain-looking at first, but she had a sparkle in her green eyes. Veronica, with her hair and eccentric clothes and jangly jewelry, was glamorous in a slightly desperate way. They both seemed like good kids, though, plucky with outsider charm.

"Have you ever been to the Angry Baker?" I said. "It's downtown. They have a bunch of vegan baked goods. I go there all the time, it's right by where I live."

"Why is it called *angry*?" Shelby said. "Are they, like, mad in there?"

"No, they're very nice," I said.

"We should go there sometime," Shelby said to her father, and he nodded.

Veronica said, "That's so cool that you live downtown. I've always wanted to live downtown. I'm applying for the Fashion Institute of Technology for college, it's in New York, in Manhattan. Which is like one giant downtown. And Shelby could move there eventually too and open a vegan restaurant and it would just be *the best*."

Shelby nodded. But there was something wistful in her face at the thought of her friend going that far away for school. That was when I noticed how Shelby looked at Veronica, a slightly lingering glance, a flutter of pure happiness in her eyes when Veronica looked back. It reminded me of the way I looked at Catherine when I first met her, all those years ago. A hopeful, hopeless crush. Veronica seemed oblivious to it, and went on talking about her plans to be a fashion designer. Shelby caught me looking at her and blushed faintly. But I smiled, a silent understanding passing between us.

TWELVE

I had known Catherine since high school myself. She was lovely and odd, the darling of the art department and on the fringes of several social circles, and I was a nearly silent B student with a reputation among teachers for being a troublemaker, courtesy of Andrew, that I didn't entirely deserve. Catherine and I had barely spoken to each other until the end of our junior year, even though alphabetical order dictated that she sit in front of me in several classes. Walsh, Weary. I spent a lot of time staring at her blond curls or the slender line of her neck and trying to decide if what I felt when I looked at certain pretty, aloof girls was envy or something else altogether. But then one day she turned around and met my eye and said, "I had a dream about you. Well, it was about your brother. But you were in it."

I didn't ask how she knew my brother. He'd graduated two years earlier. But everyone knew Andrew. "What was the dream?" I asked instead.

"We were in the library," she said, "and he was trying to get me to help him hide a bunch of butterflies. But they kept flying all over."

"As they do," I said.

The corner of her mouth tipped up. "As they do. And you were watching but you didn't say anything."

"Weird," I said.

"Definitely," Catherine said, and started to turn away. Any of the few other times we'd talked, it had been circumstantial—*do you have a pencil, what page are we on.* This was different, electric almost immediately. I didn't want the conversation to end.

"Everything in a dream," I said quickly, "is supposed to be you. That's one theory, anyway. For interpreting."

Now she leaned against the back of her chair, her arm touching the top of my notebook. I looked down at it without meaning to and she caught me looking but didn't move her arm, just said, "What do you mean?"

"You're the butterfly," I said, "and the library, and Andrew, and me."

She nodded like she liked the sound of that. "But what's the interpretation?"

"That's up to you. It's whatever it would mean to you, for you to be a butterfly."

"Or you."

"Or to be me."

But then class started, and she turned away and the moment was over. We'd talk a little before class after that, though, and she'd tell me about her dreams each morning; she told me about her family and how her father's mistress lived in their basement, though her parents were still married, an arrangement that struck me at the time as modern and practical, unlike my own father's sneaking around. She was absent a lot, and each day I let out a breath I didn't realize I was holding when she walked into the classroom. On the last day of school that year, she turned to me and said, right before she walked out of the room, "I finally figured it out. The dream, about the butterflies." Then she tossed a folded sheet of paper onto my desk. "To be you," she added, smiling slyly, "would mean I feel underestimated."

Her phone number was written on the paper. I probably fell in love with her right then.

We got close fast, an undefinably intense friendship that quickly evolved into physical contact, her hand brushing mine, eyes flashing as if daring me to move away. She told me she had kissed a girl once, just to see what it was like, when she was at an art camp in Maine. *And what* was *it like?* I asked, of course, and then she showed me, and there was no going back.

Nothing about being with Catherine was easy, nor would it ever be. Even at age seventeen she was already committed to the story lines that would define her forever: she had a boyfriend but it was for some practical reason and he was generally inconsequential to her actions; she didn't make plans and she didn't extend invitations; she would routinely keep you waiting for hours or forever, but just as often she would be unexpectedly kind; no one had ever broken up with her; she always stayed friends with her exes and kept them around her in a harem of sorts, ready and waiting and all too eager to be summoned when she was lonely or bored.

And it was all still true. I should know. She had been spiraling toward me and then away from me for half my life, on and off and off and on, disappearing to move to Chicago or New Orleans or Los Angeles. After grad school, she said she was going to be traveling in Europe for a few months and she'd write me. I didn't hear from her for three years and when she got back in town, she was married to a composer from Montreal and they bought a house in Bexley and she was *so happy,* but it only lasted for so long. It only ever lasted for so long. I knew better. But when Catherine was looking at me, I felt like the only other person on earth. It was all too easy to forget that the best anyone could hope to be was a character in a dream she had about herself.

I left the Evans house and pulled out onto Providence Street. Before I reached Clover, I caught a flash in my rearview mirror: another car starting up and edging away from the curb. My pulse quickened as the car behind me mimicked my left-hand turn toward the freeway, keeping a fair distance between us. But I only made it a few blocks east before my rearview mirror lit up red and blue. "Oh, come on," I muttered. Three run-ins in as many days. This was getting old fast, although part of me was relieved that it was just a Belmont cop and not someone with a hunting knife. But between the police down here, these phone calls, and Camo Jacket sneaking around my apartment, it felt like the universe was trying to send me one hell of a message.

If only I knew what it was.

I pulled over to the curb and slid the car into park and waited. I didn't bother looking for my registration because this clearly wasn't going to be a routine traffic stop. Finally, a tall figure got out of the car and approached me.

I rolled down my window and peered out into the cold, damp night. The man who looked back at me was fifty-five or so, barrel-chested, with a grey-blond buzz cut and narrowed, hooded eyes. He wasn't wearing a uniform, but instead a windbreaker over a pair of khaki pants. "Good evening, Miss Weary," he said. "I'm Jake Lassiter, chief of Belmont police."

I raised my eyebrows. "Let me guess," I said. "I've got a brake light out."

He actually took a step back to check, and then he looked annoyed. "Listen, I believe you've spoken with a few of my officers before."

"I have."

"About paying the professional courtesy of announcing when you'll be down here, asking questions." He draped one arm over the roof of my car and leaned in. "And yet here you are, unannounced."

I felt myself edging slightly away from the door. The air was frigid, and Lassiter was a bit too close to me for comfort. "I'm sorry," I said. "I wasn't aware that the professional courtesy was necessary any time

I set foot in Belmont. Can I just make a blanket announcement that I'll be down here off and on for a while?"

"For a while," he repeated. He looked over his shoulder, like he wanted to laugh at me with his imaginary backup. "The Cook case is solved. So you asking questions?" he added, turning back to me, his features harder now. "That stops now." He tapped his hand against the roof of my car with each word, and the hollow sound made me jump a little.

I wanted to mention that he didn't have the authority to tell me that, police chief or no. But there was very little point, not if I wanted to go home any time soon. "I understand," I said.

"Good," Lassiter said.

We stared at each other, cold air whistling in through my open window. The blue and red lights from Lassiter's car cast an eerie glow against his stony features. His expression said that he was more than happy to stand here for hours.

"May I leave now?" I said.

He watched me for another few seconds, and then he removed his arm from my car. "You have a great night," he said.

He retreated and got back into his cruiser, but he didn't go anywhere, just stayed put with those blinding lights whirling in my mirror. I put the car in gear and darted back into traffic, eager to get away before he changed his mind.

When I got home, it was about eighty degrees in my apartment. I peeled off my clothes and lay in bed with a whiskey bottle and looked up at the stars. I wasn't making any friends or any progress, and though I wasn't tired yet, I wanted to be done with the day. I listened for the sounds of anyone else nosing around my building, but I heard nothing.

Yet.

I needed to think about something else.

I took a long swallow from the bottle and scrolled through the numbers in my phone, breezing past the streak of calls from the unknown number, not wanting to think about that either. Finally I paused on the listing for Catherine's studio at home. She eschewed technology, including cell phones. I used to tell her she was nuts for that, but now I was starting to think she had the right idea.

I dialed the number and her husband answered.

I hung up.

THIRTEEN

On Saturday, I called Kenny Brayfield and told him I had some follow-up questions for him. I was looking for something that could shut down the remote possibility of Brad Stockton's involvement in Mallory Evans's death so I could move on, although I kept this to myself on the phone. He invited me to drop by his house in Belmont and when I got there, I saw that *house* was a little modest. It was easily the largest single-family dwelling I'd ever laid eyes on—a huge stone McMansion with a long circular driveway and a three-car garage, all inside a dramatic wrought-iron fence. I pulled up to the gate and rolled down my window and stated my case into a speaker, thinking the gold-flake vodka business must be damn good. But when I pulled up to the house, I saw an older, better-dressed version of Kenny in the garage loading suitcases into the trunk of a late-model Lexus, and it all made sense: Kenny still lived with his parents.

Kenny was waiting for me on the porch. He was wearing velour sweatpants and a white undershirt and was barefoot and drinking a green substance from a tall plastic cup. "Hey, you found the place."

"Hard to miss it," I said.

"Well, come in, there's breakfast. Quiche Lorraine, or you can try this, I'm doing this Superfood RX Herbal Smoothie." He waggled his cup at me and the beverage made a pond-like sloshing sound. "It's got that ginkgo stuff in it, boosts energy and focus."

I held up a hand. "Another client of yours?"

He deflated a little. "Yeah," he said. "Want to give it a try? It comes in a bunch of flavors."

I said I'd just have a cup of tea and followed him inside. The interior of the house was all vaulted ceilings and plush off-white carpet, with double curved staircases arcing away from the foyer to a second-floor walkway. The kitchen was the size of a normal house's lower level, with gleaming countertops that gave no indication food had ever been prepared in there. But a large glass baking dish of the aforementioned quiche sat on a silicon trivet, untouched.

"What do you think of the place?" Kenny said as he poured hot water from a one-cup coffeemaker. He brought it to me on a saucer, along with a tiny wooden chest of tea bags.

"How many people live here?" I said, taking a seat at the breakfast bar.

"Me and my folks, right now," Kenny said. "And my sister's moving back in a couple weeks—she's getting divorced. Plus the housekeeper."

"Cramped quarters," I said.

He grinned at me. "You're funny."

Kenny's dad came back in from the garage and, barely looking at me, said, "Okay, we're taking off. We'll be back Tuesday morning, so please no get-togethers in the house this time. Okay, Kenny?"

"Yes, sir," Kenny said, straightening up.

His dad gave a slightly irritated smile and left again. Kenny seemed a little bit old to require such a warning. But maybe with money like this, you never had to grow up at all. Without missing a beat, he said, "I'm having some people over Monday night for the Browns-Steelers game. Around seven. You should come."

I had to laugh. "Yeah, we'll see," I said.

"We have an indoor pool, it's heated to eighty-five degrees. When it's cold out, damn, there's nothing better. It'll be chill, just some old friends. I mean it, if you're around, you should come."

"Indoor pool," I said, "I bet that made for some wild prom after-parties."

He sipped his pond-water smoothie. "Oh man, you know it. This house was the place to *be*. My folks were always so cool, they were down with us having booze, no problem. My mom knows how to throw a party, that's for sure. She's the one who got me started in the promotion biz—it's like our vocation."

I wasn't sure that event promotion counted as a vocation. Rather than comment on it, I decided to use the subject to start talking about Brad. "Did Brad come to your parties?"

"Oh yeah," Kenny said. "Brad's, you know, one of those introverted-type people, and sometimes you could just see him going into this little room in his head where he could write his poems. But he was always down for whatever."

"Who else was in your group of friends?"

"Danielle," he said. "She was two years behind us in school but she could hang. And this kid Brian Zollinger, we were close with him, but he moved away junior year. We'd party with anyone, as long as they were cool as fuck."

My ears perked up. Brian Zollinger was one of the other crossed-out names on the list in my father's notebook. Plus, from what I knew about Mallory, she was a partier too. This seemed like a good place to jump in with it. "What about a girl named Mallory Evans?"

Kenny's face closed right up. So my instinct not to open with that had been correct, I thought with dismay. "Mallory. Wow, I haven't thought about her in years."

"Did you know her?"

"Sure, just from around."

"Did Brad know her?"

He seemed uneasy. I couldn't tell what, exactly, was the source of his uneasiness, but it was worth noting. "I guess. I don't know."

"She and Sarah," I said, "they were kind of similar, looks-wise?"

"I don't know. I guess."

"You know what happened to her, right?"

"Yeah, that was crazy." He set his cup down and spent a long time lining it up with the edge of the counter like a man trying to buy some time. "Why are you asking about her?"

"It's just strange," I said, "two violent crimes happening in a place like Belmont only a few months apart."

Kenny nodded but didn't say anything, even though he'd been the definition of chatty a moment earlier. I'd clearly hit a nerve.

"So Mallory and Brad," I said. "Were they in any classes together or anything like that?"

"You'd really have to ask him that, I'm not sure," Kenny said.

I could see I wasn't going to get any more out of him about that, so I tried another angle, "Did you ever hear any rumors about what might have happened?"

"You know, I'm sorry to cut out on you but I need to run some errands, okay?"

I stared at him. This was an awfully abrupt end to the conversation, after the production he'd made of offering me the tea chest. "Are you throwing me out?"

"No, no," he said, although he clearly was. He smiled halfheartedly. "I just have some shit I need to do. It's not a big deal, right?"

"No, I get it," I said.

But I didn't. I had been hoping that Kenny would steer me away from the idea that Brad could have been behind Mallory Evans's death too, but instead he steered me a little closer. He hadn't told me much, but the change in his attitude said a lot.

———

I clearly needed to talk to Brad, but when I left Kenny's house, it was too late in the day for a road trip down to the prison. Instead, I hit up a Starbucks drive-through for another cup of tea and sat in the parking lot, poaching their Wi-Fi to look into the other names that appeared with Brad Stockton's in my father's notes.

First, I nosed around on Brian Zollinger, the guy Kenny said had moved away junior year. The entry next to his name in the notebook said *Bullying, plagiarism.* That hardly seemed relevant to my case, but I pulled background info on him anyway. He lived in Chicago and posted a lot on Twitter about craft beers. I turned up a phone number for him and left a voice mail, requesting a call back.

The next name on the list was Dylan Lapka. His entry read *B&E,* which I interpreted as breaking and entering. But I determined in short order that he was dead—car accident, a decade ago.

Zero for two so far.

I had better luck on the third name: *Michael Timton, sealed JV record?* He had a Columbus address, and he also had an adult record that rendered his sealed juvie crimes irrelevant: he was fresh out of jail from a sexual assault six years ago.

Mallory Evans had been sexually assaulted.

This was worth paying attention to. Michael Timton's name was crossed out in Frank's notes—for who knew what reasons—but since he was local, I figured I could just ask him.

First, I tried his home address, a shabby James Road bungalow with an overturned children's picnic table in the yard. A skinny blond woman answered the door with an urgent enthusiasm that told me she was expecting somebody but it wasn't me. "Oh," she said, scratching at the inside of her elbow.

"Looking for Michael," I told her. "Is he around?"

"No, he's at work."

"Where's that?"

"Are you a cop?"

"I don't want to make any trouble for him," I said, a hedge that sometimes worked. "I just need to talk to him."

The woman leaned on the doorframe. She was wearing a long, ratty green cardigan over pajamas. I was willing to bet that under her sleeves, her arms were dotted with needle marks, and that the person she'd been hoping was at the door had something to do with that. She glanced at the street behind me and said, quickly, "He works at the electronics drop-off over by Walmart. Look, can you leave? I'm waiting for a friend."

"Hey, sure," I said. "Thanks a lot."

She closed the door without saying anything else.

A few more minutes of research yielded the information I needed: Powered Up, an electronics recycling center on Main Street that was run by a reentry support group, offering employment and training to recently released felons. They accepted broken televisions and fax machines and microwaves—the kind of electronics you're not supposed to throw in a Dumpster—and repaired them, then resold them in their retail storefront, which closed at 4 p.m. on Saturdays. So I hurried over to Main and found Powered Up in a mostly vacant plaza across the street from the Walmart, hoping he'd actually be there.

He was. I recognized him from his mug shot on the sex-offender registry and spotted him from the street as he wrestled what appeared to be a miniature organ out of the trunk of an ancient Bonneville and into the open door of the shop. A well-dressed, elderly lady nodded approvingly after him and then got into the car and drove away. That left the lot empty. I pulled into a parking spot and a few seconds later, Michael Timton came back out. He was big and angry-looking, wearing one of those back braces that professional movers use. His forearms were covered with tattoos, some crude and improvised. He looked like the type of person to own a camo jacket, but he didn't have any facial piercings.

"Can I help you," he said, like he had no interest in doing so at all.

I got out of the car. "Hi, Michael," I said.

He just looked at me.

"My name is Roxane Weary. I'm a private investigator and I was hoping to ask you a few questions"—here his features screwed up into an expression of pure hatred—"about someone you went to high school with." Then his face relaxed into confusion. "In Belmont."

"What?" he said.

"Do you have a few minutes to talk?"

"I don't—high school? Seriously?"

"Seriously," I said.

He folded his arms over his chest. "Who?"

"A classmate of yours, Mallory Evans. She was murdered your senior year."

"Seriously?" he said again. "Why?"

"Did you know her?"

"No. I have to go back to work."

"You didn't know her at all?"

Michael scowled at me. I opened my wallet and teased up the corner of a twenty dollar bill. He cocked his head at it. I pulled out forty bucks and held it nonchalantly in my hand.

"I didn't really know her, no," he said. He released the scowl and went back to looking confused. "I knew who she was, but we weren't in the same circles. I was a jock, she was, like, a druggie."

I didn't say anything about the woman who had pointed me here. It seemed like Michael Timton had fallen on trouble of his own design no matter which way you sliced it. "The police questioned you after she was murdered, didn't they?"

"Yeah."

"Why? If you didn't know her?"

"You'd have to ask them."

"I'm asking you."

He scowled again. He appeared to have two modes: irritated and puzzled. "There was this girl," he said, "she claimed I forced her to suck my dick at a party. Pressed these bullshit charges and everything. And then I was like on a list or something. A list of guys the police bothered any time some bitch claimed she saw someone looking at her funny."

Thoroughly charmed by him, I said, "So what did the police want to know?"

"Where I was and shit. The night she was last seen."

"And where were you?"

"I wasn't even in town. I was in Virginia with my family for my grandpa's funeral."

I let out a sigh. That seemed like a pretty solid reason for his name to be crossed out in my father's notes. "And that was the end of it?"

"Yeah." He held out his hand. "Give me my money."

I didn't feel like I'd gotten forty bucks' worth of information out of him. "What about Brad Stockton," I said, "did you know him?"

"Brad?" He almost smiled. "That dude. Yeah. You know he's on death row."

"He is."

"Why are you asking about him?"

"I heard he got questioned about Mallory Evans too," I said. "Was he like you, always getting bothered by the police?"

"I didn't know him too well. But yeah, he was in trouble a lot. I know he got suspended, because of some poem."

"A poem?"

"He was always writing these dumb poems in his notebook. He wrote one about this substitute teacher we had, about how much he wanted to fuck her. It got around and he got in big trouble for it, and then he sliced up her car or something." He looked smug, like this was an act he'd never stoop to. "She never came back after that."

I didn't like the sound of this at all. The car vandalism was bad enough, but I had been thinking it was over something like a bad grade, not a sexually explicit poem. "Imagine that."

"Look, I can't just stand out here, lady," he said. "Can I have my money?"

I held out the bills, feeling defeated.

FOURTEEN

Craft-beer enthusiast Brian Zollinger called me back as I drove home and told me he'd moved to Wisconsin in April of his junior year and he never saw anyone from Belmont again. He'd gotten a phone call from my father after Mallory Evans was found—owing, he said, to his troublemaker reputation in town—but he couldn't provide any info since he never knew her well and he hadn't even seen her in nearly two years at that point anyway.

So it seemed that Frank had a good reason for talking to Brian Zollinger, Michael Timpton, and Brad—their own troublemaking reputations—as well as logic behind crossing the first two off the list. All I could do was hope that Brad could tell me why his own name was crossed off, that it somehow made perfect sense, and that seeing Brad's name in my dad's notes about Mallory's murder was nothing but a coincidence, not a clue.

I really didn't want it to be a clue.

Once I got into my apartment, I poured a drink and stood in my dining room and looked out the window onto the alley. It was six o'clock but it was already midnight-dark. The wind rattled a loose can along the fence but otherwise, it was still quiet. In the reflection in the glass, I could see the state of the room behind me and it wasn't good. I wasn't sure that I'd ever eaten a meal in this room. It was mainly the room I walked to in order to get to the kitchen. The table was piled high with dirty clothes and unopened mail. I turned away from the window and walked back into the hallway, willfully not looking directly at the mess.

I took my drink into my office and pulled my computer out of its bag. The metal finish was cold to the touch from sitting in my car all day. I opened it, then closed it immediately when I saw that Pam Gregorio was up on the open browser tab.

"What do you want," I muttered to my empty apartment.

That was easy enough. I wanted to figure out if Mallory Evans's death was somehow related to the Cook murders, or if I was just stuck on this because of a theoretical appearance of my father's ghost. The crimes were connected, obviously, by location, and also by murder weapon. There was something weird about Brad here too, based on Kenny's sudden change of attitude. But beyond that, they weren't even similar. A young woman with a history of trouble, raped and stabbed and buried in the woods; a middle-aged couple stabbed to death in their home. And then there was Sarah, who was neither here nor there. I didn't know what it meant. But it felt very much like it all meant something.

The last thing I wanted to do was sit at home all night, thinking about what it all could mean, waiting for Camo Jacket to show up, waiting for the creepy phone calls to start again. I leaned back in my desk chair as far as it would go and let my head hang off the back of it, taking in the upside-down view of the hissing radiator and the blank square of the window above it, waiting for something else to happen. Finally, something did. The phone rang, and I nearly fell over. Then I saw that it was Catherine calling.

I knew better than to answer, but I did.

"*Hey,*" she said, like she'd been trying to reach me for weeks.

"Hey you."

"I was wondering if it did any good," she said. "The sketch."

I looked up at the ceiling. If not for the sketch and the fact that it led me to Jillian Pizzuti, I'd still be out there obliviously looking for Sarah on the streets of Belmont instead of tangled in the archives of another crime. "I think it did," I said. "Or it might have made things worse." A little like Catherine herself, always.

"Well."

"Yeah," I said.

"And," she continued, because there was usually an *and* where Catherine was concerned, "I wanted to tell you that a friend of mine is having a party on Wednesday, and you should come."

Catherine had an endless circle of friends who had parties on any night of the week and never cared who got invited. "And why is that?" I said.

"Because last I heard, you like parties," Catherine said. "And because I've been thinking about you."

I felt myself smiling, some of the defeat of the day slipping off me.

"So, are you free?"

"I'm free right now," I said.

Now Catherine was quiet.

I got a terrible idea. My heart started beating faster. "You should have dinner with me," I said.

"And *why is that*?" Her tone was gently mocking. Anyone else and I would have just hung up.

"Because it's Saturday night and you already got to W in your phone book," I said. "And, last I heard, you like passing the check."

She laughed. She had a dirty laugh, impossibly big for her quiet, demure voice. "So where are we going?" she said.

When I got to the Pearl, Catherine was already there, seated at a pub table in the window with a glass of red wine and a charcuterie board in front of her, nibbling at foie gras on a piece of bread. She was dressed all in black—a loose shift over leggings, moto boots with a tangle of silver chains around her ankles. Her blond hair was messy around her shoulders. She didn't look like she was waiting for anybody at all. I sat down and she put her hand on my thigh under the table without speaking.

"Are you going to say anything?" I said after a minute.

"I just want to have a nice evening," Catherine said. "I'm not sure talking needs to be involved in that."

We looked at each other across the table, her expression vaguely challenging. Somehow in the hour between the phone call and this moment, tension had sprung up between us. Her eyes looked a little tired, and her mood was a little prickly, and I didn't think she was on her first glass of wine when I walked in. That, and I was already feeling frustrated and unsettled. Every time someone walked by on the other side of the window, I involuntarily looked up, half expecting to see Camo Jacket staring back in at me like I had the other night. None of this was a recipe for a nice evening. But I felt a little better just being near her. So we ordered oysters and drinks and I told her all about Brad Stockton. She had always liked hearing about my cases, the small shows of bad behavior, the mysteries people thought were worth solving. She told me about a job her husband was interviewing for this weekend, in London. I'd never met him, though Internet stalking had yielded many photos of an unsmiling man always wearing a scarf of some kind, his sole personal expression to the world.

"You don't seem especially happy about that," I said.

"I'm not especially anything," Catherine said. Her hand was back on my thigh. "It's up to him if he wants to go to London or Prague or Tallahassee, Florida. I'm just not going with him this time."

"And why not?" I said. I shouldn't have. I wanted her to say something specific and she'd never do it. "Trouble in paradise?"

"Because I've moved all my shit enough times and I'm not doing it again. And there is no *trouble,* and there is no *paradise,* there's just the life I've chosen. Some days I love it and some days I hate it. But I chose it, and that's all."

I looked at the melting ice in my glass.

"Come on," she said, "you can't tell me you've just been sitting at home, crying over my senior picture all this time."

I laughed. It was a ridiculous thing to say, to act as if nothing had transpired between us since then, and she knew it. She said, "So who are you seeing?"

My thoughts flicked to Tom, and then to the smiling picture of Pamela Gregorio currently waiting for me in cyberspace. "No one," I said.

"Lies."

"No," I said, "that's the truth."

She raised an eyebrow at me.

"For a while," I said, "I was, ah, keeping company with my dad's partner. I'm not sure if you ever met him."

"Sure, yeah," Catherine said, "Tom, right?"

I nodded.

"Sort of uptight, no?"

"No," I said. "He's different, when you get to know him. But that's over with now anyway. He's seeing somebody."

"And what's she like?"

"Haven't met her."

Another raised eyebrow. "And you're not the least bit curious, either," she said, and pantomimed typing on a keyboard.

"You just think you know everything there is to know about me, huh."

She leaned closer to me. "Don't I?"

I shook my head; I didn't know what at. "She looks like a very nice person," I said.

"Lies," Catherine said again.

"Look, what's it to you?"

"I like to know you're out there, being okay."

"Well, I'm not."

Catherine looked at me like she wanted to kiss me and also like she wanted to get up and leave.

I said, "So what are you going to do about it?"

In the car, we fit together like we belonged that way, her knees over the arm rest, me balancing one hand on the doorframe, the other hand peeling away the layers of her clothes like flower petals. *She loves me. She loves me not.* Dress, cami, leggings, the black lacy nothing of her thong. The windows fogged up and it felt private, secluded, even though we were parked at a meter and every so often, footsteps passed. Catherine tasted how she always tasted, like the beginning of everything. Her hands gripped my shoulders and tugged my hair as I ran my tongue along the inside of her thigh and then back up into the sweetness of her. She came hard, a shuddering release, and then she sat up on her elbows and tipped her head back and laughed.

"You could have saved yourself sixty bucks," she said, "and just invited me out for a ride."

"Sixty bucks," I said, "bitch, please."

She laughed again. Some of the weariness was gone from her face. "I should just leave you here like this," she said, nudging me with the toe of her boot. "All hot and bothered."

"I dare you," I said. She was still breathing hard underneath me, her cheeks flushed pink despite the cold air in the car.

She unzipped my leather jacket and grabbed the front of my shirt. "You know what," she said.

"What."

Catherine tipped her head to speak low into my ear. "I never feel quite as much like myself as I do when I'm with you."

I kissed her hard. "Tell me about it," I said. For the first time in a while, I felt all right.

The feeling only lasted so long, though. I walked up the sidewalk to my apartment in a good kind of fog and unlocked the door to the building. But I froze as soon as I stepped inside. My own door was half open, one of the glass panes next to the knob neatly punched out.

I stared at it for a second, not understanding.

"What?" I heard a voice say from somewhere in the apartment. "I can't hear you, why are you whispering? She's back? *What?*"

Then the owner of the voice leaned out of the doorway to my office and looked right at me.

It was Camo Jacket. His face, illuminated by the light of his phone, flooded with panic.

"Oh, shit," he said.

"Stop right there," I heard myself say, but he darted back into the office and went for the door that led out to my enclosed porch, a voice still yelling from his cell phone. I dashed into the apartment and lunged for him, grabbing the sleeve of his coat as he fumbled for a split second with the lock, but he shrugged out of the garment and banged out onto the porch, knocking my screen door off the hinges. The intruder then vaulted over the brick ledge of the porch and dropped five or so feet to the sidewalk, immediately yelling out in pain.

Breathing hard, I looked over the porch at him. He was clutching his knee and rolling around on the ground, his face twisted up in confused agony. "Who the fuck are you?" I snapped at him.

"Help me!" he groaned.

"Tell me who you are," I said, "and then maybe I'll help you."

But a car door slammed and I heard another voice—this one a bit familiar—screaming, "What did you do to him!"

I turned to the source of the voice and nearly fell off the porch myself.

Cass Troyan.

She was dressed all in black, like she'd watched a *Mission: Impossible* movie as research for whatever gambit this was supposed to be. She ran over to him and knelt down. "Damon, baby, are you okay?" Then she glared up at me. "You hurt him. Look at him, he's hurt really bad. Oh, baby—"

"What the fuck is going on here?" I said, loud enough to make them both shut up. "Cass. What is this?"

She glared up at me defiantly while Damon struggled up into a sitting position, subdued now. "You're *not* a producer for a TV show," she said.

Shit.

"You're a liar. You lied right in my face. That's so messed up. You're a private investigator. Who do you work for?"

I ran a hand over my face, a rush of shame hitting me. I needed to retire that particular gimmick. I supposed it was bound to happen sometime, that someone caught me in that lie and tried to do something about it. But that knowledge did nothing for my racing heart. "Cass, you can't—"

"*Who?*"

"Brad Stockton's family," I said after a minute.

Cass looked pissed, but not as pissed as I might have expected. They both just looked kind of busted. "I thought maybe you were working for my dad."

"What?"

"My parents are getting divorced. It's gonna be ugly."

I shook my head. None of this made any sense. I said, "Someone needs to tell me what's going on here."

After a second, Cass spoke. "My mom said I was an idiot if I believed that we were going to be on some TV show. She said it was probably some scheme my dad cooked up. So I called that station, on your business card. They never heard of any Roxane Smith. And later, we were going to Taverna Athena for dinner, for our anniversary. And I saw your car. So we followed you, to that house on the north side. It was Damon's idea."

He nodded proudly. I thought of the minuscule diamond in Cass's engagement ring. Clearly she'd found the man of her dreams here: money *and* brains.

"He got into your car while you were there, to find out your real name. But he couldn't find anything with your name on it, so he went back to the house the next day and that old woman answered. She told him that you lived in Olde Town now."

My mother had left that part out. I gritted my teeth.

"So we drove around till we found your car, and then he got your name off your mail. So I Googled you and that's how I figured out you were a private investigator. I just wanted to know who you were working for."

As far as amateur detective work went, it honestly wasn't bad. But I was furious—at them, and at myself. After all, it was my lie that had led to this point. "Well, are you happy now?"

"What do you know about my cousin?"

"Nothing, Cass," I said. "I haven't really learned anything. I apologize for lying to you—it's just that you were about to shut the door and I wanted to speak to you. If you wanted to know more, why didn't you just ask me? You obviously have my number, right? You're the one who has been calling?"

Cass squinted in disgusted confusion.

"You haven't been calling me?" I said. "And just breathing, not saying anything?"

"No," Cass said, somewhat indignant now.

I ran a hand over my face again. I didn't believe her, not for a second.

Damon chimed in, "You owe us five hundred bucks. I need medical treatment. I didn't even touch any of your stuff, I was just looking. For, like, evidence."

I was sick of them. I put my hands on my hips. "I think," I said, "that you broke my fucking window, so we're going to call it even. Or, we can get the police here to sort it out."

Apparently those were the magic words, because Damon managed to get himself onto his feet. "No, we're good now."

"Do not come back here, understood?" I said, as firmly as I could manage.

It was one thirty when they finally left. I went back inside and locked the dead bolts on the door, a pointless act given the gaping hole in the glass. The adrenaline rush was over, leaving me shaky and exhausted and, although mildly relieved that the mystery of Camo Jacket was no more sinister than a couple of clueless idiots wound up over my own bad judgment, I didn't quite know how to deal with the aftermath. It was the middle of the night, so there was no chance of getting anyone to come out and fix the window right now. But there was also no way I could sleep with it like this. I went into the kitchen and hit the lights, wincing at the sudden brightness. I turned them off and grabbed the pizza box off the stove, where I had abandoned it when Tom was over the night before last. I dumped the old pizza into the trash and cut a square of cardboard from the bottom of the box, also selecting a broom, a dust pan, and a roll of duct tape, making do. What it lacked in security it made up for in class, I told myself.

When I had completed my expert repairs, I sat at my desk for a minute with my phone, wondering if Catherine had Ubered straight home and if she'd let me join her there if I asked. But my chest tightened when I saw another two calls from the unknown number. One that came in while I was with Catherine, and one from one twenty.

Which would have been right in the middle of my confrontation with Cass and Damon.

I closed my eyes. The vague sense of relief I'd had only minutes before was gone. I hadn't believed Cass at the time when she said she wasn't the one calling, but even I had to admit that it would be awfully hard for her to pull off such a call when she was standing right in front of me.

Maybe I was wrong about what time it was when I got back inside. I wanted to be wrong.

I'd assumed that the calls were part of the same narrative. If they weren't, that meant I knew even less than I thought.

FIFTEEN

I met Andrew at Fox in the Snow for breakfast on Sunday morning. Ten o'clock, which was on the early side both for my hangover and for him. But I could hardly turn down the offer of a free blueberry hand pie, and I needed to get moving if I wanted to attempt to beat the crowd at the prison in Chillicothe anyway.

"You look like you had fun last night," my brother said, stirring sugar into his coffee. Andrew, somehow, never got hungover, like the way some people don't get poison ivy or ice-cream headaches. It wasn't fair. "Spill."

I waved him off. Catherine Walsh was on the no-fly list in terms of conversation topics, and my late-night visit from Cass and Damon would only make him worry about me. Besides, that hardly counted as fun. I was fine, I told myself. Everything was fine. "Just working," I said. "You know I never have fun anymore."

"How's that going, your case for Matt's lady friend?" he said. Then his eyes widened as he remembered something. "I meant to tell you: Did you know he's in a band?"

I raised an eyebrow. "No," I said.

"They're called the Test Pavements," Andrew said.

I had to laugh. "What does that even mean?" I said.

He shook his head. "A construction workers' joke, I assume," he said, "it sounds like a bunch of ODOT guys playing REM covers. He told us about it on Wednesday night after you left. He has a gig at some shitty coffee shop in Hilliard this Friday and Mom said we're all going."

I squeezed the liquid out of my tea bag. "That sounds awful," I said. "A coffee shop? Will there be alcohol, at least?"

"No. Believe me, I asked. He said they have a *wholesome juice bar,* though."

I rolled my eyes. "I think I should be exempt. I wasn't there when the plan was discussed, and he clearly waited till after I left to bring it up for a reason."

"Nice try. You're going."

"A Friday night out with our mother? All this togetherness. I don't know if I can take it."

"I know," Andrew said. "It kind of makes you miss the benign neglect of our childhood, doesn't it?"

We looked at each other for a beat. Finally, I said, "You owe me seven hundred bucks. Or half that, anyway. The sink?"

"*What?*" Andrew said. "When did this happen? And how does replacing a sink cost that much?"

"I don't know," I said, "but that's what it cost. I was over there when the plumber finished and someone had to pay him."

"Shit, Rox," Andrew said. "Sorry. Wait—half? What about Matt?"

"I talked to him," I said. "He was unmoved. Also, I hung up on him. Hey, did you know that Mom hasn't been inside the office since it happened?"

"How did that come up?" my brother said, ignoring my abrupt change of subject.

"I asked her about what she did with his old notebooks," I said. "And she said they were probably still in the office but she didn't know what was in there because it was locked. But, it's not locked anymore."

Andrew sighed. "So what's in there?"

"Mostly dust," I said, "but also the good liquor."

That got his attention. "How good is good?"

"Midleton," I said. "Wild Geese."

"Nice."

"And the computer in there, I swear it's the same one they had when I was in high school," I said. Then I thought of something else. "If Mom doesn't have the key to the office, how does she e-mail us so often?"

"I think she goes to the library."

"Seriously?"

"Honestly," he said, "I think that's what she's always done."

We both fell silent for a while.

Finally, Andrew spoke again. "I'll get together some cash for you this week. But are you okay? Moneywise?"

"Moneywise, yeah," I said.

"What about otherwise?"

"I don't want to talk about it."

"Why?"

"Because my case is a mess. I don't know how to help. Or even if anyone can. And I found a weird link back to Frank and I can't stop thinking about it. Hence the notebooks."

My brother's eyebrows went up. "What kind of link?"

"Just a case he worked forever ago. It might have nothing to do with Matt's friend at all, and I'm just making it into something because, well, because I'm me and this is what I do."

"No," Andrew said, "you don't make something out of nothing. That's like the opposite of you." He smiled. "You'll figure it out."

Would I?

I shoved half of the blueberry hand pie into my mouth and chewed as dramatically as possible so he couldn't ask me any more questions.

The bureaucracy machine of the Chillicothe Correctional Institution moved a little faster since I'd already been there once. My name was called after forty minutes, and this time when Brad Stockton shuffled down to the Plexiglas booth where I was sitting, he looked flat-out shocked. "You're back," he said into the phone.

"I am. I have a few more questions for you." I wanted to say *Please please please tell me you didn't know Mallory Evans at all* but I figured this wasn't a good way to get to the truth, whatever it happened to be.

Brad shrugged. "Okay, go for it."

I smiled at him. I felt like a liar—but then again, he might very well be a liar too. "I wanted to ask you about someone else you went to school with," I said while I studied him, trying to decide if he seemed evil. "Mallory Evans."

For a beat it looked like he couldn't place the name. Then his eyebrows knit together. "Really," he said. "Why do you want to know about that?"

"I'm looking into other crimes near Belmont. Her name came up."

He thought about that for a second. His face was unreadable. "Okay. Mallory. Yeah."

"You knew her?"

"Sure, I knew her from school, but we weren't friends or anything."

"Did you hear anything about what happened after she went missing?"

Brad scratched his jaw. "Well, she dropped out junior year," he said. "I didn't even know she was 'missing.'" He put air quotes around the word. "But then when they, like, found her, people started saying all kinds of crazy things, trying to guess who she went there with."

"Went where?"

"To Clover Point."

I waited, not sure what he was talking about.

"People used to go up there to fool around, you know, like a make-out spot."

"And where's Clover Point?"

He raised his eyebrows again, like he hadn't intended to tell me something I didn't already know. "She was found in the woods, right, in this ravine? Well, above the ravine, there's a place to pull in. It used to be where you'd go, to fool around with your girl in the car because it was real quiet. No one ever went up there unless it was, you know, for that."

"Really."

"But then, after Mallory, the city put up signs that it was only open during daylight, so that kind of put a stop to it."

"Did you ever go there?"

"No," he said, going a little shifty-eyed.

"Not even with Sarah?" I said. "Are you sure?"

"Okay, maybe a few times, but mostly we just went to my house. Why are you asking about this, what's it got to do with anything?"

I took a deep breath, ignoring the question. "So after Mallory died, your classmates were trying to guess who she might have gone to the overlook with," I said. It was a simplistic view of the crime, assuming that she had been killed there—the tarp and the bungee cords said otherwise, but I wanted to hear what he had to say about it. "What was the general consensus?"

He shook his head. "It was just talk," he said. "No one knew anything. Like I said, she dropped out and that was last I ever saw of her."

"But the police talked to you, right?" I guessed.

His jaw bunched a little. "Yeah, the guy was a real asshole. Even by cop standards, you know? I'd been in some trouble earlier that year, so I guess I was on the watch list or whatever. But I mean, there used to be like four black families in Belmont. I was always getting the third degree for something."

I decided not to mention that the *real asshole* was my father. "What were you in trouble for," I said, "that got people on your case?"

His expression hardened. "It was just a stupid prank."

"A prank."

"I got suspended for a few days," he said. "It wasn't a big deal."

"Why'd you get suspended?" I said, like I didn't already know.

"It was stupid. I wrote something about a teacher, a poem. It got around, and she didn't like it. The end." He looked at me, defiant. He wasn't going to tell me any more about that.

"I heard something about slicing up a teacher's car seats," I said. I assumed it was true since I heard it from two different people. "Was that her?"

Brad shot forward in his seat, stabbing a finger in my direction. Without meaning to, I slid my chair back a few inches. "Why are you asking about this stuff?"

His unreadable expression had turned distinctly readable. Now he looked like he wouldn't mind stabbing *me*. "The car seats. Did you do that?"

"Yeah, but it was nothing. Like I said, a prank."

It didn't sound like a prank to me. "The police questioned you after Mallory Evans died," I said, "they didn't do that because of a prank."

"They questioned everybody."

I thought about what Derrow had said. *Parents would lose their minds* if the police questioned everyone in the school. "No, they didn't, Brad."

"Why the fuck are you really asking about this stuff?"

"I'm trying to get the whole story. To figure out if what happened to Mallory is somehow tied to what happened to Sarah. I need the truth, Brad. The other day you told me you never had a knife."

"You got the whole story already," he said. He shook his head and then, without warning, he stood up and slammed the phone down.

"Brad," I said, but he was already walking away.

SIXTEEN

It started to rain again on the way back toward the city, which suited my mood. It hadn't been my intention to make Brad Stockton angry to the point that he refused to talk to me, but I had. Another job well done. I still didn't understand him: he had seemed ready to give up the other day, to stop fighting. I wondered what it meant that he didn't want to fight about Sarah anymore, but he did want to throw down on the matter of a teacher's car seats. I didn't need to understand him, but I'd at least been hoping for something to definitively rule out his involvement in Mallory's death. Instead, he acted just like Kenny had, shutting down when he should have been opening up.

I had the distinct feeling that once Brad talked to his sister, I would not be employed much longer.

I headed to Belmont without much of a plan, hoping one would materialize. As I waited at the traffic light on the exit ramp I glared out at the grey landscape. *Wildflower Capital of Ohio,* the sign reminded me. But then I noticed another sign on the same pole, a brown one with an arrow informing me that the Clover Point Scenic Overlook was two miles away. The place where Mallory's body had been found. A morbid curiosity took hold of me. I wanted to see the place.

I drove east on Clover Road, past Taverna Athena, the place where Sarah Cook's house once stood, and past Kenny Brayfield's street, finally spotting another sign that directed me to turn left. The road got suddenly narrower, plastered in slick orange-brown leaves, no edge lines. Up ahead, a slight incline and a rusting guardrail. I slowed down as I drove up the hill and finally found Clover Point, which was nothing more than a gravel rectangle with space for half a dozen cars and a wooden platform perched on the side of the hill and facing the trees. There was no one else up here.

I felt around in my backseat for a Columbia rain jacket and transferred my keys and phone—which was mercifully quiet so far today—to its pockets. Then, after looking at the murky dark below, I got my revolver out of the glove box. I pulled the hood of the rain jacket over my head and stepped onto the wooden platform, grabbing on to the railing, briefly disoriented from the height. It was nearly a hundred feet of sloping, leaf-covered ground to the bottom of the ravine. I saw now that there was a set of steps leading down to the ravine from the platform I stood on. A few dozen yards away, a chain-link fence separated the woods from an access road like the one I'd taken to get here, and a cluster of orange barrels and construction equipment stood behind it.

I started carefully down the steps. They were slippery from rain and mud and leaves. Although the area was quiet now, evidence of assorted vices littered the ground: food wrappers, crushed beer cans, a condom caught on branches below a small plank bridge that spanned a dried-up creek. Why had Brad said no, he'd never come here with Sarah, and then corrected himself a beat later? Why had he told me about this place but then seemed to regret it? Peter Novotny had said that innocent clients were often the least helpful, but Brad's behavior had now crossed the line from unhelpful to something like suspicious.

At the bottom of the steps, a frayed nylon rope was tied between the hand railings, a small sign advising *No Access*. I hopped over it, put my hands in my pockets, and walked through the dense thicket of trees to the fence, through which I could see the source of the construction equipment—an apartment complex was going up over there, one of those big, impersonal ones with names like The District. Two buildings were done and appeared occupied, and two others were in various stages of completion.

I walked along the fence for a while. I didn't like it down here, but I couldn't shake the feeling that there was something here for me to see besides just the place where Mallory Evans was found. The farther away from the overlook, the denser the woods got. The muddy ground was free of footprints and trash now, like no one was interested in trespassing this far in. Five or so minutes of walking and I couldn't even see where my car was parked anymore. The rain provided a blanket of even sound, a white-noise machine.

Maybe that was why I didn't hear footsteps in the mud until they were right behind me.

I spun around, my heart leaping into my throat. A few feet up the incline, a Belmont cop peered down at me from under the brim of his uniform hat. He was a slight black guy with glasses, which were spotted with rain. He wore a billowing clear plastic poncho that made him look like he was draped in a shower curtain liner.

"Jesus Christ, you scared me," I breathed, a hand over my chest.

"Can I ask what you're up to back here?" he said.

"Can I ask why you snuck up on me?" I squinted in the low light at his name tag: *R. Meeks.*

"Sorry."

"Yeah, I can tell," I said.

But he did look like he was a little sorry. He appeared to be about my age and completely miserable in his poncho. "Come on, let's go."

"I thought it was Columbus city territory down here."

"Not anymore. Belmont annexed it a while back, and now it's private property. Hence the no-access sign, which you must have tripped over since I'm sure you aren't trespassing on purpose."

I smiled slightly. Now that my pulse was returning to normal, I put my hands back in my pockets. "The scenic overlook is private property?"

"Recently sold," Meeks said. "In nine months, all of this is going to be apartments. Now, if you don't mind, let's go on back up."

I wondered what I was supposed to do next.

I wondered if the developers of the apartment complex knew that they were about to take over what had once been a young mother's burial site.

I wondered if it mattered.

I looked at Meeks for a second. This was the fourth time I'd been intercepted by the Belmont police in as many visits to the area, and this time there wasn't even anyone around to rat me out. "How did you know I was here?"

Meeks nodded toward the steps but I didn't budge. Finally, he said, "Your car. There's a BOLO out for your car."

It wasn't funny, but I laughed. "Great," I said. "So now what?"

"Now Chief Lassiter would like to speak with you."

"About my car?"

"I don't know, ma'am." Meeks huffed impatiently. "But it sounded urgent."

I shrugged and began to follow him back toward the overlook. "How did you find my car this time?" I said.

"This time?" He glanced back at me, losing his footing a little on the rocks.

"Every time I come down here, one of Belmont's finest manages to find me. It's just interesting."

"Well," Meeks said, "I was driving by and saw your car parked up there. Every shift since Wednesday, we've been getting a little pep talk at roll call, about looking for you."

I stopped for a second as I contemplated that. The Belmont police were a bipolar bunch: they were hypervigilant to my presence even though I had literally done nothing except ask a few questions and sit in my car, and yet they also seemed to be terrible at preventing actual crime. "What is it that I've allegedly done?"

"Oh, it's nothing like that," he said, like I should take comfort in the fact that no one had accused me of anything yet. "Belmont's a close community, though. Outsiders are pretty obvious."

"I hope you realize how insane that sounds," I said, and he looked over his shoulder and gave me a little smile.

"I do. You'd be shocked at the things we get calls about on a regular basis. People are just cautious, is all. Not much happens down here, so a stranger in a vintage car sticks out like a sore thumb."

Not much happens down here. He apparently hadn't grown up in Belmont.

The air was almost a physical presence, a sheet of wet fabric. Climbing up the hill was harder than going down it had been, and I was breathing hard by the time we were halfway back to the overlook. Or I thought that was where we were, anyway. I was disoriented. The rain and the soft, sloping ground made me feel like we were in a snow globe. I glanced around us, uneasy. Leaves, fallen branches, rocks. In the fading afternoon light, the scene in front of me glowed orangish brown. I tried to picture the map from my father's notebook and wondered where Mallory Evans had been found. I remembered a curving border from his sketch—the access road or the fence, probably the former since the latter looked newer than sixteen years old. Either way, the body was discovered inside of that line, buried ten inches below the ground, covered with rocks and leaves. I tried to take in the scene through my father's eyes. I knew I only had a few minutes before we got back to the party spot below the overlook.

Leaves were everywhere.

Rocks were, too.

I was looking for a ghost.

Everything seemed suspicious, to the same extent that nothing did.

But about twenty yards past the overlook, something caught my attention: another small plank bridge running across the dried-up creek, this one oddly fortified underneath with large, flat rocks. I squinted through the misty air, noticing an unnatural object sticking out from the rocks. Something folded and shiny.

"What is that?" I said, pointing.

Meeks frowned. "What are we talking about here?"

Instead of answering him, I made a beeline for the bridge, thinking I just wanted to see, I was just curious. But I couldn't stop thinking about the tarp that Mallory Evans was buried in. The tarp that haunted my father. *That's the work of someone cold as hell,* Tom had said.

Behind me, footsteps descended on the leaf-covered steps. "Russ, everything okay down here?" a familiar voice said.

I kept walking but looked over my shoulder to see Sergeant Derrow, also draped in a plastic poncho. He gave me a seen-it-all smile. "What's going on?"

"I was just telling her that the chief would like a word," Meeks said.

"He does. An urgent one," Derrow said. "Come on along."

"Not sure why she's down here," I heard Meeks reply.

"Miss Weary, I'm going to have to ask you to come with us. Now," Derrow said.

But by then, I was already at the bridge and I jumped down into the creek bed beside the rocks. Up close, the shape became a triangle of plastic, wrinkled and mud-covered but distinctly blue. The rocks themselves were flat and and mossy. One of them lay a foot or so from the others, like it had recently dislodged itself to expose the tarp. I moved a few of them away and found myself looking at another piece of wood, flush against the bed of the creek. Only a few inches of the blue tarp stuck out from under it.

Meeks and Derrow had now caught up to me. "Let's go," Derrow said. "Now."

But Meeks was looking down at the creek bed. "Is this why you were down here?" he said to me.

"No," I said, then, "I don't know."

"What is it?"

"I don't know," I said again.

Without saying anything else, Meeks got into the creek on the other side of the bridge and peered at the rocks, toed the blue triangle. "Jack, take a look here."

Derrow stepped down into the creek bed and frowned.

"It looks out of place, doesn't it?" I said, my nerves vibrating.

Meeks started helping me move the rocks, and then Derrow joined in as well. The rocks weren't too heavy, but there were a lot of them. We began stacking them on the bridge in neat rows, like teeth.

"Maybe we should get the Parks department," Derrow said. "Looks like maybe someone didn't finish what they started. Easy to get away with it. Nobody comes this far out here anymore."

"I don't know," Meeks said, uneasy.

"What kind of Parks department project involves a blue tarp buried in the woods?" I said, but both cops looked up at me like I wasn't entitled to an opinion on the matter. Maybe I wasn't. But at least they were helping me, rather than dragging me away by my hood.

It took ten minutes or so to clear them away, and then we stared at the sheet of chipboard in silence. Wet and muddy, no more than an inch thick. It didn't look like much, but I had this terrible feeling that it was actually a hell of a lot.

"There's just going to be a hole with worms and shit under this," Meeks said, in a way that told me he knew better.

"Yeah," I said, even though I knew better too.

I held my breath as we lifted it up.

Underneath it, another layer of rocks and mud couldn't quite cover a long, blue bundle.

"Don't touch anything," Derrow said, but I was already reaching for the edge of the tarp.

"Sarah," I heard myself say.

SEVENTEEN

Chief Jake Lassiter was not happy with me. I doubted there were any circumstances under which he would have been, but he was especially irritated with me now that I'd discovered human remains inside his town's jurisdiction. More cops had come quickly, cut a bolt on the chain-link fence to allow entry to the ravine from the access road, and set up a perimeter that ran from the fence to the bottom of the cliff, and a few hundred yards north and south. I was banished to the viewing platform, where I now stood in the rain with Chief Lassiter. He reminded me of Jack Nicholson's character in *A Few Good Men* as he delivered a long, red-faced lecture to me on the importance of trusting The Justice System, a phrase he seemed to capitalize with his mouth.

"The *system*," he was saying, "doesn't *work* if just *anyone* thinks they can go around playing *detective*."

I did not remind him that I actually was a detective, that my license, though not on par with a peace officer certification, was nonetheless part of this system. I just stood there, arms folded across my chest against the chill in the air and, also, the chill in my blood—from the sight of the brown, brittle bones nestled in the folds of that blue tarp. The sparse strands of long, blond hair. My cases usually stuck to the problems of the living, to the trouble people make for each other. It seemed like a meaningless distinction, that I'd never seen anything quite so dead before, but I hadn't, and I couldn't stop thinking that.

"And you have no idea how upsetting it is for the residents of Belmont, having you sticking your nose where it doesn't belong," he added. "This is a real nice town."

At that point, I'd had enough. "Sarah Cook has been buried in these woods for fifteen years and you still want to say it's a nice town?"

He bit off a laugh, shaking his head. "Sarah Cook." He spit the name out, like he had every other time he'd said it during our conversation. "We don't even know if the remains are human."

Then it was my turn to laugh. "Are you kidding me?"

We both glanced down at the bed of the ravine, where the tarp had been laid flat on the muddy earth as Franklin County forensic technicians in white suits collected evidence into plastic bags. A ring of work lights had been set up around the tarp, casting a clinical glow through the foggy dusk. I had to look away, my stomach twisting.

"*If* the remains are human," Lassiter went on, "we will work tirelessly to identify them."

I wanted to tell him to save it for his press conference, but instead I just said, "Of course."

"And if you think you're the first hotshot who ever got the idea to take a look at the Cook case, you've got another thing coming," the chief said. "Every couple years, we get some reporter, some random crazies, people just obsessed with the whole idea. You know we used to have a citizen ride-along program? Had to close it down because we got too many people just wanting to talk about the case, see the scene, see where Bev Stockton lives—it's disgusting."

"I didn't—"

"The fact is, you never should have been down here in the first place," he finished. "I told you myself. So don't go thinking you should get some kind of a medal for discovering this today. Got it?"

I wasn't acting like I wanted a medal. I was acting like I wanted him to listen to me. But all he wanted to do was to be mad. "It's not like *I* killed her," I said. "I don't know why you're pissed at *me*."

Rage flashed through his face, like he didn't know either and it made him even madder. "No," he said evenly. "Brad Stockton did and he's already in jail."

So that was why he hated me so much, maybe: he had all the hassle of a homicide on his hands here, with none of the potential glory that could come with solving the case. I felt sick when I thought about Brad—or, not so much him, but his sister, who was stuck believing in something impossible.

"Now," Lassiter said, "I want you to get in your car and go back to the city. We'll handle it from here."

It didn't seem right to just leave. But my case appeared to be over. Brad had basically directed me right to Sarah's body. I still didn't know why. Maybe he was tired of the charade. Maybe he'd been wanting to tell somebody every day for the last fifteen years. Maybe I would never know why. I didn't like it, but it wasn't up to me. It never had been.

I passed several television news trucks on my way back down from Clover Point and I realized that if the story wasn't on the wire already, it would be soon. I called Danielle, thinking I didn't want her to have to hear about this on the news the way she'd heard the Cooks were dead in the first place, but she didn't answer.

Another job well done, indeed.

I went straight to my kitchen and poured a shot, downed it fast, then poured another. I hadn't turned the lights on and the apartment took on an eerie glow from the streetlights outside. I leaned against the counter, swallowed my second shot, and closed my eyes. I couldn't get the sight of the bones out of my head. I wondered how my father had been able to stand it for almost forty years, bearing witness to that ugliness every day. Maybe he hadn't, I realized, and that's why he was the way he was, hard and distant and drunk every night within thirty minutes of getting home. I dropped my shot glass into the sink. From the clatter it made, it sounded like there were a dozen others in there already.

I flipped the light on. It was not looking good in here: The pizza box from Yellow Brick was still sitting on the stove, though now with a square cut from the bottom. The sight of it reminded me, again, that a full day had passed and I had failed to get the door fixed. The sink was full. Someday, I told myself, someday soon, I was going to resume life as a normal person. It was easy to think of my life now as broken into two segments—before my father was killed, and after. The after part seemed like it might unfold forever. Maybe it would. Maybe every morning people like Joshua Evans and Cass Troyan woke up wondering if this was the day the *after* ended and their lives morphed into act three. Somehow, I suspected it wouldn't be that easy, not for them, and not for me.

I ran hot water in the sink; then I noticed I didn't have any sponges. Okay, fine. At least I tried. I flipped the lights back off and peeled off my damp clothes and dropped them in a pile on the laundry room floor. Then I stood under the steady stream of the shower for thirty minutes and might've stayed there all night, except the hot water ran out. I towel-dried my hair and got into bed naked and lay there waiting for something else to happen. I couldn't place what I was feeling. No one was any worse off than they had been before this afternoon, not even Sarah. But I had a sensation in my chest like we all were, and like it was my fault.

I thought about Sarah's parents. What had happened that night? What did they interrupt? I wanted to think that they died without knowing what had happened to their daughter, but it probably didn't matter. There were no silver linings here, no small bits of comfort to cling to, not for anyone. I closed my eyes but all I could see was the blue tarp, the curve of a clavicle, the blond hair.

I opened my eyes again. My apartment felt suddenly, acutely haunted. I needed something but I didn't know what. And then I wondered how long Catherine's husband would be in London and if she was alone in her house tonight too. I grabbed my phone but before I could dial her number, *Unknown* called me again.

I didn't even bother saying hello. "Who the fuck is this?"

Breathe in, breathe out.

"Cass?"

Breathe in, breathe out.

It had to be Cass after all. Brad was in jail. "Stop calling me," I snapped, hanging up.

But thirty seconds later, the phone began vibrating again. I was about to throw the device at the wall, until I saw that the universe had finally intervened on my behalf: it was Tom.

I sank back to the pillow.

"I just heard the craziest story about you," he said when I answered. "Belmont?"

I covered my face with my hand. "Is it the one where they gave me the keys to the city?" I said, and he laughed a little. "And who did you hear this from? It literally just happened."

"News travels fast around cops," he said. Then he added, "Someone I know in the coroner's office was at the scene and heard your name. Like it or not, most of the police in Ohio know who you are."

I sighed. I wasn't sure how I felt about that: the fact that people I'd never met, and probably never would, still somehow knew that I was Frank Weary's kid. He used to run into people he knew everywhere, in the city and out, once even on a family vacation to Niagara Falls. I pulled the blankets over me. "It was horrible," I said, as the image of the tarp slipped back in front of my eyes. "I thought I've seen my share of ugly already, but something like that? I don't know how you do it. I really don't."

"Listen," Tom said. "Do you want to grab a drink? An actual drink, that's not code for—you know."

I rolled over and buried my face in the pillow. Vaguely disappointed that he wasn't calling for the *you know* part, but I didn't want to dwell on it. "Right," I said, "since you're basically engaged now."

"You're never going to make anything easy, are you."

I smiled into the pillowcase. "No," I said. But the thought of not drinking alone was very appealing. "I will take you up on that offer though. I keep seeing ghosts."

He was quiet for a second. "Yeah," he said, like he knew his share about seeing ghosts, "it happens."

We met at the Olde Towne Tavern on Oak Street and I ordered shot after shot of Crown Royal while Tom nursed a single beer. He shrugged when I called him out on it. "I can't keep up with you, so there's no sense in trying. Plus, I have to drive home."

I, on the other hand, had walked over. The bar was probably chosen strategically by Tom for this reason, since he lived on the other side of the city. It was a good, old-school bar, exposed brick and pressed-tin ceiling. And it was full of people. That usually wasn't my favorite thing about a bar, but it was tonight.

"Frank and I used to drink at Bob's Bar. Do you know it?" he said after a minute.

"The Cultural Hub of the Midwest," I said, reciting the tagline of the place, a strange little hole in the wall near where my parents lived. I wondered if the proximity to Frank's house was why they drank there. Walking distance if necessary. The Weary family, in constant need of handling. "Did you stick to beer with him too?"

"That depends on why we were drinking," he said, "and what we saw that day."

I buried my head in my arms on the bar top. "Does it ever get any easier?"

"Short answer?"

I nodded.

"No."

"What's the long answer?" I said, sitting up. The bartender had refilled my glass and I downed the shot, aware that I probably should slow down. It wasn't a great sign if Tom couldn't keep up with me, considering that he drank with my father for years and years.

He thought about that for a second. "Long answer. Fuck no."

I laughed, not because it was funny, but because.

"After a while you get better at isolating it and shoving it into a compartment so it doesn't mess with you, after. But it never really gets easier, seeing what people do to each other." He took a long swallow from his glass. Then he looked at me. "Most of the time, I try to look at a scene like it's a puzzle, a series of objects to process. But sometimes you can't. Every cop has a case or two that just got in and won't get out and there's nothing you can do. That's when you drink."

I wondered what my father would have been like if he hadn't been a cop. If he'd been an electrician or a mechanic or any other profession that didn't involve seeing things you had to drink to forget. "What's the one you can't forget? Sorry—you don't have to answer that," I added quickly, suddenly afraid that he was going to say my father's death was the case that stuck with him. That was the last thing I wanted to think about today.

"It's okay," he said. He leaned on the bar so that our elbows were touching. He took a minute before continuing. "Jada Pierce. She was two. Her piece of shit father took her with him to his buddy's meth lab. She somehow got her hands on a cup of sulfuric acid—drain cleaner. It was just sitting around while they cooked up. She drank it. The acid ate through her throat, through her stomach. She might have lived if they'd gotten her medical treatment, but they didn't. Instead they panicked and put her body in a Coleman cooler and they dumped it in the Olentangy River."

I said nothing.

"About a dozen witnesses saw them, so it wasn't hard to put them away. But I couldn't stop seeing this kid, jammed into the cooler, acid burns around her mouth and a hole in her throat—for weeks, it fucked with me. I'm talking majorly here—I couldn't sleep, I was a mess. I didn't understand why everyone who'd been on the scene wasn't a complete wreck over it and I resented it. I thought I could never be the kind of person who saw that kid and felt nothing. Frank said, and I'll never forget this, he told me, *No one feels nothing. Your job as a cop is not to feel nothing. It's to neutralize what you see, so no one else has to see it, and no one else has to feel it.*" Tom paused, blinking up at the tin ceiling. "I don't know if that makes any sense to you," he added. "But it helped me. A lot."

I wasn't a cop. And what I'd seen wasn't on the same level as what Tom had seen—what he had probably seen many, many times. But it did make sense. "So it's okay to feel like shit, because there's a certain amount of shit that needs to be felt in this world, and some people have signed up to feel more of it than others," I said.

"Exactly."

I sighed and shoved my whiskey glass away. "I'm the world's worst detective. I set out to prove this woman was still alive, and instead I found her body. I was supposed to be helping my client's brother get out of jail, but instead I think I might have implicated him in another crime. I want to be wrong, but I don't know. Not now."

"No you don't," Tom said. "Want to be wrong, that is. You wish the world was different. That's something else. And the world's worst detective wouldn't have found out anything about anything, so I'm afraid you don't get to claim that title."

I stared up at our reflection in the half-moon-shaped mirror behind the beer taps. I wanted to ask how his symphony date with Pam had gone but I didn't want to know. Based on the fact that we were in this bar and not in my bed, I probably already had the answer anyway. Months of me telling Tom that it was just sex somehow left me disappointed when he finally took my word for it. I didn't even understand myself. It was no wonder I didn't understand my case. But Tom was a good guy to have on my side either way. "Look at us," I said, but then I left it at that.

EIGHTEEN

The phone woke me out of a dream again, but this time the room was still dark and the house was quiet and I hadn't been asleep long enough to be hungover. The glowing red numerals of my clock told me it was seven forty. I sat up and grabbed for the phone and my stomach dropped: Danielle Stockton. I thought about rejecting the call but I didn't, figuring I at least owed her that much.

But she didn't even let me say hello. "They found another body," she said breathlessly.

I bit my lip. She sounded way too excited about that. "I know," I said, "I tried to call you yesterday—"

"What if you were right, Roxane? About Mallory, that whoever killed her also killed Sarah's parents, and maybe now this other girl, like a pattern?"

I turned the light on, something about the darkness keeping my thoughts from connecting. "Danielle, that's not—"

"They're saying that she was a runaway, that the police didn't even look for her."

Now I pulled the phone away from my ear and stared at it for a second before responding. "What are you talking about?"

"They identified the body," she said impatiently, "her name is Colleen something and she's been missing for the last eight years."

I automatically jumped to my feet. *"What?"* I said. Thinking that eight years ago, Brad Stockton was already in prison. What the hell was going on? My heart was pounding. I immediately went into the office and booted up my computer. "Where did you hear that?"

"Kenny just called to tell me," Danielle said.

I paced the length of my office. There was still some whiskey in my system but my confusion felt separate from that. What did Kenny Brayfield know about this?

"I'm sorry, I know it's early," my client continued. "But I just, look, I know I was kind of harsh the other day, when I acted like you didn't know what you were doing. Basically, I thought you were nuts. But now—I don't know. You might be on to something."

I slumped into my desk chair and leaned hard on my hand, waiting for the wireless to connect. "Yeah, I thought so too," I said.

Promising to check in with her later, I hung up. I *had* become the worst detective in the world. Good detectives—or even okay ones—didn't go around erroneously implicating their own clients of additional crimes. The body wasn't Sarah. This realization was like a bomb blast. The location. The blond hair. I'd been so certain. And furthermore, whoever it was, Brad couldn't have killed her. Although yesterday I'd wanted to be wrong, now I just felt guilty. I navigated to the *Dispatch*'s Web site, breezing past what felt like dozens of articles about the Ohio State football team. Then, I found it:

> *Human remains found by police in Belmont development site.*

"Right," I muttered.

I scanned the article. Yeah, yeah, the future site of eight hundred luxury apartments, whatever.

> *Police Chief Jacob Lassiter says the discovery might be linked to a missing Belmont teen, but it's too early to*

tell. Acting on a tip from other law enforcement, investigators located the human remains in a wooded area late Sunday afternoon. Lassiter said dental records will be collected from the missing 18-year-old woman's parents to confirm if the remains are hers. The results won't be returned for weeks.

Other law enforcement. I guessed that was me. I was sure there were other ways that Lassiter would have preferred to describe me. The short article didn't say anything more, no mention of any Colleen. It could be talking about anyone. But it certainly wasn't talking about Sarah Cook.

The Belmont police station resembled a motel that had been built to look like a castle, an L-shaped brick building with tall tinted windows perched under dramatic notched eaves. I went in and asked to see Chief Lassiter, having assumed—correctly—that he'd be working overtime, given the developments of yesterday. I was telling myself that I was actually doing Lassiter a favor by dropping in to tell him I was in Belmont. But, of course. I just wanted information from him, a last name to go with Colleen, for starters. He probably knew I wasn't just offering a professional courtesy, and that was probably why he kept me waiting for close to an hour. I drifted from one end of the small lobby to the other, half looking at the framed pictures on the walls of various uniformed officers doing various good works in the community: teaching self-defense classes, posing with the graduates of Junior Police Explorers and *opportunity youth* programs, painting over graffiti on the siding of a Lutheran church. It was all very touching. Finally, the chief escorted me back to his office without saying anything.

Once he'd closed the door, he turned on me. "What are you doing here? Didn't I tell you to stay away from my town?"

"Look, you can't actually tell me to stay out of Belmont, you know that, right?"

His silence confirmed that he did.

"Believe it if you like, but I am not interested in making any kind of trouble for you," I went on. "I work for Danielle Stockton. She thinks her brother is innocent, and since his execution date is in less than two months, she wants to give it one last try. Now, I'll admit that yesterday, I didn't think that was looking too good for her because the whole reason I even went to Clover Point was something Brad told me, that it used to be a make-out spot."

"It did," Lassiter allowed.

I tried to sound as harmless and open as possible by laying it all out for him, in the hopes he'd relax and just tell me what I wanted to know. "He told me that the rumor used to be that Mallory Evans was not just buried there, but killed there. That she went up to the overlook with somebody. And yesterday, especially after finding those bones in just about the same spot that Mallory was buried, I was thinking that person must've been him. That's why I thought the body was Sarah. That he had killed both women."

"It's not Sarah."

"I know that. How'd they make the ID so fast? *Tentative* ID," I said, so that we didn't get into a semantic debate.

He leaned back in his chair and sighed, resting a hand over his midsection like something hurt. My act seemed to be working, because eventually he started talking instead of telling me again to get out of his town. "Yesterday at the scene, one of my guys noticed that it—she—the body—there were pins in the ankle joint. Screws. Surgical screws. Right ankle. He recalled an old missing-persons report he took, young lady, a runaway. She also had screws in her right ankle from a bad fracture. The medical examiner gave some rough guesses as to how long the body had been buried there as well as the victim's height, both of which were consistent with Col—with the young woman my guy recalled. The word got out after that."

"What was her name?" I said. But his slip already confirmed what Danielle had told me.

He shook his head.

"Sir, if there's a missing-persons report, you know I can find it."

He started shaking his head again, but this time it was a sad, existential commentary rather than a refusal. "Colleen Grantham," he said. "The report's from eight years ago, filed by her mother. But by her own admission she had no reason to believe her daughter had not left willingly. Troubled kid, history of drug use. But eighteen years old, you're allowed to leave home."

"Everyone thought Mallory Evans left willingly too," I said.

"Yes."

"But she didn't. And she was buried in the same woods."

"Yes."

"You can see the connection."

"Possibly. But what does this have to do with Brad Stockton?" He blinked at me, giving away nothing. I found it hard to believe he still didn't see the connection, but he seemed like the type to be unhelpful on principle.

"Mallory, Sarah, and now Colleen," I said. "Three young ladies from Belmont, all missing or dead."

He took a few beats before answering. "Stockton belongs in prison, don't get me wrong. But as much as he disgusts me, he clearly had nothing to do with Colleen Grantham. He'd been locked up for at least seven years by that point."

I was pretty sure he was willfully misunderstanding me now. "Right," I said. "But given the obvious connection between the three cases, what if someone else committed all three crimes? What if Brad Stockton is innocent?"

"He's not."

"You're so sure?"

"Yesterday *you* were sure that you found Sarah Cook's body, so I don't know who you think you are, to be perfectly honest," Lassiter said.

That was a valid criticism. I ran a hand through my hair. "Are you trying to tell me you don't see the connection, though?"

"I can see how Mallory Evans and Colleen Grantham could be connected, yes," he said. "But I don't see what that has to do with Stockton at all. Garrett and Elaine weren't buried in those woods. Sarah wasn't buried in those woods."

"That you know of."

He scowled deeply at me. "The area is private property. You are not to trespass there again, understood? And you're not to bother the Grantham family, either."

The phone on his desk buzzed, and a disembodied voice crackled through the speaker. "Sir, don't forget you've got the mayor coming in a few minutes."

"Ah, dammit," Lassiter said, looking at his watch with dismay. He stabbed a button on the phone. "Thanks, Dee."

Then he stood up again and calmly walked to the office door and opened it. "Okay, then," he said to me, "this conversation is over."

I didn't care for the abrupt end to it, but I didn't have a choice. He pointed out into the hallway like he was ordering a dog out of the dining room.

"Thanks for your time," I said, as insincerely as I could manage.

He practically slammed the door behind me. It echoed through the short hallway, which was empty except for a middle-aged couple sitting on a bench a few feet away. The woman jumped at the sound.

"I'm sorry," I told her as I turned to walk back to the photo gallery in the lobby.

"Wait," she said. "Excuse me."

I paused and looked over my shoulder at her.

"Are you Roxane Weary?" she said.

I turned to face her. She was a small woman with short silvery hair and she gave off the overall impression of grey: her skin, her sweater, her eyes. The man next to her was looking at me sort of sideways, like he was peering from behind himself.

"Yes," I said, curious.

The woman stood up. "My name is Erin Grantham," she said. "This is my husband, Curtis. Russ Meeks told me about you. That you were—that you were there."

I went over to them and offered a hand. I didn't offer my condolences though, unsure what was appropriate. Were they already in mourning, were they relieved, or were they still hoping against hope? My own hope was that she wasn't going to ask me to describe what I saw.

"Do you think—" Erin started. "When you found her—" She stopped, her face twisted in pain.

I quickly glanced over my shoulder to make sure Lassiter's door was still closed. I figured it didn't count against his warning about not bothering the Grantham family if she initiated the conversation.

"Is there somewhere we can talk?" I said. "Do you live nearby?"

"She never smiled in pictures," Erin Grantham was telling me thirty minutes later in the living room of her house. "Even when she was just a little thing. My sister-in-law used to tell me Colleen could model, you know, like for one of those kids' clothing stores. She was so pretty. But Colleen just would not smile. She was happy enough for the most part, don't get me wrong. But she wouldn't smile."

Colleen's parents still lived in the same house they had when their daughter went missing, a small Cape Cod just on the west side of Belmont. We sat in the living room, Erin and Curtis on opposite ends of a reddish floral-print sofa and me in an armchair. Erin handed me what looked like a senior picture—Colleen in a blue hoodie, her blond hair cut into long layers and bangs, barely smiling on a park bench. She was gorgeous, and she clearly knew it but didn't care, not even a little bit. She might have even resented it. Judging from her expression, she didn't want anyone to look at her at all.

Erin had only wanted to ask me about what I had seen in the woods and what had led me there, and I had given her a G-rated version of it. Now I was hoping I could get another lead out of her. "For the most part?" I said.

"She got in with the wrong crowd, when she started high school," Erin said. "We used to know all her friends, and all her friends' families. But then all at once we didn't anymore, and she was getting into trouble, shoplifting, cutting class."

"It seemed like kid stuff," Curtis added, speaking for the first time since we sat down. He looked like he very much needed to believe that kid stuff was an okay explanation for what had happened to his daughter. "I mean, we were upset with her, of course."

"Disappointed, more like," Erin said. "But you don't automatically assume skipping class a few times means someone is going to turn into a drug addict."

The Granthams looked at each other, Erin's mouth pressed into a thin line.

"Was Colleen a drug addict?" I said next.

"No," Curtis said.

"Yes," Erin said at the same time.

"I think I'm going to get a drink of water," Curtis said, and got up without another word.

"It's still hard to talk about," Erin continued when he was gone. "You'd think it would have gotten easier. And it did, up to a point. Then it just didn't anymore. But yes, Colleen had a drug problem. Have you heard of DXM?"

"Dextromethorphan?" I said. "The cough medicine?"

She nodded. "That was the first thing. She was about fourteen. This was before there were the buying restrictions on cold medicine, you know, you have to show your ID now. But then, kids could buy it just like candy. I went into her room to look for something, and I found a dozen empty bottles of Vicks 44." She paused and shook her head, smiling like something was almost funny but not quite. "God, I'll never forget that. It was just this horrible realization. She'd been getting moodier for months, sleeping fourteen and fifteen hours at a stretch. But, like my husband said, we thought it was just a sullen teenager phase."

"What did you do?"

"We confronted her right away, full throttle—that was probably the first mistake. We got her seeing a therapist, grounded her. But the whole idea of grounding a kid, it just doesn't make sense. She was still going to school, still seeing those same friends. So it didn't make a difference. When she was sixteen, she broke her ankle—jumping off the bleachers at the stadium, she'd been drinking. She needed surgery and they had to put pins in it, it was all very serious. And she was prescribed some narcotic painkillers, and that's when we really started to get it, that she had a problem, a real problem. But you always think you have more time to make it right."

I shifted in my chair, uncomfortable. "I know," I said. She didn't ask me how I knew, but she nodded before speaking again.

"We did what we could. We sent her to one of those scared-straight-type boot-camp programs the city puts on. We got her into a residential treatment facility that our insurance covered, but she got kicked out. For, well," Erin said, lowering her voice a little, "having sex with other patients. She was a girl out of control. After she came home from that, she was barely speaking to us. Do you have kids?"

I shook my head.

"People would say to me, *How can you let this go on? If Colleen was my daughter, I wouldn't let her out of my sight.* How can anyone say that?" she said. "Even after she left, people would still tell me that. Like it made them feel better about themselves somehow."

"You know what," I said, "fuck those people."

"I mean, seriously. What were we supposed to do? Physically chain her up in the bedroom?" She picked up the photo from the table and stared at it like she didn't recognize the girl at all. Maybe she didn't. "When she turned eighteen, she stopped going to school. She came and went as she pleased. Curtis tried to set some rules, like, if she wasn't going to school, she needed to get a job, start paying rent. He never understood what we were dealing with where she was concerned, he really didn't. Colleen said fine, she'd get out of our hair."

It was clear that Erin needed to talk about her daughter with someone. "Just like that," I said.

Erin nodded. "Just like that. A few weeks after her birthday, that's when she left."

"You weren't surprised?"

"I don't know how many times I told her I loved her, and she just looked at me," Erin said. "It was like she didn't want to be loved. I made sure she knew that she always had a place in our home. But it wasn't enough. And no, I wasn't surprised. It still hurt. It hurt in ways I can't even describe, that she would just walk out."

I hoped I never had to find out just how much something like that would hurt. "How did it happen?"

"It was a Sunday morning. Curtis and our other girls, we went to church. When we got back, Colleen wasn't home. Her purse was gone. There was nothing unusual about that. It seemed like she just went out for the day. But then she never came home."

I thought it over, not sure what I'd do in a situation like that. How were you supposed to know this time was different from every other time? "How long until you started worrying?"

"I was worried right away," Erin said, "because I could never stop worrying about her. But it wasn't until the next day that we started to feel like something was going on. She always came back in the early morning, four, five o'clock. But she didn't. We filed a police report, but she was eighteen and they said she could come and go as she wanted. And given the history we'd had with her, it wasn't exactly a secret she wasn't happy at home."

That sounded an awful lot like Mallory Evans's story, with the police not caring enough to allow for the possibility that something was actually wrong here, to take some action. "What else did you do, besides filing the police report?" I said.

"We made signs. We posted online. We tried asking her friends, or all the friends we knew she had. Curtis went through the phone bill and we called every single number to ask if anyone had seen her or heard from her or knew about her plans," Erin said. "But no one did. There was all this uncertainty, the kind that feels like it's about to end, but it didn't—and this is going to sound awful, but I have two other children, younger, and I have to be a mother to them too. I couldn't fall apart. It wasn't an option. I had to believe that she didn't want me to find her."

I wondered what my own parents would have done if I had disappeared like that at age eighteen. Even though my father was a cop, I suspected he would've been more angry than concerned, at least at first. "Where did you think she went?"

"She always talked about going out west," Erin said. Then she looked at me. Her eyes were wide and bright with tears. "I'm sure it sounds like I didn't even care, like we didn't even look. But, of course, we looked. We did everything we could think of."

I knew she cared. If she didn't, she wouldn't be talking to me now. "I understand."

"So now, thinking that maybe she didn't just walk away—it's—I don't want it to be her. But at the same time it would be such a relief, to know after so long. And I know, regardless, that the—whoever it is, if it isn't Colleen, she was still someone to another family. So there is no happy ending here."

Curtis came back into the room and just stood there without saying anything. His eyes were red.

"I think it might be best if you left now," Erin said, her voice breaking. "Let me write down our number." She patted at the surface of the end table, looking for a pen but not finding one. "Curt, hon, can you just give Roxane one of your cards?"

We both fumbled through our pockets for our respective business cards.

"Take care," Erin said. "And good luck."

Outside I sat in the car for a few minutes, not sure what to think. I pitied Erin Grantham for the impossible position she was in. She was right—there would be no happy endings, at least not for her. Either her daughter had been murdered and buried in the woods, or her daughter was still missing. Her husband didn't appear to be of much help, though in my experience, no one was, not when it mattered. I wanted to be of help but I didn't know how. Mallory and Colleen—if it was Colleen—were connected by where their bodies had been found. And Mallory and Sarah were connected, loosely, through Brad. But I couldn't connect Sarah or Brad to Colleen, and I still had no idea how Sarah's parents factored into all of it. It wasn't even a theory at this point, and barely even a story. I needed lunch, caffeine, and a stroke of divine inspiration, and not necessarily in that order. I reached into my pocket for my phone and pulled out Curtis Grantham's business card along with it, and that was when I noticed:

He worked for Next Level Promotions.

NINETEEN

I went back to the Greek restaurant—their melitzanosalata really was quite good—and sat in a booth with my laptop, pulling some background info on Kenny Brayfield. It was hard to imagine the velour-sweatpanted peddler of gold-flake vodka and ginkgo smoothies as a serial killer, but I couldn't exactly ignore it: he could be linked in some way to all three women. He'd gotten shifty-eyed when I asked him about Mallory Evans. At the time I thought he was hedging about Mallory and *Brad*, not himself. I sat with that idea for a minute, trying to decide if it worked. The knife in Brad's car, though. Why would Kenny frame his friend for the murders? Maybe it wasn't a frame, but an oversight: maybe Brad was protecting Kenny all this time. Maybe he knew. And maybe that was why he told me about Clover Point. I'd thought he brought up the overlook because he was tired of lying after all this time, and maybe that was still true—he was tired of lying about Kenny. Lying for a friend was one thing, but being willing to die for him? Brad definitely gave me ride-or-die vibes where it came to Sarah, but I didn't get the same feeling about Kenny.

I ordered pistachio baklava for dessert and looked over what I had found out about Kenny Brayfield so far. A woefully immature thirty-four, lifelong Belmont resident, two possession busts from when he was eighteen and nineteen, for both of which he received suspended sentences. No trouble in the decade-plus since.

The Brayfield family money was several generations old and seemed to come from a regional department store they founded, which Kenny's grandfather sold to Macy's in the late seventies. Kenny's father was a venture capitalist and sat on the board of two local charities. Kenny, I imagined, with his Chuck Taylors and absurd business strategies, had to be a bit of a disappointment. Up until an hour ago, he struck me as a spoiled brat but generally well-intentioned. But that didn't mean much. Anybody could seem like anything if they tried, at least for a while, and there were too many coincidences lining up to connect Kenny to the three—blond—women.

There was really only one question at the heart of every case: How can I prove it? This was going to be no different.

When I had talked to Joshua Evans the other day, I had specifically asked him if his young wife knew Brad. I hadn't asked about Kenny. At the time, I had no reason to. But that seemed like a good next move to me.

Joshua Evans was happier to see me than Lassiter had been. "God, this news," he said, ushering me inside his small house. "It's really throwing me."

"Surreal, I bet," I said. I followed him into the kitchen, where I took him up on the offer of a beer. I could hear loud, pop-punk music blaring from elsewhere in the house. "Are you doing okay?"

"Yeah, yeah. It's just crazy. I mean, first you were here asking questions about Mal after all this time. And then they find someone else in those woods. Hard to pretend they're not connected," Joshua said. He sat down across from me at the kitchen table, opening a beer that I didn't think was the first of the day.

I didn't want to get his hopes up, and I also didn't want to speak out of turn. But I figured my presence was something of a giveaway anyhow. "I think they are," I said. "I think the same person who killed your wife has killed other women, and I am going to figure out who it was."

He nodded, his nostrils flaring slightly. "Like a serial killer."

"I don't know. Something," I said. "Have the police been by to talk to you?"

"Nope." He took a long swallow of beer. "And unfortunately, I don't know what I could even add at this point. I told your dad everything I knew sixteen years ago and it wasn't much."

"I know, Joshua." Thinking of what Erin Grantham had said, I added, "And I know you have to compartmentalize a little bit in order to move past something like this, just so you can function. But anything at all you can share might help. Even if you think it won't."

He nodded again.

"The other day you told me when Mallory didn't come home, you contacted some of her friends," I said, thinking maybe Kenny was among them. "Can you remember who you called?"

He looked up at the ceiling for a minute. I followed his gaze and took in a spiderweb of plaster cracked with age. Then I looked back down. Finally he said, "Carrie. I called her, I'd say she was Mallory's best friend. She lived down the street back then, but the family moved away."

"Carrie what?"

Joshua shook his head. "Sorry."

"Okay, who were some of her other friends?"

He played with the tab on his beer can. "Marisa something," he said. "I don't know her last name either but I see her sometimes, around town. I don't know how close they were, but she called here a lot. Those two are who I reached out to. But they hadn't seen her. And you have to remember, I thought she was pissed at me. So I left it at that."

"Do you remember any of her other friends? Ex-boyfriends? The other day you mentioned you thought she was seeing someone at the end."

"Yeah. But I didn't know who. I'd just hear her on the phone sometimes, and it didn't sound like she was talking to one of her girl-friends. And she'd go out at night, all dressed up, and Marisa or Carrie might call when she was out, so she wasn't with them." Joshua shrugged. "I confronted her about it a few times, and it never went well. I didn't know how to talk to her. But I knew there was someone."

The sound of the loud music from down the hall stopped and a door opened. "Dad," Shelby called, "we're going to Target, is that okay?"

"I promise we'll be back before dinner, for completely selfish reasons," her friend Veronica added, "because I want to eat here again."

They both looked into the kitchen through the pass-through. "Oh hey, it's Roxane-with-one-'n,'" Veronica said. "So what do you think, Mr. E.?"

"Sure, go ahead," Joshua said. "LOL."

Veronica cracked up. Shelby rolled her eyes. "You're so embarrassing," she said. She looked at me. "He used to text LOL to me all the time and it, like, didn't even make sense, a text that just says LOL in response to nothing. So I asked him what he thought it was supposed to mean."

"Lots of love!" Joshua said. "I think my way is so much better."

"Now he just says it on purpose to annoy me," Shelby finished.

"It's so easy, how can I resist?"

She laughed. "Okay, we'll be back in a while." She grabbed a set of keys off the counter and then walked away.

Joshua waited until the door opened before he called out, "LOL."

His daughter groaned as she pulled the door closed behind her.

Chuckling to himself, Joshua got up and went to the fridge. "Veronica lives next door but we always joke she should get her mail forwarded, she's over here so much. She doesn't get along with her stepdad—I don't blame her for that, really. One time he asked me to cut my grass more often because he didn't like looking at my yard from his deck."

"Some people," I said.

"Yeah."

"Another beer?" he said.

"Sure."

He handed me the beer. "Cheers," I said.

"To what," he said.

"To being bigger-hearted than your neighbor."

Joshua liked the sound of that. He tapped his can against mine and we drank. "Now, where were we?"

It didn't seem like Joshua was going to mention Kenny's name spontaneously, so I decided to dig in. "Did Mallory ever hang around with this kid, Kenny Brayfield?"

His eyebrows went up. "Brayfield? Like the family that built the park?"

"What park?"

"Brayfield Park," Joshua said. "It's over by the high school."

"I don't know anything about a park," I said. "But yes, them. Kenny was a classmate of Mallory's."

He looked doubtful. "East side and west side don't really mix in Belmont," he said. But then something rippled through his eyes. "But there was this one time. I found a ring on the bathroom sink, like a diamond ring, pretty nice. It wasn't something I got her. We didn't even have wedding bands. But this ring, it looked expensive. And I asked her about it, like who's dropping money like this on you, and she got kind of weird."

"Weird how?"

"Weird like she didn't want to talk about it. But honestly, that's how all our conversations went. I could ask her what she wanted on her half of the pizza and she'd act like I was smothering her."

"You still have the ring?" I said. Half thinking maybe there was an engraved inscription; stranger things had happened.

But Joshua shook his head. "I don't know what happened to it. I only saw it that one time. This Brayfield guy, you don't think he's involved, do you? That would be a hell of a thing."

"Just following up on some ideas," I said. "I don't know yet." This bit about the ring was obviously inconclusive, but I tended to disagree with what Joshua said about east side versus west side: Kenny had been *tight* with Brad, who had described the former as a wannabe gangster, not a country club kid like he was probably supposed to be.

"I wish I could help you more."

"You're helping a lot," I told him.

He shook his head, his eyes filling up. "I still can't believe it, when I think about it. That for seven months I was thinking she was a selfish bitch, when actually she was dead. It just makes me sick now, to think that there was more than one victim."

I touched his shoulder. "I know people have told you not to blame yourself," I said, "and I know that's easier said than done. But Joshua. Do not blame yourself. You need to be strong for Shelby."

He grabbed my hand. "I know," he said thickly.

After I finished my beer, I went out to the car and sat there for a moment, thinking. I was doing that a lot lately. I could still smell Catherine's perfume on the upholstery from the other night, though that mattered less to me now than it might have otherwise. I didn't have a lot to go on: a pricey ring that may have come from Kenny or may have come from literally anyone else in the world, and the first names of two of Mallory's friends. I imagined myself trying to find a Belmont High yearbook and paging through the black-and-white pictures until I saw the name Marisa next to one of them. I wrote it down in my notebook with a question mark beside it. Then I remembered what Kenny had told me about his *Monday Night Football* party in his parents' absence today. *Just some old friends,* he said. I wondered if high school friends counted among the attendees, and if I was still invited. I put the car in gear and pulled out just as a Belmont cruiser turned down the street, slowing to a stop right beside me. I sighed. This was past the point of absurdity.

Sergeant Derrow rolled down his window and I did the same. "Everything okay here?"

"Yep," I said.

He rested his hand on the doorframe, tapping lightly. "All right, I can see you're leaving. So carry on."

I nodded, glad he wasn't going to make a thing of it. "Tell Lassiter I said hi," I said.

TWENTY

The gate at the driveway of the Brayfield house was open, so I drove in without having to announce myself. There were a dozen or so cars parked on both sides of the curve. Since I might want to make a quick getaway, I made a three-point turn and wedged my car as close to the exit as possible. Then I went into the house, the door to which was unlocked too.

Kenny was apparently unfazed by the recent crime development in Belmont. Maybe because he knew too much about it.

I stood awkwardly in the two-story entryway and looked for signs of life—from the back of the property, I heard the muffled strains of a television and, elsewhere, someone tearing through an Everclear song on an out-of-tune acoustic guitar. I unzipped my coat and headed for the kitchen, the only room I could confidently locate in the massive house.

Once again conspicuously clean, the kitchen offered a giant bowl of cheese curls and a tray of veggies. I helped myself to a red pepper slice and kept walking through a dining room with a long, polished table that could seat at least twelve people, and finally I found the den, which offered a leather sectional sofa with several good-looking women lounging on it. They were laughing about the misfortune of someone named Bridget. I'd been half expecting to see Danielle here, but I didn't. Though it was just after seven, the coffee table was covered with beer bottles and cups of gold-flake vodka. No one looked up at me.

"Hi," I said finally.

Six highly styled heads turned my way. I tried to decide if any of them looked like a Carrie or a Marisa. When I determined that I couldn't, I finally said, "Is Kenny here?"

"He stepped out for a few minutes," one of the women said. She had reddish-brown hair in a long ponytail, light green eyes.

The football game hadn't even started yet, which made it seem a little weird that Kenny was stepping out already. But I thought there was a possibility that he was a murderer. That meant everything about him was a little weird.

"I'm Roxane," I said, but no one seemed particularly interested in me. I took a seat in an armchair in the corner and they resumed their conversation about Bridget, but I noticed that the green-eyed woman was still looking at me.

"You don't have a drink yet," she said. "Let's do something about that."

That sounded good to me. She got up and stepped over someone sprawled on the carpet, a guy ignoring the group in favor of his phone, where he was furiously swiping right on Tinder.

"I'm Marisa," the woman said, leading me into the kitchen.

That sounded even better. I tried to play it cool. "Hey," I said.

"What are you drinking?" Marisa said as we stood in front of a liquor cabinet that put my father's to shame. Then she looked a little embarrassed. "I've been bartending at Kenny's launch parties for a few months, since I got laid off from my actual job. I apparently can't stop getting people drinks."

"Crown Royal, if it's not too low-class for this joint," I said.

She grinned at me. "I got this," she said. She nosed around the bottles until she found my whiskey. She was wearing jeans and a black sweatshirt with a lace panel in the back that showed off her shoulder blades, as well as the fact that she wasn't wearing a bra. She handed me a glass and poured herself some of the gold-flake vodka.

"Thanks," I said. I knew I needed to ease into the topic of her friend—and her boss—being a killer, so I started out friendly. "So what's it like, working for Kenny?"

Marisa shrugged. "Kenny's, well, he's just Kenny. I'm a travel agent, or was. But I needed a job, I have two kids. So he's doing me a favor. I don't know shit about bartending."

"You could have fooled me," I said, and she smiled. "A job's a big favor, you know him for a long time?"

"God, since kindergarten, I guess. He's a sweetheart, underneath the big pimpin' routine." She sipped at her drink. "Have you tried this stuff?"

"What is it?" I said. "I mean, what does it taste like?"

"Cinnamon," she said. "It's good. Here, try it."

"Did I stumble into some kind of multilevel marketing sales party?" I said as she splashed some into a cup for me.

She laughed. She had a good laugh. "Not that I know of," she said, "but the manufacturer is basically supporting Kenny's entire business and, thusly, me, so I hope you're willing to pay up if it comes to that."

I drank the vodka. It tasted like a cinnamon lip gloss I had in middle school, sticky and faintly caustic under the atomic sweetness. But it went down very, very smooth. "Uh-oh," I said.

"At the office, they apparently drink this all day," Marisa said. "I'm not sure how anything gets done."

"I think I know someone else who works with Kenny," I said by way of actual openers. "Curtis Grantham?"

Her eyes narrowed for a second, like she'd had a flash of something ugly. "Yeah, Curt. Finance guy."

"Did you hear about his daughter?"

"Yes, dear God," she said. "It's awful. It's absolutely awful. I didn't even know he *had* a missing daughter, but then to hear how they found her." She shuddered and looked over my shoulder at something.

"What?" I said.

"Nothing. It's not polite party conversation."

"Sorry, I didn't mean to be a downer," I said, although I did.

"No, it's not you. It's just crazy, because years ago someone I knew was found in that same part of town, the woods over there."

"Really."

"Really," she said.

"A friend of yours?"

She held up a hand and tilted it back and forth: *So-so.* "Growing up, yeah," she said. "Then in high school, she dropped out and things got weird." She tilted her head to one side. "What are you really doing here, though?" she said. "I can tell you didn't come for the vodka, or the game."

I liked her and I didn't want to keep lying to her. Or at least not entirely. "Busted," I said. "Listen. I wasn't entirely honest a minute ago. I'm trying to get some information about Mallory Evans. I'm a private investigator and I'm looking into what's been going on in Belmont. That's why I'm here."

Marisa raised her eyebrows. "Why didn't you open with that? I would have just told you."

"Sorry," I said. "Force of habit. In my line of work, people rarely want to talk to me."

"I don't know about that," she said, in a way that made it sound like she wouldn't mind if we stood here talking for a while longer, even if I was a dishonest downer. "So what do you want to know about Mallory?"

I threw out an easy question first. "How come you stopped being close?"

"Oh, it was a lot of things," she said. "When she got pregnant, she quit school and got married. The guy, her husband, he was just this big dumb loser—God, that sounds bitchy. He was a pretty nice guy, the few times I met him, but just not the kind of person you want to tie yourself to when you're seventeen. She was *miserable,* and she got kind of hard to be around."

"Do you know if she was seeing anyone? Other than her husband."

Now Marisa's mouth twisted at the corner. "Well, yeah," she said. I waited.

"Oh," she said. "He didn't tell you."

"Kenny and Mallory," I said. I had been starting to suspect as much, but the confirmation gave me a slight head rush. My cup was empty, but I was feeling warm and loose and the conversation was getting interesting. I was distinctly glad I had come here.

"Yeah." A faint blush spread across her cheeks. "Well, whatever, it's not like it matters anymore. But yeah, Kenny and Mallory were together. He used to be the guy you call if you wanted, you know, to buy weed or pills or whatever. He always knew a guy who knew a guy. Mal was way into that, so they were always kind of on the same page."

"Even after she got married?"

Marisa nodded. "That didn't really faze her much."

"Do you remember what happened when she went missing?"

"Well, I hadn't heard from her in a couple weeks," she said. "But I don't even think I realized I hadn't heard from her. But then Joshua—that's the guy, her husband—called me asking if I'd seen her and I was like, No, sorry. I thought it was him being overbearing, Mallory always acted like that's how he was. Then I didn't think much of it, till Kenny told me he hadn't seen her either."

"Was he worried?"

"I guess so. But it was like, they were seeing each other in secret, so he kind of had to respect it if she wanted to lay low. It's not like it was the love story of the century, they just got fucked up together."

I thought it was an interesting way to put it, that Kenny had to re-spect Mallory's wish to *lay low*. That made me think that no, he hadn't appeared all that worried. Because he knew Mallory was beyond being worried about? I let Marisa pour more of the vodka into my cup. "Did you ever hear any rumors?" I said. "About what might have happened?"

"I was away at school, at Kent State, when they found her. So I didn't get any general gossip from the town, but Kenny and I talked about it sometimes. He was *so* upset. He thought she went up to Clover Point with the wrong person. It made him crazy."

"He tell the police about that theory?"

"I'm sure," Marisa said, although I had my doubts about that. "You should really ask him about Mallory, though, he'll be able to tell you so much more than I can. He always does this, invites people over and then disappears."

"Oh, I'll ask him," I said. "Anyone else here who knew her? Carrie, maybe?"

"Carrie," Marisa said slowly. "She hasn't been back in a long time. And no, I'm Kenny's only friend left from the bad old days. Why," she added, narrowing her eyes at me playfully. "Tired of talking to me already?"

"Hardly," I said. I sipped the gold-flake vodka. It no longer tasted like liquor or cinnamon, just pure liquid warmth. I promised myself I was going to slow down. The fact that Kenny had been involved with Mallory Evans but claimed only to know her *from around* seemed pretty fucking incriminating to me.

I needed to talk to him and I needed to remember it.

When Kenny finally returned, Marisa and I were sitting close together on the leather sofa with the Tinder guy—Todd—and the high-heeled snob from the Next Level office, Beckett. "Aw, you guys look like the best friends ever," Kenny said.

We were not the best of friends, but we were deep into a new bottle of the gold-flake vodka, so that didn't matter much. It was somewhere after ten. Kenny had taken his time in getting back to the house.

"Does anyone want to go down to the pool?" he said.

"Oh my God *yes*," Beckett shrieked. "I have been so bored waiting to go to the pool." She stood up and took off her jeans, revealing a string bikini underneath. She was as unbearable as I would have guessed the other day, though she certainly did come prepared.

"I gotta go home, man," Todd said. He appeared on the verge of falling asleep or passing out.

I looked at Marisa, who shrugged and said, "I have my swimsuit in my bag."

"Am I the only one who's going to miss out?" I said.

"Trust me," Kenny said, "it is not a problem if you want to swim anyway."

The pool overlooked a dense, dark thicket of woods in the back of the house. One wall was a glass garage-style door that opened onto a wooden two-story deck, great for entertaining during the summer months, Kenny told me. In the November darkness, the room was illuminated only by the ashy glow of a skylight, pale and grey.

Beckett and Marisa jumped in the water right away while Kenny gave me a tour-guide spiel. "It's heated to eighty-five degrees. The floor is made from genuine Italian marble tiles."

I wished that he had returned two or three drinks ago, because now I felt like the evening was getting away from me. I eyed the vodka bottle he was drinking from, wondering how long it would take for him to get drunk enough to tell me everything. "You should have been a real-estate agent," I said mildly.

"That would be sick," he said. "But, you know, event promotion is a good living, it really is."

I pressed my palms against the fogged-up window. It was cold and wet. Then I peered through the swatch of clean glass my hand had made. "What's that little hut thing on the deck?"

"Sauna."

I laughed. "Seriously, your house has a sauna?"

"Whatever, it's the fucking bomb. I'd show you, but we can't use it in the winter."

"Some host."

"Sorry."

"I can't see anything past the deck," I said. "This is like the end of the earth."

"Basically. Just trees," Kenny said. "Deer. They're going to put apartments back there though."

I straightened up. With the subdivisions and their big, empty yards, I hadn't realized the Brayfield property backed up to Clover Point. "Isn't that where they found the body yesterday?"

"Yeah. Kinda fucked up."

He gave no indication that he knew any more about that, including the identity of the victim. That seemed to be common knowledge at this point, though, since even Marisa knew. I watched him. His eyes, grey and shallow, were like the rocks I'd moved away from the grave yesterday afternoon. He was curiously still, one of those people who didn't twitch or fidget.

Two bodies, basically in Kenny's backyard. Now this really felt like something. I said, "They found your old girlfriend back there too, didn't they?"

Kenny said nothing for a few seconds. But the alcohol had loosened him up too much for him to remember he was trying to keep secrets from me. "Like a million years ago."

"Dude, right behind your house. *That's* kinda fucked up."

Kenny shook his head so slowly he may not have realized he was doing it. "It's like she was mocking me," he slurred.

The problem was, the alcohol had also loosened me up too much as well. I wasn't used to drinking flavored vodka and it had snuck up on me. "What do you know?" I said clumsily.

He stood up. "So what do you say, want to swim?"

"What do you know?"

"I know I'm going to start wondering why you came if you don't get in the pool."

That seemed like an unreliable test of motivation. "I told you, I don't have a swimsuit."

"And I told you, it doesn't matter." He pulled off his hoodie and dropped it onto the tiles, one cuff trailing into the water. He was on the skinny side but still well built. He dropped his pants next and stood there in boxer briefs, leveling a gaze at me that felt like a challenge. It hung in the air between us, an unresolved chord.

I shook my head. I was working, I had to remind myself, and things had gotten out of hand enough already. "I'm going to take off," I said. I needed a cup of tea and a minute to think about my next move. I steadied myself against the window. I needed a minute, period. Out of the corner of my eye, I saw Marisa getting out of the pool.

Then suddenly she was beside me, dressed again and holding on to my arm, her long hair dripping on my jacket. Time had gotten slippery.

Kenny took a long swallow from the bottle, his eyes cold on me. "You don't know what you're missing," he said.

"Oh, I do," I said, or thought I said. Or thought I knew.

TWENTY-ONE

I woke up hard, like a fall from a significant height had jolted me into alertness. The room was small and bright and unfamiliar and my skull had been replaced with razor blades in an experimental test procedure I didn't remember signing up for. I sat up on one elbow and swallowed, waiting for my vision to level out.

I was in a living room, I saw now, on a futon with a grey microsuede mattress. Still clothed. My leather jacket dangled from one arm, twisted beneath my torso. Outside, it was raining. I cleared my throat. Then I heard a door opening down the hall, followed by quiet footsteps.

"Hi," Marisa said. She was wearing a Next Level Promotions T-shirt and plaid flannel pants.

"Um," I said. I rolled onto my back and covered my eyes with my hand. "What time is it?" I said, hoarse.

"Seven. Do you want some coffee?"

The thought of coffee made my stomach hurt. "Could I have a glass of water?"

"Sure, yeah," Marisa said. She got up and went to the sink. A few seconds later, she handed me a glass of water and sat down on the edge of the futon next to me.

I drank some of the water and set the glass on the floor. What, exactly, had happened last night? There was a gaping black void in my memory of the evening. I remembered deciding I wasn't going to drink too much since I was working, but that hadn't exactly worked out. I remembered the vodka, the pool. Then, nothing. I felt like an idiot.

"This is the world's most uncomfortable futon," she said. "I should know—I normally sleep on it every night. My kids have the bedroom."

"Your kids," I said, lowering my voice. "Shit, sorry, I can get out of here—"

"No, it's okay, they're with their father this week, I told you all of this last night."

I looked at her.

Embarrassment flickered through her face. "*But* you don't remember any of it." She gave a halfhearted laugh. "You're probably like, What the hell am I even doing here."

"No, no," I said quickly. I set my hand on her arm. But then I didn't know what else to say.

After a minute, she took pity on me. "I asked you for a ride home," she said, "since I don't have a car right now. But then when I wanted to leave it was pretty clear that you couldn't, you know, there was no way you could drive anywhere. So I drove us. And I let you crash here. On the futon, alone."

I drank the rest of the water. "I'm sorry," I said. "I'm really sorry."

She shrugged. "I'm kind of the worst at this though. Picking up on the signals. It's still new to me, in practice. With guys it's just so obvious where you stand."

I looked over at her. "You got the signals right," I said. "Maybe we can try again sometime."

She watched me for a second, then pulled her knees to her chest. "You're leaving?"

"I have some things to take care of," I said. I sat up too and took a deep breath. Everything hurt. But I'd already wasted more time than I cared to think about. I untangled my jacket from around myself and slipped the loose sleeve on and left her a card with my number.

Outside, the heavy grey clouds were throbbing like an open wound. I dropped into my car and shoved a pair of sunglasses onto my face. "Jesus Christ," I said to no one. I thought again of my father: Did he ever accidentally drink too much cinnamon-flavored vodka while at a serial killer's pool party? Although he certainly had his flaws, I doubted that was among them. I noticed that the whiskey bottle I bought at the liquor store last week was still wedged between the passenger seat and the gear shift. I slapped it to the floor. I never wanted to think about liquor again. Then I sat there with my hands over my eyes for a while, unable to do anything else.

I decided to go home and recover for a minute, hoping my head would eventually clear to reveal a solid next move. I drove out of Marisa's apartment complex and onto Clover Road, where I went through a drive-through for a greasy sandwich and a cup of tea, neither of which sounded good but hopefully both of which would help. I was about to join the regular people of the city on the rush-hour-dense freeway toward downtown when my phone rang. I almost didn't take it out of my pocket. The unknown number had made me distrustful of my own phone. But I got stuck at a red light and curiosity got the better of me. I checked the screen, saw that it was a known number, just one I didn't recognize.

"This is Roxane," I said, clearing my throat.

A beat of silence, and then a small, worried voice. "Hi, um. This is Shelby. Evans."

What the hell?

Something about her tone stabbed straight through the fog in my head. I put my tea in the cup holder and tried to sound normal. "Shelby, hey. What's up?"

"It's Veronica," she said, and then she began to cry. "I don't know where she is and I don't know what to do."

"She always answers her phone when I call," Shelby was saying. "Always. We have a pact. She would never not answer. Something's wrong." She was pacing back and forth in the small living room of her house, still wearing her green army coat and a heavy-looking messenger bag slung across her back. "Something's wrong."

"Okay. Shelby. Shelby? Is your dad here?" I said.

She shook her head. "He's at work and he isn't allowed to have his phone on so I called there, at the desk, and they haven't turned off the overnight greeting yet and then I saw your business card on the fridge and I, I don't know, I'm sorry if it seems like I'm being stupid but something is really, really wrong—"

"Shelby."

She stopped pacing and looked at me, her youthful features quivering.

"You're not being stupid, I don't think that at all," I said. I was trying to be calm and adultlike. But I felt sick and it wasn't only because of how much vodka I'd consumed last night. Belmont didn't have a good track record of returning teenage girls that didn't come home. "But I need you to take a deep breath and tell me what happened, okay?"

Shelby nodded and sat down in the recliner where Joshua had sat the first night I came here. "She always rides with me to school," she said. "Usually she comes over when she's ready but sometimes she doesn't, like if she's running late, and then I go there. She lives right next door. And today she didn't come and when I went over there, her stepdad answered the door and when I asked if she was ready for school he got really weird, and he was like *I thought she was at your house.* But she wasn't. And then he told me I better go to school and he would deal with her."

"Was she supposed to be at your house?"

She shook her head.

"Why would she say that?"

"She probably went to Insomnia," Shelby said. I must have looked confused, because she added, "It's a coffee shop down the street. She was telling me yesterday that this guy Aaron, his band was playing there last night, she likes him. Her parents said she couldn't go." Her eyes were on the carpet between her Doc Martens. "The show was at ten and my curfew is ten thirty, so I couldn't go either. But they always let her come over here. "

"When did you talk to her last?" I said.

"When she left here. It was like seven thirty. And I was like, Tell Aaron hi for me, but it was a joke, because she couldn't go. I thought she was just going to go home." She jumped up and resumed pacing the floor.

I didn't like the sound of this. Not at all. I couldn't help but think that yesterday evening, Kenny Brayfield had missed most of his own party. "Okay. Shelby, is this like her? Lying to her parents?"

She wrestled the messenger bag off her shoulders and flung it on chair she'd been sitting in. "I don't know. No. Her mom is, like, kind of oblivious, she just wants to get her hair done and work out all the time. Her stepdad pretty much sucks, he acts like Vee is the world's worst kid just because she has to go to a therapist. I think she just really wanted to go see Aaron."

"Insomnia," I said. "It's walking distance?"

She nodded. "If you cut through the neighborhood it's like a ten-minute walk, you just go between the houses and then you're in this big parking lot for the Kroger. It's in the same plaza."

I rubbed my forehead. The headache hadn't gone anywhere yet, but it barely mattered now. "Let's go talk to her parents, okay?" I said.

Veronica's stepdad was a short guy in a dark blue suit and tie, a pair of frameless glasses perched halfway up his nose. He threw the door open like he couldn't wait to scream at somebody—probably Veronica—and then looked confused when he saw who it was. "Shelby," he said. "And . . . ?"

"This is Roxane," Shelby said, "she's a friend of my dad's and she's a private investigator—"

He laughed, but it seemed angry. "Let's not get ahead of ourselves," he said. "Veronica is not *missing*. We both know that she's just being inconsiderate. She doesn't think about how her actions affect other people. She's probably sitting in homeroom right now."

"No she's *not*," Shelby said, her voice thick with more tears.

I took a step forward, shielding her slightly with my arm. "Sir, is your wife at home?"

"She took a sleeping pill last night. I didn't wake her up yet," he said, cold. Then his tone went from chilly to condescending. "Shelby, does your father know you haven't gone to school?"

I could see why Shelby said he sucked and why Joshua had complained about him too. "Yes," I said quickly, although he didn't yet, "and right now, I think you should be more concerned with Veronica than with Shelby."

"Who are you again?" he snapped.

"Who is it?" a voice said behind him. Then Veronica's mother appeared over his shoulder. She was tall and a brittle kind of thin, her hair frosted blond and somehow styled already even though she was wearing a bathrobe. She took in Shelby and me, her expression going suspicious.

"Mrs. Wexford," Shelby said quickly, "we don't know where Veronica is."

The woman widened her eyes, then narrowed them at her husband. "What?" she said. "Joseph. Why didn't you wake me up?"

"I didn't want you to worry, you know how you get," Mr. Wexford said.

I wanted to punch him, but instead I thrust out my hand. "Ma'am," I said, "my name is Roxane Weary, I'm a friend of Joshua and Shelby and I'm also a private investigator and I think you might want to call the police—"

"Oh my *God*," Mrs. Wexford said.

"Now, just calm down—" her husband said.

I cut him off. "Look, I'm not trying to alarm you, but Shelby hasn't heard from your daughter for about twelve hours." Mrs. Wexford covered her mouth with her hand when I said *twelve hours,* but I kept going. "We have reason to believe she went to see a band play at Insomnia, but we don't know why she didn't come home. Shelby says that it's not like her to not answer her phone. So we should act quickly here, find her as soon as possible."

"We?" Veronica's stepdad snapped. "Do you even *know* Veronica?"

"Can we come in, please?" I said.

He opened his mouth as if to say no, but his wife put her hand on his shoulder and begrudgingly he stepped away from the door.

TWENTY-TWO

Officer Meeks was the first to arrive at the Wexfords' house. He sat on the sofa talking with Veronica's mother—Amy—while her husband, Joseph, banged around in the kitchen, allegedly making coffee for his wife. I stood with Shelby at the front door. She kept looking outside for her friend or her father, who was on his way home from work. He'd asked me to stay with her till he got back. I didn't blame him, given what was going on, given what had already happened. Joshua knew, perhaps better than anyone, what could occur if you chalked up someone's absence to being inconsiderate.

"She's going to be so mad at me," Shelby murmured to the glass panel in the storm door. She kept going back and forth between feeling certain that something was terribly wrong to convinced that her friend would hate her forever for blowing her cover. A self-preservation impulse, that. But there was no harm in it, or at least not yet.

She turned back to the street as a silver Toyota pulled up and squealed into the driveway of her house, shocks crunching as it clipped the edge of the curb. Joshua jumped out of the car, eyes frantic. Shelby ran outside and across the yard and Joshua grabbed her hard in a hug that looked like it hurt. Their relationship was sweet. But it was entirely foreign to me. My father had been the last person I'd ever reach out to for comfort. I had to turn away.

"No," Amy Wexford was saying to Meeks, "her last name is Cruz. C-R-U-Z. Joseph is my second husband."

"Okay, Cruz, I got it. Is her father in the picture?"

"They're not close. He lives in Dayton."

"Has she ever done anything like this before?"

Amy nodded. "We've had problems. My daughter has a form of bipolar disorder. But everything has been pretty good for the last year. She's stable when she's on her medication."

I closed my eyes and leaned against the wall. It was only getting worse. In a regular missing persons case, Veronica's age and the history of mental illness would flag her as high-risk, a critical missing—suicide, some kind of break with reality, or risky manic episode. All very real concerns. But I knew, like I had known about the rocks under the bridge at Clover Point, that this was something else.

"Is she on it right now?" Meeks said. "Her medication."

"Yes," Amy said. "She knows it helps her."

I listened to them discuss Veronica's stats for a few minutes: seventeen years old, five-eight, one-ten, dyed red-violet hair, brown eyes, ears pierced three times each, no tattoos or birthmarks, vintage coat with fur collar. When Amy got up to look for a photograph, I motioned Meeks over to me.

"I need to tell you something," I said quietly. "It's going to sound a little out-there."

"Shoot."

I took a deep breath. "I think something is very wrong here."

He gave me a reassuring policeman smile. "Look, we get this all the time—"

"No," I said. "Something is wrong in Belmont. The body we found the other day. That didn't happen in a vacuum. There are others. Shelby, Veronica's friend? Her mother Mallory Evans was murdered sixteen years ago and her body was found in the same woods. In both cases, it was assumed that they left home voluntarily."

His brows inched toward each other.

I went on. "And there's another girl who's been missing since 1999, Sarah Cook. So I don't think anyone should be wasting time thinking this is just a case of irresponsible-teenager syndrome."

He sighed at that. I shouldn't have said *wasting time.* Or maybe I shouldn't have dumped the whole mess on him at once. "Are you saying you have a better idea than talking to her mother?" he said.

I knew I should stop there, but I couldn't. "Do you know the Brayfield family?"

"Yeah, of course, why?"

"Okay, this is the crazy part," I said.

He put a hand up. "Do I want to hear this?"

"You need to hear it." Based on his expression, I figured I had another minute before he wrote me off like Lassiter had yesterday. "Kenny Brayfield can be connected to the three girls I just mentioned. He dated Mallory Evans and didn't come forward with that information after she was murdered. He was good friends with Sarah Cook's boyfriend. And he works with Colleen Grantham's father. These girls, all blond, who all went missing—"

"I don't—" Meeks started. "*Kenny* Brayfield? What are you even saying? Sarah Cook was the daughter of that family, they were killed ten, fifteen years ago. The guy who did it is in jail."

"No—"

"And what does any of this have to do with Veronica Cruz? What's the supposed connection to her? She's not even blond."

He wasn't listening to me. I needed to try a different tack. "Look. You were there with me in the woods."

"Yes."

"Was I wrong?"

He sighed again. "No."

"I think Kenny Brayfield has been hurting people in Belmont for the last sixteen years," I said. "Young women. Seventeen, eighteen years old. Like Veronica. Please. You have to see the connection. Two days after we find those bones and another girl is missing?"

Now he shook his head, leaning in closer to me. "Don't talk about that around these people."

"Do you hear what I'm saying?"

But then Amy Wexford walked back into the room, holding a five-by-seven plastic frame. "This is from picture day at school," she said. "Will this work?"

Meeks and I both looked at the photo.

Veronica's hair had been honey-colored at the beginning of the school year, cut into bangs. I tried to catch the cop's eye but he wouldn't let me.

"Let's make a list of your daughter's friends, how about," he said, turning away from me altogether.

I ground my teeth together so hard my sinuses ached. Then I pushed out of the house, unable to stand still. I walked across the Evanses' lawn, bits of dew-damp grass sticking to my boots, and I was about to knock on the door when Joshua pulled it open and grabbed my arm. Despite the cold temperature, he was sweating and the hand gripping my elbow was trembling slightly like he was tapped into the same well of concern that I was, only he had gotten there by way of personal experience rather than professional instinct. I wasn't feeling very professional though. I felt like a disaster zone. I followed Joshua into the house.

"Are you doing okay?" I said.

He sat down heavily in the recliner. "Roxane, I don't know how to do this," he said. "I don't know how to tell my kid to stay calm, it'll all be okay, because I've lived through this before and—"

"Hey." I crouched on the carpet in front of him and took his hand. "I know. I know what you're thinking right now. I'm not going to give you the Pollyanna routine. But I do want you to stay calm for Shelby, okay? Let me do the worrying."

"I hardly know you," he whispered. "I can't ask you to do that."

"Sure you can," I said. "And you knew my father. People have been telling me I'm just like him my whole life. So we've known each other forever, Joshua."

He nodded, squeezing my hand. "Okay."

"I want you to stick close to your daughter until we find Veronica."

"Okay."

"I need to talk to her for a few minutes and then I'm going to leave to go check into some things," I said. "But you can call me if *anything* happens, and I'll be back later."

"Okay. Thank you. Thank you for—" He stopped. "Thank you."

By my estimation, all I'd done for anyone so far was stir shit up in Belmont. But I nodded and stood up, my head pounding.

"Shelby's in her room," he added, pointing toward the hallway.

I found her sitting on a bed with a bright orange bedspread, an old, greying black Lab sprawled there beside her. The dog looked at me without interest. Shelby's face was illuminated by the screen of the computer propped on her lap. "I'm looking on her Facebook and Twitter and Instagram to see if she posted anything," she said as I stood in the door. "But she didn't."

"Can I come in?"

Shelby nodded. She put the computer down beside her and stroked the dog's head.

"I want to ask you some things," I said. "And please be honest— don't worry about getting Veronica in trouble."

"Okay."

Thinking that Colleen Grantham and Mallory Evans both had another connection besides Kenny, I said, "Does Veronica use drugs?"

Her eyes got wide for a second. "Not really," she said softly. "She used to smoke weed but she has to take lithium now so basically everything messes with her. So she doesn't anymore."

"Does she have a boyfriend?"

"No."

"Crushes? Maybe on an older guy?"

"Just Aaron."

"Do you know his last name?"

"No. He works there, at Insomnia. He's just this guy with long hair and a pierced lip. I don't even know why she likes him."

"Do you think she might have gone there with anyone else?"

"No. Everyone else sucks here. She had—she used to be kind of popular, like more popular than me, and then at the end of sophomore year she started getting these mood swings really bad, she'd be happy and singing and dancing in class one day and then the next— she used to keep this, this little razor blade in her purse and she'd . . . you know, she hurt herself sometimes, she would cut her thigh. And I didn't know what to do because she didn't want to talk about it." She looked down at the bedspread. "And then one time we were at the mall with some people and she had this total panic attack and they called an ambulance for her and stuff. She had to go be in a hospital for like the rest of the school year. And after that everybody kind of treated her like she was broken. She's not *broken,* she's not crazy, it's just brain chemicals and stuff. But she pretty much only hangs out with me now. She—she knows I worry about her, though. That's why she promised she would always answer her phone." Shelby took a deep breath and blurted, "I love her. And not just like a friend." Her voice was wobbly, vulnerable.

I briefly closed my eyes. This poor kid. I could tell that she'd never said this to anyone before, not even Veronica. I thought about being seventeen myself, when Catherine's absence from school felt like the world was ending. And that was nothing like this. Shelby had to feel like her universe had flipped over. I wanted to say something reassuring, so I tried, "Shelby, it's okay."

She covered her face with her hands, not buying it. "What is?"

I took a deep breath. I doubted that I'd ever been the kind of person who would know what to say here, but I especially wasn't that person right now. I said, "I don't want to sound like an after-school special, with the whole *it gets better* thing. So I'll tell you that falling in love is always the worst. But as far as it goes with liking girls? It does get better. I can tell you that from experience."

"I don't know what to do," she said. "My dad, I can't tell him. About . . . me. And I know he's just thinking about my mom right now and that's so messed up, what happened. I don't remember her. I don't want to think about that. But I want to go out and look and he won't let me and he doesn't understand anything and I'm just going to go crazy, I swear to God."

"Look," I said, "you're going to get through this. You just have to stay as calm as you can. I know that's a tall order, but making yourself sick with worry isn't going to help her. After we find her"—I said it with optimism I didn't feel—"then you can deal with the rest of it. Okay?"

She didn't say anything. But she did take her hands away from her face.

"And if you tell me where you want to look, Shelby, I'll go to every single one of those places since you can't."

"I don't even know," she whispered.

"Do you have a recent picture of her?"

Shelby looked up at the wall behind me, nodding quickly. She reached for her phone and thumbed the screen for a few seconds. "This is from the other day," she said, holding the device out to me.

The picture was a good one: Veronica smiling hugely in the seasonal aisle of a grocery store, clutching a bizarre silver ceramic turkey to her chest. Her reddish-purple hair was braided into pigtails and she was wearing that coat with the ermine collar.

"Send this to me?"

She nodded, typing.

"I'm going to go look into a couple things," I said as my phone vibrated in my pocket with the image she just sent. "If you hear anything, let me know. And I'll come check in later."

It was the exact same thing I promised her father. Shelby finally looked at me. Her eyes, blue-green and bloodshot, were wide with anxiety. "Thank you for helping me."

I wanted to tell her not to thank me yet, but there didn't seem to be a point. "Hang tight for a bit," I said instead.

Back in the car, I felt around in the glove box for a bottle of aspirin but couldn't find it. "Dammit," I said out loud. I looked up at the Wexford house; nothing was happening yet, but Meeks's cruiser was still parked out front. I took the lid off my now-cold tea and grabbed the Crown Royal bottle from the floor. Then I changed my mind and shoved it under the passenger seat, preferring to pretend that I hadn't just contemplated having a drink at nine in the morning.

TWENTY-THREE

The Brayfields' housekeeper buzzed me through the gate, and once I was in the house, she pointed me toward the TV room we'd been in for most of last night. Kenny was lounging on the couch in a blue bathrobe, another pond-scum smoothie his hand. "Hey, it's you," he said, his voice a little hoarse. He sat up, pausing the animated show he was watching. He didn't look too happy. "What's up? Did you forget something last night?"

I had thought about what I wanted to say to him on the drive over, but seeing him here with his stupid robe and his cartoons made me feel crazy and I blew it right away. "What's up," I said, "is there's another girl who didn't come home last night, Kenny."

"What are you talking about?" He put the smoothie down, palming the scratchy stubble on his jaw.

"Mallory," I said. "Sarah. Colleen. Now Veronica."

"Who's Veronica?"

"Where did you go last night?"

"What?"

"Stop it. Tell me where you went last night."

"Kenny, is everything okay in here?"

His father paused in the doorway, eyes narrowed. Once again, he didn't look at me.

"Fine, Dad," Kenny said. "We're just talking."

Mr. Brayfield walked away, but I had a weird feeling I hadn't seen the last of him.

"Last night, you missed half your own damn party," I said. "Where were you?"

"I—look, what's it to you? I had some work I needed to do. I own a business—I'm always working."

I took a few steps into the room. "Where did you go?"

Kenny sat up, holding the front of his robe closed. "Jesus, what is your problem? I told you, I had some work to do. I was checking on a display. I'm, like, really busy."

"Busy," I repeated. I wanted to throttle him. "Why aren't you at work now, then? What are you doing home?"

"Because I feel like shit," he snapped, "for reasons I'm pretty sure you follow. And anyway, I don't see how that's your business."

"Kenny, I was in your *house*," I said, regretting that I hadn't taken a few minutes to calm down before coming here. I was too fired up. "Did you bring her here?"

Now he jumped to his feet. "What the hell are you talking about?"

I resisted the urge to back up and changed tactics. "Why'd you lie when I asked you about Mallory Evans on Saturday?"

"What? I didn't."

"You did, Kenny. You conveniently failed to tell me that you used to date her."

"You didn't ask about that!"

"Are you kidding me?"

"No, I'm not finding this funny at all," Kenny said.

"Me either. But on Saturday when I asked you about her, you acted like you barely knew her. That's a lie."

"Okay, fine, I knew her."

"So why'd you lie about it?"

"Because I don't like talking about her, okay?" He paced the length of the room, his hands clasped behind his head.

"No, it's not okay. Give me a real answer."

He stopped pacing and turned to me. His eyes were flat and hard. Without the jovial, slightly daft smile, his face was angular and tough. "I'm not giving you anything."

"Where's Veronica?" I tried again.

"I don't know any Veronica."

"Is she here?" I scanned the room, catching a glimpse of the two-story deck through the windows. "Outside, maybe?" I remembered the small shed I noticed last night, the sauna.

"I think you should probably leave," he said.

"I'm not leaving," I said, just as I heard heavy footsteps in the kitchen behind me.

"You're leaving now," Jake Lassiter said.

I spun around and took in the police chief standing there with Mr. Brayfield. They looked ready to physically remove me from the house. I'd been there for only a few minutes, so this was a new record in terms of the Belmont cops intercepting me.

Lassiter said, "Ken, you were right to call me. Miss Weary here has been stirring up trouble in town for the last week or so, despite quite a few warnings from my department. I apologize on her behalf for the inconvenience. She'll be on her way now."

I opened my mouth to speak, but Lassiter's expression made me close it again.

"Let's go, Miss Weary."

I took a step, Lassiter nodding at me like I was a good girl. But I turned back to Kenny with my phone out, snapping a quick picture of him. "What the—" Kenny said.

"Okay, that's enough," Lassiter said. He grabbed my upper arm and dragged me into the kitchen. To Kenny's father, he said, "You're not going to have a problem again. I'm very sorry, sir."

But Mr. Brayfield was looking at his son with a combination of disdain and dread. "What is she talking about now?" he said.

"*Nothing,* Jesus, Dad." Whatever he said next was lost to me as Lassiter yanked me by the arm out through the foyer and down the steps of the porch.

"Let go of me," I snapped, pulling my arm out of his grip.

He took a step closer to me, a pointed finger in my face. "What the hell is wrong with you?"

I brushed past him, trying for my car. But he stepped back into my path, grabbing my bicep again.

"Get your hands off me. You told me to leave, and I'm leaving."

"What are you doing here?"

"Which is it?" I exclaimed, my breath visible in the cold air. "You want me to leave or you want me to talk?"

"You can't just barge into a house like this, with your questions—"

"No one barged anywhere."

"Stop arguing with me," Lassiter said. He hadn't let go of my arm yet. He had eight inches and a hundred pounds on me, not to mention the legal authority to throw me in a cell for the rest of the day. I had to concede the moment to him. I spread my hands in surrender and he released his grip on me. "Now, why are you here?"

I rubbed my arm. I could feel a hand-shaped bruise forming already. "Veronica Cruz didn't come home last night."

"I'm aware."

"I'm worried that whoever buried Mallory Evans and Colleen Grantham in the woods is the reason why," I said, "and I believe that person is Kenny Brayfield."

He laughed at me like I'd just told the world's worst joke.

Not caring if he liked what I had to say, I ticked off the reasons for my theory. "The woods backs up to the Brayfield property. He used to date Mallory. He was friends with Sarah's boyfriend. He works with Colleen's father—"

"Belmont's a small town," he said. "Everyone is connected to everyone else."

"*And* Kenny lied when I asked him about Mallory the other day, he was unaccounted for last night when Veronica went missing, and they were awfully quick to call you just now when I started asking questions about it—"

He took another step toward me. "The Brayfield family is entitled to police protection from nosy outsiders, just like anyone else in this town."

I shook my head. The man had a singular way of responding to exactly the wrong thing. "Not just any police protection, though," I said. "You. Did he call you directly so you could rush over?"

"Listen to me," he said, waving a hand as if to silence me. He was back to just wanting me to leave. "I know you probably think you're helping, but we don't want or need your help here. We'll figure out where she went, we will leverage all of our resources to solve Colleen's murder, and we will deal with the other dozens of small police matters that pop up each week in Belmont, and we'll do all of that without your involvement. This connection you're clutching at just doesn't exist."

"You're not even listening," I said.

"Go back to the city," Lassiter finished. "You don't belong here."

I wanted to tell him that it wasn't a matter of belonging, but maybe it was. And in that case, I was glad I didn't belong in Belmont. I went around him and got into the car. If I was right, there'd be some way to prove it. Finding out the truth about what happened to Sarah Cook and her parents and the other women might be impossible after so much time, but I'd just seen Veronica yesterday. I might not have a paying client who expected answers from me anymore. But after what I'd stirred up down here, I needed to get those answers all the same.

Insomnia was a cozy little space with navy-blue walls, yellow area rugs over a scuffed wooden floor, and eclectic-chic mismatched furniture.

I could see why Veronica, what with her experimental outfits, probably liked it here. Metric's "Poster of a Girl" was playing over the speakers at a volume that seemed a little loud for the suburbs and the hour—eleven in the morning now—but the smattering of patrons didn't seem to mind. While I stood at the counter waiting for someone to notice me, I looked at the baked goods in the glass case: lots of muffins and cupcakes, some with a little card in front identifying them as vegan. I had to resist the urge to lean on the case with my head in my arms. It was the right height.

"If you're on the fence, definitely get the chocolate chip." The barista emerged from the back room, wiping her hands on her apron. She had a shock of greenish-blue hair and a tattoo of swirling lines on her chest peeking out from behind her uniform apron. "They're made in-house every day. Well, all of them are. But that one's the best."

"Not today," I said. Though my greasy breakfast sandwich had been abandoned when Shelby had called, I didn't think I could eat. "Could I just have a peppermint tea?"

"Absolutely."

She turned away, pouring hot water into a chipped mug.

"Hey," I said, "is Aaron working today?"

"Yeah, but he's doing an interview right now. He's the manager on duty."

"Were you working last night?"

The barista turned around and looked at me curiously. "I was."

I pulled my phone out of my pocket and navigated to the picture of Veronica. "Do you remember seeing this girl?"

She squinted at the screen. "She comes in here all the time," she said, "but I don't know if she came last night. There were a ton of people, mostly, you know, girls like that. Aaron's band has a bit of a following."

"So I gathered." I was hoping she just had a bad memory, that

Veronica had been here, had spent all night talking to Aaron in his car somewhere. That there was still going to be an easy resolution. "She didn't come home last night, and I'm trying to find her."

The barista dropped a tea bag into the mug and pushed it across the counter toward me. "Shit." Then, "Wait, are you her mom?"

"No, no," I said quickly. "God, no." I was more accustomed to being mistaken for a cop than for someone's mother. "Friend of her family. What about him, did you happen to see him?" I showed her the picture I'd taken of Kenny.

The barista laughed. "Is he wearing a bathrobe?"

I needed a better photo of him. "He wouldn't have been wearing the robe last night."

"No, I've never seen him before."

A short line had formed behind me, so I stepped aside. "When Aaron's interview is over, can you tell him I'd like to talk to him for a second?"

The barista nodded. I took my mug of tea and sat down in a worn leather armchair, the kind manufactured in the era before furniture was filled with the cheapest synthetic materials possible. I used my phone to search online for Kenny Brayfield, hoping I could find a picture of him wearing anything but a bathrobe. Next Level's Web site featured his photo, but he was wearing a blazer and looked like a different person. His Facebook profile pic showed his eyes only and the rest of his photos were private. I found a decent one on Next Level's Instagram account though, of Kenny grinning in front of a tower of vodka bottles. I took a screenshot of it. He looked like a minor deviant to me, a harmless troublemaker. But maybe that was part of his thing. Maybe the women would go with him willingly, this mildly charming rich kid they'd known forever, offering a ride or a drink or whatever.

The connection to Mallory and Sarah was solid—he knew them well. I wasn't sure how well he might have known Colleen Grantham, if her father would have ever introduced his teenage daughter to his boss, or if Curtis had even worked for Next Level at the time. She was about ten years younger than Kenny was, though it sounded like they had converging interests—in Belmont's drug trade. Veronica was the biggest question mark—how did Kenny know her? I wondered darkly if Kenny had kept an eye on Mallory's daughter all these years, if he had seen Shelby and Veronica together. It all sounded crazy, even in my head. But there were too many connections here to write any of this off as a coincidence, not to mention the fact that Kenny's father had Jake Lassiter on speed dial. Brad had told me that Kenny got out of a lot of trouble growing up because his family was loaded, and it seemed like nothing had changed.

Nothing except the nature of his crimes.

I drank some of my scalding hot tea, gasping a little when the liquid hit my throat just as a kid in an apron walked over and sat down across from me. He was probably nineteen, sleepy-eyed and with dyed black hair that looked like it had been styled with a sock. "Hey," he said. "I'm Aaron. Maura said you wanted to talk to me."

I cleared my throat and sat up. "I'm a private investigator," I said, holding out my phone. "I'm looking for this girl, she came to your show last night. Did you see her?"

Aaron looked down at the picture. "Veronica," he said, "right?"

"Yes," I said, perking up a little. It seemed like a good sign if she'd made it to the show, although she was still gone. "Was she here?"

His mouth twisted. "I don't *think* so? I didn't talk to her, anyway. She comes to a lot of my shows and she always comes up to me and says hey or whatever, afterward. It was crowded though, so I'm not sure."

I showed him Kenny. "Okay. How about him?"

"No, but I know that dude, he came in here once and wanted to put a flyer on the community board, for some flavored vodka or something. I told him, it's for community events only."

That sounded about right. "Thanks," I said. "That's all I wanted to know."

He started to stand up, but I added, "Wait, one more thing. Have the police been here to talk to you?"

"The police?"

I nodded.

"Nope."

He walked away and I finished my tea, barely tasting it or noticing the temperature. It had been hours since Shelby gave Meeks her information about where Veronica might have gone last night. Even if she went somewhere else, they should have been checking, they should have been looking. They were mighty quick to attend to *my* whereabouts, but not a missing girl's. I returned my mug to the counter and went back outside. Maybe the police didn't feel like looking, but I sure did.

TWENTY-FOUR

Insomnia sat in a strip mall with a grocery store, a dry cleaner's, a tutoring center, a dentist, a small, crusty bar called the Varsity Lounge, and a hair salon. With the exception of the grocery store and the bar, they had all been closed on Monday night. But I went into each store, asked about security cameras, and showed my two photos. The dry cleaner's, tutoring center, hair salon, and dentist did not have cameras that faced the parking lot. The grocery store had cameras, but they weren't allowed to show them to me without a warrant or written authorization from their corporate loss prevention department. But the Varsity Lounge had lot-facing cameras without any such policy attached. I offered the bartender twenty bucks if he'd let me look at them.

"I don't know," he said.

But the twenty had already disappeared into his pocket. A social contract had been made. I waited. He waited too. So he agreed to the terms, and it was a matter of price. I opened my wallet and teased another twenty out.

"I could get into a *lot* of trouble," he said. He was a tall, broad fellow with a bushy red beard. I didn't exactly buy him tolerating any trouble with anyone. But I still pulled out the twenty and a ten. That was all the cash I had on me.

"It's this or nothing."

"Okay," he said.

The bar's office was a storage closet stacked high with beer kegs and papers. "Don't touch anything else," he told me officiously, nudging the computer mouse to wake up the machine. "There's payroll stuff back here."

"You just took a bribe," I said, "be nice."

After he left, I sat down at the computer terminal. It was an old system with a jerky frame rate of five or so per second, but the interface was straightforward and I clicked through the folders of the previous day's video files. The bar had six cameras: two on the sidewalk, facing each other so that I had a clear view of several yards in either direction; two inside, one in the front and one in the back; and two in the rear of the bar. I focused on the front sidewalk cameras, starting with seven o'clock last night. Veronica had left Shelby's house at seven thirty, and though the show at Insomnia wasn't until ten, I thought maybe there was a chance she had walked over early, intending to kill time somewhere before it started. I didn't expect to catch a crystal-clear picture of Kenny luring Veronica into his late-model Lexus, but I was at least hoping for something: a sign that would help establish more of the timeline, something that the Belmont police couldn't ignore.

At eight ten, I got my wish: Kenny Brayfield walked up the sidewalk and into the bar.

"Holy shit," I muttered.

I felt my jaw tightening as I navigated to the interior cameras and watched as he went up to the bearded bartender, pointed, and shook his head. The bartender shrugged, turned away. A minute or two later, Kenny left.

I went back to the outside cameras and saw him walk back in the direction he came, and that was it.

I sped up the footage and watched through three hours of the bar's Sunday-night business in a half hour. Then I stood up and walked back into the bar, the picture of Kenny pulled up on my phone. "You told me you didn't see him," I said.

The bartender was muddling an orange for someone who was obviously feeling lofty. He stopped what he was doing and looked at the picture. "I didn't."

"You did," I said. "He came in here, and you talked to him. It's on the camera. He was probably asking you something about that cinnamon vodka with the gold flakes in it."

"Oh," he said. "That guy."

"Yeah, that guy."

"He wanted to know why it wasn't on the top shelf. I told him because no one who comes into this bar is ordering that shit."

"That's it?"

"That's it," he said. "He said he talked to the owner about placement, that's his word, *placement*. I was like, Whatever, dude, we're busy, go away."

"I thought bartenders never forget faces."

"No, we never forget a *drink* order. Faces, eh."

I watched him as he finished the old-fashioned with a generous whiskey pour. I shook my head as he tipped the bottle in my direction. "Okay," I said, flipping back to the pic of Veronica, "if she didn't order anything, you wouldn't remember her either?"

The bartender said, "No, I'd remember her. She's hot. I mean, you're not bad yourself, but—"

"She's seventeen," I told him, not in the mood. "And she's missing. Look at this picture. Are you sure she wasn't in here?"

He looked. "Positive."

I went back into the office and resumed my stop-start watching of the video footage, but I reached the two o'clock county-wide closing time without seeing Kenny or Veronica or anything else out of the ordinary. Then I navigated back to his appearance on the sidewalk cameras and inserted the jump drive from my key ring into the computer, copying the files. Kenny hadn't exactly been lying earlier—he *was* doing some work. But his work took him pretty damn close to Veronica's probable location.

I needed more than that before I could try again with Lassiter, but at least no one could tell me this video footage didn't exist.

I left my car where it was and walked across the parking lot to where it backed up to a row of trees. There was a clear path worn into the muddy ground from people making a habit of cutting through, just like Shelby had said.

I followed the trampled grass through the trees and came out in the backyard of a yellow split-level. The sky was grey and the air was wet and no one was around except a German shepherd that regarded me balefully as I hiked up the slight incline of the yellow house's backyard. When I got out to the sidewalk, I saw that I was on the far end of Providence Street. About a dozen houses down, I could see two Belmont police cruisers now parked in front of the Wexford home. But no one was out canvassing, so I turned around and went up to the porch of the yellow house and knocked on the door.

I heard signs of life—shuffling and banging and then a prolonged period of someone struggling with the dead bolt. Finally, an old guy in a plaid shirt flung the door open and scowled out at me, leaning heavily on a cane. "Did you just walk through my yard?" he snapped.

"I did," I said. "I'm sorry. People do that a lot?"

"All the goddamn time."

I showed him the picture of Veronica. "Her?"

He grabbed my phone and held it an inch or two away from his face. "Oh, yeah, sure," he said, "she lives up the street or something."

"She does. How about last night, did you see her last night?"

"Last night?" From his tone of voice, last night might as well have been last month.

"Yes, around seven thirty, eight o'clock?" I sensed his interest was flagging, so I added, "You seem pretty sharp, I bet you notice everything that goes on around here."

He seemed to like the sound of that. "Last night?" he said again.

I smiled politely and waited while he thought about that.

"Right at the end of *Wheel of Fortune*." He nodded. "Seven fifty-five, then. Someone went by. I got a light on a motion sensor."

"And it was her?"

"I can't swear to it, but I think so. That hair, it nearly glows when that spotlight goes on."

So Veronica had likely passed through the trees at around eight. At eight fifteen, Kenny was walking out of the Varsity Lounge. Their paths would have converged right after that. I had no idea what had happened next, only that Veronica likely hadn't made it as far as Insomnia, and Kenny didn't get back to his house until ten.

After that, I tried the surrounding houses, but most yielded no response to my knocks—the residents either at work or hiding from me. Fair enough. When it started to rain, I headed up the street to Shelby's house. The two cruisers in front of Veronica's hadn't moved, but I saw that one of the cops had gotten behind the wheel of one, ready to drive away. That is, until I got closer. Then he got out. It was Pasquale, the muscular guy who'd given me a hard time at the gas station last week.

I held up my hands in a *don't shoot* gesture as I climbed the steps to the Evanses' porch. But Pasquale didn't buy it. His expression told me he knew about my encounter with Lassiter already somehow. "Ma'am, the situation is under control."

I didn't believe for one second that anything was under anything. But I didn't want to get stuck explaining my way out of any more conversations with the Belmont police. "Oh, I know," I said, knocking on the front door. "I'm just visiting a friend."

"Oh, a friend?" Pasquale said, doubtful.

Fortunately, Shelby opened the door right then and invited me inside. I resisted the urge to look over my shoulder and stick out my tongue. Instead I just followed her into the house. Joshua was in the armchair, talking on the phone, but he raised a hand to me in greeting. They both seemed slightly more relaxed, which made me wonder what spin the police were putting on Veronica's absence now.

"He's talking to my grandma," Shelby told me as we went down the narrow hallway to her bedroom. "She lives in Indiana. He wants us to go there to stay with her but I don't want to go anywhere, I want to stay here." She sat down on the bed and spun her laptop screen around so I could see it. "I'm making a poster. I don't know what else to do. Dad talked to the police and they told us we should stay home in case Veronica tries to come back and she gets nervous because of the police at her house."

"Yeah," I said. I was willing to bet that Lassiter was responsible for that brilliant excuse, but I supposed it didn't matter. There was nothing Shelby could do yet anyway. I nodded at her poster. "That looks good. Listen, I'm going to show you a picture and I want you to tell me if you recognize the person."

"Okay."

I showed her the image of Kenny, and she immediately nodded.

My heart jumped into my throat. "You recognize him?"

"I think he lives around here," Shelby said. "I've seen him driving by."

My mouth had gone dry. Kenny didn't live anywhere near Shelby's street. East side, west side. "Shelby, when was the last time you saw him driving by?"

She thought about that for a second. "We saw him on Friday, I think. Yeah, Friday, it was the day you came over the first time."

"Have you ever talked to him?"

"No."

"Has Veronica?"

"No. I mean, not with me. He's just some guy."

He wasn't. He wasn't just some guy. He was hanging around on Shelby's street often enough for her to notice. I was not going to let the Belmont police pretend that this was nothing anymore.

"Why?" Shelby said next. "Who is he?"

"I don't know yet," I said. I ran a hand through my hair and tried to breathe. "You're listening to your dad, right? Staying inside?"

She nodded.

"Good."

TWENTY-FIVE

I could see clear through to the end of Kenny's street from Clover, the main drag. A cop car was parked at the Brayfield house, in front of the gates, like a warning. I kept driving and turned on the access road that had taken me to the overlook the other day. The rain was steady now, slanting against my windshield as I pulled over along the back edge of the Brayfield property. The wrought-iron fence made it easy to spot. I switched from my leather jacket to my raincoat, transferred my phone and keys to the pocket, and, in a last-minute inspiration, grabbed my revolver from the glove box, hoping this act would not draw trouble to me. *More* trouble. I snapped the magnetic holster onto my jeans at my right hip and pulled my hood over my hair.

I probably looked like I was up to no good, which I was. I had no idea how the situation had escalated to this point. Danielle Stockton had hired me to track down a woman she saw at a gas station, but she was really asking me to save her brother. Everything else sprang up around this like a cage I couldn't get into. Or out of. But Veronica Cruz was somewhere, and I had reason to believe Kenny knew where. I looked up at the fence, almost waiting for it to talk me out of this. I told myself that I *would* go through the front if I could. But I couldn't. And something had to be done. If the Belmont police weren't willing to look everywhere, I sure was.

I got out of the car and went up the slight hill to the fence, which was comprised of square-shaped iron beams about the width of a quarter, spaced roughly ten inches apart. They stood a good eight feet tall and tapered to a point on the top. The fence was old, the metal going rusty on the edges. I looked past them at the house, a hundred or so yards ahead. There was a light on above the pool, and it cast a murky glow over the water and through the floor-to-ceiling windows. The house was huge. There were endless places to conceal a person in there. Was that what had happened? Had Veronica been in the house while I was drunkenly looking out the window by the pool? I rested my forehead against the fence. I'd never forgive myself if that was the case. But there was really only one way to find out.

I considered whether or not I could squeeze in between the gap between bars in the fence, experimentally putting one foot inside to see if I could get my hips through. But I didn't get far before I heard a faint creaking sound behind me. A cop's utility belt was the only thing that made that sound. I pulled my foot back and turned around to see Jack Derrow a few feet down the embankment. His face was partly in shadow from his own raincoat hood. Somehow the coat made him appear bigger than he was.

"We've got to stop meeting like this," he said. "You know this is private property too, right?"

"I know," I said. I wondered if he'd help me, as he had on Sunday. But something in his face told me he'd already gotten the download from Lassiter. I would just go back to the car and wait for him to go away. "I was about to leave."

I took a step, but he moved into my path.

"I'm afraid you used your freebie the other day," he said. The smile was gone. "I'm going to have to ask you to put your hands above your head."

"I'll seriously just go—"

"You're under arrest for criminal trespass," Derrow said. "Hands above your head."

"A fourth-degree misdemeanor," I said. A current of panic vibrated through my body. I was no use to Veronica if I got arrested, something I probably should have thought more seriously about. But I hadn't. "I don't think this is necessary, is it?"

"I don't make the rules. Put your hands above your head."

I exhaled slowly, disbelieving, but I did want he wanted.

Derrow went behind me, so close he stepped on my heel. I could hear him breathing. "Do you have anything on your person that I should be aware of?"

"Handgun, right hip," I said.

I felt his hands on my torso. Then one arm snaked up as he reached for the zipper pull on my coat. As a reflex, I found myself stupidly reaching down to hold the collar closed.

"Do *not* move," Derrow said, all business now. He jammed his elbow between my shoulder blades, forcing me face-first against the fence. My cheekbone cracked against the iron beam and the rough metal tore into my skin.

Derrow continued shoving his elbow into my back as he used his other hand to reach into my coat, his fingers brushing the bare skin of my hip as he unfastened the holster.

"You're hurting me," I said.

"No, I'm not," he said. "You got a CCW permit for this, or are we adding to the charges?"

"I have a permit," I snapped. Rain had immediately begun to soak my shirt.

"Thank God for small blessings, right?" Derrow said. He pulled off my hood and continued the pat-down. "I'm going to cuff you now, and then we'll get you to the station."

"Then what?" I said as he jerked my hands down to the small of my back and tightened a set of handcuffs around my wrists, the cold metal biting into me.

"I think that depends on you," Derrow said. "Doesn't it."

"What is that supposed to mean," I said. The rain was running down my face now. My cheekbone was on fire and I tasted blood.

"It means you might want to start behaving yourself," he said, "because you've got some people pretty pissed off."

First he made me wait, wet and handcuffed, on a bench in the holding area of the police station while he slowly removed his raincoat and hung it up. Then he uncuffed me and directed me to empty my pockets onto the counter. I complied and just tried to breathe evenly. Anything else seemed likely to make the situation worse. That was a self-preservation tactic I wished I'd discovered about thirty minutes sooner. Derrow examined my driver's license, then put my phone, keys, wallet, and the handgun into an envelope, which he tucked under the counter.

"Okay," he said then, "come on."

"Come on where?" I said. I had hoped for one naïve second while he was at the counter that I could pay a fine and get back to my search for Veronica. But that wasn't going to happen.

He grasped my arm just above the elbow. "I'm going to need you to sit tight," he said, steering me into a painted concrete holding cell.

"Wait," I said. The small cell had a buzzing overhead light, a short row of cloudy glass-block windows near the ceiling, and a long stainless-steel bench that looked like it belonged in a slaughterhouse. The same instinct that made me try to hold my coat closed in the woods now made me dig my heels into the floor.

But he pushed me inside and pulled the metal door closed. "I'll be back in a bit," he said, and then he smiled.

He walked around the corner and went out of sight. I exhaled violently. What, exactly, did *a bit* mean? I sat down on the bench but stood right back up again, too wired to be still. I paced the length of the cell, maybe fifteen feet from end to end. The wall opposite the windows offered a metal toilet and a tiny matching sink. I went to it and bent over the sink, peering at my blurry reflection in the shiny surface. It was hard to see much, but I could tell that my cheekbone was bruised already, bleeding from a vertical laceration directly below my eye. I didn't need to see my reflection to tell that, though. I grabbed a wad of tissues, the cheap kind that disintegrate if you so much as look at them, ran water on it, and used it to gently wipe my face. The paper came away tinged with pink and dotted with dried blood and dirt and rust. I repeated the process until the tissue came away clean. I dropped the bloody tissues into the toilet. Then I sat back down and waited for the *bit* to end.

It didn't.

TWENTY-SIX

I had never been arrested before, but I had been around enough criminal cases to know that this was not how it was supposed to work. There was supposed to be a process to it: intake questions, finger-prints, mug shots, a pay phone for collect calls.

Eventually I stood up and went to the barred gate of the cell and tried from different angles to see anything around the corner. From the far end, I could see the desk and the envelope that contained my possessions. I could see a clock on the wall, the kind that looked like it belonged in a high school. I squinted at it until the time came into some semblance of focus: two p.m. From the other end of the cell, I could see a security camera mounted near the ceiling just outside the gate.

I paced for a while longer, then sat on the bench again, then got up and squinted at the clock.

Two thirty p.m.

I took off my raincoat, which had gotten wet on the inside when Derrow had unzipped it in the woods. Removing it felt like giving in, accepting that I was not just going to be able to pay the fine and then be on my way. I turned the coat inside out and draped it over one end of the bench to dry out. Then I took my shirt off and attempted to wring water out of it over the sink, aware of the security camera at my back.

Three fifteen.

I put the still-damp shirt back on and stretched out on the bench on my back. The ceiling of the cell was disgusting, dotted with wads of gum and dead insects. I contemplated who was directly responsible for my current predicament. Maybe Chief Lassiter had me followed. Maybe Kenny had seen me through the woods. Either way, I felt pretty certain that I was stumbling in the right direction now.

Or was, before I was sidelined here.

Four o'clock.

I tried to distill my theory down into an elevator pitch that I could deliver to the next human being I saw. Kenny Brayfield had been killing women in Belmont for sixteen years. Two of the women had been written off as runaways, until they turned up dead. It was thus wildly negligent for the police to pretend that another missing girl had left of her own accord, especially when Kenny had been hanging around the street where Veronica lived. Especially when he was at the Varsity Lounge at the exact moment she would have been walking by.

I wasn't sure where Garrett and Elaine Cook fit into my elevator pitch.

I wasn't sure how long an elevator pitch was supposed to be.

I needed a pen.

Four thirty.

I invented a game: try to guess when exactly five minutes had passed.

It was virtually silent in the cell. Every so often, I heard the faint crackle of a radio dispatch or a murmured conversation from somewhere else in the building, but no one so much as came down the hallway. I realized I could hear the ticking of the clock if I sat very still.

Some game.

At five o'clock, I went to the gate and cleared my throat and shouted, "Hey."

Nothing.

"HEY."

Nothing.

I took off one of my boots and banged it against the bars as hard as I could, still shouting.

Finally, I heard footsteps in the corridor, and a second later, Officer Pasquale appeared in front of me. "You're making quite the racket," he said helpfully. His eyes drifted from my cheekbone to my chest. "Cold in here, huh?" he said.

"Is there any news about Veronica?" I said, ignoring him.

"Nope," he said. "Is that what you're making all this noise for?"

"When can I get out of here?"

"Not my call."

"Listen," I said. "I've been in here for three hours and I haven't been booked yet and I haven't gotten to make a phone call or anything. Can you tell me when that is going to happen?"

"Let me go see what's going on," Pasquale said. "I'll be right back."

He wasn't.

I wadded up my raincoat and tried using it as a pillow, but the thin nylon provided little cushion. My headache was coming back, but this time it was different, deep and grinding. I was hungry—I hadn't eaten today. I went to the sink and attempted to drink out of it, but it was too shallow to get my mouth under the stream of water. I managed a few sips from my open palm.

Six o'clock.

I took my boot off again and banged it on the bars and yelled for Pasquale. This time it was Meeks who came down the hallway.

"Shit," he said when he saw me. "What happened?"

"I've been here for four hours and I haven't been booked or gotten to make any phone calls, is what happened," I announced. "Is there any news about Veronica?"

Meeks's eyes narrowed slightly when I said *four hours*. "I tried to—" he started, but then he seemed to realize this wasn't the time for an I-told-you-so. "There's an Amber Alert out now. Everyone's looking."

"Twenty hours after she was last seen," I said, "that's fantastic. What I told you earlier, about Kenny Brayfield—"

"What did you do? Who brought you in?" he said.

This seemed familiar. I sighed. "Derrow. Look, I promise not to do it again or whatever if you let me out of here." I had no intention of keeping that promise, but my options were limited and I had zero leverage.

"Okay, let me go see what's going on. I know you're trying to help."

He turned to walk away.

"Wait," I said. He looked back at me. "Can I have a pen?"

He shook his head. "Sorry."

"Wait," I said again when he turned back around. "Can I have something to eat? Or at least something to drink?"

He looked at me. "What were you brought in for?"

"Criminal trespass," I said. "Yes, a fourth-degree misdemeanor."

"And you've been back here since two?"

I nodded.

He did seem slightly concerned about this. "Let me go see what I can find out," he said. "I'll be right back."

He wasn't. My headache was getting worse. I tried lying on the bench with my legs up the wall. I tried putting my raincoat over my eyes to shield from the aggressive fluorescent light.

I wondered where Mallory and Colleen had been killed and how long it took.

I wondered how in the hell Sarah's parents fit into this.

I wondered how Shelby was doing. I hoped she wasn't out there wondering about me.

Seven o'clock.

"I need help," I yelled, throwing both boots at the gate without getting up.

A few minutes later, I heard the squeak of footsteps and then Meeks reappeared. He held a bottle of water and a single clementine.

"What's this," I said, steadying myself on the wall. I got a little dizzy sitting up.

Meeks didn't say anything.

I took the water and the fruit. "What's going on here?" I said.

"Someone should get to your report soon," he said stiffly.

"When?"

"Soon."

"What time?"

"Soon."

"Is Derrow still on duty?"

"No," Meeks said.

I leaned against the bars and closed my eyes. "You can't do this," I said. "It's illegal."

"You'll be brought up on charges or released within seventy-two hours. That's the law."

"Seventy-two hours?" I felt like I would undoubtedly be dead within seventy-two hours if I had to stay in here. The reality of the situation was too big to contemplate all at once.

"Yes."

"You can't hold someone here for seventy-two hours without food," I said.

"I just brought you an orange."

"This is from your lunch and don't pretend it isn't," I said.

At that, he gave me a slight smile. "It is."

"Thank you."

He nodded.

"Can you please tell me what's going on?" I said.

He looked down at the ground. "Chief Lassiter said he talked to you this morning about not interfering."

"I'm not interfering."

"Not right now, you aren't. But you were. We're doing everything in our power to find Veronica. We don't need a civilian getting involved, trying to sneak through fences onto private property—"

"Honestly, enough with the private property! Meeks, listen to me. These women are connected. Kenny Brayfield is the link. Talk to Shelby Evans. She's seen him *hanging around* on her street. For no reason. On top of everything else, isn't that enough to warrant a conversation with him?" I couldn't remember my elevator pitch. That was why I had needed the pen. I ran a hand over my face, forgetting about the cut on my cheekbone. "You can't tell me you don't see it."

He saw it. But he looked uneasy. "There are different rules where the Brayfields are concerned," he said.

"Different rules."

"Yeah."

"What does that mean?"

Meeks shook his head. He wasn't going to say any more about that. "Look," he said, turning down the volume on his radio as it crackled to life on his hip. "You just have to be quiet. They'll let you go after you're quiet."

Then he walked away.

Quiet.

I sat back down and drank half the water in one gulp and felt immediately nauseous. But I peeled the clementine and ate it in two bites. Then I leaned back against the wall and closed my eyes, a gnawing pit of dread opening up at the center of me. I finished the water, but I didn't want it. I wanted a drink.

Seventy-two hours.

In seventy-two hours, every trace of Veronica could be gone.

Nine o'clock.

I was physically anxious, my body begging me for an explanation. I retrieved the clementine peels from the sink and studied them to see if there were any more pieces of edible fruit stuck to them. I wondered if eating a clementine peel would kill me, decided probably no. My headache was more likely to finish me off. I experimentally chewed on one. It tasted like shit. I spit it out. I really wanted a drink.

Needed.

It was starting to scare me, how much I needed a drink.

Ten o'clock.

I banged my boots on the gate and yelled some more. My voice was starting to fray.

I counted to a thousand. Then two thousand. I made lists.

New York, Los Angeles, Chicago, Houston, Philadelphia, Phoenix, San Antonio, San Diego, Dallas, San Jose, Austin, Indianapolis, Jacksonville, San Francisco, Columbus, Charlotte, Fort Worth, Detroit, El Paso, Memphis.

Royals, Giants, Red Sox, Giants, Cardinals, Giants, Yankees, Phillies, Red Sox, Cardinals, White Sox, Red Sox, Marlins, Angels, Diamondbacks, Yankees, Yankees, Yankees.

Ardmore, Buffalo Trace, Crown Royal, Dewar's, Eagle Rare, Four Roses, Glenlivet, Heaven Hill, Inchgower, Jameson, Knob Creek, Lagavulin, Midleton, Oban, Pappy Van Winkle, Queen of the Moorlands, Redbreast, Sazerac, Talker, Usquebach, Very Old Barton, Wild Turkey, Yamasaki.

I tried to fill the water bottle up at the sink but could only get a few inches in before the water flowed back out, again because the sink was so small. Fill, sip, fill, sip. My hands were shaking.

Eleven o'clock.

I filled the bottle as much as I could, then touched it to the bars on the cell door and dragged it back and forth. It made an awful noise, jarring but satisfyingly loud. It made me feel like my head was about to cave in, but I kept at it until someone came over, this time a mean-looking guy my age with so much gel in his hair I could smell it.

"Is there a woman on duty?" I said, trying a different approach. I wanted to speak to someone reasonable.

"Huh?" he said. His name tag read Shanahan.

"Is there a woman on duty," I repeated. "I'm having, you know, woman problems."

"Like you need a tampon?" he said brightly.

"Yeah," I said. "Like that."

"Nope," he said. "Sorry."

He walked away but returned a few minutes later with a tampon in a crumpled pink wrapper and thrust it at me sheepishly.

I sighed. I regretted wasting a wish on a tampon I didn't need. "Hey," I said. "Can you tell me if there's news on the missing girl? Veronica Cruz?"

He cocked his head. "From what I understand, you're not supposed to be asking about that." But then he said, "Hasn't turned up yet. We've got every agency in the county on the lookout, though."

They didn't need to be on the lookout across the entire county. They needed to look a hell of a lot closer than that. I didn't say anything. I just lay back down and thought about what kind of incendiary device I might be able to make with a tampon, a water bottle, and a clementine peel.

Midnight.

I needed a drink.

I wiped a thin layer of perspiration off my upper lip.

My father was showing me how to handle a revolver. I was ten. "You always check to see if it's loaded," he said. "Even if you're sure it isn't, you always check. That's how you know what kind of beast you're dealing with." He snapped the barrel open and showed me the empty slots. "Now you know it's a harmless one." He pointed it at me. Bang, bang.

I woke up as the cell door slammed open and I nearly fell off the bench. A new uniform was shoving a twentyish girl into the cell with me. She was dressed in an impossibly tiny black dress and patent spike heels and she reeked of vodka. It cleared my head for a second, just the smell of it, and I felt better, and then I felt worse.

"Hey," I said to the cop before he closed the cell door.

He acted like he hadn't heard me.

"HEY."

Behind me, the girl's phone rang and she answered it. "Fuuuuuuck," she drawled, "where the fuck have you been."

The fact that she was allowed to keep her cell phone in here made me feel insane. The cop was now walking away like he hadn't even seen me. I pulled the tampon out of my pocket and threw it at him.

"This is illegal," I said. My voice was nearly gone now.

The cop came back to the cell door. His name tag said *Kowalski*. He smiled at me coldly. "Not your brand?" he said, holding up the tampon.

"This might fly for punk suburban kids," I said feebly, though I was in no position to be making demands of any kind, "but it's not going to work here."

"It seems to be working okay," he said.

"I need to make a phone call."

"No."

"One phone call."

"No."

"She gets to keep her phone with her and I don't get to make one fucking call after ten hours in here? Eleven?"

"She's just waiting for a ride," Kowalski said. "Keep it down."

The girl, meanwhile, had pushed my raincoat onto the floor and stretched out on my bench.

"Can I use your phone?" I said.

She kept talking like she hadn't heard me either. "So *I* said, if she wanted to put her skank ass up in his face, she could just—" She stopped and stared at me. "*What?*"

"Can I please use your phone?" I said. "Please."

She blinked at me. "Yeah, I'm still here. Some trainwreck in here is, like, trying to steal my phone. *I know.*"

I paced from one end of the cell to the other and back, then stared into the throat of the toilet for a while, trying to decide if I was hungry or sick or actually dying. The floor was filthy but I grabbed my raincoat and curled on my side, my face buried in the still-damp lining. I could feel my pulse in my hands. Anything could have happened out there in eleven hours. I didn't know what to do.

Then my father was dragging me out of the house by the sleeve. Catherine started to open her car door, but Frank hip-checked it closed. "Don't rub it in my face," he hissed at me. I could almost taste the whiskey on his breath.

Then I was at his funeral, clinging to Andrew's arm while the spindly heels of my borrowed shoes sank into the muddy area around my father's grave. The officiant asked for a moment of silence and then, through the cold air, the crackle of radios and a voice rang out, clear and strong.

"Forty-one three oh one . . ."

My father's badge number. This was the last radio call, the tribute my mother had selected instead of a three-volley salute, not wanting to hear gunfire. Around me, a ring of faces contorting.

"Forty-one three oh one . . . Calling number forty-one three oh one . . .

"This is the last call for radio number forty-one three oh one.

"No response from Detective Frank Weary. The time is sixteen hun-

dred hours, February eighth. After thirty-eight years and four months of police service, radio number forty-one three oh one is ninety-seven on his final assignment. Forty-one three oh one is ten-seven forever. Rest in peace, brother. We'll take it from here."

My whole body hurt, like each word was a car accident.

And then it was two days after the funeral and I didn't have any food but I did have whiskey so I just went with that. Tom called ten times and I couldn't answer. I couldn't move. But then he was there, the front door still unlocked from when he had left. He climbed into my bed with me and embraced me from behind. "Can I just stay here with you for now? I don't know where else to go," he said, and I nodded that he could.

Crown Royal.

Crown Royal.

I wasn't sure if I was awake or not. A matronly female cop was unlocking the door for a bald guy in glasses and a rain-spattered trench coat. "Come on, Kira," he said.

"But I'm so tired," the brat who took my bench whined.

I sat up. My eyes were watering from the headache. I rubbed a hand over my face, temporarily forgetting about my cheekbone again. The sharp pain helped me focus. I cleared my throat. "Are you a lawyer?" I said.

Trench Coat looked at me warily. "Yes—"

"Because I've been in here since two o'clock yesterday afternoon," I said quickly, "and I haven't even been booked yet. I haven't been able to call anyone. Please help me."

The guy looked at me, then at the cop. Her eyes were wide.

"You haven't been *booked,* even?" she said.

I struggled to my feet. "No."

"Well," she said. "Well. Let me see what I can find out."

I'd heard that before. "Can I have my phone back, please?" I said.

"What?"

"She got to keep her phone. Can I at least have mine back?" I said.

"Kira, come on, please," Trench Coat was saying.

"I just had no idea this was going on back here," the cop said. "But it you weren't booked yet, why don't you have your phone?"

"He put it under the counter, in an envelope," I said.

She went around the corner while Trench Coat grabbed Kira's arm and pulled her to her feet.

I heard the cop set my revolver on the counter, muttering, "What the . . ." But she came back a second later and handed the phone to me and locked the cell door again after Trench Coat and Kira had made their way out. "I'm going to figure out what's going on, okay?" the cop said.

I sat down on my bench, cradling the phone like it was a precious artifact, which it was. I had six missed calls and a dozen texts but the battery was at four percent and I didn't waste power looking at them.

Instead I called Tom.

TWENTY-SEVEN

When the cell door opened again, it was after five in the morning and Jake Lassiter was scowling at me from the hallway. He looked rumpled and furious that he'd been woken up to deal with this. "You're free to go," he said.

I sat up shakily.

"You can collect the rest of your belongings at the front desk."

"Has Veronica been found?"

"You can collect the rest of your belongings at the front desk," he repeated. I assumed that to mean no. If she'd been located safe and sound, a guy like Lassiter would have relished telling me so.

"Is that all you have to say to me?" I said.

"It sure is," Lassiter said.

I didn't have the energy to deliver the lecture I'd fantasized about. I just brushed past him and out to the lobby, where Tom was sitting with his eyes closed. He looked like he was asleep, but he jumped up as soon as I walked in. "Hey," he said, giving me half of a smile. Then his expression hardened. "What happened," he said, tipping my head up gently with a knuckle under my chin as he studied my cheekbone.

"It's fine," I said quickly. His touch sent a sharp spiral of pain from my jaw down to my sternum. "I need to get out of here."

"Right, of course," he said.

I pushed outside into the rain and took a series of breaths so deep my lungs hurt, hoping I could breathe out all the tension. But I couldn't. I didn't feel any better and I didn't understand. Or maybe I did, which was worse.

"Are you all right?" Tom said.

"Yeah, yeah," I said quickly. Act normal. "I just—that was—thank you, Tom, really. What did you have to do? I hope I didn't cost you any favors."

"Oh, you know, I just had to make some empty threats, generally pretend I'm more important than I am," he said.

"Typical Wednesday."

"Typical Wednesday," he said. "Roxane, are you okay?"

"I'm fine," I said. "Just ready to be done with this portion of my day."

I followed him to his car and sank into the passenger seat, which felt like the clouds of heaven after fifteen hours in that cell. I pulled the seat belt across me and the buckle rattled in my trembling hands as I tried to fasten it.

Tom turned to me, touched my forearm. "You're shaking," he said.

"I'm fine," I said again, too quickly. "I think I'm just hungry," I added. I wasn't. My stomach felt like I had swallowed a bottle opener. "I haven't really eaten since Monday."

"Can I get you some breakfast?"

"No, no, that's okay," I said, "you've already done enough, coming down here in the middle of the freaking night."

"I don't mind," Tom said as we turned onto Clover. "I'm in urgent need of coffee anyway. Today's going to be rough."

I didn't want to have breakfast. I wanted to get back to my car, to the whiskey bottle that I had shoved under the passenger seat. "I thought cops were used to hours like this."

"Coffee willing," Tom said.

Inside the restaurant, I asked him to order me a cup of tea and the same as whatever he was having to eat. Then I went into the rest-room and locked the door, leaning against it as I tried to breathe evenly. I caught sight of my reflection and winced—my cheekbone was a swatch of black and blue, the cut red and angry. My skin was pale and my hair was tangled and greasy. I hadn't showered since Monday either. No wonder drunk Kira called me a trainwreck. I washed my hands and patted my face with a cool, damp paper towel.

An hour.

An hour, tops.

I could do that.

I went back into the restaurant and sat down across from him and gulped at the bitter black tea, then folded my hands in my lap so he couldn't see them shaking.

"Are you going to tell me what started all this?" Tom said.

I looked at him. I didn't want to talk about it. I didn't want to talk at all. I wanted to put my head down on the table and weep from ex-haustion and embarrassment. But Tom was in my corner, unlike the cops I'd been dealing with all night. "A girl is missing," I said. "She didn't come home Monday night. She's actually a friend of the daughter of that woman I had you pull case info on. Frank's case."

He leaned on his hand, watching me. "Okay."

"I know when we talked the other day, I was afraid I'd just found Sarah Cook's body, that Brad Stockton had led me right to it. But it wasn't her. It was another girl. She was thought to be a runaway, eight years ago. But she wasn't. Someone killed her. While Stockton was in prison."

The waitress brought our food, waffles and bacon and grits with a slick of neon yellow butter pooling on the top. I wanted to throw up. But I continued, "That made three girls—Frank's case, Sarah, and the body I found. Now a fourth, with this girl who didn't come home. It's been nearly thirty-six hours. And there's one guy who is con-nected to all of them, a piece of shit named Kenny Brayfield. But his parents paid for some city park in Belmont and now the police won't even listen when I try to bring it up."

Tom nodded, chewing. "So you got arrested for what, for criminal implying?"

I knew I was supposed to smile, so I did. "Well, that. While in the act of trying to see if I could fit through a fence."

He looked at me like I should know better, which I should have. Which I did. Or maybe I didn't. "Why?" he said.

I cut off a tiny piece of waffle and chewed it slowly but it was like a mouthful of sand. "I think he took this girl. Her name's Veronica. I think he took her and if she's not dead already, he's keeping her somewhere. The police don't care—"

"What's your evidence? I mean, it's a small town. I know you're a city girl but connections abound in places like this."

I looked up at the ceiling. I didn't have any evidence, not really. Just a bunch of anecdotes and Kenny Brayfield appearing on the security tape at the Varsity Lounge, which wasn't really proof of anything except the fact that he had been at that bar. I still had no clue where Sarah's parents fit in. But taken as a whole, the collection of anecdotes told a very convincing story. Right? Things were getting blurry. I wouldn't have been surprised to wake up and find myself at home in bed, or still in that cell, or ten years old, or dead.

Tom added, "I'm just saying, devil's advocate, without evidence, you might just come off like a lunatic calling a tip line, right? Police departments, especially small ones, don't like it when citizens try to tell them how to do their jobs."

That annoyed me a little. I was clearly aware of this point. "I'm not telling them they need to install a traffic signal in front of my church," I said, "I'm talking about a missing teenaged girl."

"No, I know, I get it. She's been gone how long?"

Then, on the table next to Tom's plate, his phone lit up.

He glanced down at it, and so did I. A text, from Pam G. *Is she okay?*

"You told her about this?" I said, my voice coming out harsh.

Tom looked surprised. "I did," he said. "I'm sorry—I didn't know it was top secret."

I sighed and shoved my plate away. "This is just—I hate that the first time she hears about me I'm calling you from jail."

"Well, it's hardly the first time she's heard about you," he said. "But it was a little hard not to tell her, I mean," he added, "I was at her place when you called. Like, sleeping."

Of course. I ran my hand over my face, forgetting about the bruise again. "Why did you answer the phone then?" I said.

"What?" Tom said. Now he looked confused. "I assume you wanted me to answer."

"Only if you weren't busy," I said. I didn't know what I would have done if Tom hadn't answered. But that did not seem important at this moment. "You're not supposed to answer the phone when someone you're fucking calls you, if you're in bed with someone else you're fucking."

His eyebrows went up. "Roxane, I seriously don't understand how you're mad at me."

"I'm not," I said. I tried breathing slowly but even that wasn't working now. I needed that drink. "I'm not. You're right. I did want you to answer. You can tell her I'm fine, I'm fucking fantastic."

He was looking at me like he could tell something wasn't right here. He was a detective, after all. "What happened?" he said. "Really."

"I need to get my car," I said, unable to deal. "Now. Can you give me a ride or should I call a cab?"

Tom let out a heavy sigh. But he pulled out his wallet and dropped a twenty on the table. "Let's go get your car."

We rode in silence through the dark, wet streets. The traffic lights made streaks in my vision like vapor trails. I knew I needed to say something, but my thoughts were a blank white square. As we pulled up behind my car on the access road, Tom said, "What are you going to do?"

"What am I going to *do*?" I repeated. "About what?"

"Well, you just told me you got arrested trying to sneak through a fence," he said, nodding at the wrought-iron fence caught in the glow of his headlights, "presumably this one, and I just want to make sure you aren't going to try that again."

I stared at him, irrationally annoyed at the implication that he had the power to *make sure* I did or didn't do anything at all. "Whatever I decide to do, it's not your problem."

He made a face. "I'm trying to help, here. That's not what I was saying. "

"No, it was," I said. I felt the tug of gravity in this conversation, a free-fall plummet. But I couldn't stop. "You think you get to give me a lecture because you got me out of a jam, is that it?"

"No—"

"Well, I don't need it. I don't need a lecture and I don't need any help. I don't even know why you answered the damn phone."

"*You* called me."

I put my head in my hands as he spoke.

"I don't know what this is really about, but I'm not playing a game with you. Don't call me if you don't want me to answer," he said. "Because I'm always going to."

"Stop it."

"If it makes you feel any better, it's because I promised."

"You didn't promise anything," I said to my lap.

"I promised Frank," he said after a minute, his voice softer. "I promised Frank. That I'd look out for you."

I took in his profile in the dashboard light for a second, my heart hammering in my head. The last person I wanted to hear about in this moment was my father. I got out of the car and steadied myself against the rain-dotted hood.

Tom opened his door and got out too. "Roxane, come on."

"You *promised*?" I said, spinning around. "What did you even promise? And when? He's bleeding to death and he asks you to *baby-sit* me? Is that what we've been doing for the last nine months?"

"No, of course not—"

"I don't need you to do me any favors, okay?" I said. "I can take care of myself."

"I know you can."

I was going to crawl out of my skin. "Then why are you throwing that in my face?"

His eyes were worried and confused and a little mad too. "I'm not throwing anything in your face," he said. "I'm concerned—you're not acting like yourself, you're honestly not making sense, and—"

I couldn't hear any more. "Thanks for whatever you said to them, at the police station," I said curtly. I fumbled through my pocket for my car keys, my hand shaking.

"Roxane, wait."

His voice made my chest hurt. I knew I was being unfair, but I didn't know how to stop. "Take care," I told him. I ignored the hand he skimmed along my arm as I walked over to the driver's side of my car. He didn't say anything else and neither did I.

There was a parking ticket on my windshield. I snatched it off and threw it into the ditch. Then I got into the car and felt for the bottle on the floor of the passenger seat, still aware of Tom's headlights shining on me. I ripped the cellophane off the top of the bottle, waiting for him to leave. I didn't dare look up into my rearview mirror. Finally, he pulled a three-point turn on the access road and went back down to Clover Road. I took a long swallow of whiskey and squeezed my eyes closed. I thought of the first time I'd ever tasted Crown Royal: I was nine, sneaking a sip from the liquor cabinet in the middle of the night, curious about what it was that my father liked so much better than all of us. It burned my throat and my gums, a forest fire that made me cough so hard I saw stars, so hard that I didn't hear my father coming down the steps to see what was going on. "You like that, huh?" he said, startling me. I expected him to be mad but he wasn't, just tiredly amused, probably still drunk himself. "Tastes nice and quiet, doesn't it?" he added. I didn't know what he meant by that at the time; there was nothing nice or quiet about the big, ugly flavor of that sip. He sent me back to bed after I swore not to ever touch anything in the liquor cabinet again, a promise I thought I'd have no trouble keeping even into adulthood. But at some point I forgot how gross I thought it was, and at some point after that I realized he was right. It did taste nice and quiet. It was the only thing that did. Now, in the car, I swallowed a little more and tried to pretend that everything would be okay.

For a second, I could almost believe it. The liquor was warm going down and it numbed everything it touched. Unfortunately, that didn't apply to my brain. Or to my white-hot anger, my anger at Tom, at the Belmont cops, Kenny, my father, myself, everyone, no one. I had no intention of driving anywhere yet, but I turned on the car and cranked the heater. I felt around in the dark for the cord to my phone charger and plugged the device in, but the screen told me it needed to charge before it would turn on. I dropped it onto the seat beside me in disgust.

And then I saw a figure dressed in black coming quickly down the hill toward me.

TWENTY-EIGHT

He opened a gate in the fence. I didn't have time to process the existence of this gate and how it might have changed what happened yesterday. I automatically shook my gun from its holster and was out of the car just as he reached me. "Take another step and I'll shoot you right here," I said, aiming at his chest. The gun, I realized, felt curiously light.

"Whoa," Kenny said. "Holy shit. What is that. No, I just—"

"Keep your hands where I can see them."

"Roxane, whoa, come on—"

"Do you think I'm kidding?" I said, stepping forward. "Because I'm not."

His thin face was white with fear. Real fear. "I just wanted to see if you were okay," he said.

That threw me. "What?"

"I was worried! I saw what happened yesterday," he said. "Like from the windows upstairs. You can see all the way down here." He gestured around atmospherically.

"What?" I said again. There was no space in my head to understand this. "You saw what happened. Me getting arrested."

"Yeah, I saw it, and I was like, I wasn't dressed yet. So by the time I got dressed and came out here to say it was okay, he didn't have to take you in, you were already gone. But I saw your headlights just now and I wanted to make sure you were all right."

I stared at him. This didn't exactly fit with my theory. But then again, Kenny had been fooling people for years. He hadn't fooled me though, which was why it felt strange that he seemed credible now. I'd already determined his poker face was shit. "Kenny," I said, trying to sound calm, "where is Veronica Cruz?"

"I don't *know* Veronica Cruz."

"Yeah, you do. You drive up and down her street. Providence Street."

His jaw bunched up. His eyes were still on my gun.

"Tell me what you're doing on Providence Street."

"Look, can you put that away?" He nodded at the gun.

"No. You need to start giving me some answers, Kenny."

He pressed his lips together in a thin, hard line. He didn't look angry. He looked afraid. Of me. "She hangs out around Mallory's daughter, right?" he said.

"You tell me."

"I've seen—shit, Roxane, do we have to do this?"

"Yeah, we do," I snapped, taking a step closer. "What do you know?"

"I don't know anything! I saw her on the news. Veronica. And I've seen her, with Mallory's daughter."

"How do you know Shelby?"

"I sometimes, I don't know, I just like to make sure everything's okay over there."

"What the hell are you talking about?"

"Can you please put that gun away?"

I had a suspicion that the cylinder of my revolver was empty anyway, but he didn't know that. I kept it where it was. "What are you talking about," I repeated.

We watched each other for a few seconds.

"When Mal told me she was pregnant," he said, more quietly, "I didn't react too well."

Oh my God, no. I felt like I was waking up from one of those dreams where you tumble off a bridge.

"I said, are you sure it's, you know, mine? Because there were a lot of guys, there was no getting around that. And I don't know how she could have known. But I still shouldn't have said it. She was coming to me for help. She wanted to get an abortion, like before anyone found out." He looked down at the muddy ground. "We argued and then I didn't see her for a while, she dropped out of school, and I heard she married that mechanic and they were going to have a family. And I just felt relief, okay, I was a junior in high school at that time, I didn't know shit."

I thought of Shelby and Joshua and how close they were. This was not happening.

"And eventually, Mallory came around again and we started, you know. Started back up with being together. She told me the guy, Josh, she said he was dumb as a box of hair but he loved the daylights out of that little girl. So she obviously made the right choice, going to him." Kenny wiped at his eyes. "I said I'd always, you know, support her. Them. If they needed it. I gave her money, but that usually went right to drugs. When she disappeared, she was using a lot. Heroin. I don't go there, I don't mess with that. And then she was just gone one day, she just didn't call me and she never picked up the phone when I tried to get her—I can't even tell you how many times I hung up on her husband, when he answered. I figured she needed a break, from, you know, life. She always had that free spirit thing going on."

"You're telling me you didn't know what happened to her."

"No, I had no idea. I thought she just took off. But I'd drive by that little house sometimes, though, during those few months when she was gone, and I'd see Josh and the little girl and they both looked so happy to be together, and that just made me feel good. Like *good*. If Mal and I had tried to raise a kid together—there was no way. There was no way anybody would turn out happy."

The free fall I'd felt when I was talking to Tom was far from over. I felt like I was only gaining velocity. "Why didn't you tell me any of this the other day?" If it's true, I added in my head. Although my arm was beginning to tremble, I kept the gun trained on him.

"Because I don't like talking about it," he said. "Shit, I'm sure you can see why."

"You never talked to the cops investigating her death. Did you?" I guessed.

He shook his head. "The lawyer told me not to."

I rubbed my forehead with my free hand. "The lawyer."

"Mort. Uncle Mort. I mean, I told my dad first, that I knew Mallory. Then he had me tell the lawyer."

It took a certain kind of family, I thought, to have a lawyer named Mort, let alone one close enough to be called *uncle*. "What did you tell him?" I said.

"I told him that we used to hang out, get high, you know, that kind of stuff. And he had me talk to Mr. Lassiter, who told me to just keep that to myself."

"The police chief just kept that secret for you?"

"My dad and him, they go way back," Kenny said. "He's kept me out of a lot of trouble, over the years. And listen, it's not like I feel good about this. It fucking *haunts* me, what happened to Mallory."

This really could not be happening. I wasn't sure which was worse: that Lassiter had the nerve to jam me up for interfering with an investigation when he was clearly capable of the same, or that after everything in the last twenty-four hours, I was starting to believe what Kenny was telling me.

"Talk to me about Colleen Grantham."

He shook his head. "I didn't know her, Curt's only been working for me for a year. I didn't know he had another daughter. I've met his other two, but not Colleen."

"Where did you go Monday night? During the game."

"I had to check on some displays, I told you that. I went to this bar, the Varsity Lounge. And to Kroger, it's in the same plaza, and to the liquor store on Clover. I needed to make sure they had the right displays set up because my client, the owner of the vodka company, he was coming to town yesterday to have dinner with my dad, and they wanted to check it out."

I lowered the gun slowly, unable to keep my arm up anymore. Kenny visibly relaxed. I didn't know what to think of any of this, the way he seemed to have an answer for everything all of a sudden. But he was no longer tripping any of my shiftiness detectors the way he had been before. "Why do you still drive down Mallory's street?" I said. I snapped out the cylinder of the revolver and saw that it was indeed empty. I wondered which of the Belmont cops had relieved me of my bullets.

He rubbed a hand over his face. "I don't know," he said. "It's like, I just like seeing her kid. She looks exactly like Mallory. Like exactly. And I like knowing that she's okay. It makes me feel, I don't know, calmer. Please, you have to believe me. I'm sorry I didn't tell you all this the other day, and I'm sorry my dad called Mr. Lassiter and set all of this in motion. But I am telling you the truth. And if I could help you find that girl, Veronica, I would. I would help you in a second."

"You didn't see her when you were at the Varsity Lounge."

"No."

"You didn't drive down that street on Monday night."

"No."

"How did you know the body in the woods was Colleen Grantham?"

"Mr. Lassiter," Kenny said. "He came and told my dad, because my dad's an investor in the apartment development back there. He thought he had a right to know, before it came out in the news."

I sagged against my car, barely feeling the damp, cold metal.

I wondered if Lassiter had told Mr. Brayfield before he even told Colleen's parents. There was not a single person in this story who came out looking good. I finally said, "Kenny, you can never tell anyone what you told me. About Mallory's daughter. *Never.* Joshua Evans is her father."

"I know that."

"I mean it."

"I know."

I opened the car door. "I will destroy you if you ever say anything."

He nodded at me like he believed me. And although it was the last thing I wanted to admit, I was pretty sure I believed him now too.

My phone, now that it was powered up, told me Joshua Evans had been three of the six missed calls and five of the texts. Shelby was two of the calls and the rest of the texts. No real news, just a handful of operational updates—such as the Amber Alert—followed by apologies for bugging me. Danielle Stockton was the sixth call, a detail I could not consider at the moment. No calls from the unknown number while I was in the cell, a small blessing. I drove back to Providence Street and parked in front of the Evanses' house. It was just before eight. Joshua's car was still in the driveway. A light was on in the living room. I hoped he hadn't been up all night. He answered the door about two seconds after I knocked, as if he had been waiting for hours for someone to show up. At first he looked relieved that it was only me, but then he looked confused as he took in my face. "What happened to you?" he said.

"I'm sorry for the radio silence," I said. "I got arrested."

"What . . . ?"

"It's a long story. But I hope I didn't add to your stress."

"No, I just wasn't quite sure what to think," Joshua said. "You were here, and then you weren't."

"I'm sorry. I was trying to help."

We looked at each other. It seemed like he had indeed been up all night, his eyes bleary but wild. He was wearing a too-tight Ohio State sweatshirt with a coffee stain on the front. "There isn't anything new," he said softly. "Last night, there were police all over the block, talking to everyone. A neighbor down the way thinks he saw her cutting through to go to the Wildflower Plaza, but that's the last anybody saw. The police have been real helpful, real on top of it. Amy Wexford's in bad shape, though." He shook his head. "I can't even imagine, your kid missing."

My face burned. *This man is her father,* I repeated in my head. "I know," I said. I didn't know how anyone could think the police were doing a good job here. But I didn't want to take that small comfort away from him. Not when I had nothing to replace it with. "Is Shelby at school?"

"No, she's in the shower. I told her she didn't have to go to school. Just thinking about what you said, to keep her nearby. We're going to go out, put up some flyers. We did some last night, but Shel's been making a list of other places Veronica likes to go. You, uh, you're welcome to come with us," he finished.

It broke my heart, the way he said it. The way he still thought I could help them. I wanted to stay, even if I couldn't help. But I could only make things worse at this point, what with the entire police force hating my guts. I needed to go home and regroup and try to figure out another connection between the girls. A real connection this time. "I can't," I said, and he nodded quickly, embarrassed. "I just wanted to check on you guys this morning. But can I take some flyers?"

"Sure, yeah, yeah," Joshua said. He went into the kitchen for a beat and then returned with a stack of printouts. *MISSING.* Below the headline, Veronica smiled out from the same picture Shelby had given me yesterday, the one with the ceramic turkey.

We both looked at the photo. Everything about it looked impossibly normal.

Except Veronica was gone.

She was gone, and I was here. It didn't seem fair.

"Keep me posted," I told him.

But on the street, a Belmont cruiser was parked next to my car. "What do you want?" I snapped at the street, although I couldn't see who was inside the car. If it was Jake Lassiter, I was going to scream.

But the door opened and Meeks got out, holding his hands up like *calm down.* "I didn't call this in yet—"

"Call in what?" I crossed the lawn in a few strides. "Is there no *parking* on this street? Tell me what the fuck you could possibly call in."

He looked slightly afraid of me. "You can't be here. Lassiter is adamant that you be arrested on the spot for disorderly conduct. And charged, this time."

Disorderly conduct was a blanket charge that covered any number of wrongdoings. Still a fourth-degree misdemeanor. But the Belmont police clearly weren't just talk where it came to their misdemeanors. I felt my teeth grinding together. "I just want to find this girl."

"I know. But listen, so do we."

I shook my head, smiling out of disbelief.

"We do, Miss Weary," Meeks said. "There's an Amber Alert. We're checking area hospitals, jails, bus stations, you name it. We are on top of it. The best thing you can do for Veronica Cruz is just leave us to it, okay? Every cop in town is looking for her. We don't need to waste time looking for you too."

"That's on your boss, not on me," I said, but the meaning of his words was clear. And I realized that he was right. It was absurd that

Lassiter was doing this, but I couldn't deny that he was. Even the three minutes we'd been talking here meant three minutes Meeks hadn't spent on Veronica. I didn't think it was possible to feel worse, but I did.

"We will find her," Meeks said. "I promise."

He couldn't promise that, not to me, not to anyone. I got into my car without saying anything else.

TWENTY-NINE

I slept all day. When I woke it was after six and my room was dark. The experience in the jail cell seemed crazy enough to be a dream, but it wasn't. I hurt all over. But I got out of bed and checked my phone, running a quick Google search to see if Veronica had come home. She hadn't. I sighed. Then I pulled on clean clothes, because I was due at my mother's house for our weekly dinner.

I made a point of not looking at the cardboard square still taped to the front door as I walked down the hall. I would deal with it at some point—soon—but not right now. In the bathroom I considered my cheekbone in the mirror, my seldom-used makeup bag in hand. Then I decided not to bother. The bruise was too big to effectively conceal with makeup, and the cut was still painful to the touch. The rest of my face was pale. I dragged a brush through my hair, which was tangly and strange because I'd gotten directly into bed after taking a shower. I would be impressing nobody tonight. But my family, now that my father was gone, could be counted on to accept me more or less as I came.

Or so I thought. When I walked into the house, it was clear that this was not the place to be if I wanted to take my mind off my problems. Matt was parked on the couch and barely looked up from ESPN, while I could hear my mother's and Andrew's raised voices from the other room.

"I don't see why you can't just leave it!" my mother was saying. "How many times do I ask you for anything?"

"Are you happy now?" Matt muttered.

"Me?" I said.

"Yes, you," he said.

"What's the difference?" Andrew said. "Nobody else is going to drink it."

"Oh," I said, realizing what was going on: Andrew must have freed the liquor stash from the office.

Matt looked up at me now. "What happened to your face?" he said.

"I tripped." I dropped my coat on a chair and went into the kitchen. "Hey, Mom."

"Hello," my mother said, voice cool.

"Jesus, what happened to you, Rox?" Andrew said.

"Watch your language!" my mother said, but then she looked at me and gasped. "Honey, what happened?"

"It's okay, it's nothing," I said. "I tripped and fell, it looks worse than it is."

"That's almost never true," Andrew murmured to me, which was correct. I met his eye. He flicked his glance at the source of all the present trouble, the Midleton bottle on the table, and I nodded.

My mother turned back to the stove in a huff. "Did you see a doctor?" she said.

"No," I said, impatient, "it's just a cut."

"Just a cut," she said, "Roxie, you could need plastic surgery!"

"No one *needs* plastic surgery," Matt called from the living room. "That's a total vanity procedure."

"What, are you going to med school now?" Andrew called back. "Shut up."

"And where did you fall?" my mother said. She turned around again, brandishing a wooden spoon at us. "And didn't you try to catch yourself?"

Matt appeared in the doorway to the kitchen. "Were you drinking, when this happened?" he said, watching as Andrew poured the Midleton into a rocks glass and passed it to me.

"No."

"Sure."

"Matt," I said flatly. "Don't worry about it." I brought the glass to my lips.

"Are you sure you want to drink that?" Matt said. "Because you never have to take another—"

"Jesus, shut the fuck *up*," Andrew snapped.

"Language!" my mother said.

"Thanks, all, for your concern," I said, downing half the whiskey, "I was out for a hike and I tripped on a branch, okay? The subject is now closed."

"A hike?" Andrew said.

I spun at him. "Please, don't you start with me too," I snapped.

He looked a little shocked. I never snapped at Andrew. I held up a hand in silent apology.

My mother made ham and green beans and crescent rolls for dinner, one of the five or so meals in heavy rotation from when I was growing up. She had always wanted to be more creative in the kitchen, as evidenced by the series of ethnic cookbooks she checked out of the library all the time, but my father liked things a certain way. My mother still read the cookbooks, but to my knowledge she hadn't cooked anything new since he died.

I didn't blame her for not wanting anything to change where Frank was concerned—not the sink, not the food, not the liquor—but I didn't understand it.

Like I was ten years old again, I pushed soggy green beans around on my plate and listened to the conversation going on around me. I kept hoping my phone would ring, but it didn't. My mother reported that she'd invited Tom to dinner and he said he might try to make it later, which sounded like the worst thing possible right now. Meanwhile, my brothers argued blandly with each other, all of us in a petty bad mood tonight. "I'm telling you, Trabue Road turns into Renner at Hilliard-Rome," Matt was saying.

"No, it's east of there," Andrew said. "Your sense of direction is fucking terrible—remember how you got us so lost going to Michelle Lindstrom's party that one time?"

"I didn't get us lost—you wrote down the address wrong because you were stoned."

"Oh, please," Andrew said, "I didn't even have her address, she was your friend."

"You were stoned."

"It turns into Renner *east* of Hilliard-Rome, Matt."

This had been going on for ten minutes. What started as a discussion on where the Test Pavements were playing that weekend had devolved into a meaningless rehash of every other argument they'd ever had.

Veronica was gone and my brothers were fighting about nothing.

"Why are you even arguing about this?" I said. "It's objectively one way or the other. Look it up."

"You drive all over the city, which is it?" Andrew asked me.

Matt scoffed. "She's obviously going to agree with you," he said.

"Did you put some bacitracin on it, at least?" my mother chimed in, still worried about the scrape on my cheekbone. "That could really scar."

"Yes," I lied.

"Because I have some, in the first-aid kit upstairs."

I took a deep breath. "Mom, I'm fine."

"I don't even understand why you were out hiking, the weather's been terrible," she said.

It had not been the greatest of cover stories, I realized now.

Matt and Andrew had their heads bent over one of their phones, the former looking pissed. "Well, whatever," he said, as if it no longer mattered now that he'd been proved wrong.

"I'm sure the Test Pavements will be so devastatingly brilliant that I'll forget all about this," Andrew said.

"Shut up," Matt told him. "I don't even want you guys there."

"Come on, Matt," my mother said. "We're *all* going to be there. Right, Roxie?"

"Can't wait," I said flatly.

"Oh," Matt said, tapping at his phone. "I talked to Danielle today."

"Okay?" I said. How perfect it would be, I thought, if after everything, my brother had been instructed to fire me. I pulled out my own phone, thinking maybe I'd accidentally switched it to silent. I hadn't. But I saw a missed call from Tom and dropped the phone facedown on the table.

"She's been trying to get ahold of you, I guess. And you never called her back."

I sighed. "It's on my list for tomorrow."

"Isn't that sort of unprofessional?" Matt said. "To wait that long?"

I wanted to stab him with a bread knife. "Matt, thanks for your concern for how I run my business, but you don't know anything about it."

"I know that. I also know that I referred her to you and instead of helping her, you're just getting shit-faced with people she went to high school with? She told me one of her friends met you at some party and you were practically incoherent. I should have known better. Aren't you getting a little old for that?"

I wanted to tell him that helping Danielle was the least of my concerns at the moment. "Why did you refer her to me at all then, if you should have known better?" I said.

"Because you used to be good at it," he said.

A tense silence settled over the table. I took another deep breath, about to let it go and continue pushing my food around on my plate.

But then I couldn't. "You know what," I said, "Matt, you're right. It's unprofessional. I'm going to go call Danielle back right this minute. Thanks for dinner, Mom."

"Oh Roxie," my mother said, "he didn't mean anything by that, please, sit down, your brother's just worried about you."

I gave her a quick hug and walked out, adding Matt to the list of people I was currently, acutely mad at. Even though he was right. It wasn't just something to say, either. I'd always been preternaturally good at finding things and finding things out, even as a kid, and Matt had benefited more than once. A wallet, the name of a girl he liked at the Y. Later: a witness to a hit-and-run car accident that left him with a broken leg, a stolen bike for one of his girlfriends. It was the only thing I was ever good at. And I'd been successful, until I wasn't anymore. Until my father died and I forgot how to do my job at exactly the moment when I needed most to do it well.

Outside I pulled my coat on, feeling startled by myself, like an animal spooked by its own reflection. I needed to put Veronica Cruz out of my mind. It didn't matter, I tried telling myself. I didn't know her. I didn't know Shelby or Joshua. They were just people I'd come across on a case. Veronica probably just ran away. She had big dreams—fashion design, getting out of town. She described Belmont as a shithole, after all. That's all this was. I started walking down the street to my car, but then Andrew called my name.

I turned around and said nothing.

He was lighting a cigarette. "Seriously," he said. "What's going on?"

I opened my mouth, then closed it. I didn't know where to start. "I'm just not in the mood for his sober-living bullshit tonight," I said instead, wondering for maybe the first time ever if Matt actually had a point.

Andrew kindly let me off the hook. "Yeah, he's in rare form," he said. "Before you got here, I wanted to beat him with that Midleton bottle. She didn't even see me bring it down, but of course Matt finked on me."

"You know she's going to pour every drop of it down the sink later," I said.

"If I don't get any," Andrew said, in a decent approximation of my father's voice, "nobody gets any."

It wasn't even funny but I laughed, a sad, quiet laugh that made me feel like my ribs were imploding.

"That sink," my brother said next. He pulled out a wallet and counted out seven hundred-dollar bills. "Here. Paid in full."

"You only have to cover half," I said.

"Don't worry about it," Andrew said. "You can make an appointment for the plastic surgeon on me. Listen, do you want to get into something?"

"Like what?"

"Food, maybe, since you didn't eat America's Bounty in there."

"We should probably go back in."

"No, no, we already made it out," he said. "Besides, you don't want to risk being there if Tom shows up, do you?"

I cleared my throat. For the first time, I shared Andrew's feelings about that. "Not a chance," I said.

We went to Little Palace and sat at the bar. I ordered the fried chicken sandwich and a side of mac and cheese and a whiskey on the rocks. The food was good and greasy and made me feel slightly more human. It was pleasantly loud and crowded in the restaurant, and no one looked twice at my cheekbone.

"I knew I should've said no to this case," I said. "I had a weird feeling at the beginning."

"I remember," Andrew said. "You told me you thought it might turn into something, and you were afraid you'd mess it up."

"And I did."

"What have you messed up?" Andrew said. "Other than Matt's imaginary chances with this Danielle."

I pointed to my eye. "In a development that will shock no one," I said, "this did not happen while hiking."

Andrew smiled. "I'm scandalized," he said. "So are you going to tell me?"

"I got arrested."

"What, for getting into a brawl at that party?"

"Trespass," I said. "And, resisting arrest, I guess. That's where this comes in."

My brother stopped smiling. "Shit," he said. "A cop did that to you?"

"Belmont police," I said, "yeah."

"Shit," he said again. "What did you do, exactly?"

"I *was* trespassing," I said. "But the reason I was there, the thing I thought could have happened—I don't even think it happened now, and it had nothing to do with Matt's friend even if it did. So I wasted ten days, got my ass kicked, and I didn't solve shit. That's what I messed up." And a seventeen-year-old girl has been missing for forty-eight hours, I didn't say. That wasn't my fault, but I sure as hell hadn't helped.

"Did you file a complaint?"

I just looked at him.

"Well, don't let old Test Pavement rattle your confidence, Rox. If he knew you got hurt while you were working on this, you know he'd feel terrible."

I didn't care if Matt felt terrible or not. "You're never going to get over the name, are you?"

"The Test Pavements. No. Never. It's the single greatest slash worst thing I've ever heard. I cannot wait till Friday."

"Yeah, well, I'm not going," I said.

"Yes, you are."

"I don't want to drive all the way out to Trabue *or* Renner Road."

"I'll drive you, then. It'll be great. And he didn't mean it, what he said."

"Why are you defending him?"

Andrew finished his drink too. "You have to forgive people for being who they are," he said. "Otherwise you'll just make yourself crazy. Do you want to do another here, or do you want to go somewhere else? Guy from the hotel is doing a poker night tonight."

Veronica was gone and we were talking about poker. "I don't like cards, you know that."

"We'd clean up," Andrew said. "He's an idiot."

I shook my head and chewed the rest of my ice. I wanted something else to happen, some other kind of stimulation I could stuff into my brain to stop the looping thoughts about Shelby, her father, Veronica, the assholes of the Belmont police department whom I had no choice but to trust to find her. If she wanted to be found at all. Which she probably didn't. Right? She was probably in Manhattan by now, eating a vegan cronut and doodling in her sketch book. "Let's go to this party I heard about," I said.

"Whose party?"

I looked down at the smear of mayonnaise on my empty plate. "Friend of Catherine's," I said.

Andrew didn't say anything right away. "So she's a thing again, then," he said.

"No," I said. "I don't know."

"You really want to go to a party looking like you just got mugged?"

"Oh, whatever, a minute ago you wanted me to go to a stranger's poker game."

"Roxane, you're a grown-ass woman and you can do whatever you want," he said, "but you're also my baby sister and I worry about you.

Catherine isn't a good person. I mean, she's just not. She's a selfish cunt."

I didn't argue that. "What about forgiving people for being who they are?" I said.

"*If* you were to subscribe to that all of a sudden," he said, "Catherine Walsh is not the one you should start with."

"Well, I'm going," I said. It was a bad idea. But I wanted Saturday night again, a switch flipping on to make me okay. I needed it. "Do you want to come or what? There's bound to be plenty of borderline-personality art school girls there."

My brother sighed and dropped a fifty on the bar. "How can I resist that," he said.

The condo at the Dakota was one of those lofts with high ceilings and exposed ductwork and beautiful, uncomfortable furniture that looked like it was looted from a Swedish train station. Neither of us needed anything else to drink but Andrew procured us some and we sat on a low leather ottoman near the windows, people-watching. There were lots of tattoos, experimental haircuts, and drapey black garments in attendance. The crowd a mix of art people—the ones standing near the twelve-by-fifteen-foot vagina painting on the wall and discussing its composition—and hipster lesbians—the ones discussing who the owner of said vagina might be. The consensus was that it belonged to Thao's fiancée, who was presently in LA on a grant for building a public sculpture out of reclaimed plastic flatware, though there were murmurings that it could be Thao's teaching assistant. I assumed Thao was the hostess. I saw a few people I sort of knew and collected two condolences about my father, plus one inexplicable compliment on my hair.

I didn't see Catherine.

Classic.

"If she was a guy," Andrew was saying, "you'd write him off as a complete dick so fast. You'd never put up with it. This is boring."

I rolled my eyes at him. "Oh, so I'm being sexist?" I stood up and held a hand out for his empty cup. "I'm getting us a refill and then we can go."

He nodded, looking tired. But as soon as I walked away, a redhead in a sequined bustier and satin pants sat down in my spot, and Andrew's mood appeared to improve. I went into the kitchen and found the bottles but I felt a hand between my shoulder blades before I could pour.

"There you are," Catherine said in my ear.

I turned around to face her. She was wearing a claret-colored dress that brought out the green of her eyes and she smelled like whiskey and clove cigarettes. If anyone could take my mind off the Belmont situation, it would be Catherine. Or so I hoped. "I was starting to think this was some kind of trap. When did you get here?"

Her eyebrows went up slightly when she saw my face. "I've been here," she said. "I was upstairs. What happened to you?"

"The first rule of Fight Club," I said. We looked into each other's eyes. Hers were bottomless. Everything seemed off-kilter, like a dream where you're in one place that looks like somewhere else. "What's upstairs?"

"Quiet," Catherine said. She nodded at the two cups in my hands. "Make a friend already?"

"Andrew came with me," I said.

She laughed that big laugh of hers. "You brought your brother to this? Christ, you need to get a life."

Andrew was right about her, per usual. "That's a shitty thing to say."

She poured whiskey into the cups I was holding and took one of them, tossing it back quickly. "Drink up," she said. "And come on. I want to introduce you."

I looked out at the ottoman where Andrew and I had been sitting; it was now vacant. Andrew and the redhead were over by the vagina painting, and he met my eye and winked.

I followed Catherine out of the kitchen toward the balcony, which looked like it might have been occupied past fire code, twelve or so women crowded into a space the size of a bathtub. The center of attention was an Asian woman with bluish hair and white plastic-framed glasses and an elaborate tattoo peeking out from the V-neck of her paint-spattered T-shirt. When she saw Catherine through the window, she pushed out of the pack and reentered the apartment.

Catherine said, "Thao, Roxane. My first true love."

"Dude, the famous Roxane from Saint Bleeding Heart's or whatever," Thao said, taking my hand in both of hers. She had good collarbones, a good, wry smile.

"I thought the two of you might get along," Catherine said. I was confused for a second. Was this a fix-up? To puzzle me further, she linked her arm through mine, the curve of her hip pressed against my elbow.

"Cat always thinks everyone will get along," Thao said, which was the truth. "And ten minutes later, someone's sobbing in the elevator. You look like an interesting type, though."

"Thao, you should get your camera," Catherine said. "Wouldn't Roxane be perfect for the series?"

"No," I said. I didn't know what she was talking about. But if there was a camera involved, I wasn't interested.

"Ah, you're one of those girls who hates having her picture taken," Thao said.

"Thao's doing these great portraits," Catherine said. "Large format, straight-on angles. Think Richard Avedon, except naked dykes."

I almost choked on my drink. "I thought you were a painter," I said.

Thao grinned at me.

"No," I said again.

"You think you hate getting your picture taken. But getting, like, a driver's license photo taken isn't the same as really being photographed," she said.

"I'm sure there are plenty of other people here who'd love the attention," I said. I swallowed the rest of the whiskey in my cup. It wasn't helping me forget about Veronica. It wasn't doing anything.

"Oh, it's not about attention," Thao said. She brushed my hair away from my cheekbone. "It's about telling the truth. What happened here?"

"I jumped out of a moving vehicle," I said, and they both laughed.

"Maybe you could do us together," Catherine said.

Thao nodded. "Hold that thought," she said. She took my empty cup and headed for the kitchen. "This calls for more liquor."

I looked at Catherine. "Is this why you invited me?" I said. "Some fucked-up art project?"

"No, of course not," she said. "But then here you are, looking all scrappy and hot?" She slipped her hands inside my leather jacket. "So sue me." Then she pulled away, her eye on something over my shoulder. "Andrew, hi," she said.

I turned around. My brother was holding his car keys and the redhead was behind him, pulling on her coat. "Are you cool if I go?" Andrew said.

"Yeah, of course," I said. "She looks fun."

He raised an eyebrow. "We'll see," he said. "Hey, call me tomorrow?"

"To let you know I survived?"

"She'll survive," Catherine said.

Andrew squeezed my shoulder, then walked away without saying a word to her.

"Wow," she said. "What's his deal?"

But Thao returned with my drink and thrust it at me. I had the distinct feeling that once again, the evening was getting away from me. Catherine slipped her hands back into my jacket. I closed my eyes and focused on her touch, like maybe enough contact with her could erase my memory. And I kept drinking. I didn't know what else to do.

THIRTY

I woke at seven in a room thick with darkness. My limbs felt like I had spent the night folded into a metal suitcase. I ran a hand over my face and winced when I touched my cheekbone. I wasn't sure where I was. I heard kitchen noises coming from far away and quietly got out of the bed. I didn't feel hungover so much as fragmented, like half of my thoughts had been forcibly removed from my head. My throat was raw. I looked at my phone but the battery was dead again. My jeans were inside out on the floor, shed like a skin. I was still wearing my shirt. I looked through the open doorway and saw another bedroom with the door closed, an alarm clock bleating, ignored, inside. Over the metal railing, the lower level of the loft looked like the scene of a disaster movie, so many plastic cups and paper napkins and a smear of something on the wall by the vagina painting that was either hummus or vomit. A woman with long black hair was passed out on the ottoman, snoring faintly. Catherine was in the kitchen drinking coffee and her dress was unzipped. I pulled on my jeans and boots and went down the spiral staircase.

"Good morning," I said.

She smiled but it didn't touch her eyes. She had always been like this, all over me one minute, then struck down by the blackest of moods the next. "You were totally out up there," she said. "I was surprised you stayed."

I thought that was a strange thing to say. "She stayed," I said, pointing to the snoring girl. "You stayed."

"Um, yeah, I did," she said like I was stupid.

"So what, ah, happened?"

Catherine looked at me. "Funny," she said.

I shook my head, grabbing on to the counter for stability as I did so. "Seriously," I said.

"Seriously, I think you drink too much if you don't even fucking remember. Thanks for coming. We had a good time."

I felt my face getting hot. I looked at her in the thin morning light. Her eyeliner was smudged and her hair was tangled and standing there in this big, modern kitchen, she could have been anyone.

We.

That *we* wasn't Catherine and me. It was Catherine and Thao.

It made sense, all of a sudden.

I fumbled with the zipper of my jacket. I needed to not be in this apartment anymore. I should have known better than to think that Catherine could fix anything. I gave up on the zipper. My hands were shaking too much. "You couldn't have said something?" I said.

Catherine set down her coffee mug and it clattered against the granite countertop. "What does that mean?"

I stared at her in disbelief. "It means the other night, I asked you where your husband was, if you'd stoop to having dinner with me," I said. "I guess the more relevant question is where Thao was."

"Don't get mad," Catherine said. "The other night was great. Last night was great. Either way, I'm attached. So what's the difference?"

She knew exactly what I meant. I could see it in her eyes. "The difference," I said, even though I knew I shouldn't bother, "is last year you said you wanted to work on things with him."

"Yeah."

"And I said when you were done with all that, come find me."

"Yeah."

"And you said you would," I said. "But instead you found her? You're choosing her? How long has this been going on?"

"It's been a few months." She folded her arms over her chest. "And I don't know what you're talking about, *choosing*. Come on, Roxane, you know how things are. It's not like you and I owe each other anything."

It sounded a little like what I'd told Tom last week, except I liked it less when it was directed my way, and especially when I realized in both cases it was about sleeping with someone other than me. I blinked hard. "This is perfect," I said. I felt every second of the last forty-eight hours pressing down on my heart. "Why would you invite me here?"

She picked up her coffee cup again. "I wanted to see you." Her tone was infuriatingly innocent.

"You don't get to want that," I snapped at her. "Not when you don't give me all the information."

She laughed, like anything could possibly be funny. "Oh, you," she said. "Trying to tell me what I'm allowed to want."

I turned around and walked out.

No one chased after me this time.

After a forty-minute shower and two cups of tea, I still wasn't ready to face things. I lay in bed with the blinds drawn. I wanted to sleep for a year and wake up sober and entirely happy. But I couldn't even sleep for five minutes. Finally I looked at my phone and considered the damage from the past day.

Calls from: Danielle (confused), Marisa (concerned, having heard from Kenny about what happened to me), Danielle again (annoyed),

Tom (concerned/apologetic), Matt (inviting me to an AA meeting with him), my mother (with the phone number of her dermatologist), Joshua (no update), Shelby (no message). The unknown number remained silent.

Even it had determined that I had no next move, that I proved no threat to anyone.

I stared at the stars on my ceiling, willing them to tell me what to do. Either they didn't know, or they weren't saying. Finally I got up and took my tea into the office and called Danielle.

"I'm sorry for the delay in getting back to you," I told her. "I have no excuse. But it won't happen again."

"Listen, Roxane," she said. "I don't think this is working out."

I pressed the heel of my hand against my forehead. "Danielle—"

"It's nothing personal, really," she said, "and I don't mean to be judgmental about whatever, um, problems you might have. But my brother is running out of time. Literally. He doesn't have any time to waste. I hired you to help him, and instead you spent the last week trying to pin some other shit on him?"

So she'd finally talked to her brother. I felt my face get hot again, even though I was alone. "I wasn't trying to *pin* anything on Brad," I told her. I stood up and paced the length of the hallway. "I was trying to figure out how these events were connected. In my line of work, you have to explore everything. Even when it looks ugly. Even when it's the opposite of what you set out to do. I know—"

"No, I don't think you do." Danielle cleared her throat. "Brad had Columbus police detectives in to visit him the other day, about that Mallory Evans girl you asked me about. They didn't just spontaneously decide to revisit that."

Fuck you, Tom, I thought unfairly.

"So I can't work with you anymore," she finished. "That's all I wanted to say."

I couldn't even argue with her. I walked back to the office, once again refusing to look at the square of cardboard on the front door. "Okay."

That seemed to throw her a little. "Okay?"

"I'm sorry, Danielle," I said. "I don't know what else to tell you. You didn't see Sarah Cook at the gas station that night. I thought I could find another way in to helping out your brother, but I can't. I don't know what happened. I don't know where else I can look. You should hire someone else, some ex-military guy with a buzz cut and an illustration of a shooting-range target on his business card and maybe he'll have some entirely conventional approach with better results. And don't hold this against my brother. He's nothing like me."

I hung up and went back to the bedroom. But instead of getting back under the covers, I leaned against the doorframe for a while. I had no idea how I had gotten here: what started as a search for a potential witness to a very old case had turned into a missing teenager, circa now. Along the way I had two viable suspects that were, in retrospect, not all that viable. I'd lied to Sarah's cousin and wound up with a broken window as punishment. I'd never been able to make sense of the Cook murders at all, which was the very thing I set out to resolve. I'd made a series of connections that maybe didn't exist, that could too easily be chalked up to small-town syndrome. Maybe too much time had passed to be able to prove anything either way. Maybe none of it was connected in the first place. Maybe the woods below Clover Point were a notorious dumping ground for murderers across the entire Midwest because of the indistinct jurisdictions and general isolation.

But the blue tarp.

The image of the bones rose into my mind.

It almost didn't make a difference if any of it was connected, not anymore, I tried to tell myself. Mallory and Colleen and Sarah's parents were still dead, even if no one ever figured out what really happened.

Except that wasn't true. Of course it mattered. It mattered to Brad and Danielle. And it mattered to Veronica and Shelby and Joshua.

And really, it mattered a whole hell of a lot to me.

THIRTY-ONE

Shelby was making grilled-veggie sandwiches for lunch when I got to their house. "I have an extra one," she said, "are you hungry?"

"Sure, that sounds great, thank you," I said. It was warm in the house, and I took off my leather jacket and hung it from the back of a chair at the dining table.

"Guess you had a feeling she was coming, huh, Shel?" Joshua said.

Shelby didn't say anything. We looked at each other and I could tell that the sandwich was really for Veronica, a hopeful, hopeless gesture. "It's probably not going to be very good," she said. "We're out of garlic and he wouldn't let me go to the store to get more. So the flavor is like nothing."

"Shelby," her father said, an uncharacteristic note of warning in his voice. To me, he added, "She's getting a little stir-crazy."

Shelby slammed a skillet down on the stove. "Stop *saying* that. God," she said, brushing past us on her way out of the kitchen. A beat later, her bedroom door slammed.

Joshua shook his head. He hadn't changed his shirt from yesterday and it looked like he still hadn't slept. "She's never like this," he said. "But she hates me right now. I wouldn't let her go to work at the restaurant. I wouldn't let her go to the store, I wouldn't let her go make more copies. She acts like that means I don't care about Veronica, but of course I do. She's practically another daughter to me, that girl. The police said there's nothing we can do except stay safe ourselves."

"I know."

"I'm sick over this."

"I know."

"Shelby doesn't remember her mom," he added. "So it's like something that didn't happen to her. But it happened to me. I remember. And this—I just—" He stopped and brought his fist down on the table, hard enough to knock over his beer bottle. It was empty, but it rolled onto the floor where it clinked against something. Glancing over his shoulder, I saw quite the collection of empties in a brown paper bag.

So that was why he hadn't just driven her to the store for more garlic. *This man is her father,* I reminded myself, my chest tight.

"Joshua," I said, "if Shelby wants to make copies, I'll go with her. It might be good for the two of you, to have a little space. You don't need to be at odds with each other at a time like this. She'd be safe with me." And I'd reloaded my revolver, I thought but did not say.

"Oh, you don't have to do that. I know you have your own life." But there was gratitude in his eyes.

"I'd be happy to," I told him. "Really."

He nodded. "Thank you, Roxane."

I patted his shoulder and left him sitting at the table and went down the hall to Shelby's bedroom. I knocked on the closed door. "Can I come in?" I said.

"Whatever."

That wasn't much of an invitation, but I went in anyway. Shelby was sitting cross-legged on her bed, arms crossed. Her computer was open on the blanket next to her, Veronica's Facebook page on the screen. She didn't look at me.

"Shelby," I started.

"I thought you were mad at me or something," she blurted,

beginning to cry. "Or you thought I was so stupid. Because you went away and stopped helping us."

I closed the door and sat down next to her. "No," I said. I felt sick. "No, that couldn't be further from the truth. When I left the other day, I thought I knew something about what might have happened, and I went and made a really stupid choice, and because I was interfering with what the police were doing, I got arrested."

She finally looked at me, her eyes going wide.

"That's why I didn't answer when you called," I added. "And yesterday, once I got out of jail, I was feeling really bad and I didn't know how to help you. Your dad said the police were doing everything they could, and I thought I should leave them to it. But then I realized if it was my friend who didn't come home, it wouldn't matter to me if the police were doing everything they could. I'd want to do everything *I* could. Even if that was just something small. So that's why I came back, to see if I could help you today. Your dad said you want to make more copies of your flyer. I'll go with you, if you want me to."

Shelby covered her face with her hands, nodding. "Thank you."

"Why don't you finish making lunch for your dad, and we can go. Okay?"

I sprang for five hundred copies of the flyer at a print shop by the high school. Then I let Shelby navigate for the rest of the afternoon. We expanded the canvassing area well beyond Belmont to include other places Veronica liked: the Drexel movie theater near downtown, a few vintage clothing stores on High Street—Flower Child in the Short North, the Boomerang Room in Clintonville—and the gift shop at the art museum. I didn't think Veronica had disappeared for going on seventy-two hours in order to go shopping, and no one we talked to remembered seeing her. But we distributed flyers liberally. It didn't hurt to widen the net.

Later I took Shelby to the Angry Baker, the vegan place I'd told her about last week. We got chai lattes and sat at a small round table in the window, watching in silence as cars splashed through the puddles on Oak Street. It had stopped raining, but the city was atmospherically wet and felt like it would be forever. There was no reason to bring her here, except I was trying to cheer her up. I didn't know what else to do.

"Veronica would like it in here." Shelby cupped her hands around her mug. "We never come to this part of downtown. My dad says we shouldn't because it's a bad area."

"This is my 'hood, kiddo," I said lightly. "Does it look like a bad area to you?"

Her eyes flicked to the boarded-up building across the street and over a few houses but she kept quiet.

I had to laugh. I opened my mouth to say something about Belmont and how it looked nice on the surface but was far from it. But the moment wasn't right for such horizon-broadening. "Has your dad ever been up here?" I said instead.

"Probably not. He basically only leaves our neighborhood to go to his job."

"Well, there you go."

"When Veronica gets back, I'm going to bring her here," she said.

When Veronica gets back, like she was currently on a camping trip.

Shelby looked into her empty mug for a while. "He asked me if it was possible that she hurt herself. Killed herself. It's not. It's so not. She would never do that to me." She paused again before finally speaking. "My dad probably doesn't know what he's talking about, he doesn't know everything. She's coming back. Right?"

I didn't know what to tell her. There were so many life lessons contained in that one question. I was the last person in the world to be giving advice to anyone right now. I didn't want to lie to her. But I didn't see any way around it. In that moment, Shelby needed reassurance more than she needed straight shooting. "Yes," I said. One way or another, at some point, she'd be found. "She is."

On the way back to her house, we tried the Book Loft and a big thrift store on South High and then, as it neared seven o'clock, Shelby said she wanted to hit up the Belmont Public Library. "Not that Veronica really likes libraries," she said. "I mean, I do, she doesn't. But they have a place where you can post flyers and I always see people reading them."

"Good idea."

It was cozy and quaint inside, a small space arranged around an actual hearth. An old card catalogue stood in one corner as a museum of sorts, along with a deeply earnest poster about the history of the Dewey decimal system. While Shelby asked for permission to post her flyer, I looked around, trying to picture Brad and Sarah at their weekly writers' group in this space. But it was hard for me even to imagine their faces. I felt like a physical manifestation of a jammed signal. Nothing was getting out, and nothing was getting in. Shelby turned away from the counter, giving me a thumbs-up as she took her flyers over to the community board. I doubted that any librarian in the world would refuse to post a missing-persons flyer; librarians were, in my experience, some of life's finer human beings. But it was good to know that there were still some decent people left in Belmont.

I sensed the library doors opening behind me, so I took a step toward the card-catalogue museum. But then I heard the telltale utility-belt creaking of a uniformed cop.

I spun around and came face-to-face with Sergeant Jack Derrow.

"I'm just waiting for someone, come on," I said, spreading my hands wide. It was hard to believe that I thought he was friendly the first time I met him.

"Maybe I'm just here to check out a book."

"Why do I get the feeling that you're not?"

His eyes flicked to my cheekbone he but didn't comment on it. "I'm sure you understand, I was doing my job."

"Yeah, of course," I said. "Good work. Go ahead. Go get your book."

"What are you doing here?"

"I told you, I'm waiting for someone. Pretty sure that's not a police matter." I semi-seriously considered if the cops had LoJacked my car while it was parked on the access road behind the Brayfield house. BOLO or not, the speed with which they seemed to locate me each time I came here was out of control.

Derrow watched me for a minute like he was waiting for me to commit a crime in front of him. But I wasn't trespassing this time. I wasn't even loitering. And he'd have a lot of witnesses to refute any disorderly conduct claims. Then his gaze traveled over my shoulder as Shelby came up to us.

She looked at Derrow, then down at her shoes. "They let me put out twenty of them and they said they would make more copies if it runs low," she said, almost whispering.

"Awesome. You ready?" I said.

"How are you holding up, Miss Shelby?" Derrow said. "How's your dad?"

"We're okay," she said. "I'm ready."

We walked back out into the cold, Shelby slightly behind me and walking close to my heels. I glanced behind me and saw that her face was bright red.

"Hey," I said. "Is something wrong?"

She shook her head, pulling at the handle of the car before the vacuum lock had released. Once it did, she jumped inside and pulled the door closed while I was still standing outside. I got in too. "Shelby," I said. "What? You're blushing."

Shelby's hands went to her knees, fingers digging into the fabric of her pants. "I—" She didn't any anything else.

"You can tell me," I said.

"I blush, sometimes. I can't help it."

I waited, one hand on the ignition.

Then she said, "I just don't like him, is all."

"Derrow?"

"I don't like him," she said, more resolutely. "Veronica always said he was so weird in shock."

I let go of the ignition and turned to her. "In shock," I repeated, not understanding.

"She had to take this class, her stepdad made her. After she stole, like, one lip gloss from Target. The police run it. Self-discipline, honor, opportunity, um, the 'c' is . . . character. And knowledge. It's like a, what's the word, acronym. SHOCK."

I suddenly felt like I was staring into the barrel of a gun. "Veronica took the class," I said slowly. Danielle had told me Mallory Evans had taken a class like that. *This boot-camp program that the city runs for messed-up kids,* she'd said. Colleen's mother said she'd been sent to *one of those scared-straight-type programs the city puts on.* Was this the same program? Had Derrow taught those girls too? I shook my head, trying to slow down the racing thoughts. "Weird how? What did Veronica say he did?"

Shelby still looked embarrassed. "I don't really know. She said he was always staring at her boobs. I don't know about that, sometimes Veronica can be melodramatic that way. Her mom always says, *Veronica, you think the whole world is in love with you, just wait till you find out it's not.*"

Veronica's mother sounded like a bitch, although I'd known girls like that growing up too. But my heart was beating hard in my ears. I suddenly remembered the conversation the girls had been having when I first encountered them at Joshua's house last week.

On a scale of one to ten, how frequently did he ogle all the girls in class?

And it wasn't just that. Shelby was clearly picking up on something about him too.

"Shel," I said. "Listen. I know that sometimes something might make you feel weird, and other things just make you feel bad. And as a woman, you have a little sensor in your brain that tells you which one it is, right?"

She nodded, watching me watching her in the reflection in the passenger-side window.

"You owe it to yourself to pay attention to that sensor, always, always," I said.

Shelby nodded again. Then she turned and faced me. "I don't like him," she said again. "I don't like how he looks at me."

"And how does he look at you?" Something dark began to coil around my chest.

"Like—I don't really know how to explain it. Like he knows something about me. Except he doesn't, he doesn't know me at all," she said.

"Overly familiar, like," I said.

"Yeah," Shelby said. "I guess that's what it is. He came into the restaurant one time," she said. "And he sat at the bar and every time I was seating a party, he smiled at me. Wow, that sounds so stupid. *He smiled at me.* So what. I don't know. I just don't like it."

She shivered in the cold, so I finally turned the car on. Her color had returned to normal. She didn't seem to realize that what she told me was still exploding in my brain. In the rearview mirror, I saw Derrow slowly drive away, pointedly not looking at me.

When we got back to the house, Joshua had shaved and changed clothes and had taken the collection of beer bottles out of the kitchen. He looked bright-eyed and rested. "Thank you," he said. "I mean it."

He invited me to stay for dinner—pizza delivery was on the way— but I couldn't wait to get out of there. I felt nauseous and crazy and like anyone could read it on my face, that I was terrified of my own conclusion. Derrow hadn't blipped on my radar at all until now. At first, he was helpful. Then at the Brayfield house, he'd been aggressive with me but at the time, I thought it fit with the context. But the unknown calls had started immediately after I met Derrow for the first time and—I realized as heat spread across my face now—the calls had stopped once I was arrested. He didn't call while I was locked up because he knew I wouldn't answer, and he didn't call after that because I did exactly what he wanted: I gave up and went home. My cheekbone throbbed. Trying to force a connection hadn't gone very well for me before. But sometimes the connection insists on making itself. The universe sends you the same lesson over and over until you learn it. The world is a series of patterns on its own; the coincidence is only in the discovery of them.

Can't go over it. Can't go under it. Can't go around it.

Gotta go through it.

The lobby of the police station was empty at nine o'clock. I walked in and went directly to the photos in the lobby, the ones I'd spent an hour looking at while Lassiter kept me waiting the other day. Five-by-sevens with little engraved plaques on the bottom of each frame. *SHOCK, 2015.* About twenty kids in matching green T-shirts. I squinted at the image and saw Veronica Cruz in the second row, smiling halfheartedly. Jack Derrow stood behind the kids, his arms folded over his chest. I went back in time, guessing when Colleen Grantham might have been in the program. *If* she was.

Of course she was.

SHOCK, 2007. The year she disappeared. She stood in the front row, looking uncomfortable. Jack Derrow was in the background of this shot too.

I went back a few more years. Mallory wasn't in the class of 1999, the year she was murdered. But she would have dropped out of school by then, already married to Joshua. I looked further back and found her in 1997, a dead-eyed stare from the back row. Jack Derrow was directly behind her.

I took a deep breath and sat down on a bench. This was a connection that was hard to ignore. Derrow had been involved in five of the welcome receptions I'd received in Belmont. He knew all three girls. I thought about the way he'd acted during my arrest, his hand slowly snaking up my chest to unzip my coat.

But what about Sarah? She hadn't been a troubled kid.

Then it hit me.

The Cooks were personal friends of his.

He had told me this himself.

The lounge at the Westin was packed tonight. I took the last open seat at the bar and nodded at my brother as he held up a hand to indicate that it would be a minute until he could get to me. While I waited I thumbed the screen of my phone, debating. I wanted to call Tom. Some part of me was still pissed at him. But he'd know what to do next, or he'd know how tell me to drop it, that I'd finally lost my mind after nine months of not thinking very clearly anyway. But at any rate, he'd know.

I couldn't do it.

My contact list was a wasteland of people I no longer spoke to. Cops, lawyers, a woman from the county sheriff's office whom I'd gone on two miserable dates with a year ago. I put the phone away.

"You," my brother said, sliding a shot across the bar, "were supposed to call me today."

"Isn't in person better?" I said. I downed the shot and pushed the glass back for another.

"It is," Andrew said, "but right now you just want something."

I laughed. "Me?" I said.

He grinned at me. "What is it?"

"I want to borrow your car," I said.

He refilled my shot glass and poured one for himself, looking at me with mild concern. "What happened to yours?"

"Nothing," I said. "I mean, I want to trade cars. Just for a few days. I need to go incognito."

"I told you that car would be shit for surveillance," Andrew said.

"And I told *you* to get the Escape because no one would ever think somebody in a beige compact SUV was up to no good," I said. "Which is exactly what I need."

We swapped keys. A woman in a grey suit at the opposite end of the bar rapped her snifter sharply on the polished wood, and Andrew rolled his eyes. "I hate these fucking people," he said. "All night it's been like this."

"It's okay," I said, "go. I'll take good care of your baby, I promise."

He started to walk away, but then turned back. "Roxane," he said, "I don't give a shit about the car. Take good care of you."

THIRTY-TWO

I got to the Radio Shack in the Shops at Wildflower Glade right as they opened on Friday morning. I had a plan this time, having already learned my lesson about pursuing leads without thinking it through. I wasn't about to get thrown into a cell for another fifteen hours. I didn't have time for that. And neither did Veronica Cruz, if she had any time left at all. Either way, I was going to prove that I was right about Derrow. But first I wanted to be able to tell where he was.

After looking around helplessly for a while, I allowed a pimply but enthusiastic kid wearing a tie with a saxophone on it to talk me into a five-hundred-dollar police scanner. Far from the cheapest, it was also not the most expensive one in the store, which I thought showed restraint on his part. But it was the correct tool for the task of listening to the Belmont police radio broadcasts from anywhere within the city's thirteen square miles.

"A lot of departments are still on the analog systems," the kid told me excitedly, "but the police here just got a brand-new communications center last year, everything upgraded. Before that, you could have gotten into scanning for way less. And they've got apps for it now too, but you can't listen to all the channels that way. Too bad, huh?"

I thrust my credit card at him, even though I had no one I could bill this expense to. "Bad for me, good for you," I said. "Maybe don't rub it in."

I asked if he could program it for me and he said to give him thirty minutes. Then I went into a sports-apparel store and tried on a series of baseball caps, finally settling on the grey Ohio State hat that made me look the most forgettable.

"You know we have ladies' hats," the cashier told me at the register, pointing to a rack of pink ones in the back of the store.

"*Ladies'* hats?" I said loudly, slapping my card down on the counter.

I went back to Radio Shack, where Saxophone Tie gave me a brief lesson on straight repeater operation and trunking radio systems and talk groups. Much of it went over my head, but the gist was that the scanner automatically tuned itself to the frequency someone was speaking on within the talk group, but I would have to manually check one talk group at a time. Then I took my overpriced new toy out to Andrew's car and stretched out in the backseat.

One thing was immediately clear: people in Belmont called the cops *a lot.*

Even shortly after ten in the morning, there were complaints about noise, about traffic jams at afternoon kindergarten drop-off at the Montessori school, about a suspicious individual entering a neighbor's house.

(*"I advised the caller that the individual was actually the neighbor, wearing a new coat."*)

I heard a few familiar voices, namely Meeks and Pasquale. I didn't hear Derrow yet. So I lay there and drank some tea and waited, paging through the scant information I had found about him.

On paper, he was conspicuously inconspicuous. John "Jack" Derrow. Fifty-six, born and raised in Belmont, a lifelong resident apart from six years spent in the navy following high school. After a general discharge, he joined the police department. Married early on to

Theresa Marr, a fellow Belmontian, divorced four years later. No kids. No social media profiles. No search results at all beyond the occasional police-beat item and, in 2003, the race results from the Capital City Half Marathon. Two hours and six minutes, in the bottom third for his age group. But that told me nothing, of course. None of it did.

It was around eleven when his quiet rumble of a voice came over the radio. He was driving car one-four, the same vehicle he'd driven when I had the pleasure of riding with him. I listened as he responded to a traffic-accident call and then an identity-theft complaint on the far eastern edge of the town. I drove over there and parked a block away from Derrow's cruiser. Once he emerged from the victim's house and had radioed in that the call was resolved, I pulled out my phone and called the police dispatcher.

"There's a woman taking pictures of people in Brayfield Park," I said in my most concerned tone of voice. "Like from a car. She's in an old blue Mercedes. I don't know what she's doing, but there are *children* here."

I described myself—dark brown hair, leather jacket, maybe a black eye?

"Thanks for the tip, ma'am," the dispatcher said. "Can I get your name?"

"Pam Gregorio," I said.

A minute or two later, I heard the call come across the scanner. "Anybody near Brayfield Park? Got another report of the chick in the blue Mercedes. Sounds like she has a camera this time. Concerned parent called it in."

Derrow answered immediately. "This is one-four, I'm right around the corner. I'm on it."

He snapped on his lights and sirens and took off in a flash. I followed. He lost me on Clover Road, going far too fast for me to follow without looking suspicious. But I knew where he was going. And the thing was, he wasn't right around the corner. He was clear on the other side of town.

So everyone, including the dispatcher, was aware to be on the lookout for me, but Derrow's interest was a little stronger than most. Strong enough to tear across Belmont, sixty in a thirty-five-miles-per-hour business district, and—as I observed when I caught up to him—to systematically approach every person in the park that afternoon. It was damp and chilly out, so there weren't that many people in attendance, but he spent close to thirty minutes looking for me or someone who had seen me. I watched from the safety of my brother's nondescript vehicle for a while and then left him to it before he made his way to the side of the lot I was parked on. Ten minutes later, his voice came through the scanner as he radioed in clear, apparently giving up.

I contemplated calling in again—maybe I could be harassing people at the skate course this time—but decided to reserve the only trick I had for later, when it might count more. I parked at the library and listened to the voices on the radio for a while. Pasquale pursued a kid who'd stolen three cans of spray paint from the art-supply store but lost him; Derrow caught a speeder with expired tags; Meeks followed up on a tip about an individual lurking around the closed-for-the-season pool of the Holiday Inn Express.

There were no mentions of Veronica Cruz, I noted.

Sure, the police were doing everything they could.

I caught up with Derrow around three, when he cleared a security-system call near the center of town and then radioed in for a meal break. I followed him in Andrew's car to a Lowe's near the mall. He went inside and emerged eight minutes later, carrying two plastic bags that appeared heavy. He put them in the cruiser and pulled out of the lot, heading west.

I kept after him. In the middle of the day, traffic was heavy enough to make tailing him easy. Plus, he wasn't looking for me in a nondescript beige sport utility vehicle. That helped too. But eventually he made his way to 665 and we went west for six miles, and he turned in to a tangle of narrow country roads. I had no choice but to fall back. But the black-and-white cruiser was hard to miss, and eventually I was able to spot it through the almost-bare November trees, parked in the gravel driveway of a white clapboard Victorian with a *SOLD!* sign out front.

It was a little eerie out here, foggy and quiet, the sky the color of wet concrete. And this wasn't his house, or at least not his regular address, which was back in Belmont proper. I slowed down as I passed the road the house sat on. I couldn't see Derrow or anything else. So I kept going, pulled a U-turn, and parked on the shoulder. I dug through the bag I'd brought—gun, computer, notebook, flashlight, camera, binoculars, flask—and got out the binocs and checked out the house. It was pretty rough, the white paint worn off around the eaves, roof tiles missing or flapping loose like errant buttons. The windows had no curtains, but they were too dirty to see through at this distance.

He came out of the house five minutes later, the blue Lowe's bags crumpled and empty in his hand. This time when he drove away, I didn't follow. I got out my revolver and a flashlight and walked up to the house and rapped on the front door. I heard nothing but hollow silence. Then I lapped the perimeter and peered in all the windows. Clearly no one lived here, not yet. From what I could see, the wood floors were dirty and littered with tacks and flaps of glue from stripped-out carpet. The kitchen, though newly linoleumed, was missing a part of a countertop and all the appliances.

I stood in the sloping backyard and looked around. Everything was brown and grey and hopeless here. There weren't any neighbors within eyeshot. If he'd brought Veronica here, no one would have seen. No one would have heard. No one even knew this house existed, except for whoever had owned it last. What had been in the blue bags, and why was it so important he bring it here, during his lunch break? My pulse was racing. I couldn't shake the feeling that there was something for me to find here. The way I had in the woods. This was concerning, since that feeling had ended with a discovery that I couldn't get out of my head.

I didn't want to find Veronica that way.

But I had to find her.

Although I had vowed I wasn't going to do anything else stupid, I considered the cheap knob on the back door—loose in the strike plate, its finish worn off from age. I looked at the hinges next, to determine if the door swung inward. It did. Otherwise, it would be next to impossible to kick in. I took a step back, steadied myself, and kicked hard, driving my heel of my boot into the door just above the lock. It splintered without giving way, so I kicked it again, the shock of it vibrating up through my leg.

That took care of it.

There was no turning back now.

I stepped into the house. The air was cold and dusty and smelled like adhesive and cigar smoke. "Veronica?" I said.

I heard nothing in return.

I walked slowly through the house. Floorboards creaked and my boots crunched over the renovation-related debris that was scattered everywhere. But I didn't hear anything else. I flipped a light switch but nothing happened; no power. So I covered the lower level in fading afternoon light: empty living room, empty dining room, bathroom with an army of dead bugs in the sink and a stack of tools arranged on the lid of the toilet. Without even the faint hum of electricity, the house seemed isolated, sealed off from the world entirely.

It wasn't a good feeling.

Second floor: patchy blue carpet, browning wallpaper peeling off in strips. There were visible rectangles at eye level where picture frames had hung, protecting the wallpaper from the cigar smoke that had discolored the rest of the house. The bathroom up here held a shower with a mildewed white liner. The sight of it made me suddenly, acutely afraid.

And then it twitched.

I froze where I was.

Every horror movie I'd ever seen flashed through my head. It was easy enough to write those off most of the time, but not when you were standing in a creepy house like this and not when you'd discovered human remains only days before. One sweaty palm on my revolver, I lunged forward and yanked the shower curtain back, barely suppressing a shriek when I saw two pale grey mice book it down the rusty mouth of the drain.

"Jesus," I said, shoving the curtain away in disgust.

I checked the rest of the house, including a search via flashlight of a horrifying basement with concrete walls and floor painted reddish-brown, but I found nothing except more rodents and a random collection of old Atlas mason jars in a cabinet.

No one was here.

It was five thirty and the sun had set. Outside, I shined my light on the splintered door and pulled it closed as much as possible, not wanting my fruitless little visit to be any more noticeable than it already was. Then I went back to my brother's car and turned the heat on high. I was freezing and unsettled, but more importantly I was no closer to figuring anything out.

There was no way I was wrong this time.

Derrow was personally acquainted with Mallory, Colleen, Veronica, and the Cooks.

There was no way.

Or was there?

It would all fit together perfectly, except I still had no idea what had happened with Sarah and her parents. Mallory Evans had been sexually assaulted and stabbed to death. I didn't know exactly what had happened to Colleen, but she obviously hadn't wrapped herself in a tarp before dying in her sleep. There was a cold calculation involved in burying those women in the woods. By contrast, there was passion behind Garrett and Elaine Cook's death. Not planned, not well-thought-out. Derrow knew them, which made it simultaneously harder to fathom but easier to understand. What had happened? Did the Cooks walk into their house and find Jack Derrow attacking their daughter? Was she already dead? Was she buried in the woods too?

Maybe with enough evidence, the police would rip up all of Clover Point to find Sarah's body.

Maybe I could convince Kenny Brayfield to ask them to.

It wasn't funny, but that made me laugh out loud, a strained, demented laugh that probably would have made anyone worry about me if they'd heard it. My heart rate still hadn't returned to normal, even though I'd been out of that house for ten minutes now.

I put the car in gear and drove back to Belmont. A lot of things could happen with enough evidence. But I had to find it first.

I located Derrow's actual house, a well-maintained but ugly two-story with an attached garage and green siding and black shutters. Most of the yards on the street were still covered with a thick blanket of fallen autumn leaves, but Derrow's was just an expanse of grass. I drove past it and parked a few houses down, where the street widened into a cul-de-sac. Two women in patterned leggings and neon jackets with reflective trim were speed-walking on the other side of the street, engaged in a loud, breathless conversation about low-fat slow-cooker recipes. I tried to tune them out as I looked at Derrow's place. There were lights on in the lower level, glowing pale yellow behind miniblinds. I hadn't heard Derrow on the scanner since I got back to Belmont, so I didn't know if he was home or not.

If Veronica was in there, I didn't think she was calmly reading next to a table lamp.

My head was pounding. The speed walkers had stopped on the sidewalk to finish their conversation before parting ways. "Go away," I muttered. I wanted to check out the house, but I didn't want anyone to see me and call the police. It seemed likely enough that someone might call on me just for sitting here for too long anyway.

The house looked so normal. Like just a house. I felt nothing when I looked at it, unlike the old house earlier today. Did that mean something? I looked through the binocs but it was too dark to see any detail. On the scanner, there was a scuffle between teenagers at the skate park, a complaint of someone smoking too close to the door of the mall. Shanahan caught another fender bender on Clover Road.

I wondered how many fender benders on Clover Road there were each week in Belmont.

I wondered if the dispatcher somehow screened the calls before even putting them on the radio, because I'd heard no actual crime all day, which was a little weird even for a suburb. Especially one as fucked up as Belmont.

I wondered if I could return the overpriced scanner to Radio Shack for a refund and spent a minute looking for the receipt, but gave up.

I looked at my phone—a text from my brother asking me if my Mercedes took diesel, another call from Tom. He didn't leave a voice mail this time. I texted *yes* to Andrew and dropped the phone onto the seat. I rubbed my eyes, forgetting again about the scab on my cheekbone.

"What are you doing," I said out loud, not for the first time recently.

No one ever solved a case from staring at a house.

I went back to my notebook. I'd written hardly anything down.

Red sedan.
Big green pickup.
Long wool coat.
Marisa?

No one ever solved a case with notes that looked like this.

I dropped the notebook on the passenger seat and massaged my forehead, waiting for a clear thought to shake loose.

Derrow had been involved in the SHOCK program for at least eighteen years. Based on those pictures hanging in the lobby of the station, I guessed an average of fifteen students per class. That was a lot of kids, a lot of girls. The department surely kept records. I thought for a minute about how I could wheedle a list out of them, track down Derrow's former students to establish a pattern. But I could spend months on end tracking down a few hundred formerly troubled teens. And Veronica didn't have months. Just like Brad didn't have months.

I thought about Derrow's friendly little wave when he drove past me on Shelby's street Monday night. When I said to tell Lassiter hello for me. What if that was when he got the idea? The other day I'd consoled myself with the knowledge that Veronica's disappearance wasn't my fault, but maybe it was. I got the flask out of my bag and ran my thumbnail back and forth over the cap, debating. Whiskey might kill the edges of the feeling I had, but it wasn't going to help Veronica. I put the flask down. Then I scrolled through the names in my phone, pausing for a second on Tom's again. But I couldn't. I still felt something hot and dark squeezing my insides when I thought of it, my father using his dying breath to remind me that I didn't know what I was doing.

The speed walkers hugged and went into their separate houses.

A garage door behind me opened and a rusty Chevy Nova wheezed down the street and turned left onto Clover just as another vehicle turned onto Derrow's street.

I squinted against the LED headlights, momentarily blinded.

Then Derrow's garage door went up, and the vehicle turned and the headlights were no longer shining right at me.

I saw that it was a green pickup truck.

My hands squeezed into fists.

A dark green pickup.

One of those big new ones, just like Danielle Stockton had said.

What if Sarah wasn't buried somewhere in the ravine?

What if she was alive?

THIRTY-THREE

I fumbled around on the seat for my phone as the garage door closed again and glanced at Tom's number but scrolled to Peter Novotny's instead. "Who do you know in the sheriff's office?" I said when the old PI answered. I was thinking I needed to go bigger than Belmont. To an agency with the authority to swoop in over their heads. "Or the Ohio BCI?"

"Wait a minute, wait just a minute," Novotny said. He sounded confused. "What's going on? Are you in trouble?"

"Not in trouble, no," I said. "But I need a name. Someone you trust."

"Listen, honey." He cleared his throat. "You sound a little wound up. Tell me what's going on."

Derrow's garage door opened, and he dragged out some long sheets of drywall, which he leveraged into the truck with some difficulty. I took a deep breath. "I think there was a Belmont cop involved in the Cook murders," I said. It was like ripping off a bandage and then waving around the open wound for all the world to see.

Novotny didn't say anything for a while. Then he cleared his throat and said, "Why?"

"Petey, listen, I don't think Sarah Cook is dead. I think she's in his house. Right now. I don't know if she helped with the other girls or not but—"

"Roxane," he said slowly. "Have you been drinking?"

I ground my teeth together. "No—"

"Because you sound like you're out of your goddamn mind. I know I drink a little too, and so did your daddy, and it's fine. But you have to learn to keep work and whiskey separate, okay?"

"Listen—"

"No, you listen, I mean it," he said sharply. "You don't play around with stuff like this."

"I'm not playing—"

"Oh, you're not playing, okay," Novotny said. "So you've got evidence, then?"

"He knew all the girls. He's driving the same truck that Danielle saw that night at the gas station—"

"*Danielle* is your frame of reference? That's not a point in your favor. And what other girls are you even talking about?"

"Please," I said. "Do you know anyone in Ohio BCI?"

"You just got a wild idea and I know it sounds right to you, but that's just the booze talking. Shit, I could tell you all kinds of stories, cases I was sure I cracked after a drink or five."

I didn't have time or desire to hear any of his old war stories. "No—"

"Where are you? Can I come get you? Believe me, you'll thank me in the morning."

I hung up and I covered my mouth with my hand and screamed until my throat ached. My heart was hammering at the base of my skull. The irony of it was, I felt like I was thinking clearly for the first time in months. I watched as Derrow went back into the garage. A second later, his driveway was illuminated by the truck's taillights. Then he backed out.

I got the car in gear but I didn't follow. Instead, I waited until he'd turned off his street and then I parked in front of his house.

———

The doors to Derrow's house were all newish and secure. I wouldn't be kicking these in, not unless I wanted to break an ankle. The basement had four subterranean windows, the kind set in a half-moon-shaped egress well. The windows in the front of the house were glass-block and would be difficult to break without making a hell of a racket. The ones in the back were made of single glass panes, though. I lay on the cold, wet grass and shone my flashlight into each, trying to gauge what might be down there. But the windows were old and caked with grime and I couldn't see much. Finally, I just picked one.

I punched the handle of my flashlight through the glass and used it to clear away the jagged shards left clinging to the frame. Then I waited for a second, to see if neighbors came outside or porch lights turned on.

Nothing.

No one cared.

There was *really* no turning back now.

It was nine o'clock. I figured I had at least an hour before Derrow made it back from his new home in the woods. That would have to be enough time.

I looped the flashlight to my belt and lowered myself into the hollowed-out space in front of the window, hands bracing against the concrete lip of the foundation, my legs hanging down into the house. Then I slid forward and let go.

It went better in my head than it did in practice. The basement floor was farther down than I expected and I came down sideways, my left hip crunching against the concrete. I immediately wanted to throw up, flattened by a wave of pain. I lay there for a second on the cold, dusty floor. I was in over my head already. I reached into my pocket for my phone. Tom could get here in thirty minutes, maybe less. He probably wouldn't even make me explain myself—if I said I needed him to come, he would. But my phone was toast: a spiderweb of broken glass and bleeding colors was all that remained of the touch screen.

"Have you been drinking," I muttered to myself.

I struggled to my feet. Once I was up, I was okay. There would be a hell of a bruise in the morning, but at least I wasn't paralyzed in Jack Derrow's basement. And at least I hadn't landed on my other hip, where my gun was holstered. I flipped the flashlight on and bounced the beam around the room. There wasn't much to look at—boxes, neatly sealed up with packing tape; a weight machine that looked like it actually saw some use, unlike the ones in most people's basements; a long white deep freezer, an ironing board stacked high with folded uniforms. I crept to the bottom of the steps and listened.

Nothing.

The house was dead silent.

I went up the creaky wooden steps, my hip protesting. I stopped every few feet to listen but still heard nothing, just my own anxious breathing. At the top of the staircase, I opened the door slowly, holding my breath and half expecting someone to stop me, but no one did. I closed the basement door behind me.

The house was neat and orderly, a small eat-in kitchen with speckled blue countertops and plaid wallpaper, a living room with sculpted blue carpet and fake wood paneling on the walls. Leather recliner, big entertainment stand with a tube television, the kind so heavy you needed three people to lift it. The only light on was the one I'd seen from the street, a lamp beside the recliner.

The house was outdated, but not out of the ordinary.

It looked like a boring, lonely person lived here.

I bounced the beam of the flashlight around, hoping to find a landline phone. But there wasn't one, just an exposed jack mounted on the wall between the kitchen and living room.

If I was keeping someone hostage in my house, I probably wouldn't have a working phone line either.

I still heard nothing, not even a breath.

But then it began to get weird.

The front door of the house had a metal bar across it, secured with a padlock. The floor creaked as I walked over to it and tugged on the padlock.

Ordinary houses didn't have a door like this.

I stared at it for a long time, almost disbelieving my own eyes. Half expecting, after all of this, that there was nothing to find in the house, that I was wrong again.

But I knew better now. I might have been a lot of things, but wrong wasn't one of them.

The sight of the door made me feel like a caged animal, panicky. I checked out the other doors: the one leading out to the deck at the rear of the house was secured with a similar lock. But the door off the kitchen that led to the garage, the one that Derrow used to come and go from his house, was just a regular door. I opened it and shined my flashlight around the garage. There was nothing to see, just typical garage fare: lawn mower, snow shovel, an oily, dirty smell. A peg board where tools had once hung from individual nails. Before he moved them to the new house, maybe. More boxes here too, stacked neatly against the wall.

Derrow was nothing if not orderly. I went back into the house, and that was when I heard the sound.

A gentle keening, an urgent whisper. I spun around with the flashlight, hitting all the walls. But it wasn't coming from in here. I entered the foyer and stood by the barred front door, listening as I turned for the first time to the carpeted staircase that went the second floor.

At the top of the steps: another door, grey metal.

I crept up the steps and shone my flashlight on the door, taking in the knob of a dead bolt installed at eye level. Installed backward, so that you'd need a key to get down the steps but not up. I turned the knob and pulled open the door, taking care to disable the dead bolt so it didn't lock behind me. Then I stopped and observed. There was a strange smell up here, musty and sour. The sound was getting louder.

"Veronica?" I said. "Sarah?"

The noise stopped and silence filled up the darkness again. But this time it was the soundless tension of listening. I swept the flashlight around the upstairs hallway. Four doors. Two of them had the backward dead bolts at eye level, again to keep something *in* the rooms rather than out.

"Veronica?" I said again, louder this time.

The wind blew outside, bare tree branches scraping against the house.

That was the only sound.

And then it wasn't.

"In here, in here, in here," a scratchy voice pleaded. There was a clang of metal on metal, the muffled thump of pounding on a wall.

I ran to the end of the hall and yanked open the dead-bolted door. "Veronica," I said.

Seeing her in the beam of my flashlight was shocking, even though I had been looking for her for days.

Abruptly, she stopped pleading, just stared at me. She was sitting on a bare twin mattress on the floor, clutching a sheet to her chest. She appeared to be naked beneath it. Her red-violet hair was tangled. Her lips were dry and peeling. She was looking past me somehow, as if she expected someone else.

"Veronica," I said again.

"Shhhhh," another voice whispered from somewhere else in the house.

I whirled around in the dark, but the room was empty.

I went over to the bed. "Veronica." I knelt down in front of her, holding the flashlight between my elbow and my rib cage. "Veronica."

"It's a trick, don't say anything," the other voice hissed.

Veronica blinked at me, her eyes wide with confusion and stunned fear. "Wh—" she said. Then she stopped.

"Veronica, are you okay? Are you hurt?" I reached for her shoulder but she jerked away from me. Then she pulled the bottom of the sheet up, exposing her legs. Her ankles were shackled together, the skin around the cuffs scabbed and bruised deeply. The irons were attached to a long length of heavy chain, which was bolted to the floor. The mattress was stained and the room smelled like blood and sex and urine and I bit my lip so hard I tasted metal.

"Veronica, listen," I said to her. I stood up and scanned the room. The only window was boarded up, the curtain smashed against the glass under a sheet of plywood. The chain tying Veronica to the floor was long enough to get to a bucket in the corner, which appeared to serve as a toilet. I grabbed the chain and pulled against the bolt, but it was fastened tight. I knew from the other whispered voice that we weren't alone in the house but I needed to focus on getting her out of there. I dropped the chain and knelt in front of her again. "I met you at Shelby's house," I said, in case the horror of her last few days had wiped her memory. "You can trust me."

"I remember," she whispered numbly. I wondered if she was drugged. "One 'n.'"

I smiled, or at least tried to. I hoped it was reassuring but it felt like anything but. "Yeah, that's right. Roxane, with one 'n,'" I said. "Girl, am I glad to see you. And Shelby's going to be so happy too. I'm going to get you out of here, okay? Is Sarah here?"

"Shelby," she said.

I tried again. "Where is Sarah?"

"Other room."

"Okay, Veronica? Veronica. Do you have clothes?" I said. She just stared at me. I looked around the room again. No clothes. Nothing except the bucket in the corner. Hoping Sarah might be able to assist me in some way, I went back into the hall and pulled open the other dead-bolted door. It led into another small bedroom. A very different bedroom. This one had a lamp and a bed with pillows and an actual blanket, a section of floral fabric hanging over the plywood on the window, a small television, two stacks of books and journals on a dresser.

And there was Sarah Cook, crouched in the corner, her hands on her belly.

She was pregnant.

Very pregnant.

I dropped to my knees in front of her and we stared at each other. She was wearing sweatpants and a grey T-shirt. Her ankles were bare, no shackles in sight. She looked to be in much better shape than Veronica did, except for the obvious. She did not seem happy to see me, however.

"You tell him I was good," she whispered. "You tell him I was good because I was."

"Sarah, I'm here to help you. I want to get you out of here, both of you," I said, approaching her slowly.

Sarah shrank back into the corner. She was shaking her head, muttering *no no no no no no*. In the other room, Veronica was crying.

"I know Brad," I said. "Brad Stockton. That's why I'm here."

She stopped muttering, her nostrils flaring. "Brad," she said.

"I don't know what happened here but it's over, Sarah," I said, "please, help me. Help me with Veronica and we can get away from this place and you can see Brad."

She shook her head and didn't move. "I'm not stupid anymore," she said.

I wanted to ask what she meant. But there wasn't time to ask. A digital clock on her nightstand said it was almost ten. I winced as

I stood up and looked around the room for something I could use on the chain, running my fingertips over book spines and dirty plates and the base of the lamp. It was cheap metal, but it had some heft to it. I yanked the cord out of the wall, plunging the room into darkness.

Sarah drew in a sharp breath.

I stumbled over something on my way out of the room—a laundry basket. I grabbed a shirt and sweatpants from the stack and took them in to Veronica. She was still silently weeping, her tears sparkling grimly in the pale glow of my flashlight. She picked up the sweatpants and just looked at me like *What the fuck am I supposed to do with this.*

"Right," I said. "Okay." I sat on the floor above the bolt and drove the base of the lamp against it with all my strength once, twice, three times. On the fourth, the lamp fractured into four pieces while the chain remained untouched. I threw what remained of the lamp against the wall, feeling sick as I stood up and paced the length of the small room. Veronica was still on the bed, but she had lowered the sheet to her lap as she struggled into the shirt. Her torso was blotchy with bruises.

I was not going to cry.

I went back to the bolt and thought about putting a bullet through it. But the chain was iron and there was no telling what might happen if I shot at it—I imagined a slug ricocheting around the house and killing us all. I tried yanking on it again with my bare hands.

If only I had called Tom instead of Peter Novotny with my last remaining moments of sanity.

If only I hadn't broken my phone.

If only I had a clue what I was doing.

"I don't like the dark," Sarah whispered, close to my ear. I spun around, jumping slightly at her shadowy figure. "You took my light."

"I'm sorry," I said. "Here." I placed the flashlight on the bed next to Veronica so that it lit up the floor in front of Sarah. I shrugged out of my leather jacket, sweat pouring off of me as I picked up the chain again. "Okay. I need some help. Please."

Sarah looked at me. She was physically in better shape than Veronica, but mentally, maybe far worse off. Fifteen years was a long time. She'd been in this house for almost as long as she'd ever lived outside of it. "You can't be in here," she said. "He isn't going to like it."

"I know." I yanked at the chain, my arms trembling. "That's why we need to get out. Do you know where the key is for this?"

"You have to leave."

"Sarah. Can you go to the neighbor's house and get help? The garage door is unlocked."

She shook her head over and over. "He's going to come back and I'm going to be good."

My hands squeezed into fists as a current of desperate frustration coursed through me. I didn't know how to reach her, how to make her understand that the past fifteen years were not real life. It would probably take a very long time before she could see that. But I needed her to get it *now*. I had to try something else.

"Sarah," I said. "Did you know that Brad is in jail?"

She said his name again, clutching her belly.

"He's in jail for murdering your parents," I continued. I wiped a slick of perspiration from my forehead. My mouth was bone-dry. "But he didn't do that. Did he?"

She said nothing.

"Once we get out of here," I said, "and you tell the police what really happened? You can get Brad out of jail. You can take your life back. You can be in control. None of this has to count."

"The police," she murmured, miserable. She looked from me to Veronica. Then Sarah sat down on the bed, her hands balled into fists. "This isn't what was supposed to happen," she said.

I moved the flashlight so it was facing the bed and I crouched in front of her. "What's supposed to happen?" I said.

"He said," she began. "He said that in the new house, it would be better and we could be like a family and he wouldn't lock the door upstairs. And I could go outside sometimes, into the yard. And there could be a swing set and a garden, that's what he said. It's a big yard. He showed me." Her eyes welled up and overflowed.

I wondered how often Derrow had taken her out of the house. Maybe dozens of times over the last decade and a half, and everyone in Belmont was too self-involved to see. Maybe he'd gotten cocky, assuming nothing could ever touch him. Or maybe—probably—he was out of his mind. A family? How was that supposed to work? I felt the minutes rushing past like water down a drain. "Sarah, he's not a good guy. You don't want to stay here."

"It's not as bad anymore," she said. "Now that he trusts me, almost."

"He made you a prisoner," I said. "He'll never let you be anything other than that, not until you get away from him."

"He told me I love him."

"You don't, Sarah," I said. But she didn't look too sure about that. She didn't look like she believed me at all. "Listen," I said, desperate. "He trusts you. Because he tested you before and you didn't fall for it. Right?"

She nodded.

"He even took you to see the new house, right?" I guessed.

Another nod.

"You were at a gas station about two weeks ago," I said. "That's why I knew you were here. Someone saw you."

"How do you know that?" she whispered.

"Because I've been looking really hard for you. That's how you can tell this isn't another test," I said. "Because he already trusts you. He wouldn't test you again, not after he trusted you enough to let you get out of the truck at the gas station. Right?"

The sideways logic appeared to reach her. She looked up at me, her head tipped to the side. "But you knew about Veronica," she said. "Brad wouldn't know about Veronica."

"No, Brad doesn't know," I said. "But I found out, while I was looking for you. I found out a lot of things. He's killed other women."

Sarah continued to stare at the floor. "It's because of his sexual problem," she said, like what was wrong with Jack Derrow just needed a prescription remedy. "He can't help it. He can be okay. He doesn't chain me up anymore when he leaves, and he lets me use the bathroom now. And take showers. He's not so bad."

"Sarah, yes, he is." I went to the window. I didn't want to leave to get help myself in case Derrow came back sooner rather than later, but maybe I could get someone's attention. The plywood covering the window was nailed down every two inches. I grabbed at the edges, hoping for a weak spot.

"He said we could be like a family."

I looked back at her. "He *killed* your family. Didn't he?"

She nodded. "He—" But then she stopped.

"What happened," I whispered.

"He gave me a ride," she said after a minute.

I yanked on the plywood as hard as I could, but nothing gave way except my fingernails.

"I got a flat tire on my bike, and I saw him driving by, and, and," she said, shaking her head, "he stopped to help me."

This was how it had gone down, I realized, for Sarah and the other women. Out and about in Belmont, maybe in some kind of distress, maybe not. There was nothing weird about a cop pulling over, especially one that you knew. On the street below, I heard a car approach, but it kept going past Derrow's house. I let out a breath I didn't realize

I was holding. He could return at any moment. I abandoned the idea of opening the window and went back to the bolt that secured Veronica's chain to the floor. I squinted at it in the near-dark and considered the Swiss army knife on my keychain. Although I'd managed to get my father's office door open with the Swiss army knife the other day, I'd need better tools than that if I was ever going to get this sucker open. A better light, too. Steady hands. Lots of time. And maybe not even then.

"He was my dad's friend," Sarah continued. "So I knew him, so I let him give me a ride home. And he took my bike in and his hands got all greasy from the chain and I said he could come in, to wash his hands."

"Sarah, it wasn't your fault." I stood up and looked at her. Sarah's eyes were wide, glued to the floor in front of her. I needed to get her to do more than talk. "Please. Help me."

But she continued, "And then in the kitchen, he had, I saw he had an erection." She stopped and wiped her eyes. "It made me really uncomfortable and I was going to go upstairs. But then my parents got home. And Jack went outside to help my dad with something on the car." Now she looked right at me. "I told my mother about what I saw. And then he walked back in. Mom started yelling at him to get out, and she was calling for my dad, screaming his name. Jack got this knife out of his pocket and he just snapped his arm out and then my mom was clutching her throat. There was so much blood. So much. My dad came running in and Jack stabbed him too. He hit me and then I woke up here." She pressed the heel of her hand against her mouth again, hard. "He told me he didn't want to kill me, because I was good, I was a good girl. But he said he would do if it he had to because it was all my fault."

"Sarah," I said, my voice cracking. I had no idea how much time had passed but it felt like a year. "It isn't your fault. You have to believe that. You can change the story, starting now. You *will* change it. But we need to act fast here. Please."

She sat there without saying anything for a moment, just looking down at her hands. Then she reached out to me like she wanted to give me something, and she dropped a small silver key onto my open palm.

THIRTY-FOUR

Sarah turned on every light switch as we made our way into the hall-way and down the steps. She was scared of the house, or scared that Derrow was waiting for her around every corner. So we went slowly. Veronica, surprisingly strong despite her drugged condition, clutched my elbow. Sarah, two steps in front of us, held the flashlight in both hands. She had shoes, a pair of ancient women's sneakers. Veronica had no shoes, the articles of clothing she was wearing when Derrow grabbed her nowhere to be seen. But it didn't matter. My brother's car was in front of the house, across the street.

Less than a hundred yards away.

But when we made it to the kitchen, I heard a sound that made my heart stop.

The garage door going up.

Derrow had returned.

Sarah let out a strangled sound and said, "He's going to kill us he's going to kill us he's going to kill us," over and over.

The door to the garage was the only one without the padlock. Now there was only one way out of the house—back into the basement and through the window I broke when I came in.

Not only that, but there wouldn't be much time before Derrow realized something was going on. If the car parked in front of his house wasn't a dead giveaway already, he'd know it when he saw that every light in the lower level was on.

I opened the basement door and ushered the two women inside. Derrow's giant truck gunned into the garage, then turned off. Then there was the sound of a key in the lock a few seconds later. The garage door stayed up.

"Come on," I said. I pulled the door closed behind us, Sarah shrieking as we were plunged into darkness. I carefully felt for the next step, my whole body trembling.

But she fumbled with the flashlight and dropped it, and it bounced down the steps and went out.

"Oh my God," she whispered.

"We're going to be fine," I told her with a confidence that I in no way felt.

We had to take the stairs even more slowly now in the pitch-black of the basement. I undid the snap on my holster and gripped the handle of my gun. My palms were wet. Veronica leaned heavily on my arm, her long hair brushing my wrist. Sarah's breathing was ragged in my ear but I listened hard for an idea of where Derrow was, what he was doing.

He wasn't doing anything, not even walking. The floorboards weren't creaking. He was just standing there, probably just inside the house, listening too. Then he took four heavy steps, crossing the room quickly with his long strides. He stopped at the basement door, turned the knob, but didn't open it.

"Why couldn't you just stay away?" Derrow said through the door, his tone as dark and cold as the concrete walls around us. "You were afraid, on the phone. I could hear it in your voice."

I said nothing.

"I should have dealt with you. I knew I should have. You're not a good girl. You broke into my house. Both of my houses. Didn't you?"

I still kept quiet.

"And you're trying to turn my Sarah against me now?" he said.

I didn't say a word, too busy trying to formulate a new plan. If Derrow opened the door and we were still on the steps, we'd all be dead in seconds.

"You miserable bitch," he said. "I could shoot you through this door and what could anybody even say? Self-defense. Not a doubt in my mind you have that little revolver of yours in your hands right now."

Sarah yelped a little. I got the three of us off the steps in case he decided to do just that. I wanted to shoot him through the door myself but my eyes hadn't adjusted to the darkness yet, and I couldn't be sure exactly where the door was, or if he was behind it or beside it. "That's the least of your problems right now," I said, forcing my voice to sound strong. "But you're right, I do have my little revolver in my hands. I reloaded it, by the way. And if you open that door, all eight shots are going into your chest."

I grabbed Sarah's upper arm and pointed at the broken window, where the palest hint of moonlight illuminated the area on the floor just below it. She looked at me with confusion but then took Veronica's arm and they shuffled toward it.

"The least of my problems?" Derrow said next. His voice sounded slightly farther away, then closer as he added, "I wouldn't worry about *my* problems right now."

I heard a scraping sound, and then the door rattled in its frame. He was wedging something under the doorknob, like a chair. He must have thought I broke into the house through the garage, not the basement window.

"But *your* problems," Derrow said. "I'd like to see you talk your way out of this one."

Then I heard him walk away.

I ran up the steps and jerked at the doorknob, but it wouldn't even turn. The sweat snaking down my spine went ice cold. A beat later, his heavy footsteps returned, accompanied by a wet, sloshing sound.

Then the sharp tang of gasoline.

I half ran, half tripped back down the steps and over to the window, where Sarah was just standing, staring up at the freedom beyond the small, open rectangle. Veronica was at the weight bench, hopelessly trying to drag it across the floor. But at least she was trying.

"No, this is too heavy," I said. I tried to think of what else I had seen in the basement. There were boxes, which might be sturdy enough to support Veronica's weight but not mine or Sarah's. And then I remembered.

The deep freezer.

I felt my way along the wall until I bumped into it, Veronica at my heels. I pulled the cord out of the wall and tried to drag it, but the thing weighed a ton.

"We need to push it," I said.

Veronica and I went to the other end of the appliance and pushed and pushed, and it barely budged three inches.

From upstairs, I heard a faint crackling sound, smelled smoke in addition to gas. A smoke detector began to peal.

"Oh my God," Sarah said.

"What the hell is in this thing?" I said. I threw open the lid to the freezer and was met with a blast of cold, wet air and a smell that instantly made me gag, and Sarah shrieked.

"Don't open that, don't, don't," she said. "Theresa is in there."

Veronica recoiled and I slammed the lid shut, unwilling to reach inside.

Theresa.

I remembered the name from my background check. His ex-wife. My thoughts were going everywhere at once, a swarm of insects. And I had never been more afraid.

"Focus," I said out loud.

I got lower to the ground, my hip screaming at me, and pushed as hard as I could. Veronica did the same. We got it moving, slowly, but steadily, until I heard it crunching over broken glass from the window.

"There, that's good." I held back a cough as I helped Veronica and Sarah get on top of the freezer.

As soon as I saw her standing at eye level with the window, I realized that there was no way Sarah would fit through the small opening with her pregnant belly. She realized it too, blind terror in her eyes as a smoke detector somewhere in the basement started going off over the anxious hiss of flames right above us. Smoke must have been seeping through the crack under the basement door.

"You're going to leave me here," she whispered.

"No. Sarah, I'm not."

"You are. You are you are you are."

She coughed so hard she had to lean against the wall for support. I felt sick. Sarah had lived through hell on earth only to now face dying in a house fire. And that was because of me.

"Veronica," I said. I had to raise my voice over the growing crackle of the flames. I braced against the freezer as I pulled off my boots and thrust them at her. "Can you run to one of the houses and get help?"

She was bewildered for a second, but then she nodded and stepped into my boots.

"It doesn't matter which house. Just get help. Say—" I stopped for a second, not even sure now. "Say there's a fire. There's a fire and you need the fire department and the sheriff's department, okay? *Not* the Belmont police."

She nodded. "Okay."

I scrambled on top of the freezer and helped Veronica up through the window. Then she stood there in the damp grass of Derrow's backyard and looked down at me like a mistake had been made.

"What is it, Veronica?" I said. "Do you see him?"

She shook her head.

"Okay," I said. "Just go. Run."

She turned and ran.

"Sarah," I said, turning to her now. Her shoulders were heaving, her breath coming way too fast. The air was too tight in my own lungs, and the chill from the open window seemed to increase as the temperature in the basement crept up. "You need to calm down."

"I'm going to die down here," she said. She grabbed on to my forearm, not for comfort but as if to prevent me from leaving. "And this, my—" She looked down at her belly.

"You're not going to die down here," I said. I wiped roughly at my eyes, watering from the acrid smoke. Heat radiated from the ceiling. I squinted through the darkness, hoping for a sign that Veronica was able to get help. I didn't know how long it would take until the basement filled with hot, black smoke, until the air was unbreathable. I didn't want to stick around to find out. "*We're* not going to die down here. We're going to be fine. I'm not going to leave you. We're going to get out of here together."

Sarah was shaking her head. "All the times I wished for it, that I just wouldn't wake up," she said. "And now, now—" She leaned against the cinder-block wall, coughing. "Why did you even do this?"

I gritted my teeth and said nothing. The fire above us was angry now, raging, hungry for fuel. Over the roar of the flames, I heard him dragging something across his kitchen to the garage. It sounded like a suitcase. He had an escape bag packed. He was prepared. I wasn't. Sarah was right. I wasn't helping her at all.

"Sarah," I said, grabbing her by the shoulders. "I'm going to get us out of here."

She looked back at me, her nostrils flaring, furious.

"I know I just made things worse for you, but I'm trying to make them better. I'm going to. You have to trust me."

She said nothing.

"If I go up there, I can get back into the house and open the door," I said.

Sarah shook her head, still holding on to my arm with all the strength she had.

"I will do that," I said, "I will come and open the basement door so you can get out. Okay?"

She didn't believe me. I wasn't going to leave her until she did.

"I will," I said. "You have to trust me."

Finally, she let go of my arm and leaned against the wall. She started to slide down into a sitting position on top of the freezer, but I caught her by the elbow.

"You have to stay by the window, you have to keep breathing," I said.

She stood up again, her face tense in the moonlight.

"I will be right back," I told her.

I holstered the revolver. Then I set my palms on the concrete lip of the foundation and pulled myself up until my torso was in the well. It wasn't easy. I balanced on my pelvis against the foundation and pushed my elbows up to the grass until I had enough leverage to pull my head above ground, then get my knees up into the well. Then I could stand, dizzily gulping lungfuls of clean night air as I pulled my gun out again and ran around the side of the house and into the garage—

I got there just as Derrow opened the door from the kitchen and stepped out.

A handgun in one hand, a suitcase in the other.

He looked at me, angry and stunned as he raised the arm with the gun.

I shot him twice.

They weren't good shots, but I hit him. Once in the shoulder and once in the thigh. He went down, blood spurting from his leg. The gun he was holding clattered to the concrete floor and I grabbed it before he could. I left him moaning in the garage and pushed into the house, which was no longer even a house but instead a wall of black smoke and orange flames, the floor a roiling plane of heat. I felt the vinyl flooring stick to my wool socks. I couldn't see a thing. I pulled my coat over my head and dashed through the kitchen, trying to remember how far down I needed to go. Luckily, not very. I bumped into a chair, the one Derrow had wedged under the knob of the basement door. I shrieked at the touch, the chair metal and white hot. Using my coat to protect my hands, I wrenched it out of the way and threw the door open. "Sarah," I coughed, "come on."

I didn't see her through the smoke, so I ran down the steps. The basement was at least forty degrees cooler than the upstairs. "Sarah."

She was still standing on the freezer, her face tipped up to the window. Her expression was one of eerie peace.

I grabbed her hand, and she turned to me, startled. "You came back," she whispered.

I helped her down from the freezer and gave her my coat to put over her head. "Follow me," I said. "There's no time."

Her hand in mine, we ran back up the steps and into the kitchen. The curtains had caught now, flames shivering up the wall. She followed me out into the garage, gasping at the sight of Derrow bleeding on the floor. There were sirens approaching, lots of them, fast.

I fell to my knees in the yard, just as a squad car flew down the street and jumped the curb, stopping inches from me. "Put down the gun," a sheriff's deputy was shouting, and it took me a minute to realize he was shouting it at me.

I lowered it slowly to the grass, then felt his weight on top of me as he pushed me face-first to the ground, followed by the bite of handcuffs. Sarah was screaming *no* over and over. The rest of the sirens wailed down the street and cast a flickering light show across the pavement.

It was almost beautiful.

THIRTY-FIVE

I told the story so many times I lost count. In the back of a squad car, on the bumper of an ambulance between breaths through an oxygen mask, while I received treatment for third-degree burns on my left hand and wrist, in a dimly lit interrogation room at the Belmont police station. I told it to people from the sheriff's department, the Franklin County prosecutor's office, BCI, since the Belmont police, I assumed, had no say over the situation anymore. I wrote it in long-hand on a legal pad and signed a printed copy of a statement and agreed to be videotaped. It was a hell of a story, one that even I would think strained against the limits of the plausible had I not just lived through it. And in between the tellings, there was a lot of wait-ing. I put my head down on my arms when I was in the interrogation room, and it didn't feel like I slept, just drifted in and out on a burnt cloud of memory, but each time the door opened, I jerked upright, gasping and coughing.

Light was slanting in through the window near the ceiling when a man in a three-piece suit came in and sat down across from me. He was even wearing cuff links, though it couldn't be much past eight in the morning yet. That's how you know someone is important, I thought mildly.

"I'm David Homza," he said.

The name was familiar. I looked at him: salt-and-pepper hair,

Elvis Costello glasses. I didn't know him. But then I remembered why I had heard of him. "You prosecuted Brad Stockton," I said. My throat was scratchy from the smoke. I smelled like I had set the fire myself, and bits of ash kept falling out of my hair.

"I did," he said. "And you're Frank Weary's kid."

I leaned on my good hand, my stomach flip-flopping. "I am."

Homza watched me for a minute. "Do you need anything? Coffee, soda?"

I asked him for a Coke. He nodded and stood up.

"And is there any way I could get a bit of whiskey in that?" I said when he opened the door. Someone in the police station was bound to have a bottle stashed in a desk drawer, and I figured that if Homza knew my father, he might not judge.

He smiled and left the room, returning a few minutes later with a can of Coke still cold from the vending machine and a coffee mug with a quarter inch of whiskey in the bottom. "Will that do it?" he said.

"It will," I said. I opened the can one-handed and poured the soda into the mug and took a sip. This was the only drink I was going to have today, I told myself. I was so happy for a second, the sugar and caffeine and liquor giving me a rush as good as any narcotic high.

"You had quite the night," Homza said a minute later.

"Yes," I said. "How are Veronica and Sarah?"

"Good," he said. "Well—you know. Good, considering. They've both been sexually assaulted, Veronica pretty violently and recently. They have been admitted to Mount Carmel East for the time being. You'll be happy to know that they corroborated your account of tonight."

I nodded. But I hadn't even been thinking about them corroborating my story. I was just glad they were okay. "Did someone call Veronica's family?" I said. "And Shelby Evans?"

He nodded.

"What about Sarah's family? She has an aunt in town, and a cousin."

Homza leaned back in his chair. "No," he said. "I wasn't aware that she had family left and she didn't say anything."

I thought about that for a second. Maybe Sarah wouldn't want to see Elizabeth Troyan, since her somewhat exaggerated testimony had put Brad Stockton in jail. But it might be good to have someone there. "I have their numbers," I said. Then I realized I didn't—my broken phone was a useless chunk of metal and glass and I didn't even know where it was.

"It's up to her," Homza told me. "It's likely they've already heard—this is a media circus and a half."

I nodded. I hoped my client had heard too, because her phone number was lost to the ages as well. I was a detective, though, and maybe an okay one after all. I could probably figure it out.

"Derrow's going to make it, too," Homza said.

"Hallelujah."

"He's in stable condition. But the bullet shattered his femur. They might have to put pins in it," he added.

"That's just terrible," I said. It wasn't that I'd hoped I had killed him, although I wouldn't have lost too much sleep over it. I just didn't want to hear anything else about him. I remembered the pins in Colleen Grantham's ankle. Maybe someone would find Jack Derrow's body in a ravine during another lifetime and identify him because of the pins.

"And," Homza said, "he's talking."

That got my interest. I sipped my drink and said, "Tell me he made a full confession."

He raised his eyebrows. "He did."

My jaw dropped.

"I know," Homza said. "I was surprised too. I guess he knows when he's been beat fair and square, sick bastard. And he's a coward.

The first thing he said was he'd cooperate if we won't consider this a capital case."

I drank a little more. "What did he confess to, exactly?"

He sighed. "Quite a few things. The murder of his ex-wife, Theresa Marr, in 1995, for starters. She apparently moved to Florida after they got divorced. She was reported missing down there, but no one knew she'd come back to Ohio. He also confessed to murdering Mallory Evans, Garrett and Elaine Cook. Kidnapping Sarah and planting the knife in Brad Stockton's car. Then the murder of Colleen Grantham, kidnapping of Veronica Cruz. And there was another student of his, before any of this started, he said he raped her."

I shook my head. I almost asked if Derrow said why, but that was a stupid question. There was no why. I might never get any more answers than I already had. "Lassiter had to know about some of this," I said instead. "The rape? Was that reported? There's a lot going on here that isn't exactly aboveboard."

"That," Homza said, "is something I can't comment on. It will be looked into."

"Seriously?"

He spread his hands. "Sorry."

"Okay, what about Brad," I said. "What's going to happen to him? Can you comment on that?"

He gave me a pained little smile.

"I hope you have a good apology planned," I added, although it wasn't exactly fair of me to put it all on him. It took a village to orchestrate the railroad job against Brad Stockton.

"Trust me," Homza said, "no one is more horrified over this than me."

"Except Brad. And Sarah. And Veronica."

We stared at each other for a long time. He didn't argue with me on that point. He said, "You look just like him, did you know that? Your dad."

"I've heard," I said.

"Tell you what, your dad would be proud of you today," he added. He touched my arm and then stood up. "You're free to go."

I looked into my mug, blinking hard.

Before I was actually free to go anywhere, I had a number of practical concerns to deal with: I had no shoes, no coat, and no car. I walked stiffly to the lobby in my socks, freezing in place when I saw the crowd outside the police station, a gaggle of reporters with television cameras. Homza wasn't kidding about the media circus. One surly uniform was losing a battle to keep them all away from the door. And just inside the lobby, Jake Lassiter was hurriedly removing picture frames from the wall.

The ones with Jack Derrow smiling behind his groups of students.

Lassiter spotted me and almost didn't stop what he was doing, but then he did. We looked at each other for a long moment. He'd aged five years since I saw him two days earlier. Learning you'd harbored a killer for more than twenty years probably did that to a person. I wondered how much longer he'd even have a job. He looked down at the picture he was holding, and then pitched it into the trash.

"You might want to go out the back," he said, clearing his throat.

"Yeah," I said.

I waited for a second, in case he wanted to say anything else. He didn't. So I kept walking. Then he cleared his throat again. "Ask Dee in the dispatch office to show you the lost and found," he said. "I'm sure there's a pair of shoes in there."

I turned back to him, but he didn't look at me again. Maybe offering me a pair of stranger's shoes was his version of an apology. I decided to assume that it was. Besides, in that moment, I needed shoes more than I needed anybody's *I'm sorry*. He threw two more photos away and I left him to it. I'd spent more than twenty-four hours in this terrible building in the last week. After I got a hoodie and a pair of canvas sneakers from the lost and found, I started looking for the back door of the police station.

Then I heard my name.

"Roxane?"

I turned around at the familiar voice and Tom was there, jogging down the hall toward me. He grabbed my arm, relief flooding his face. I thought maybe no one had ever been happier to see me in my life. "You're okay," he said.

"What are you doing here?" I said. I wanted to be mad at him for showing up like this, but I couldn't. I placed my good hand over his and held on tight.

"I—" he began. He shook his head like he had no idea what to say to me. His tie was loose, his hair sticking up from running a hand through it one too many times. "I had to meet this badass detective who closed Frank's case."

My face felt weird, but I tried to give him a smile. "That's right, I did," I said. Somehow, in all of the excitement, I had forgotten that part. Mallory Evans. My father's case.

"Your phone is off," Tom said, "and we kept getting conflicting information on what had happened, and I needed to know. For me. I needed to know if you were okay."

"We?" I said.

"I probably speak for much of the city with that we," he said, "but I meant my squad. All of Crimes Against Persons, actually. I told you, cops are gossipy as fuck."

"Really," I said.

"Like a bunch of sorority sisters," Tom said. He grinned at me, but there was something nervous about it. "So you're a little banged up," he said, glancing down at my bandaged hand.

I nodded. It didn't hurt, or not yet, anyway. But it would, once the adrenaline wore off. "Indeed, and someday soon, we can get together for a drink and I'll tell you all about it."

He took a deep breath. "But today is not that day," he said.

"Today is not that day." I squeezed his hand and then let go. "I just, I don't know, Tom, I can't. I can't talk about it any more right now."

"Hey, of course, of course."

We watched each other for a few beats. I could no longer even remember exactly why I thought I was so mad at him.

"So," I said. "I could use a ride back to the car. Again."

He laughed, and the sound put me a little more at ease. "Do you want to ride in the backseat?" he said. "And I can wear a little chauffeur hat?"

"As much as I would love that," I said, "I'll just settle for the ride today."

"You got it," he said. He set a hand lightly between my shoulder blades and steered me down the hall. "I figure you'd rather skip the press junket."

"It's like you know me or something."

Once we got in the car, I told him where to go, and then we rode in silence for a while. But it was a better silence than the one we endured on Wednesday. I closed my eyes against the bright morning sun, even though I couldn't sleep. I wondered if I would ever be able to sleep again.

"Listen," Tom said as he turned onto Derrow's street. It was still mostly blocked off by cop cars, but not as many as earlier. "About the other day."

I shook my head. "Tom, it's okay," I said. "That was all me. Really. *I'm* sorry. Let's just forget it."

"No, I don't want to," he said, "I need to say this."

He parked the car and turned to me. I thought about just getting out and walking away. But I didn't. I assumed I had already made it through the hardest part of my day.

"I know you and Frank didn't have the easiest relationship," he said next, catching me off guard. "I know you think he didn't respect you, that he was always trying to undermine you. I know that. But Roxane, I spent ten-plus hours a day with the guy for almost ten years, and I think I knew him better as a person than you did."

My chest was starting to ache. "Please don't," I whispered.

But he did. "He was my best friend," he said. "So I know what I'm talking about when I tell you that when he asked me to promise to look out for you, he didn't mean because you couldn't look out for yourself. He meant it because he loved you." His warm brown eyes were bright, and he blinked hard. "And I promised, because I loved him. And I do take that promise seriously."

I said, "It's fine." But I didn't know what was fine or who I was telling.

"But the other day," Tom said, pinching the bridge of his nose, "I didn't handle it well, what I said. But I didn't know how else to tell you."

"How to tell me what. What else is there?" I said.

His jaw bunched and his eyes filled up and I felt my sinuses getting tight too. I pressed a hand over my mouth.

"How important you are, Roxane," he said. "To me. That there's a big space in my world for you no matter what. You've been very clear that it was just sex, and maybe that's true. But that's not all you are. You were there when no one knew how to be there."

I was shaking my head. "But I didn't do anything," I said.

"Are you kidding?" Tom said, and then he was crying and I was crying and I didn't know what was happening. "All the nights you let me talk about him even though I know you didn't want to? All the times I didn't even want to talk but I didn't want to be alone? You always knew what to do." He leaned toward me, so close our foreheads were almost touching. "I would not have made it without you. I feel like we went through a war together, Roxane, like I trusted you with my life. That matters more than anything. That's bigger than everyone else. That's why I always want you to call, and I always want to answer. It doesn't matter why or where you are or where I am, okay?"

I squeezed my eyes closed. "No."

"No what? No you don't want somebody on your side?"

I was being ridiculous. I did need somebody on my side, probably now more than ever. "I'm sorry I'm impossible," I said.

"You're not. Sorry, that is," he said with a smile in his voice, and we both laughed a little bit. "You're impossible just like he was."

"I always hated it when people said I was like him," I said, "but it's true."

"It is true, Roxane. But that's something you can be proud of. You can leave the parts you don't like."

"It doesn't work that way."

"Says who?"

"I don't know." Over the last nine months, we had talked about my father a lot. But we hadn't talked about me. I didn't want to. I thought I could skip over that part and come out on the other side, already over it. But I couldn't. Probably no one could. "I don't even miss him but I feel like a part of me is gone," I whispered. "So I guess I do miss him."

"It's okay to miss him," Tom said.

We sat like that for a long time, until his tears stopped and then mine did and then he kissed me on the cheek and pulled away. "I'm going to hold you to it, about that drink," he said. He rubbed his face like he could get the sadness off of him that way. "Soon."

I nodded quickly. "Very soon."

"And I want you to meet Pam."

"You're going to have to give me a minute for that," I said. I wiped my eyes. "I hope she knows what a delicate flower you are."

He grinned. "No, she thinks I'm stoic and tough. I guess that's her type."

"You'll have to break it to her eventually."

Tom shrugged. "I figure I can come find you when I need a good cry."

I met his eye. It was hard to believe that less than a year ago, we'd barely known each other. Now it felt like I had known him forever. "Any time," I said, and then I squeezed his shoulder and got out of the car.

The morning was bright and cold and it hurt my eyes and my lungs as I walked down the street to my brother's car. Jack Derrow's house was half gone, the garage a sagging black hole. I paused and stared at it for a second but then turned away, unwilling to give him another second of my attention.

THIRTY-SIX

There were reporters at the hospital too, but they didn't appear to notice me. They were much more interested in who might be coming out of the hospital than who might be walking in. I passed a lot of cops as well, what looked like half the police in the county standing around with their arms crossed. Part of me was glad to see them, like it made the hospital somehow safer. The rest of me wanted to tell them to get back to work. I stopped in the gift shop, stared at the racks of balloons and teddy bears and magazines. But I hated all of the things they sold, so I just went up to the third floor empty-handed. A Belmont uniform was guarding the end of the hall where the women's rooms were located. As I got closer, I saw that it was Shanahan, the guy who'd brought me the tampon. He nodded at me and gave me a sheepish smile before he stepped aside and let me pass.

I wondered if Veronica and Sarah would ever be able to look at a police officer again without fear.

No one could blame them if they couldn't.

Veronica's door was closed. I knocked, and Joshua Evans opened it and gasped. His wide face lit up and then crumpled almost at the same time as he dropped to his knees in front of me. "You're an angel," he whispered into my thigh.

I touched his arm. "Joshua, it's okay."

After a few seconds Joshua got to his feet and pulled me into

Veronica's room. She was asleep, clutching a fluffy pink teddy bear that someone who didn't hate everything from the gift shop had purchased. Her mother was sitting beside the bed and she glanced up at me, stunned. She looked like she had no idea what to say to me, but that was all right. I smiled at her reassuringly. She didn't need to say anything. I hoped that the absence of her jerk husband might be permanent, for her daughter's sake.

"Veronica hasn't talked much yet," Joshua told me. "But the doctor, he said—he said she's lucky. That she'll get better. It just takes a bit of time, maybe."

A bit of time. That seemed like the understatement of the year. Although Veronica looked peaceful sleeping there in the hospital bed, I couldn't shake the hollow-eyed expression she had in that house. "I'm glad to hear it," I said anyway. "Is Shelby around?"

"Yeah, she was just here. Want me to call her and get her back in here? I know she can't wait to talk to you."

This man is Shelby's father, I repeated. "No, it's okay, I'll be around for a while," I said.

Joshua nodded. We looked at each other. "How did you know?" he said finally. "About him. He's so, he just seems like the nicest guy. He was one of the officers who responded when I reported her missing—Mallory—I just—"

I embraced him and let him cry on my shoulder for a minute while that sank in. That Derrow had been the officer to take Mallory's missing-persons report, after he had taken *her.* It almost made me wish I'd shot him in the head. "I know, Joshua," I said. "Derrow fooled a lot of people."

"But not you," he said. "You're amazing."

I didn't feel amazing. I felt lucky. And Derrow *had* fooled me at first. But I supposed I should take the compliment. "I'm going to check in on the other woman," I said. "You ever need anything, though, you call me. That goes for you, Shelby, Veronica, or her mom, okay?"

He nodded. "People say that," he said, "but I actually believe you mean it."

"That's because I do."

When I got to Sarah's room, I was surprised to see Shelby Evans sitting next to her bed. They weren't speaking, and Sarah was just staring at the wall, her arms resting over her stomach. When Shelby saw me she jumped up and ran over and threw her arms around me.

"How did you know?" she whispered into my shoulder, just like Joshua had. Behind her, Sarah didn't even look up.

I wiped my eyes. "You helped me figure it out," I said. "I couldn't have done it without you. How come you're down here?"

"Veronica went to sleep. And I thought it was sad, that Sarah doesn't have a family to come be with her," Shelby said with a glance over her shoulder. "Veronica said she was nice to her. But I don't think she wants me here."

"Oh, Shelby," I said. "It's not you. It's very sweet of you to sit with her though."

"Veronica said she thought she was dreaming," she said next. "When she saw you. She didn't understand."

"I know."

"It was horrible, wasn't it?"

"Yeah, it was."

"She didn't really talk about it."

"Listen, Shelby, I want to tell you something."

Shelby looked at me. "Okay."

"Veronica is going to need time," I said. "Probably a lot of time, before she's back to herself, okay?"

"I know," she said.

"You just have to be patient. This is a happy day, and the worst is over now, but not all the hard parts are finished."

She nodded.

"Can you make sure you're patient with her? That you don't lose hope if she needs time? That goes for her mom too. I know you're strong, kiddo, so that's why I'm putting this on you."

"I know."

"And as for you," I said. "We can always be friends, okay? If you ever need to talk—about her, about some other girl, whatever. I mean it."

She nodded again. "I'm really glad I met you."

"Me too," I said. It felt good, knowing that I had helped to clear Brad Stockton's name. But it felt even better that I had told Shelby I would help her, and I did.

She hugged me again and went back down the hallway, shooting me a smile over her shoulder as she walked. I hoped that she'd be tough enough to get her father and her friend through this. I thought she was. She just had a look about her. Then I went into Sarah's room and sat down. Her gaze was still pinned to the wall. In the bright light of the hospital, I could see that she had dark circles under her eyes, a sallow cast to her skin. Her hair was tangled and frayed, her fingernails broken and peeling. An IV was taped to the back of her hand.

She looked miserable.

But she was out of that house.

That was not nothing, even if it was still hard.

Neither of us said a word for a long time, which was okay. And then she finally spoke. "They did an ultrasound," she said. "I'm going to have a little girl. In five weeks. They said she looks healthy."

I gave her a big smile. "Sarah, that's such good news."

She nodded. But there was ambivalence in her eyes. "But she's his."

"No, Sarah, she's yours," I said quickly. "He has no rights. He's never going to hurt you again," I said. "He's going to jail and he'll never get out. Never. You don't have to waste another thought on Jack Derrow for the rest of your life."

She looked down at her belly. She didn't tell me that was a stupid thing to say, even though it was. She'd probably think about Derrow forever, and probably so would I. We fell into another stretch of silence. Activity hummed behind us in the hallway, comforting in its normalcy.

Today was an ordinary Friday for the rest of the city.

"Is Brad still in jail?" she said after a minute.

"Yes," I said. "It'll take a bit of time. But he will get out." Then I added, "He still loves you."

She thought that over. "I guess we have even more in common now. We both had our lives stolen by the same person," she said. For a second I caught a glimpse of the happy, bright girl she once was.

"That's exactly right," I said.

Sarah nodded. "Maybe I could see him," she said. "Maybe."

I ran into Danielle Stockton in the parking lot of the hospital. She almost hustled right past me, her nose glued to her phone. But she looked up at the last second and her eyes went wide. "You're here," she blurted. She was keyed up, a good kind of jumpy. "I went to the police station looking for you and they said maybe try here. Oh my goodness, Roxane, you—" But she stopped there, shaking her head, unsure of what she wanted to say.

"I guess I owe you an apology," I said lightly, "for trying to tell you the woman you saw wasn't Sarah."

She laughed, nervous. "Right, you owe *me* the apology. I'm the one who fired your ass."

"You were not out of bounds. But I guess it's a good thing I didn't quite listen."

"It really is." She kept shaking her head in disbelief, her hands clutching at the folds of her scarf. "I don't know what to say. *Thanks* doesn't quite seem to cut it."

I smiled at her. "Have you talked to your brother?"

Danielle looked up at the clear blue sky, smiling. It had probably been a long time since she'd smiled when she thought about Brad. "Yeah," she said. "I'm headed down there later today with my mom, but he called a little bit ago. His lawyer says they can't just release him, they have to have a hearing and all that." She let out a long, shell-shocked sigh. "I sound like I'm complaining, but I'm not. Believe me. I know what you did for us. I might not ever be able to repay you, but I know what you did."

I could tell the reality of the situation hadn't sunk in for her yet. When you're stuck inside something for so long, it's hard to believe it could ever be over, even when it is. Once Brad was home, it would hit her like a ton of bricks. "Go be with your family, Danielle," I said after a few beats. "And maybe get Matt off my back—that would be repayment enough. Fair?"

I held out my good hand, and she shook it.

"Fair."

THIRTY-SEVEN

I took a shower when I got home, with some difficulty—holding my bandaged left hand outside and trying to do everything with one arm. There was a reason, I supposed, that everyone made such a big deal about teamwork. Then I made a cup of tea and lost it somewhere in the apartment, and then I went to bed.

For the second time in a week, I slept all afternoon. This time when I woke up it was because someone was knocking on my front door. The clock said seven thirty. I rolled over and pulled a blanket over my head and hoped they would go away. But they didn't. I got up, my hip loudly making its objections known, and I pulled on a shirt. "I'm coming, hold the phone," I called.

It was Andrew. He was holding a bouquet of white roses and a ten-dollar bill.

"What's this?" I said.

"I don't know, it was in front of the door. And speaking of, what happened to your door?"

"Don't ask."

"So are we going, or what?" my brother said. "And Jesus, what happened to your hand now?"

I hadn't even heard anyone at my door all day. I took the flowers and the ten dollars, which had a sticky note attached.

I'm sorry, doll. I should have known, it said, and was signed *Petey*. The flowers had a note as well: *You're my local hero. Let's talk.—C*

I thought about tossing them directly into the trash, but I dropped the flowers on the table in my entryway instead.

I hadn't looked at the news coverage but it seemed I was some kind of star. Andrew apparently hadn't seen the news either. Chances were, he had just woken up too. "Going where?" I said.

"The Test Pavements?" Andrew said, pantomiming a backward electric guitar. "I called you but I think your phone's off."

"The other way," I said, and he grinned and switched hands. My phone was not exactly off. Broken and lost somewhere forever was more like it. "I forgot about that," I added. "Shit."

"How could you forget about the Test Pavements?"

I rubbed a hand over my face, also forgetting, for the millionth time, about my cheekbone. "Sorry," I said as I winced. "Let me get ready." I turned around and went back into the bedroom.

"Rox, are you okay?" The floor creaked as Andrew walked past my open door and back to the kitchen.

"Yeah," I said. My clothes were scattered all over the floor, in various states of cleanliness. I looked into my closet and saw nothing but bare hangers. I sat down on the bed and sighed and it started me on a coughing jag, my lungs still scratchy and tight from the smoke.

"You sound terrible," Andrew said. He reappeared with a whiskey bottle and two shot glasses. He filled them and handed one to me. "Are you getting sick?"

"I'm fine." I put the shot glass on my nightstand without drinking it and shook my head when Andrew looked at me quizzically. I took a slow, deep breath. "I think I need to pull back, where that's concerned."

It was scary to say it out loud, especially to my brother. But he just looked at me for a second and poured himself another shot.

"To each her own. You may change your mind later on, though," he said. "The band that plays before the Test Pavements is apparently a Christian rock group."

"Orange Barrels for God?" I guessed.

Andrew laughed. "Divining Roads," he said.

"We cannot go to this," I said. It suddenly seemed impossible that I was even here, laughing with my brother. Last night had happened to someone else. I had just fallen asleep during a horror movie and woke up unscathed, credits playing.

"Are you kidding me? It's going to be fucking amazing."

I started coughing again.

"But look," he said, "as much as I want to make fun of him all night with you, if you're sick, it's okay. Mom would understand. She'd ask if you saw a doctor yet, naturally, but she'd understand."

I placed my good hand over my chest, trying to coax my lungs into stillness. It would be so easy to say yes, I was sick, and sleep for another seven hours. But I didn't want to, I realized. I wanted to be around my family tonight. "No, I'm good. I just need to change and we can go."

"Are you sure you're okay?"

"I am," I said.

Andrew took the whiskey bottle back into the kitchen and I put on a bra and a cleanish shirt. I ran a brush through my hair without looking in the mirror. I didn't even want to know at this point.

"Mom told me yesterday that she sent Tom an e-mail about to-night," Andrew said from the hallway. "Inviting him. I hope that even he has the good sense to stay away from this *important family event,* but who knows."

"Hey," I said. "Do you think we could lay off Tom?"

Andrew leaned into my bedroom. "What?"

"He's good people," I said. "And he was probably closer to Dad than either of us ever was. I think he's just doing the best he can."

He raised his eyebrows but he didn't ask. "Sure," he said.

"We can still make fun of Matt, though, don't worry."

"Good."

Andrew was waiting by the front door. "Do you want to put these in water?" he said, with a nod to the roses from Catherine. "Who are they from, anyway?"

"Mind your business," I said. I slapped his hand as he nosed through the folds of cellophane for the card. "And no. I don't think it was meant to be a lasting sentiment."

He looked at me. "What's really going on?" he said. "You look beat to hell, your door has a pizza box taped to it, what happened?"

I tossed him his car keys. "I have a story," I said, "but I only want to tell it once tonight."

"Fair enough," Andrew said. "Ready?"

This was one of the reasons I loved my brother. He was kind, and not curious. He didn't need to know every last secret. He would trust you to tell him in your own time. In that way, he was my exact opposite, and it meant that he could find peace. I wasn't sure that I could ever do that. I wasn't sure I even wanted to. Not if it meant completely turning off the part of my brain that made me go into that house. But maybe there was a way to do both. I thought about what Tom had said earlier, how you could leave behind the parts you don't like. He meant the parts of my father's memory, but I wanted to think the same could apply to parts of yourself, that you could choose who you wanted to be, that every moment could be different. That, like I told Sarah, nothing counted, not unless you wanted it to count. I said, "Ready enough."

ACKNOWLEDGMENTS

This book would be nothing without Kellye Garrett, whose support, guidance, humor, plotting brilliance, and reminders about thought process were nothing short of transformative to the story and to me as a writer. Thank you, thank you, thank you.

Thanks also to Brenda Drake, for everything she does to support emerging writers via Pitch Wars. And speaking of which, I'm so grateful to everyone I've met from the PW community, especially Elle Jauffret and Jenny Ferguson for their rational advice when I was in full freak-out mode, Sonia Hartl and Roselle Kaes for their generosity and feedback on my manuscript, and Lisa Schunemann, my writerly drinking buddy.

Massive gratitude to my agent, Jill Marsal, and to my editor, Daniela Rapp, for believing in this story and for all of their work on my behalf. Also, thanks to Marla Cooper for putting me in touch with Jill in the first place.

Thanks to Bill Kerwin, for always reading.

I also want to thank Jessica Adamiak for her sharp editorial eye and her patience while reading approximately one zillion of my stories, novels, and pieces and parts thereof over the years. And for teaching me that *getting ink* means don't give up yet.

And finally, thanks to Joanna Schroeder, my best reader, listener, sounding board, and my partner through this and all other adventures.

Read on for a sneak peek at
Kristen Lepionka's next novel

What You Want to See

Available May 2018

ONE

Urban renewal was in the air on Bryden Road. The dilapidated house across the street from my apartment had been condemned, foreclosed, and eventually purchased by a fighty grad-student couple who appeared to be using the renovation process as experimental marriage counseling. Then my upstairs neighbors moved out and were replaced by a twentyish hipster with a name I could never remember and dreams of starting a farming collective in the building's narrow backyard. I knew this because she had long, loud phone conversations about it all day long.

It was a Tuesday, the kind of perfect June day that made it easy enough to forget how undesirable the weather was in Ohio most of the time. I was on my porch, listening through her open windows to Bridie or Birdy—whatever her name was—talk about the Brahma chickens she was thinking about buying for her farm. As annoying as she was, there was something compelling about it, like a hipster radio drama playing out one floor above me.

It goes without saying that aside from being pathologically nosy, I was also currently unemployed.

I was finishing my second cup of tea when the car pulled up. Tan Impala with no hubcaps and LED light strips behind the grille, easy enough to spot as an unmarked police-issue vehicle. A regular old cruiser was a more common sight in Olde Towne East, but an unmarked one wasn't out of the ordinary either.

Upstairs, Birdy said, "There are cops on the street. Again. Do you think it's, like, safe here?"

I thought about calling up to her, "Not for Brahma chickens."

But I decided against it when the passenger door of the cop car opened and Tom got out.

That meant they were here for me.

Tom didn't look happy about it. Neither did the other guy, who was short and dense with salt-and-pepper hair razored into a bristly buzz cut like a vacuum attachment. I didn't know him, but his expression said that he knew something about me.

I put my mug down on the ledge and stood up. "I didn't know I was getting company."

"Hey, Roxane," Tom said. His face was unreadable. "This is Detective Sanko. You got a few minutes?"

"To?"

"Chat."

"About?"

The vacuum attachment scowled at me. "You talk just like your dad did," he said. "And you look like him, too."

I sighed. "What's up, friends?"

Sanko said, "Do you want to do it out here, let everybody on the block know your business?"

Upstairs, Birdy was silent for the first time in what seemed like days. "Why don't you come in, then," I said.

I led my visitors into the front room of my apartment, which served as an office of sorts. I tried to catch Tom's eye but he still wasn't playing. "So what's this about?"

Sanko looked around my apartment, his eyes sweeping over an end table piled with laundry and a nearly empty bottle of Crown Royal. "Nice place you got here."

"Ed, don't be a dick," Tom said. He looked at me, finally. There was tension in his face.

"Marin Strasser," Sanko said once he finished his inspection. "You familiar with her?"

I stared at him.

Although I had no idea why they were here, I never would have guessed it'd be about her.

Until a few days ago, I'd been following Marin Strasser everywhere she went. Her fiancé had hired me to find out if she was cheating on him. She wasn't, not so far as I could tell. Which wasn't very far, because less than a week into the case, the man's retainer check bounced and that was the end of it.

Or so I thought. "Yes."

"How?"

"I recently did some work for her fiancé. Why?"

They exchanged glances. "Because she's dead," Sanko said.

A week earlier, I had met with Arthur Ungless at the print shop he owned on the north side. It was in one of those stucco office parks where rows of one-story buildings housed an oddball mix of businesses; the print shop was nestled between a bulk candy distributor and a karate studio. The office smelled like ink and paper and had a pleasant hum of activity murmuring from somewhere on the other side of Arthur's closed door. Business was apparently good: a slow but steady stream of cars coasted past the window behind his desk. "Norm said you were very discreet," he was saying. "And easy to talk to. I need that. Telling a complete stranger that I think the love of my life is having affair. This is all very uncomfortable, see. Embarrassing."

"I get that," I said. I did a job here and there for Norm Whitman's personal-injury law firm, surveillance stuff that fell on the dirtier end of the spectrum of the cases I took on. But money was money, and I valued Norm's business enough to take a referral from him seriously. "But you've got nothing to be embarrassed about. I'm on your side."

Arthur smiled faintly. "Well, you do seem very professional," he said. "I like that."

I straightened up in my seat. I wasn't sure how professional I seemed. I was wearing a black T-shirt, jeans, and an old olive-colored military jacket I'd had for fifteen years that had sort of come back in style recently. But I'd brushed my hair for the meeting, and I was sitting here instead of having this conversation amid the laundry in my home office. So compared to my past self, maybe this *was* professional. "Why don't you tell me about your fiancée?" I said.

Arthur nodded somberly. He was about sixty, short, barrel-chested, with reddish hair going silver, a wide mouth, and washed-out hooded eyes. The cuffs of his blue Oxford shirt were dotted with ink and rolled up to his elbows, revealing a faded Marine Corps tattoo on his left forearm. He struck me as a hardworking, friendly guy. By contrast, the woman in the photograph on the desk between us was coldly pretty, a well-dressed blonde at least fifteen years younger than him. "Marin," he said. "Marin Strasser. You're probably thinking what the hell does she see in me, good-looking woman like her."

"No, no," I said. But I could see what he meant. If *leagues* were a real thing, Marin would be out of his. I wrote her name down in my notebook and underlined it twice. "What makes you think she's cheating on you?"

Arthur sighed and leaned back in his executive chair, idly fiddling with the end of his tie. "Well, we got engaged last October. We were at dinner at M when I asked her. You been there?"

I nodded. "Romantic."

"She was so happy, just over the moon. We've had some real good times together, me and her. Trips and such. This year we've done Palm Beach and Vegas already, and we're talking about Mexico for Christmas. I like taking her places, taking care of her." He paused, his expression clouding over. "But honestly, something's different now. She's different. I can just tell. She's distracted, and jumpy. She'll get phone calls at all hours—that's not really new, her clients are very demanding—but she'll get up and leave the room sometimes too."

I glanced down at the photo again, wondering briefly if she was an escort. "Clients?"

"Marin's an interior decorator," Arthur said, and then I felt like an asshole. "That's how we met—she came in here to get new business cards." He shook his head briefly. "Anyway, when I ask her about it, ask her what's going on and all that, she says it's just the stress of wedding planning. I don't know. Feels like more than that. And I gotta be sure, about her. I can't get married feeling like this. Doubting her, doubting myself."

"Do you have any suspicions about who she's seeing?"

"None," Arthur said.

I waited.

"Marin doesn't have a lot of friends. Neither of us do. That's partly why we got close so fast."

I looked down at Marin's picture. I highly doubted a woman who looked like that had few friends. "Okay," I said, "if you don't know who, do you have any thoughts about when or where?"

He shook his head again. "We live together, so I'm with her every night. But during the day, I don't know exactly what she's up to. No idea. She doesn't keep an office or anything. I know she spends a lot of her time buying for her clients, so she's in and out of furniture stores a lot."

I tapped my pen on my notebook for a second, then wrote *furniture stores* down under Marin's name. So far it was not shaping up to be the case of the century. "So you'd want me to keep an eye on her during the daytime hours."

"Yeah. I usually leave home around seven, and I get back home by eight. Weekends, I usually only work in the mornings."

I restrained an unprofessional sigh. "Arthur," I said, "cases like this can get expensive fast. Especially if you're hoping to have someone on her for thirteen hours a day. Say it takes a few days, or a few weeks, even. Are you prepared for that?"

"Trust me, money is not a problem."

I told him my hourly rate, and he didn't bat an eye. So maybe that was what Marin saw in him: either his unwavering dedication, or his bottomless pockets. I figured she was probably having an affair. Part of me wanted to tell him to save his money, because the very act of hiring me more or less meant he'd never be able to trust her again. But if he was determined to pay somebody for answers, it might as well be me.